D0676539

Born in Glasgow and now a dual UK/US citizen, **T. F. Muir** is currently working on his next Andy Gilchrist .... other story suffused with dark alleyways, cobbled s....s ... all things gruesome.

Praise for T. F. Muir:

'Everything I look for in a crime novel.'

Louise Welsh

'Rebus did it for Edinburgh. Laidlaw did it for Glasgow. Gilchrist might just be the bloke to put St Andrews on the crime fiction map.'

Daily Record

TOOTH
FOR
A TOOTH
T. F. MUIR

Constable • London

CONSTABLE

First published in Great Britain in 2012 by Robinson,
an imprint of Constable & Robinson Ltd.

This edition published in 2015 by Constable

Copyright © T. F. Muir, 2012

3 5 7 9 10 8 6 4 2

The moral right of the author has been asserted.

All rights reserved.
No part of this publication may be reproduced, stored in a
retrieval system, or transmitted, in any form, or by any means,
without the prior permission in writing of the publisher, nor be
otherwise circulated in any form of binding or cover other than
that in which it is published and without a similar condition
including this condition being imposed on the subsequent
purchaser.

A CIP catalogue record for this book
is available from the British Library.

ISBN: 978-1-78033-777-7 (paperback)
ISBN: 978-1-78033-778-4 (ebook)

Printed and bound in Great Britain by Clays Ltd., St Ives plc

Constable
is an imprint of
Constable & Robinson Ltd
100 Victoria Embankment
London EC4Y 0DY

An Hachette UK Company
www.hachette.co.uk

www.littlebrown.co.uk

To the memory of Craig Martin Stevenson

RENFREWSHIRE COUNCIL	
140637521	
Bertrams	11/10/2016
	£8.99
BIS	

ACKNOWLEDGEMENTS

In almost every work of fiction an author will seek the assistance and guidance of others in an effort to improve the authenticity of the tale. In that respect, this book is all the better for input from the following: Jan den Dulk, Gloria del Carmen Echeverria and Simon Vilarasau Slade, for Spanish translation; Gayle and Kenny Cameron of Fife Constabulary and Sheriff Jim Bowen of Saratoga County Sheriff's Office, NY, for police procedure; Rob Dinsdale for editorial and plotting advice without which this story quite simply would never have been published; Jenny Page for exacting editorial assistance; Al Zuckerman for expert guidance in fine-tuning structure and plot; Krystyna Green for having the courage to take me on board; Nicola Jeanes and other staff at Constable and Robinson for working hard to see this book make it into the bookstores; Heather Holden-Brown for her tireless efforts when other literary agents would have dropped me like a brick; and finally Anne, for putting up with me, believing in me, and loving me all the way.

This book is a work of fiction. Those readers familiar with St Andrews and the East Neuk may notice that I have taken creative license with respect to some local geography.

Any and all mistakes are mine.

CHAPTER 1

October 2004

Detective Chief Inspector Andy Gilchrist stood alone at the back of the chapel as the curtains closed on the coffin of his ex-wife. He barely heard the prayer of committal as he watched his son, Jack, in the family group in the front pew, place an arm around Maureen. Beside them shuddered the grieving figure of their stepfather, Harry. Even now, at the moment of Gail's final parting, Gilchrist could not find it in his heart to forgive Harry.

As the chapel emptied, Gilchrist held back, tagging on to the end of the mourners, each giving their condolences to the family line as they shuffled through the vestibule.

Jack gave him a sad smile of surprise. 'I didn't see you.'

'Late as usual,' Gilchrist offered.

Jack's grip was firm, a son-to-father handshake meant to assure Gilchrist that Jack would be strong for all of them. The tremor in his chin said otherwise.

Gilchrist pulled him closer, gave him a hug. 'Mum's no longer suffering,' he said.

Jack nodded, tight-lipped, as they parted.

Maureen went straight for a hug. 'I wasn't sure you'd come.'

Even through her heavy coat he could feel her bones, her body light enough to lift with ease, it seemed. She was thin, too thin. He tried to say something, but found he could not trust his voice. Instead, he hugged her tighter, breathed her in, pressed his lips to her ear.

'We'll miss Mum,' he managed to say.

'Oh, Dad.'

He gave Harry a firm handshake and a wordless nod, conscious of Maureen's eyes on him, searching for signs of forgiveness. Then he was down the stone steps, marching across the car park, avoiding eye contact with family friends he did not know. From his car, he watched Jack and Maureen leave the chapel hand in hand, Harry in front, defeated, alone. And something in that simple formation told Gilchrist that Harry could never fill their paternal void.

He caught Maureen's eye as she prepared to step into the funeral car.

Are you coming back? she mouthed to him.

He nodded as she slipped from his view, then he powered up his mobile and saw he had two missed calls, both from Stan.

'What's up, Stan?' Gilchrist asked.

'Thought you might be interested in a skeleton, boss. Just been dug up.'

Gilchrist switched on the ignition, slipped into Drive. 'Keep going.'

'In Dairsie Cemetery. Uncovered while the lair was being opened for another burial. No coffin, and not six feet under, boss. So we're definitely thinking murder.'

Gilchrist eased his Mercedes SLK Roadster forward. Ahead, the funeral car cruised through the crematorium grounds, grey exhaust swirling in the October chill. The wake was being held in Haggs Castle Clubhouse, the golf club where Harry was a member. Gilchrist knew he should attend, for Jack and Maureen, for Gail's memory, too. But the thought of faking a face for Harry decided it for him.

'I'm on my way, Stan.'

Gilchrist walked through the gate in the old stone wall and into the cemetery grounds.

By a gnarled willow tree in the far corner the forensic tent was erected. Yellow tape looped around it from headstone to headstone. As Gilchrist approached, Stan broke the connection on his mobile with a slap of its cover.

'This skeleton,' Gilchrist said, as he pushed his feet into his coveralls. 'Is it in good nick?'

'Right thigh bone chopped through by one of the gravediggers. But other than that, it seems perfect.'

'Whose plot were they preparing?'

'A local by the name of Lorella McLeod. Fair old age of eighty-seven. Passed away at the weekend and was to be laid to rest in the family lair next to her husband, Hamish. He died in '69. So the grave's not been touched for thirty-odd years.' Stan shook his head. 'Already checked our misper files for '68 to '75, and came up empty-handed.'

'What about the PNC?'

'Got Nance doing that, even as we speak.'

Gilchrist pulled his coveralls up and over his shoulders, his mind working through Stan's rationale. 'Did the McLeods have children?' he asked.

3

'None. Mrs McLeod lived alone.'

'For the last what, thirty-five years?'

'So I'm told, boss. But I haven't confirmed that yet.'

Gilchrist looked away. Tree-covered hills were already greying with the coming of winter. It seemed unimaginable for someone to live by themselves for that length of time, and he wondered if the end of his life would be as destitute. Sadness swept through him at that thought. *The end of his life.* Or more correctly, *part* of it. Gail was now gone, and he worried he would spend even less time with Jack and Maureen. He forced his mind to focus on the present, and eyed the forensic tent.

'So, Stan, it looks like we're dealing with a thirty-five-year-old murder.'

'Bit soon to jump to that conclusion, boss. The body could have been buried any time since the burial of Hamish McLeod.'

Gilchrist zipped up his coveralls. 'But why was it buried in *that* grave, Stan? Have you asked yourself that?'

Stan scratched his head. 'It's difficult to imagine a more perfect place to hide a body. I mean, who would look for it in a cemetery?'

'But why that particular grave?'

'Boss?'

'Because it would have been *fresh*, that's why. And if there is no coffin, there was no funeral. And if there was no funeral, no one knew about it. Therefore, we have a thirty-five-year-old murder on our hands.' He stared off to the edge of the cemetery and the open fields beyond. Scotland in the sun was like no other place on earth. But its blue skies offered only false promise of a fine day. 'Not exactly thriving, is it, Stan?'

'Dead centre of town, boss.'

4

Gilchrist almost smiled. 'Ever been here before, Stan? In this cemetery?'

'No.'

'Neither have I. Which makes me think neither have a lot of people. So start off by making a list of all those who attended McLeod's funeral.'

Stan livened. 'I'll get on to it, boss. Door to door, discreet like, see who knows what,' he said as he walked away.

From the outside, the *Incitent* gave the impression it would be cramped and dark, but the interior was suffused with a yellow light that seemed to lend a reverential quietness to the scene. Gilchrist counted four transparent plastic bags next to the open grave, each filled with bones the colour of mud. A row of larger plastic bags, full of earth, lined one wall like in a garden centre. A camera sat on a silver metal case. Four Scenes of Crime Officers worked in silence, while Gilchrist watched.

One SOCO sifted through a heap of soil at the side of the grave. Another placed more muddied bones into a fifth bag, while two more scraped soil from the bottom of the opened grave with the focused intensity of biblical archaeologists. As Gilchrist stepped forward, one of the SOCOs in the grave looked up. Despite coveralls that hid his balding pate and made his face look round and tight, Gilchrist recognized Bert Mackie, not a SOCO but the police pathologist from Ninewells Hospital in Dundee.

'Any luck, Bert?' he asked.

'I expect you mean have we found any items of identification?'

'That'll do for starters.'

'Afraid not, Andy. All we have at the moment are bones. No watches, no jewellery. And the clothes have deteriorated to rags.

5

Looks like she was wearing some sort of nylon jacket, but it's difficult to say at this stage—'

'She?'

'The bra gives the game away. Unless *he* was trying it on for size. Interestingly,' he added, scowling at a muddied bone, scraping at it with his thumb, 'she appears not to have been wearing any knickers.'

'Could they have rotted away?'

'I'd expect to find traces of elastic.' Mackie shook his head. 'None so far.'

Gilchrist wondered if that was important. Why wear a bra, but no knickers? Had she just had sex, perhaps a *quickie*, and something was said that ended in violence? Had she been raped, then murdered? Or did she simply like to walk around feeling free and airy, so to speak? 'Any ideas on her age?' he asked.

'I'll be in a better position to confirm that after a full postmortem, of course. But if I was pushed, I'd say late teens, early twenties.'

Gilchrist squatted by the open grave. 'This no knickers thing,' he persisted. 'Any thoughts?'

'Sex is always a grand motive,' said Mackie. 'He wants some. She doesn't. He's drunk. They argue. Turns into a fight, and before you know where you are he has a fit and batters her to death.'

Mackie's explanation seemed brutally simplified, but Gilchrist had heard of less compelling motives. 'Too early to have a stab at cause of death?'

'Neil,' snapped Mackie. 'Skull.'

The SOCO by the plastic bags removed a dirty-brown skull from one of them, which he handed to Mackie as if passing over the Crown jewels.

Mackie took it without a word, and Gilchrist noted that the teeth looked perfect. The skull's deformed shape confirmed the cause of death as blunt trauma. 'See here,' said Mackie, pointing to a jagged hole in front of where the right ear would have been, the skull indented, networked with cracks. 'Best guess would be a single blow to the temple. And to crush the skull like that, she was most likely dead when she hit the deck. Definitely unconscious. From the damage here,' he said, and ran his finger over the bone, 'to here, I'd say not a hammer. The impact dent would have been more circular. And not an axe. The skull's been crushed, not cut.'

'Blunt axe?' offered Gilchrist.

Mackie shook his head. 'Something broader, more rounded. If she was killed at home, perhaps the base of a heavy table lamp. Now that would do it.' Seemingly satisfied with his theory, Mackie offered the skull to Gilchrist.

Gilchrist folded his arms. He had never been comfortable handling human remains. Not long after joining the Force, he had once held the skull of a man shot through the head, and found himself struggling to control his emotions as he visualized the bullet thudding into the forehead, ripping through the brain and exiting in an eruption of blood and gore. Had the man felt any pain? Or just a numbing thud, followed by blinded confusion then death? At what point in the bullet's passing had the man died? Gilchrist had managed to hand back the skull before vomiting over the mortuary floor. From that point on, he made sure to keep a safe distance.

'It's a classic wound for someone murdered on the spur of the moment,' said Mackie. 'Face to face. A heavy blow that crushed her skull and sent her flying, either dead or dying.' He gave a slow-motion demonstration, holding an imaginary weapon and striking at the skull.

'Left-handed, I see,' said Gilchrist. 'Unless she was struck from behind, of course.'

'Of course,' said Mackie.

Gilchrist stared at the battered skull. Had sex been the motive behind this young woman's murder? Had she put up a fight that ended in her death? Regardless of how she was killed, her disappearance would not have gone unreported. Someone would have missed her – her parents, boyfriend, sister, brother. She could not have vanished without some stirring in the local press. But Stan had found nothing up to 1975. Maybe Nance would have better luck with the Police National Computer.

Mackie handed the skull back to the SOCO.

'Dr Mackie, sir?' shouted the other SOCO, scraping around the exposed ribcage.

Gilchrist found himself on hands and knees, leaning into the grave.

'It looks like a metal case, sir.'

'Camera,' ordered Mackie, and flapped a hand to his side.

The SOCO by the plastic bags obliged.

The camera flashed as Mackie pried more soil loose and eased a rusted lump of metal from the rotted remains of clothing. 'Ah-hah,' he said, holding it to his face. 'Looks like we've found ourselves a cigarette lighter.' Mackie rubbed the lighter's rusted surface with his thumb, holding it as if about to light up. 'Don't suppose it works,' he said.

'Shouldn't think so.'

Mackie reached for a metal box beside the moss-covered headstone and removed a magnifying glass. He turned his attention to the lighter. 'Looks as if there's some marks here,' he mumbled, 'scratched on the side. Difficult to say. Could be damage to the case, of course. Or just natural deterioration.'

'May I?' asked Gilchrist.

The case was about three inches long by two wide, scarred black with rust. Gilchrist supposed it had been silver-coated at one time. He studied it through the magnifier, tried to make sense of the markings, but the metal was too rusted after all that time. 'They could be anything,' he said, and handed the magnifying glass and lighter back to Mackie. 'Can you clean it up?' he asked. 'I'd like to know if they mean anything. You never know.'

'Let me see what I can come up with.'

Gilchrist thanked Mackie and stepped from the tent.

Outside, the crisp air and bright sunlight failed to lift his spirits. Somehow, the discovery of the cigarette lighter troubled him. Seven years earlier, a child's body had been discovered on a stretch of dunes, a pair of matching footprints stamped into the sand close by. Gilchrist's suspicion that they had been set there to lead them away from the murderer had been proven correct in the end. And now he had that same feeling with the cigarette lighter.

It seemed so innocent, it rattled alarm bells. They had found no watch or jewellery of any kind on the woman. Only the lighter. If the killer had removed her jewellery, if in fact she had ever worn any, why leave the lighter? Gilchrist grimaced at the thought. Had the lighter been overlooked? Or was he searching for clues where there were none?

As he unzipped his coveralls, he struggled through his rationale.

Was it possible the lighter had been deliberately left in the woman's clothing? If so, did that mean the killer had known

Hamish McLeod, had known that the family lair would be reopened in the future to bury Lorella, and the body found? It all seemed possible. But more troubling was the thought that for thirty-five years the murder had gone unnoticed, as if the young woman had simply been forgotten by all who had ever known her.

Had her parents been alive? Would they not have missed their own child?

Would she not have had friends, or siblings, someone who would have reported her missing? And now her remains had been found, would her killer worry about her murder investigation commencing? That thought troubled Gilchrist.

After all these years, what secrets from the past was he about to uncover?

CHAPTER 2

By the time Gilchrist left the cemetery the day was dying, clear skies turning a murky grey. A chilling dampness in the air hinted of rain to follow. The woman's remains had been removed and bagged, as had the soil from the grave. Other than the rotting remnants of some clothing and the cigarette lighter, nothing of any real significance had been found. Somehow, just thinking about that lighter gave Gilchrist an urge to feel the hot hit of a cigarette. To change his thoughts, he called Nance, but ended up leaving a message.

He stopped by Lafferty's. Six thirty, and night had already begun.

Fast Eddy winked as he caught his eye. 'Usual, Andy?'

'You talked me into it.' Gilchrist rested his elbow on the counter and eyed the pint of Eighty-Shilling as its creamy head filled the glass and threatened to foam over the top.

'First of the day?'

'And gasping for it.'

Fast Eddy machine-gunned a laugh. 'All that sunshine works up a right thirst,' he said. 'Enjoy it while you can. It's supposed to be pissing by the weekend.' He eased the pint from under the tap. 'I'll never understand why you don't put on any weight. You stopped eating or something?'

'Stopped smoking.'

'I had a cousin who gave up smoking. Put on three stone in three months. That's a ton of beef, let me tell you. Three stone? He'd love to know your secret. What are you now? Ten? Ten and a half?'

'Almost twelve last time I looked.'

'Get out of here.' Fast Eddy mouthed a silent whistle and glanced at a blonde who had risen from the bench seat that backed on to the street window. 'With you in a sec, love,' he said, giving her a smile and a wink. He slid Gilchrist's pint over. 'Here you go, Andy. This one's on me.'

Gilchrist raised his eyebrow. 'What's the occasion, Eddy? My birthday's not until the end of the year.'

'I think I'm about to get lucky, if you know what I mean.'

Gilchrist lifted his glass to his lips. 'Thought you were settling down with Amy.'

'A man would be a fool to fight nature, Andy. Shagging to a man is as natural as breathing. It's his instincts, is what it is.' He winked, then lowered his voice. 'Now what would a man do with that, I ask myself.'

Gilchrist thought the blonde looked over-tanned. With her mobile phone to her ear, and navy-blue jacket and trousers, she looked every bit the businesswoman. She caught his eye at that moment, and he gave a quick smile, then returned his attention to his Eighty-Shilling. The beer tasted cold and creamy, and he had just opened the sports page of the *Daily Record* when he sensed someone beside him.

'I was told I might find you here.' Her jacket heaved with

sunburned cleavage. She thrust out her hand. 'Hi,' she said, her lips twisting in a crooked smile that warned Gilchrist to be careful. 'I'm Gina.'

He caught her American accent, placed her somewhere in the New York area. Her grip felt businesslike, firm and brisk.

'Andy,' he said.

'And I'm Eddy. Nice to meet you, Gina,' he offered, giving one of his best Irish smiles.

She kept her eyes on Gilchrist. 'Detective Chief Inspector Andrew James Gilchrist,' she continued, 'of the St Andrews Division of Fife Constabulary's Crime Management Department, to be precise.'

'Quite a mouthful,' said Gilchrist.

'Quite a title.'

Gilchrist ran his fingers over his lips. 'Well, Gina, you have me at a disadvantage.'

'Which doesn't happen often, I hear.'

'You seem to know more about me than I do about you.'

'We could change that.' She turned to Fast Eddy. 'I'll have a double Tanqueray and tonic. Ten, if you've got it. And plenty of ice.'

'No Ten, I'm afraid. Just regular.'

'You need to get Ten in.' Then back to Gilchrist. 'Pint of Eighty-Shilling, is it?'

'I've just got one.'

'And another Eighty-Shilling for Detective Chief Inspector Gilchrist.'

'Must be my birthday,' he said. 'That makes two.'

'Your birthday's not for another two months.'

Gilchrist paused mid-sip.

13

'Born December thirty-first, nineteen fifty-six, to Jack and May Gilchrist. Lived in St Andrews most of your life. Married Gail Jamieson from Glasgow at the age of twenty. Have two children, Jack and Maureen, both now living in Glasgow. Divorced your wife eight years ago for adultery.'

Gilchrist clapped his pint on the counter.

Fast Eddy stopped slicing his lemon.

'My name is Gina Belli,' she said, 'and before you let me have it, I'm not prying.'

'Define *prying*.'

'I'm an author. And a psychic. I write true crime stories for a living. You may have heard of me.'

'*The* Gina Belli,' chirped Fast Eddy, placing her gin and tonic in front of her.

She raised one eyebrow. 'What was the title of my last book?'

'Slipped my mind. But I'll be buying a copy if you promise to sign it.'

She chuckled, raised her gin and tonic to Gilchrist. 'To my next case study.' Her dark eyes twinkled as she eyed him over the rim of her glass. 'DCI Andy Gilchrist.'

'I always told him he would be famous one day,' Fast Eddy said. 'Didn't I tell you that, Andy? And let me tell you something, Gina, my darling. Never has there been a finer detective chief inspector to cross my threshold. Write that down in your book, darling. There you go, Andy.'

Another frothy pint of Eighty slid across the counter, but Gilchrist only stared at it.

'You don't look pleased,' she said. 'Which is not uncommon. You're suffering mixed emotions. Anger at what you consider to be the violation of your private life, although as a prominent member of Fife Constabulary that seems pretentious. Flattered at my interest in writing you into my next book. And curious as to why.'

'I can assure you I'm neither angry nor flattered, although I am a little curious. But I'm also not interested.'

She shook her head. 'Doesn't matter. I'm going ahead whether you're interested or not, with or without your approval. Of course,' she added, and slid closer so that her chest pressed against his upper arm, 'I always find it more gratifying working with someone who approves of what I'm doing.'

She looked older, close up. Her powdered skin hid tiny acne scars that punctured her cheeks. He saw, too, how her eyebrows were black, thinned and powdered to lighten them. Her blonde hair seemed clear of dark roots, so he assumed she'd been at the salon in the last day or so. Gina Belli, it seemed, was not from old money, but gave the impression of having clawed her way to the peak of whatever pile she thought she now stood on top of.

Gilchrist shifted his stance, freed his arm from the pressure of her chest.

She breathed him in. 'Is that Aramis?'

'No.'

'Must be Dunhill, then.'

Gilchrist thought he kept his surprise hidden.

She laughed, stepped back, finished her gin with a flourish. 'Give me another,' she ordered, then lowered her head and eyed Gilchrist over the top of imaginary glasses. 'I could get to like you, Andy.'

He finished off his beer and surprised himself by lifting the second pint. 'Well, Ms Belli,' he said, 'before I leave, I'd like to ask a question.'

'Gina. Please.'

'Why me?'

'You're famous.'

'Since when?'

'Since you solved the Stabber case.'

'I was only one of an entire investigation team—'

'Who was suspended and battled on alone.'

'It took the entire Force to—'

'Modest, too. I like that,' she said, and before Gilchrist could complain, added, 'And photogenic. I've seen some press coverage. We can do better than that. But most important of all, people will *pay* to read about your uncanny ability to solve difficult cases.'

Gilchrist almost laughed. 'I really don't think so.'

'That's where you're wrong, Detective Chief Inspector. I'm good at what I do. One of the best. And so are you. You're a best-seller just waiting to be sold, and you don't even know it.'

Gilchrist took one long sip then pushed his half-finished pint away. 'Listen, Ms Belli. I'm flattered. Truly I am. But I'm not inter-ested. It was nice meeting you.' He turned from the bar. 'Catch you later, Eddy.'

'Gotcha, Andy.'

'Before you go.'

Gilchrist stopped, but knew he should have kept walking.

'Grant me exclusive permission to write about you and your cases, and you get a percentage of the royalties. And we're not talk-ing paltry sums here.' She shook her head. Her face seemed to harden. 'No permission, no percentage.' She shrugged and smiled. 'Sorry, but that's the way it is.'

Gilchrist made to push past.

'Wait.' She slipped her hand into her bag and took out a business card. When she realized he was not going to take it she pushed it into his shirt pocket. 'My mobile's on twenty-four seven.'

Outside, the temperature had dropped close to freezing. Stars glittered in a cloudless sky, giving prelude to a bitter night. Gilchrist removed Gina Belli's card from his shirt pocket, was about to rip it up, when something stopped him.

Instead, he slipped it into his wallet and kept walking.

She caught up with him as he stepped into Market Street, and surprised him by slipping her arm through his.

'Do you mind?' she asked. 'It's cold.'

He resisted pulling free, and said, 'Well, in that case . . .'

He said nothing as they strolled across the cobbled street.

'Where are you taking me?' she asked.

'Nowhere.'

'Never been there.'

As they neared PM's, the vinegary smell of fish and chips helped lift the misery of his day and reminded him he had missed lunch. 'How about a fish supper?' he asked her.

'What about my figure?'

'It looks fine to me.'

'You should see it naked.' She chuckled, her voice rasping like a smoker's cough. 'I'll make you a deal,' she went on, tightening her grip. 'Skip the fish and chips and take me to a favourite pub of yours, and I'll buy the rounds.'

It sounded more like a command than a request, but Gilchrist, to his surprise, heard himself say, 'Just the one, then.'

'The one what?' she asked, eyes glinting with mischief. Then she tugged at his arm as if in reprimand. 'I see I'm going to have to watch what I say to you. You take everything so literally.'

'A fault of mine,' he said.

'One of many, I'm sure.'

Like a long-standing couple, they entered Union Street arm in arm. The air felt cold and damp on his throat, and he adjusted his scarf. Her fragrance, a perfume he knew he had smelled before, but could not place, teased with his senses. Her grip felt firm, not too tight, as if she feared that giving him any slack would let him flee. Their breath puffed hard in the night air, and they fell into easy step with each other, her thigh bumping against his.

'Penny for your thoughts?' she asked.

What could he tell her? That he had let Maureen and Jack down by not attending the wake? That he should have called to explain? That he regretted the bitter end to his marriage with Gail? That the last time he visited her, they had argued? He shrugged. 'Thought you were a psychic.'

She tugged his arm as if in annoyance, then carried on in silence.

They reached the Dunvegan Hotel as light rain started to fall. Gina brushed a bejewelled hand through her hair as she stepped into the bar. If Gilchrist had not known better, he would have sworn the room stilled for an instant. Gina looked in her element, like a star in the limelight toying with the cameras. She slipped off her coat, then her jacket, to reveal a matching waistcoat – no blouse – that exposed lean arms and tight muscle tone.

'I'm going to have a Glenfiddich,' she said. 'On the rocks. Want one?'

'It's Glenfiddich with an ick, not an itch.'

'There's that perfectionism again. So you'll join me?'

Gilchrist seldom drank whisky, but said, 'Why not?'

'Two double Glenfiddichs,' she said to the barman. 'On the rocks.'

While Gina studied the gantry, Gilchrist studied the lounge. He recognized a number of regulars, nodding to them when they glanced his way.

'You're a popular kind of a guy,' she said.

'It's a small town.'

'And you're the small-town hero.' She handed Gilchrist his whisky. 'I tell you, it makes you almost irresistible.' She raised her glass. 'What do they say in Scotland? Up your kilt?'

'Something like that.'

'Up your kilt, Detective Chief Inspector Andy Gilchrist.' She chinked her glass against his, then took more than a fair mouthful.

'I'm off duty,' he said. 'Andy's fine.'

She grinned, white teeth against tanned skin. 'I didn't want to sound too intimate in a crowded bar.'

'Do you always do this with your subjects?' he said. 'Act the vixen?'

Something flashed behind her eyes. Anger, irritation, he could not say. She seemed like a crackerjack filled with emotions, as if she could burst into laughter one second then attack him with clawed fingernails the next. But the moment passed.

'My latest book was about the case of Frankie Hannerstone,' she said.

'Never heard of him.'

'Her.'

'Still drawing a blank.'

'Frankie went to work one morning, four years ago, and never arrived. Her husband reported her missing later that night. By the time I was called in, she'd been missing for two years in the Carolinas. The FBI suspected her husband had killed her, but he had a rock-solid alibi. Plus, no body. He claimed she'd been threatening for years to leave him. So he supposed that's what she'd done.'

'You were called in?'

'Huh?'

'You said you were called in. Why?'

'As well as writing, I'm a psychic-detective. I assist law-enforcement officers throughout the States in solving cold cases. Three out of every four I'm involved in get closed, or are progressed significantly.'

'That's an impressive record.'

She eased closer, as if to confide in him. 'It all depends on how my sightings are received, and what the police do with them. Whether they take them seriously enough to consider throwing resources at it, or not.'

'Sightings? As in, I see dead people?'

'Yes.' She took a sip. 'Does that scare you?'

'No,' he said. 'Just hard to believe.'

'I'm used to disbelievers.'

'Do you see any dead people now?'

She nodded to a group of four ruddy-faced caddies at the corner of the bar. 'The guy at the end,' she said, 'has just lost a family member.'

'Male or female?'

'Female.'

'You can see her?'

'It's not as simple as that. But, yes, I *see* her.'

Gilchrist studied the caddies. They seemed to be enjoying

themselves, not exactly mourning the loss of a family member. Somehow, just looking at them caused the hair on the nape of his neck to rise. He returned to the safety of his drink. The whisky warmed his throat, the ice chilled it.

'So, this Frankie Hannerstone,' he said, 'did you find her?'

'In a storage locker on the outskirts of Vegas. Her body had been chopped up and kept in a deep freezer.'

'How did you discover it?'

'I didn't. I gave the police clues from her personal effects.'

'You rub your thumbs over a photo or two, then tell them where to find the body?'

'Buy my book. Check it out. Call up the Sheriff's Office. They'll confirm it.' She paused, as if trying to read the disbelief on Gilchrist's face. 'And what about *your* cold cases?' she asked him.

An image of the skeleton burst into his mind. 'What about them?'

'*It*,' she said.

'Now you've lost me.'

'That's the author in me.'

Maybe it was the effects of the whisky, or the cosiness of the bar, or the look in her eyes, but Gilchrist surprised himself by saying, 'Which case would you like to discuss?'

'Tell me about your brother Jack,' she said, without missing a beat.

Something shifted in Gilchrist's chest. 'That's out of bounds,' he grunted.

'You were only twelve when it happened. Surely—'

'Look,' he said, struggling to keep his tone even, 'I'm happy to have a drink with you, but if you don't want my company, keep this up.'

21

Her gaze danced over his, as if searching for the strength of his conviction in one or other of his eyes. Then she glared at him. 'You're serious.'

'I'm glad we agree on something.'

'Come on, Andy. I can help you.'

'You're surprising me.'

'In what way?'

'You're not as smart as I first thought.'

Her look changed at that moment, and she set her whisky on the bar with a force that should have cracked the glass. She pulled on her jacket, threw her coat over her arm. 'It's such a pity,' she snarled. 'I was getting to like you.'

When she left, he ordered a pint of Eighty. But it did little to cheer him. Somehow, Gina's departure felt like a replay of all his past relationships, as if reaffirming how he would spend the rest of his life; standing alone in a bar, with his pint. He took no more than a sip before he shoved the glass away.

As he stood to leave, he caught the hotel owner's eye. 'Sheena,' he said. 'These four at the end of the bar. Anyone in mourning?'

'Danny,' she replied. 'His sister was killed in a car accident last weekend.'

Gilchrist pulled his scarf around his neck. He thought he caught a look of mourning in Danny's eyes as he pushed through the crowd.

CHAPTER 3

The following morning, Gilchrist arrived at the office just after 6.30, and almost bumped into DI Walter 'Tosh' MacIntosh as he pushed through the entrance doorway.

'Only the wicked get in this early, Gilchrist. Kicked you out of bed, did she?'

Gilchrist's half-nod and snarl for a smile was all he could offer the man.

'Some dog you picked up last night, was she?' Tosh said, pushing past him and out into the morning chill. 'That cock of yours is going to land you in trouble one day.'

Gilchrist strode towards his office, Tosh's laughter ringing in his ears.

It took a good thirty minutes before he managed to push all thoughts of Tosh from his head and, after checking his email and catching up with the latest reports on his investigation, none of which told him anything new, he reached the Victoria Café by eight o'clock. He ordered only a pot of tea, and was lost in the *Courier* when Stan arrived. At six foot two Stan was one inch taller than Gilchrist. But where Gilchrist was slim-framed, Stan had shoulders wide enough to hang a suit on. He pulled up the chair opposite and flicked open his notebook.

'Here's what I've got,' Stan said. 'Some of the older folks remember McLeod's funeral.' He ran a finger down the page. 'Most are in their seventies and eighties now, and those I spoke to offered a few more names until I have what I think is the full list. Well, at least of the locals. But I think that's it. The McLeods had no children, no living relatives.'

'No living relatives thirty-five years ago?'

Stan blinked, then scribbled in his notebook. 'That I don't know yet.'

'Keep going.'

'As best I can tell, twenty-two people attended McLeod's funeral. Of those, twelve are no longer around . . .'

'Dead? Or left the area?'

'Eleven dead. One in England. Nance is chasing up on that. Which leaves ten.'

'And?'

'Most interesting was old Sammy Wilson, now eighty-six. His wife passed away last year at the age of ninety.' Stan looked at his notes. 'Sammy says he went to McLeod's funeral so he would know where to go when he wanted to shite on someone's grave.'

'Charming.'

'His own words. According to Sammy, Hamish McLeod was a miserable bastard who deliberately died so he wouldn't have to cough up the fiver he owed him.'

Gilchrist grimaced. He had seen fights start in bars over change that would not buy a book of matches.

'Then there's Tam and Liz Docherty,' Stan said, studying his

24

notes. 'Could barely remember each other's names, let alone what went on thirty-odd years ago. Then Bernie Bingham.'

'Bingham? Is that the Bingham who—'

'The very same. His wife, Betty, committed suicide not long after. But he looks like he's lost all his marbles now. Just sat there staring into space.'

Gilchrist felt something shift in his gut. The decomposed bodies of both Bingham children had been found in an abandoned well twenty-four years ago.

'Jack and Doreen McGinlay,' Stan went on. 'They're still alive. Barely. No luck there. Then we're on to Dan Simpson. He was able to tell me he went with a couple of his drinking buddies – Billy McLeod, no relation to Hamish, and Jimmy Patterson – but they couldn't tell me anything new.'

'You said ten,' said Gilchrist. 'That was nine.'

Stan closed his notebook. 'Douglas Ewart was there.'

For a fleeting moment, the name did not register. 'Dougie?' Gilchrist finally said.

'The very same. He was a medical student at the university back then. Says his family knew the McLeods.'

'You've spoken to him?'

'Phoned him last night around midnight. Said he couldn't speak, his wife was asleep. I pissed him off a touch. But he agreed to meet. If anyone can remember what went on back then, he can.'

Stan's bacon roll was served, and Gilchrist poured two cups of tea, recalling what he could of Douglas Ewart MD.

Dougie once worked with Bert Mackie as assistant police pathologist in Ninewells, but left in the early eighties to set up a private practice in Cupar. Apparently the sight of one too many dead bodies forced him to change career, and as coincidence would have it, it had been the bodies of the Bingham children that caused him to move. Though he had no children of his own, he had found the task of performing a post-mortem on their mutilated and decomposed bodies too much to stomach. Two weeks rotting in the stinking mud of an abandoned well would do that to human flesh.

As far as Gilchrist knew, Dougie was a private man who went through life with the minimum of fuss, never ruffling feathers, doing his job to the best of his ability. He was not a high-flyer, more of a plodder, and someone you could trust.

'He said he had a break in his morning schedule at nine thirty, which gives us . . .' Stan looked at his wristwatch, '. . . ten minutes to finish breakfast.'

They arrived at Ewart's surgery five minutes late. The building looked drab and uninviting, a box extension on to an old stone complex. The receptionist led them down a hallway that ended at a white door. She knocked, pushed the door and stepped to the side.

Ewart crossed the room with the single-mindedness of a lion chasing a gazelle. 'Come in, come in,' he said, and shook Gilchrist's hand. 'Good to see you again, Andy.'

Gilchrist introduced Stan, and Ewart grabbed his hand.

Ewart's office was small and square and uninteresting. Two windows, framed by white venetian blinds, kept out the sunlight. Glossy prints of various parts of the human anatomy hung in a haphazard arrangement on walls that could have used a coat of paint. Ewart appeared to be a man who wasted no money on luxuries, which matched Gilchrist's earlier memories of him. Ewart drifted behind his desk and gestured at the seats.

'Right,' Ewart began. 'How can I help?'

'Apologies for calling so late last night,' said Stan. 'I'm sure you understand.'

'Afraid Millie was not a little displeased, I have to say. Beauty sleep, and all that.'

Gilchrist thought he caught a hint of annoyance in Ewart's eyes, nothing much, but enough to pique his interest. 'Your wife?'

'Second wife. Nothing like Megs. Different animal altogether. Day and night.'

Gilchrist nodded. 'Of course.'

'No problem. I'll prune the bushes at the weekend. Keep her sweet.' Ewart rattled out a laugh. 'Millie loves the garden. Keeps me on my toes.' He wrung his hands. 'So, what's this all about?'

'We want to ask you about Hamish McLeod's funeral,' said Gilchrist. 'Back in February '69. I believe you were there.'

Ewart's gaze settled on something over Gilchrist's shoulder for a long moment, then returned. 'What about it?'

'How well did you know Hamish?'

Ewart frowned, shook his head. 'Hardly at all. He was a friend of my parents. Worked in the Post Office with my father. For some reason, neither he nor my mother wanted to go to his funeral.'

'Why not?'

'No idea. Never asked. Just did as I was told. Went along to represent the family.'

'Your parents still alive?' Stan asked.

'No. Both gone over ten years now. Within a year of each other.'

'I'm sorry,' said Gilchrist.

'Thank you.'

'Did you know Mrs McLeod died three days ago?'

'No. I didn't.'

'Can you remember who was at Hamish's funeral?'

27

'Not really,' he said. 'They were mostly friends of my parents, and older than me. I didn't want to go. But duty called. It was a miserable affair. And a miserable day, too. Dull and raining. Umbrellas up. I can still see Mrs McLeod standing at the graveside. She seemed strong, in control of her emotions. Not crying. And her daughter, too. She was there.'

Gilchrist paused. 'The McLeods didn't have any children.'

'They didn't?' Ewart frowned. 'Well, that goes to show how well I knew them.'

'Why did you think she was her daughter?'

'She had dark hair, dark eyes and looked Italian. So naturally I assumed she was her daughter. I wonder who she could have been.'

'She looked Italian?'

Ewart almost smirked. 'Mrs McLeod's family was from Italy.'

Gilchrist leaned forward. 'I thought you hardly knew the McLeods.'

Ewart looked straight at Gilchrist, hands flat on his desk. 'My father told me,' he said. 'Mrs McLeod came to Scotland as a young woman not long after the war.'

'Did you speak to her after the funeral?'

'No. I went home.' Ewart tried to give an embarrassed shrug. 'Most of the other students lived in rented accommodation. Being a local boy I stayed at home with good old Mum and Dad.'

Gilchrist forced his thoughts back on track. 'Can you recall how many people were there?' he asked.

'What's this about, please?'

Ewart's response seemed more challenge than question. Gilchrist placed his elbow on Ewart's desk and moved closer. 'Yesterday,' he said, 'a woman's skeleton was discovered in Hamish's plot.'

28

Ewart grimaced. 'Was anyone reported missing back then?'

'Back when?'

Ewart seemed to freeze, like a child trapped in the telling of a lie. 'You did say skeleton. So I'm assuming it's been there a while.'

Gilchrist nodded, oddly deflated.

'Well, was there?' Ewart asked.

'We're looking into that,' said Stan.

'Do you know who she was?'

'That's why we're here.'

'Here?' Ewart's face adopted a look of pain. 'Are you in any way suggesting—'

'No. Not at all,' said Gilchrist, and returned Ewart's firm look with one of his own. 'We're trying to establish who was at the funeral, what they saw, what they can remember. We intend to talk to everyone who was there.'

Ewart settled, seemingly satisfied. 'Well, I've told all I know.'

Gilchrist prodded a few more questions, but Ewart could offer little more. Gilchrist stood, and offered his hand. 'Thanks for your time, Dougie. You've been very helpful.'

'My pleasure.' Ewart shook Gilchrist's hand as vigorously as before. He smiled, a short flash of teeth that folded into a grimace. 'If there's anything else I can do . . .'

'We'll be in touch.'

Outside, Gilchrist and Stan walked across the car park in silence.

The Merc's lights flashed as Gilchrist pressed his remote and opened the door.

Gilchrist swung his Roadster around the end of a row of parked cars and drove back past Ewart's office. 'Don't be too obvious, Stan, but second window from the right. What do you see?' Gilchrist eased along the car park and pulled to a halt at the exit.

From that location, Ewart's office was out of sight. 'Anything?' he asked.

'Someone peeped through the blinds, boss.'

'Dougie?'

'Maybe.'

'Now why would he do that?'

'Happy to see us leave?'

'That would be my first guess.' Gilchrist pulled into the flow of traffic.

'Have to say, boss, that I thought he had a good memory. All those years ago and he can still remember what the weather was like.'

'Meaning?'

'That if I didn't know any better, I'd say he was ready for your questions.'

Gilchrist gave Stan's words some thought. But an image of Dr Douglas Ewart in the throes of murdering someone, and a woman at that, simply refused to manifest. 'You got Sammy Wilson's address?' he asked.

Stan slapped his pocket. 'In my notebook, boss.'

'Good,' said Gilchrist. 'I'd like to talk to him.'

CHAPTER 4

Sammy Wilson lived in a council house on Tom Morris Drive, south of the West Port. The garden either side of the slabbed path looked neat and tidy, but on closer inspection had about it the look of an old man's face after shaving in the dark.

Sammy answered the door wearing a worn woollen coat and flat cap, its tip finger-blackened smooth. For a moment he struggled for recognition, then showed his false teeth. 'It's yourself, son,' he said. 'In yous come.'

'Were you going out?' asked Gilchrist.

'Naw. The bloody place is freezing. Have to wear a coat to keep the heating bills down.' He turned and stepped down the hall, his voice echoing, thickened with phlegm. 'Scandalous, so it is, the bloody price of stuff.' He gave a cough that seemed to shake his body to his toes. 'Can hardly afford to buy myself a bloody half these days.'

Gilchrist walked along a dark hallway redolent of burned toast. Doors lay opened to bedrooms long since transformed into storage rooms. Cardboard boxes, plastic crates, clothes folded badly, rows of leather boots, shoes, half a library of paperbacks, bicycles

31

by the dozen, littered the floors and climbed the walls. In the far corner by a curtained window he glimpsed a scythe, its curved wooden handle grey with age.

They followed Sammy into a room with drawn curtains. The floor was cramped from more junk, except for a cleared space in the middle of a threadbare carpet. A television sat on an upturned milk crate, a wire aerial perched on top. A fuzzy black-and-white picture filled its screen, faced by a wooden chair with a single cushion.

'I'd offer you a seat. But I've only got the one.'

'We're used to standing,' said Gilchrist.

'Do yous golf?'

Gilchrist followed Sammy's gaze to a bundle of knotted plastic bags on the floor that bulged with the pimpled swelling of what had to be hundreds of golf balls.

'A way to make some spare cash, son, without the taxman knowing. I walk the golf courses, like. But I'm no stupid. I know where to look. See?' He tapped the side of his head. 'Gives me money for beer.'

'How much do you sell them for?' Stan asked.

'Three for a pound. Thirty-five pee each.'

Stan peered at the rows of bags. 'Any Titleist Pro V-1s?'

'Aye, son. But they're a good ball.' Sammy coughed again, a heavy burst of phlegm that had Gilchrist thinking the old man had pneumonia. From a box behind him, Sammy pulled out another plastic bag. 'I have to charge fifty pee each for these ones, son. That's two for a pound. Take as many as you like.'

Stan took hold of the bag.

'While Tiger's going through the stash,' Gilchrist said, 'I'd like to ask a few questions. We're here about Hamish McLeod's funeral.'

Sammy scowled. 'I hope they make as much fuss about my funeral as they're making about that miserable old sod's.'

'What was your relationship to Hamish?'

'I wisnae related to—'

'I know that, Sammy. But why did you go to his funeral?'

'As a mark of respect, like.'

'I thought you didn't like him.'

'It wisnae out of respect for that thieving bastard,' growled Sammy, his eyes taking on a distant look. 'It was for Lorella. She was a fine-looking woman, son,' he said, and stared at some spot on the wall.

Gilchrist thought he now understood the reason for Sammy's dislike of Hamish. He waited until the old man's gaze returned to him with a couple of blinks, as if surprised to find he was still alive. 'We're trying to establish the names of everyone who attended the funeral. Could I ask you to go through them again?'

'I done that last night, son.'

'Maybe a name or two came back to you in your dreams.' He tapped Stan on the arm. Stan pulled out his notebook.

Sammy shut his eyes and recited each name in turn, Stan ticking them off as he did so. The old man's eyes flickered as if watching some action on the back of paper-thin eyelids, each name followed by a nod. At last, he looked at Gilchrist. 'Of course, my Jenny was alive back then.'

Gilchrist waited while Sammy dabbed a thick thumb to the corners of his eyes. 'Take your time,' he offered. 'You're doing wonderfully well.'

Sammy grimaced. 'There was two more. But I didnae know their names.'

'Can you remember what they looked like?'

33

Sammy shook his head. 'I didnae pay them any attention, mind. I just clicked that they was there, like.'

'Male? Female?'

'A man and a woman. Students, I think they was.'

'Young, were they?'

'Aye.'

'Were they together?'

'I don't think so.'

Dougie Ewart, thought Gilchrist. And Mrs McLeod's *'daughter'*. 'Did you see the young woman console Mrs McLeod?'

Sammy frowned, causing skin to corrugate the length of his forehead, letting Gilchrist see the full age of the man. 'Everybody was consoling her, son.'

'But the woman who stood beside her,' nudged Gilchrist. 'The one who was hugging her and talking to her. Can you remember her, Sammy?'

Sammy turned his head and stared at the heap of domestic junk, as if each box was a book of memories from which he could retrieve an image.

Gilchrist placed a hand on Sammy's shoulder, felt the hard lump of bones beneath the coat. 'If you can't remember, Sammy, it doesn't matter.'

'Sorry, son. It's just too long ago.' He coughed again, a barking sound that echoed from somewhere deep inside his chest.

'I think you should see the doctor, Sammy.'

'Cannae stand the buggers. A hot toady's what I need.'

Gilchrist handed over his card. 'If you remember anything else, give me a call.'

'I'll take the lot,' said Stan. 'Sixteen Pro V-1s in here. That's eight quid.'

34

Gilchrist pulled out a twenty and handed it to Sammy. 'Keep the change, Sammy.'

'Son?'

'Buy yourself a bottle and have some hot toadies. You've been a great help.'

They spent the remainder of the day checking local misper files and the Police National Computer reports for mispers around the time of McLeod's funeral.

Local records turned up nothing. Two teenage boys had disappeared from Crail in October of that year. Gilchrist had vague memories of the incident, being only twelve at the time. Ten years later, one of the boys returned, having lived in London with his missing friend who was then working in a bar in St Tropez.

The PNC files offered more promising leads and Gilchrist downloaded photographs where available, or asked the local police to fax or email him what they had. By the end of the day, they had a few more mispers to look into.

'That's nine possibles,' said Stan. 'And I'd say at least five of these are long shots. But we still don't know for sure that she went missing in '69.'

'It's all we've got,' Gilchrist conceded. He picked up one of the photographs. The date confirmed the girl had been missing for nineteen years. She looked to be in her teens, hair dark, untidy, with eyes that could have been borrowed from an older woman. What had he been doing when she had vanished? Back then he and Gail had been happy. At the moment of the girl's disappearance, had he and Gail been laughing, crying, making love? Playing with their own children? He studied the image. Thin lips stretched tight over teeth almost hidden from the camera, but parted just enough to confirm that one of her front teeth was decayed black. He handed the photograph to Stan and pushed himself to his feet.

'Where're we off to, boss?'

'We're not. You stay put and get dental records for every one of these.'

Stan's face almost slumped.

Gilchrist pulled his Mercedes into the car park of the police mortuary in West Bell Street, Dundee. Inside, he entered the post-mortem room and found Bert Mackie already hard at it, his attention held by a skeleton on the closer of the two PM tables. Gilchrist had never become accustomed to the smell of the mortuary, a fragrance thick enough to taste. He slipped an elasticated mask over his lower face as he approached the table.

Mackie glanced up. 'Been expecting you, Andy. Come see our lady.'

In front of him lay a disconnected skeleton, bones washed clean and tinged red from soil that now lay like mud in a bucket on the tiled floor. Gilchrist tried to picture the skeleton covered with skin and, in doing so, imagined the woman to be slim.

'What do we have?' he asked Mackie.

'The thirty-plus-year-old skeleton of a young woman. More than likely killed by a blow to the head. See here?' Mackie ran a finger around the cracked indentation in the skull. 'No new bone growth of any kind, which suggests she died immediately, or shortly after, assuming of course that she was alive at the time of the blow.'

Gilchrist leaned closer.

'Slightly taller than average. Five-ten,' went on Mackie. 'Slight in build. No fractures, no broken bones of any kind. Except this.'

He ran his hand down the skeleton's lower left leg and stopped at the ankle. 'See here?' He removed a bone from the foot. 'This has been cracked and healed, somewhat poorly, I have to say. See this ridge? The fracture is an injury normally associated with a sprain. She could have twisted her foot stepping off the pavement. It's impossible to determine exactly how long before death the fracture occurred, but I'd say no more than a year, maybe less.'

'Anything else?' Gilchrist asked.

'Teeth.' Mackie returned to the top of the table and picked up the skull. 'All thirty-one of them are perfect,' he said. 'Not a single filling. The top right wisdom tooth never came through.'

'Could she be coloured?'

'The shape of the skull suggests Caucasian.' Mackie held the skull in profile, staring at it with almost morbid fascination, before returning it to the head of the skeleton. 'I'd say she was a common-or-garden white woman.'

Gilchrist felt his body give an involuntary shiver. When she had been killed, she had been younger than his daughter, Maureen. And something in that thought sent a cold frisson the length of his spine.

He turned away.

On the other table, a white sheet bulged in the shape of a bloated belly. Was the body simply fat, or swollen by the gases of putrefaction? A set of scales stood nearby, their trays glistening wet with slime, and Gilchrist marvelled at Mackie's apparent resilience to the daily revulsion of his profession – skin that glistened black and blistered like overcooked meat, or peeled from the bone at the touch of a finger, or burst open like ripened fruit.

He forced his attention back to the skull.

He stared at it, trying to imagine skin, nose, lips, eyes, hair, all

37

the superficial tissue that forms the human face. He found his gaze pulled to the eye sockets, and wondered what her eyes had last seen. Had she watched her killer strike? Or had she been taken by surprise? Was her last living image that of a word in a book, or a view from her window?

And her perfect teeth. What had her mouth been like? Had her lips been full or thin? What words had passed between them? Had she called out the name of her killer? Had she screamed? Was that the last sound she made?

Someone must have known her. Someone must have missed her.

'Anyone from the science lab expected over?' he asked.

'Later, they tell me.'

Gilchrist eyed the skeleton. The Police Forensic Science Lab Dundee – PFSLD – had specialists expert in skeletal examination. But *later* was not fast enough. Besides, he needed to ID the woman, and knew someone who might be able to help.

'Is Heather Black still one of the best?' he asked Mackie.

'Glasgow University?'

'That's the one.'

'Last I heard.'

'Overnight the skull to her, would you?'

While Mackie returned his attention to the ankle bone, Gilchrist stared at the skull. If anyone could put a face to this missing woman, Dr Heather Black could. Until then, he would have to go with what he had.

'Did you find anything on the cigarette lighter?' he asked.

Mackie shook his head. 'One of those lighters you used to buy for ten a penny at Woolies.'

'What about the markings?'

38

'Inconclusive. Rusted to buggery. The scratches don't spell out the name of the killer, if that's what you're asking.' Mackie slid the ankle bone back into place, then brushed a finger over the healed fracture as if trying to determine how painful it must have been.

Something in that action had Gilchrist wondering if it was ever too late to change careers. Rather than experience hardening him, Gilchrist found he had developed a weak stomach for the sights and smells of the mortuary. The memory of one recent post-mortem was still fresh in his mind. He had been at a fiftieth the night before and consumed too many beers, as usual. The following morning, pale and heavy-stomached, he faced the decomposing body of a woman recovered from the River Eden and missing for ten days. When Mackie slapped her brain on to the scales with a splashy flourish, it was too much for Gilchrist. He had turned, too late, and vomited as he staggered away.

Relief surged through him when his mobile rang, then sank when he recognized Mo's number. He tried to keep his voice light. 'Hi, Mo.'

'Why didn't you come back to the clubhouse? Everyone was expecting you.'

'Everyone?' he said, pushing through the door. 'I didn't know anyone.'

'It's not like you'd have had to have a political debate or anything.'

He resisted reciting his usual excuse of being too busy. 'I know, Mo. I'm sorry.'

'If you ever gave Harry a chance, Dad, you'd like him. I know you would.'

Gilchrist burst into early-afternoon sunlight, the sky bright through a narrow clearing of clouds. Harry's name being spoken by his daughter still fired some primitive instinct through his system. Gail had left him for Harry, had taken their children with her. Why would Maureen think he would ever give Harry a chance? He tried to keep his voice level. 'I'll make a point of talking to him next time we meet.'

'Don't give me lip service, Dad. I don't like it.'

'I'm not, Mo, I'm—'

'Mum and Harry were married for seven years, Dad. They were happy together. Did you ever think about that?'

All the time, he thought. 'I know Harry was good for Mum,' he said. 'He's going to miss her. We all are.' He opened his car door, sat behind the wheel, pleased that his words appeared to have quietened her. He tried to shift the subject by asking, 'How are you and Jack holding up?'

A sniff, then, 'OK. How about you?'

'Hanging in there.' He stabbed the key into the ignition, gave a twist and the engine fired into life. 'Thinking back on the good times,' he went on. 'When you both were little.'

When Maureen next spoke, her voice was as tight as a child's. 'Mum tried to put a face on it, Dad. But she was so ill. It was awful. Just watching her. There was nothing we could do.'

Nothing we could do. He remembered intending to call last week, then deciding against it. What could he have done? In the end they had all felt helpless.

'When did you last see Mum?' he asked.

'The Sunday before . . .' Her breath brushed the mouthpiece.

'Was she asleep when she died?' Why did he have to know the details?

'Mum slipped away,' she said. 'It was peaceful at the end.'

He caught an image of Gail glaring at him through eyes sunk deep in a skeletal face.

'Will you speak to Harry?' she said.

Her question surprised him. 'I don't see the need.'

'Not even to convey your condolences?'

'We shook hands at the crematorium—'

'Barely, Dad. That doesn't count. You almost ran out of the place.'

The speed with which Maureen's emotions shifted never failed to amaze him. It was like listening to Gail all over again. On the upside, it was a sign of Maureen's recovery. He had to take that from it. Then it hit him with a clarity that stunned him that he was through trying to understand why Gail left. He had was through trying to work out why she hated him. He was just through. Gail was gone, now nothing more than a memory, her face and body and barely remembered smile only images on long-forgotten photographs. He wished he had called at Christmas, spoken to her at New Year, maybe even paid her one last visit in the summer.

'You're right, Mo. I should've been more considerate.'

'Harry loved Mum. He really looked after her.'

Gilchrist struggled to keep quiet.

'And *she* loved *him*,' she pressed on. 'Don't forget that.'

He almost asked why she would tell him that, as if she blamed him for their divorce. After all, Gail was the one who'd had the affair. But he had travelled that road with Maureen before and knew he was on a losing ride. Instead, he said, 'I know.'

His submission seemed to work. 'I know you loved Mum, Dad,' she said. 'I'm sure you must be hurting, too. But Harry took care of her, you know.'

Hearing those words hurt. If he had been there for Gail, been there when she needed him, instead of working the case of the day, would their marriage have survived?

'Mum didn't want you to visit because of the way she looked.'

'It wouldn't have mattered to me how she looked.'

'It mattered to Mum.'

Gilchrist stared across fields that stirred alive with the shadows of tumbling clouds. Beyond, on the horizon, the black silhouette of a ship seemed anchored in time. He felt an inexplicable urge to be standing on board, facing the wind, breathing in the promise of—

'Mum was only a shadow of herself.' Maureen's voice cut into his thoughts like a cold wind. 'She couldn't keep her food down. You would hardly have recognized her.'

Gilchrist pressed his thumb and forefinger into the corners of his eyes, surprised by the sting. Gail had always been a fighter, and she had fought for every one of those final closing days. 'I'm sorry, Mo,' he offered. 'I'm not thinking straight. The whole thing's come as a shock. Are you all right?' He listened to another sniff, then said, 'I'll be in Glasgow this evening. We could meet if you'd like.'

'I can't.'

No explanation, just a statement that dared him to challenge her. But what hurt was the thought that she might prefer to visit Harry rather than spend time with her father. He forced those thoughts away. She had somewhere to go, friends to see. Not Harry.

'Let's talk later,' he said.

'Sure.'

He hung up, but not before Maureen.

He gritted his teeth. After Gail and Harry moved to Glasgow, taking Jack and Maureen with them, he often felt he was out of touch with his children. He promised himself he would call more often, spend more time with them, now Gail had gone. Not that they needed him, if the truth be told, but that he needed them.

With that thought, he called Jack, but could only leave a message, asking him to get back for a chat. He eased the Mercedes off the grass verge and called Stan as he accelerated into traffic.

'Listen to this, boss. Nance visited the university, like you asked.'

Gilchrist pressed the phone to his ear. Nance could be as tough as a bulldog when she got her teeth into something, and twice as determined.

'She spoke to the dean of the geography and geosciences faculty, who said that female students often formed clubs that provided each of its members with a token of membership. Pens, diaries—'

'Cigarette lighters?'

'Correct, boss.'

'And get this,' Stan went on, failing to keep the triumph from his voice. 'They were often initialled.' A pause, as if to let the statement settle. 'I'm willing to bet we'll find initials on the cigarette lighter.'

'Willing enough to try to clear the twenty quid you owe me?'

'Done.'

'Sorry to burst your bubble, Stan, but Bert doesn't think the scratches are initials.'

'Come on, boss. They must be.'

'That's forty. Keep this up and you'll be applying for a mortgage soon.'

'Aw, shit. What are they, then?'

'Bert couldn't say for sure. Probably random scratches.' Gilchrist listened to Stan curse under his breath. 'Great try, Stan. Did the Dean know which club gave out lighters?'

'No, boss. That's problem number two. Some of them were secret, with only three or four members. Some even swore to life-long secrecy.'

'Have Nance stick with it,' he ordered. 'Get her to find out which club gave out what. I want names, addresses, phone numbers, the lot. OK?'

'Got it, boss.'

'Any luck with the dental records?' he went on.

'Yes and no. The good news is they'll be sent through soon. The bad news is that none appear to match. None of her teeth have fillings. They're perfect. Did she never eat sweeties?'

'Maybe her father was a dentist.' Again, Gilchrist wondered why her parents had not reported her missing. Had they been alive back then? Were they alive now? And in a town of sixteen thousand residents, maybe only ten or twelve thousand in '69, why had no one at all reported her missing?

'Nance has come up with a few names, boss. Three students who were all members of the same club. Years ago, Nance's old dear worked as a waitress in the Central Bar of all places, for about ten or twelve years.'

Gilchrist frowned. The Central was one of his regulars, had been for the last thirty-plus years. He'd had his first pint there at the age of sixteen. Underage by two years, but his height helped him pull it off. Besides, the place was always flooded with students, and back then he blended in. If Nance's mother worked in the Central, he must have come across her. *Nancy Wilson. Wilson.* Gilchrist wracked his brain for a face to a name. Then he had it. A small woman, overweight, with dirty blonde hair. 'Her name Phyllis?'

'That's her, boss.'

'I never knew she was Nance's mother.'

'Small world, boss. But listen to this: according to Nance, her old dear remembers a group of girl students who came into the pub at least three times a week. Once a month, on a Saturday night, they would each order up four double Moscow Mules, and on the last one light up cigars.'

'Cigars?'

'It was a bit of a ceremony, boss. They were all pished, of course.'

'Four Moscow Mules?' said Gilchrist. 'Which year was this?'

'Late sixties, early seventies, as best she can remember.'

Gilchrist tightened his grip on his mobile. 'Anything else?'

'She remembers one of the girls' names because it was Grant,' Stan said. 'The same as her husband. Jeanette Grant.'

'Where's this Jeanette Grant now?'

'Nance is still trying to track her down.'

'Get her to call me with an address.'

'Got it, boss. And one other thing.'

'What's that?'

'Gina Belli's called the office three times today, asking to speak to you. Nice voice. Very sexy.'

'You wouldn't like her, Stan. Believe me. She's way too old for you.'

'Could have fooled—'

'Get someone to help Nance. And get her to give me a call.' He hung up.

Gina Belli. *Nice voice? Very sexy?*

He slowed for the mini-roundabout at City Road, was about to turn right when the lights of the Dunvegan caught his eye. *Just the one*, he thought, and accelerated up the hill.

He found a parking spot in The Scores and five minutes later was standing at the bar, a creamy pint of Eighty-Shilling in his hand. It somehow felt odd having stood on that same spot the night before with Gina Belli, all eyes turned her way while she stripped off her jacket. He wondered if the real reason for stopping at the Dunvegan was his secret hope that she would be there, that he was looking for her, this Gina Belli, the psychic detective in the business suit with waistcoat and no blouse and a tan that pronounced to all who ogled that she was a woman from another part of the world. And don't you forget it.

His mobile vibrated.

'Stan said you wanted me to call,' said Nance.

'Only when you found something.'

'I've got a few names and addresses that might give us a start.'

'Let's have them.'

'Well, working on your theory that the body was buried at the same time as Hamish McLeod, that works out to be the year Jeanette Grant entered her second year of university. I concentrated on that year first, then the year either side of that. If we draw a blank with these names, I can dig into other years.'

'So, what have you got?'

'Eight in total. All now married. Six in Scotland, two in England. One lives near here, in Cupar.'

As he listened to Nance go through her list of names like a roll call, he thought of the cigarette lighter, and wondered if that was reason enough to focus only on the four cigar-smoking students who drank Moscow Mules in the Central—

'Stop,' he snapped. 'Go back, go back. Who was that?'

'Agnes Bullock, née McIver?'

'No, no. Before that.'

'Margaret Ewart, née Caulder?'

'That's the one,' he said. 'She lives in Cupar. Right?'

'You know her?'

'Douglas Ewart's ex-wife. Megs, he called her. Ewart was at McLeod's funeral.' He caught the bartender's eye and gestured for a pen and paper. 'You and Stan talk to Megs,' he said, 'and I'll visit Jeanette Grant. Is that her married name?'

'No. Jeanette Pennycuick.'

'How d'you spell that?' he asked, and wrote it down. 'Telephone number?'

He noted the Glasgow code, which had him thinking he could kill two birds, maybe three, with the one stone. 'Once you've talked to Megs,' he said, 'get on with the others.'

'With all due respect, Andy, this is only one avenue,' Nance said. 'We've nothing to confirm the skeleton was even that of a student.'

'Any other suggestions?'

'Have you thought of digital reconstruction?'

'That's why I'm going to visit Pennycuick.'

A pause, then, 'I don't follow.'

'Glasgow University, Nance. And Dr Heather Black of the Computing Science Department and the Turing Institute.'

'Is she any good?'

'Pioneering, I think you would call her. But until we have a visual to work from, I'm afraid it's good old-fashioned detective work. Talk to people. Ask questions. Poke and prod. All right?'

'I'm on it.'

'What are you doing tomorrow night?' he tried.

A pause, then, 'I'm busy, Andy. I can't.'

'Sure,' he said. 'Keep me posted.'

He tried Jeanette Pennycuick's number, but after six rings a woman's aristocratic voice ordered him to *leave a number and some-one will return your call*.

He eyed the scribbled address, knew enough about Glasgow to know it was located in the West End, where Jack lived. He had not visited Jack for a couple of months, so he asked Sheena if he could borrow a bottle of The Macallan 10.

He left his Eighty half finished and stepped into the damp October chill.

CHAPTER 5

The drive to Glasgow cast up more images of Gail.

Gilchrist had thought, perhaps even hoped, that at the moment of her passing he and Gail would somehow make peace with each other, for the memories they shared, for the love they once had, for the children they brought into the world.

From the moment he first set eyes on her he had loved her. He had loved her cheeky irreverence of things authoritarian. When they had staggered across the golf course and she stepped from her knickers in the Valley of Sin and giggled at the look on his face as she lay down on the damp grass, he had loved the simple symbolism of that action. This is my life, she was saying to him. No one can tell me what to do. Come share it with me. He had loved her for that. He had loved her through a short but torrid courtship and nineteen difficult years of marriage that swung with discomfiting ease from passionate to indifferent.

And he loved her still. He would always love her.

But the truth was that Gail's love for him had changed like the clicking of a switch. She had cast him off like an old winter coat as she welcomed the fresh summer winds of her new lover, Harry.

Harry. God, how he hated the sound of that name, a name that cast up images of extramarital sex behind locked doors in the hospital administration building, rushed and desperate and kept out of sight of all and sundry. But although Gilchrist had not once strayed, he saw that his love affair with his job had caused the death of his marriage.

When Gail's affair started, their marriage was already dead.

That thought calmed him. Detective Chief Inspector Andrew James Gilchrist of the St Andrews Division of Fife Constabulary's Crime Management Department had no one to blame but himself.

He had just slipped on to the M876 when his mobile rang from a number he did not recognize.

'You're a hard man to track down.'

He grimaced at the American accent. 'And you're a hard woman to lose.'

Gina Belli laughed, a grating sound he found unattractive. 'You hiding from me?'

'Trying to. I like to keep my personal life personal.'

'You almost made the cover of *Newsweek* after the Stabber case. Did you know that?'

'Does that matter?'

'To people who write biographies, yes.' She paused. 'Where are you?'

He ignored her question, wanted to ask how she found his mobile number, but heard Stan's voice say, *Nice voice. Very sexy*, and already knew. 'You need to stop calling me,' he replied.

'What are you doing tonight?'

'I'm out of town.'

'Tomorrow night?'

'I think I'm losing you. You're sounding faint.'

50

'You can do better than that, Andy. If you want to disconnect, just say so. But I'll be in the Central tomorrow night at seven. I'd like to ask you something.'

'Ask away.'

'Not on the phone,' she said. 'And one other thing . . .'

Gilchrist waited.

'I don't bite.'

He arrived at Jeanette Pennycuick's at five to seven. The cold stone building looked dull and imposing, all the more uninviting seen through a damp drizzle that hung in the air like an east-coast haar.

He stepped from his car and pulled his collar up.

He pushed open a heavy metal gate that groaned on rusted hinges, and walked along a pathway lined with the skeletal branches of pruned autumn bushes to a dark door sheltered by a portico with twin stone columns. A matching pair of flowerpots shaped like lions sat on the first step and guarded the door. The brass doorknob resembled a roaring lion with a ring knocker like an oversized nose-piercing. A dim light on the door frame led his fingers to the doorbell, beneath which lay a polished brass nameplate.

Geoffrey Pennycuick.

No mention of his having a wife.

A deep chime echoed back at him when he pressed the doorbell. A dim light warmed the ceiling of an upstairs room. If not for that, he would have said the house was deserted. Late October was the time for the mid-term break. Maybe the Pennycuicks were away on holiday with their children, if they had any children. Or perhaps they had gone out for the evening. If they were not to return until after midnight, he would have a long wait. Mind made up, he

51

stuffed his hands into his pockets and returned to his car, intent on paying them a visit first thing in the morning.

He wound his way through night-time traffic to Jack's flat in Hillhead. Unable to find a parking spot, he abandoned his Merc in a cobbled lane opposite and hoped he would not be clamped.

Jack's flat was one of a terraced row of tenement buildings; whose façade had been sandblasted clean within the last year. Despite the communal door being freshly painted black, the starless Glasgow sky doused the area in misery. He climbed the footworn steps. From somewhere beyond the bottom of the road, he heard the sound of breaking glass, people shouting. He eyed the junction but saw only passing cars, their lights piercing the night air like laser beams. He pressed Jack's doorbell.

Several seconds later a tinny voice said, 'Heh.'

'Jack?'

'Who's this?'

'Your father.'

'Heh, Andy, didn't recognize the voice. Up you come, man.'

The lock buzzed, and Gilchrist stepped into a dark close that echoed with the sound of his footfall. The door thudded behind him. On the third-floor landing, Jack was waiting. They hugged, tight, and when they parted Gilchrist dabbed a hand at his eyes. Jack faced him, eyes glistening in the chilly landing air.

'How are you holding up?' Gilchrist asked.

Jack shrugged. 'Over the worst of it. Pity you couldn't make it yesterday.'

'Got an urgent call. Pressure of work, and all that.'

'Turned out to be a good do. Well . . .' Jack gave a twisted smile. 'If you could ever call a wake good.'

Gilchrist tightened his lips, held out The Macallan 10. 'It's a bit

52

early for Christmas,' he tried, forcing a joke. 'But anyway, Merry Christmas.'

'Any excuse'll do, right?' Jack studied the label. 'This looks good enough to open right away.'

'I see you still take a lot of persuading.'

'Only where drink's concerned.' He placed a hand on his father's shoulder and pressed him towards the open living-room door.

Gilchrist stepped into a room he remembered as being dull and drab. Now, woodwork sparkled with off-white gloss. Bold oil paintings of indeterminate subject hung from ceiling to floor on every wall and brightened the room in blues, greens, reds, yellows, with shapes that swirled and swooped like some multicoloured maelstrom. He recognized Chloe's work.

'Can never sell them,' said Jack, and placed two tumblers on a bleached coffee table stained with enough paint for Gilchrist to think it doubled as a palette.

Jack cracked open The Macallan 10.

'How are her exhibitions going?' Gilchrist asked, and almost cringed at his question. He had promised to come along to the most recent one, but had called off at the last minute, tied up with the case of the week.

Jack poured a hefty measure. 'Great,' he said. 'A lot of interest in her work.' He handed the glass to Gilchrist. 'But they pissed me off in the end.'

'They?'

'All those wankers who think they know a bargain when they see it.'

'You don't like her work?' Gilchrist asked, failing to hide his surprise.

'I love her work. She's brilliant. *Was* brilliant. I told them that.'

Jack held out his glass, chinked it against Gilchrist's. 'Cheers,' he said, and threw it back as if it was a shot, then grimaced. 'How good is that?'

'Good enough to savour?'

'Always like to slam the first one.' Jack refilled and took a measured sip, licked his lips. 'Well, this one guy in particular. A real English plonker. Fancied himself as some art connoisseur. A right prick. With the grey-haired ponytail and the bow tie and the public-school voice. Offered me ten grand for the lot. I told him to fuck off.'

'I can't imagine that going down well.'

Jack chuckled. 'He kept upping it, as if that was going to make me change my mind. When he told me twenty-five was his final offer, I told him I wouldn't sell even one of them for that. He looked at me like I was crazy. Just like you're looking at me now.'

'Twenty-five thousand's a lot of money.'

'And your point is?'

With Jack it was never about money. It was about freedom of expression, the exploration of self, the discovery of the new or even the old. Jack would never change. But paintings did not pay bills, and Gilchrist worried that Jack always appeared to live a penny or two above the poverty line. Chloe's display, rather than putting money in the bank, was also keeping Jack locked in the past, not letting him move forward.

'How's your own stuff selling?' he tried. 'Last I heard you were back to painting some of your own.'

Jack chinked his glass to Gilchrist's. 'Like me to show you?'

Glass in hand, he followed Jack into a back bedroom that felt arctic-cold. The sharp tang of turps and paint caught the back of his throat. The room was stripped of wallpaper, carpet and furnishings. Their footfalls echoed as they crossed the floor. A bare window stretched almost from floor to ceiling, next to an artist's easel on which rested an unfinished painting, nothing more than brush strokes of bright colour that converged in the middle and gave the impression of being sucked along some kaleidoscopic corridor.

'What's it supposed to be?' he asked.

'Whatever you want it to be.'

Gilchrist cocked his head. 'I suppose the colours are bold, refreshing even. But . . .'

'You don't like it.'

'I wouldn't go as far as that.'

'Wow. Andy *almost* liking my stuff.' Jack grinned. 'Now that's a first.'

'I didn't say I liked it,' objected Gilchrist, then chuckled. Despite recent events, it was nice to see Jack so relaxed. A noise from the hallway, the metallic clink of a key being inserted into a lock, diverted his gaze.

'That'll be Kara,' Jack said, and walked from the bedroom.

In the hallway, Gilchrist met a fresh-faced woman with blue eyes and fine blonde hair hanging straight to the shoulders of a grey business jacket. A black skirt came to just above her knees, revealing slim legs that stopped at a pair of running shoes. Jack closed the door behind her. She put her leather briefcase and canvas bag on the floor, then approached Gilchrist with an extended arm.

'I'm Kara. I've heard so much about you.'

Her grip felt firm. 'All good, I hope.'

'And I'm sorry to hear about Gail,' she said. 'It was a blessing in the end.'

Gilchrist nodded, tight-lipped. She had not accompanied Jack to the crematorium yesterday, and the first-name familiarity seemed odd to him. Perhaps she had gone along to the clubhouse later.

As if sensing a need to lift the mood, Kara said, 'I see Jack's already got you on his favourite subjects. Drink and art.' She gave off a laugh that brought colour to her cheeks. 'Let me get out of this lot, and I'll join you.'

'Working overtime?' Gilchrist asked.

'Had to stay late, finish a report for a case that finds in court tomorrow.'

'You're a solicitor?'

'That'd be the day. I'm a paralegal. I do all the dirty work, while others get to stand up in court and take all the glory.' She tugged a strand of hair behind her ear. 'The hours are long and the money's poor. But it pays the bills.'

Gilchrist thought he detected a hint of resentment. 'What would we do all day if we didn't have to work to pay the bills?' he tried with a smile.

'Paint?' she offered.

Gilchrist felt himself cringe on Jack's behalf.

'Kara's a bit like you, Andy. Thinks I should go out and find a proper job.'

'One that gives a bit of financial security,' she added.

'You're only as safe as the length of your notice,' Jack said. 'And in this climate, who knows whether their job is safe or not. At least I'll always paint.'

'Yes,' Kara said, 'we'll always have that.' She glanced at Gilchrist. 'Excuse me,' and picked her bags up from the floor and disappeared into the bedroom opposite.

'Don't worry about Kara,' Jack said. 'She takes her work too

56

seriously. And to make matters worse, some plonker in her office treats her like shite.'

'Charming,' Gilchrist said.

'Needs taken out the back and beaten up,' Jack snapped, and something in the flare of his eyes, the set of his jaw, had Gilchrist wondering if Jack had changed.

'Seems like she can look after herself,' Gilchrist offered.

'When push comes to shove, she chickens out.'

'Probably afraid of losing her job.'

'And therein lies the problem,' Jack growled. 'See what I mean? Everyone's got to suck up to everyone else so they don't get canned.' He shook his head, finished his whisky, grabbed the bottle for a refill. 'That's what's wrong with this fucking place—'

'Glasgow?'

'Planet Earth.'

'It's all we've got—'

'Not for much longer, the way we're fucking it up.'

Gilchrist held Jack's blazing eyes for a moment, before saying, 'Are you all right?'

''Course I am.' He spilled some whisky on the table. Gilchrist watched him flourish his glass, thought he must have had a drink, maybe two, before they met. 'All this money talk. It's all everyone thinks about. Instead of all these rich capitalist bastards making more money than they could spend in ten lifetimes, they should be taxed to the hilt and the money put back into the environment—'

'To save Planet Earth?'

'We should abandon the monetary system. Go back to trading. That'd sort the fuckers out.' He tilted his head back, almost emptied his glass then faced Gilchrist with a knowing grimace.

57

'You know,' he said, 'it's been a while since I got arseholed. Fancy a pub crawl down Byres Road?'

'What about Kara?'

'She'll catch us up. Come on.' He drained his glass, opened the bedroom door and shouted, 'We're going down the pub. Meet you in Curlers if you're quick.'

But Kara didn't make it to Curlers, or Tennents, but caught up with them as they were ordering a second pint in Jinty's in Ashton Lane.

'Sorry I'm late.' She went on tiptoe to give Jack a peck on the cheek.

'Didn't know we were in a hurry,' Jack said, and pulled crumpled notes from his jeans. 'What're you having?'

'The usual.'

'Can't persuade you?'

She shook her head. 'Just bottled water. None of that fizzy stuff. And no ice.'

'Very sensible,' Gilchrist said. 'Wish I had your willpower.'

'Both my parents were alcoholics. So I keep well away from it.'

He thought that standing in a pub, surrounded by drink, soaking in the alcohol-fuelled atmosphere contradicted her stance. And he noticed the past tense – *were alcoholics* – which had him thinking her parents were dead. While Jack pressed through the crowd to the bar, he asked, 'So, how long have you known Jack?'

'Several years, but we've only been together for about four months.'

Gilchrist nodded, and wondered why Jack had never mentioned her in all that time.

'Jack's upset,' she said. 'I've never seen him cry before.'

'Excuse me?'

58

She searched the bar, as if ensuring Jack was out of earshot. 'His mother,' she said. 'She was very young.'

'Forty-six,' he agreed.

'I lost one of my sisters to cancer,' she went on, her voice as soft as a whisper. 'I still can't believe it. She was much too young to have died.'

Gilchrist held her gaze. Her eyes were the lightest blue, like a frosted sky on a winter morning. 'How old was she?' he asked.

'Twenty-two.'

Twenty-two. Kara's sister had been around the same age as the girl in McLeod's grave when she had been murdered. And older than Gilchrist's brother when he had been killed in a hit-and-run. And he saw that he and Kara must have shared the same emotional pain, probably even the same tear-filled dreams. He wondered what life would have been like if his brother had not been killed, and how his own mother had put a brave face on it and struggled through the remainder of her life. And that thought made him realize something more troubling than an unsolved murder.

Had the girl's parents been alive when she disappeared? Had they lived every year, every month, every moment since, torturing themselves over what might have happened to their daughter? And if they had been alive then, were they alive now?

'Here we go, Andy.'

He took hold of a low-ball glass that glowed golden and chinked with lumps of ice.

'And don't try and tell me whisky's a warm drink. That's just another example of trying to fit everyone into the same mould. This is the way it should be taken. Just like the Russians drink their vodka. Ice cold. Even better straight from the freezer.'

'I thought you drank Pernod.'

'Just a phase we go through,' said Jack, and glanced at Kara as if seeking approval. 'We're Scottish. So we should be drinking Scotch. Right?'

'Becoming patriotic in your old age?' Kara said.

'And proud of it.' Jack lifted his glass to Gilchrist. 'To Mum,' then to Kara, who held hers up in silent salutation.

'And to the memory of the good times we used to share,' Gilchrist said, and felt his throat burn as the whisky wormed into his system. He watched Kara ease her tumbler towards Jack's, then take a sip, and something in her hesitancy warned him that all was not well between Kara and his son.

Gilchrist and Jack spent the next hour reminiscing, with Kara silent on the sidelines. They touched on life together as a family, Gilchrist recalling the fight Jack and Maureen had over who was going to sit first on the swan potty, and how in the end they sat on it together. The sight of their two little faces straining in unison had sent Gilchrist into fits. Looking back, he could see that, even then, Gail had begun to lose her sense of humour. The swan potty had disappeared not long after.

Gilchrist revealed to Jack how, on the first night after Gail's departure, he had ended up drunk and flat on his back in the Whey Pat Tavern, where his relationship with Gail had first begun, and how he had struggled to hold back his tears. He was surprised when Jack told him Gail had cried, too. And throughout their reminiscing, Gilchrist was conscious of Kara being sidelined. She seemed to brighten when he suggested they return home, and after Jack swallowed his third one-for-the-road, they set off.

Back home, Jack did his best to finish The Macallan 10 before midnight, and all the while Kara sat on the edge of the sofa, like some stranger seated on the periphery of a family gathering. Just after midnight, she excused herself, and was about to step from the living room when Gilchrist stood.

'S'too early for bed, Andy. Come on, man. Sit. Have another one.'

'I'll be leaving first thing in the morning,' Gilchrist said to Kara.

Kara stretched up to give him a peck on the cheek. As he watched her slim figure leave the room without acknowledging Jack, he lifted his hand to where her lips had pressed, not sure if the dampness he felt on his cheek was from her lipstick or her tears.

He stared at his refilled glass. The Macallan 10 was almost done. He turned to Jack, wanted to ask him about Kara, but the effort to speak seemed too much. He tried a sip, but the whisky no longer slid down his throat like warmed oil, and had to be forced back with a painful grimace. Heartburn nipped at his gut. He would suffer for this in the morning.

He pushed his glass to the side. 'I've had it,' he said.

Jack held up the bottle. 'C'mon, Andy. Still some left.'

'It won't go to waste, Jack. Goodnight.'

As he left the room, he caught Jack topping up his glass.

Morning hit Gilchrist with the shock of a blaring radio alarm and the dazed realization that he was in someone else's bed. He turned his head to the tinny din. Pain shot through his neck. He tried to swallow, but his mouth felt as dry as cardboard. He tried to lick his lips, but his tongue felt thick and stiff as if it belonged to something else.

He struggled on to his side and managed to switch off the alarm. The display read 6.33. Why had he set it so early? Could he have just ten more minutes?

When he next looked, the alarm clock read 7.39.

He pulled the continental quilt to the side, felt a rush of cold air hit him. As his feet hit the floor he felt some measure of comfort that he'd had the sense and the decency to undress before going to bed.

He made it to the bathroom without stubbing his toes on unfamiliar furniture, or throwing up. Scrunching his eyes against the bright light, he grimaced into the mirror. An old man stared back at him, skin grey and salted, eyes creased and bagged. He combed his fingers through his hair, turned on the hot tap. It ran cold, and he splashed some into his mouth where his tongue soaked it up like a desiccated sponge.

He shaved using Jack's razor and a new blade he found in the cabinet. Then he showered, hot steaming water that he let filter every pore. He lifted his head to the spray, opened his mouth, gurgled and spat. Not a pretty sight, but ten minutes later he felt almost ready to take on the world – or Jeanette Pennycuick, at least.

In the kitchen, he found some fresh orange juice and Irn-Bru and poured himself a large glass, peachy-pink. He burped as Kara entered the kitchen. She looked young and fresh, her pale skin enhanced by cream silk pyjamas, through which the tips of her nipples pressed. She stood in bare feet, her toes as long and slender as fingers.

'Sorry,' he said. 'Stomach.'

'At least you apologize.' She held the kettle under the tap. 'Tea? Coffee? You mustn't miss breakfast.'

Gilchrist glanced at his watch. 'I'll catch something later.'

He was about to step from the kitchen when Kara said, 'Could I talk to you?' She shook her head. 'Not now, I mean. Later. When you've got some time.'

'Sure,' he said, and gave her his mobile number. 'Call any time.'

'I care for Jack,' she said. 'I don't want to lose him.'

'Why do you think you'll lose him?'

She held his gaze, as if deciding whether or not to tell him. 'You'd better go,' she said. 'You'll be late.'

He nodded, then headed for the door, wondering if the changes he'd seen in Jack were what would cause Kara to lose him.

CHAPTER 6

Outside, low clouds seemed ready to smother the city.

Gilchrist found his Roadster where he had left it, relieved to find it had not been clamped. When he sat behind the wheel, he knew from the way he breathed and coughed that he was well over the limit. Before closing the door, he spat a lump of phlegm to the ground, and swore he would never drink whisky again.

He eased the car from the lane in search of a coffee.

Jeanette Pennycuick's home looked more imposing in the cold light of day. He pulled up behind a silver BMW, then took another sip of his Starbucks. Tall latté was about as hard as he could stomach. It tasted warm and milky and cut through the slag in his mouth. He stuffed the container into the holder in the console, then tore open a packet of chewing gum he hoped would keep his breath fresh, or at least rid his mouth of the residual taste of stale alcohol.

He strode up the gravel path. The grass either side lay neat and trim, and what he had at first taken to be a dark and dingy building was in fact an old stone residence that had been maintained with care. Window frames glistened with fresh paint. Plant beds looked dark and fresh and free of weeds. Even the lion flowerpots seemed more tame, the doorknob harmless.

He pressed the doorbell, coughed his throat clear as the door cracked open.

An attractive woman, who looked to be in her early fifties, stood before him.

He tried a smile. 'Jeanette Pennycuick?'

'Yes?'

He held up his warrant card. 'Detective Chief Inspector Andrew Gilchrist,' he said, choosing not to mention he was with Fife Constabulary. 'I'd like to ask you a few questions.'

'Questions? What about?'

'Routine enquiry.'

She frowned, as if uncertain whether to believe him or not.

'Inside might be better,' he suggested.

'We're running late.'

'I won't keep you.'

'Problem, darling?' The man's voice blasted from the depths of the hall a moment before he, too, appeared in the doorway.

'It's the police, Geoffrey.'

He was a good six inches taller than his wife, and glared down at Gilchrist like a Roman emperor about to give the thumbs-down. Gilchrist almost expected the petrified lions to spring to life. 'Is there some problem?'

'Routine enquiry.'

'We're running late.'

'I won't keep your wife long.' Gilchrist wondered if they could see through his alcoholic glaze and know he had been pretty much legless the night before. He chewed his gum, but the fur persisted like moss in grass. Then, with a speed that almost made him start,

Pennycuick removed a mobile from his suit pocket, a gesture at which his wife stepped back as if in resigned agreement.

As Gilchrist followed her into the front lounge, he heard her husband bark into the phone that all his appointments should be pushed back one hour. Just how late were they running anyway?

The front lounge looked and smelled of money. Cornicing bordered the high ceiling. The walls were dark, papered in a rich burgundy. A Bechstein grand piano stood in the corner by the curved bay window, cleared of clutter and glistening with the fresh sheen of varnish. Side tables, four in total, dark wood and polished, accompanied the seating, their tops littered with framed family photographs.

Jeanette held out her hand, directing Gilchrist to a sofa close to the piano. As he sat, she took the chair opposite, conjuring an image in his mind of her listening to her husband playing.

Gilchrist nodded to the piano. 'Do you play?'

'No.'

'Your husband?'

'The children.'

On the table to his left, a gallery of framed photographs stood like a phalanx of some two-dimensional army. He eyed the closest frame. 'Is this them?'

'Yes.'

'Names?'

'Penny and James.'

The boy looked frail and tired, barely smiling at the camera. Beside him stood a young girl, more attractive than beautiful, and he wondered what kind of parents would dare name their daughter Penny Pennycuick.

'Gone to school already, have they?'

'They're both through university.'

Pennycuick entered the front room, stuffing his phone into his inside jacket pocket. 'Right,' he said, 'I have a busy day ahead. What's this about?'

Gilchrist rested his elbows on his knees, tempted for a moment to ignore him. 'I'm here to talk to your wife,' he replied. 'So don't let me keep you from your office.'

'Hospital. I'm a consultant at the Western. And I drive my wife to the city centre. Who did you say you were with?' he ordered.

'I didn't. But I'm with Fife Constabulary.'

'Fife?' He frowned. 'Are you not out of your jurisdiction?'

Gilchrist pulled himself to his feet. At six-one, he stood a couple of inches shorter than Pennycuick. 'I can obtain a warrant, if that would make you feel more comfortable. Then we could talk at Police Headquarters in Glenrothes in a day or so.' He let his words settle. 'Or we can talk now. Informally.' He smiled at both of them in turn. 'Whichever way's fine with me.'

'How can we help?' It was Jeanette.

Gilchrist decided to remain standing. He explained about the skeleton, and how the police were now tasked with identifying the woman they guessed had been in her late teens, early twenties when she had died. Both Jeanette and her husband listened in silence.

'You were at St Andrews University in '69.'

'Yes. I graduated in '71 with a first in English Lit.'

He asked her where and when she was born, where she lived as a child, what her parents did, why she chose St Andrews, and all the while her husband shuffled around in the background with barely masked impatience. Gilchrist strode past the piano and looked out of the bay window. On the opposite side of the street, a row of terraced houses staggered up the shallow incline. 'Nice view,' he said. 'A bit different from life as a student.'

'In what way?'

He turned, surprised by her question. 'Living the life of penury,' he said, and let his gaze drift around the room. 'This is a palatial home.'

'My parents are wealthy,' she explained. 'I've lived in moderate luxury most of my life.'

'Even as a student?'

She shook her head. 'My parents wanted me to learn a bit about life, or so they told me. I lived in a rented flat in St Andrews. Bit of a dump, really. They paid all the bills, so what I learned I really don't know.'

'Any room-mates?'

'Three.'

'Names?'

'Oh, my goodness. Now you *are* testing my memory.'

Gilchrist's own memory for names was not the greatest, but he could still remember the person with whom he first shared a flat. Sammy McFarland. Laugh-a-minute Sammy. Drink-a-minute, too.

'Betty Forbes,' she said. 'Betty and I were best friends back then. Inseparable, I would have said. But we haven't spoken in almost five years.' Her gaze flickered over Gilchrist's shoulder, and he detected a stiffening in her posture.

'Did you and Betty fall out?' he tried.

She gave a stuffy little chuckle. 'That's putting it mildly.'

'What happened?'

'She tried to have an affair with Geoffrey.' Her nostrils flared. 'But Geoffrey would have none of it.'

Gilchrist felt his gaze tug to his right. Pennycuick stood with his lips tight, eyes blazing. He seemed to puff out his chest, and Gilchrist wondered if he was doing so in offence at the memory, or from guilt at the thought of infidelity. He forced his thoughts back on track by asking, 'Can you remember the names of the others?'

'There was Ella. Big Ella, Betty and I used to call her. She stayed with us for two years, as best I can recall. But I can't remember her last name.'

'And the fourth?' he asked.

She shook her head. 'The fourth came and went. Betty and me were in the same year, so we earned some spending money by taking in the occasional student, then flinging them out when we got fed up with them.' Her face seemed to sag, as if in remorse at the unkindness. 'We could be bitches when we put our minds to it.'

Geoffrey coughed.

'Can you remember any of their names?' Gilchrist asked.

She shook her head. 'Denise rings a bell. Maybe Alyson. But I really couldn't say. Just the two of us for certain.'

'All Scottish?'

'The occasional Englishwoman.'

'Any foreigners?'

'None that I recall.'

'Good teeth?'

'Excuse me?'

'Do you remember if any of them had good teeth?'

'Can't say that I do. Why?'

'Just a thought.' He then told her about the list of names Nance had prepared, and offered to send her a copy for her review. Maybe one might jog her memory.

'Here's my email address,' she said, removing a business card from her purse.

'Anything else, Inspector?' It was Pennycuick.

'You drank in the Central,' he said to Jeanette.

She frowned. 'One of many pubs, I'm sure.'

'What about the cigars?'

She looked at him as if he had cursed. 'Cigars?'

'And the Moscow Mules?'

Then it dawned on her. 'Oh, that,' she said. 'Just some student stupidity.'

'An initiation of some sort?'

'I don't follow.'

'Friends can be cliquish,' he suggested. 'Form gangs, clubs, that sort of thing.'

'None of us joined any gangs,' she objected, 'or clubs. Not to my knowledge, anyway.'

'Did you form one of your own?'

Pennycuick stepped into the centre of the room. 'How much longer is this going to take?'

'Not much.' He faced Jeanette. 'Why once a month?'

'I beg your pardon?'

'Why did you smoke cigars and drink Moscow Mules once a month?'

She seemed to give his words some thought, then shook her head. 'I've often heard about policemen like you, who look for clues in the strangest of places only to find nothing.' She gave a tired smile that evaporated to leave a hard face.

'You haven't answered my question.'

'Oh, for goodness sake. Must I spell it out for you? Our menstrual cycles. Women living together often tune in to each other's monthly cycles. It was our way of combating the dreaded rag week.'

Gilchrist turned to the window. The cold from the glass felt good against the warmth of his face. Their periods. How bloody simple. Why had he not thought of that? Would Nance have worked it out? Or Stan? He faced the room again.

'How did you light your cigars?' he asked.

'This is preposterous,' snapped Pennycuick. 'What on earth has lighting cigars got to do with anything? I think we've heard quite enough.' He held out his hand. 'Jeanette?'

She looked at him, but made no attempt to stand.

He glared at her for a moment, then growled, 'I'll be in the car. And I'll be leaving in exactly one minute.'

Gilchrist waited until it was only the two of them. The room seemed larger without Pennycuick's presence. And Jeanette seemed smaller, too, almost insecure. 'Where do you work?' he asked her.

'The city centre.'

A car door slammed. Gilchrist glanced out the window. 'I can give you a lift, if you'd like.'

Jeanette stood, patted the creases from her skirt. 'If you have no further questions,' she said, 'I'd rather Geoffrey dropped me off.'

Gilchrist nodded. 'After you.'

He followed her along the hallway where a cold wind blew in through the opened front door. As he stepped outside, he caught sight of Pennycuick's flushed face through the windscreen of his BMW. He waited until Jeanette locked the front door.

'You never did answer my question,' he said.

'I didn't?'

'How did you light your cigars?'

'With a candle.'

She stepped down the slabbed footpath, her heels ringing in the icy air.

Gilchrist wrapped his arms around himself to fend off the chill. Somehow the air in Glasgow felt colder than in St Andrews, as if the west-coast dampness could infiltrate the heaviest of garments. 'A candle,' he repeated. 'I don't remember the Central Bar ever having candles on the table.'

'We brought our own.'

Gilchrist almost stopped. 'But why would you bring a candle?'

She smirked as she stepped through the gateway. When he followed, she pulled the wrought-iron gate towards her, closing it with a hard metallic clang. 'Now, why else would nice girls carry candles around with them, Inspector?'

Gilchrist stepped aside as she opened the passenger door and slid on to the seat, her skirt riding high on stockinged thighs. He watched the BMW accelerate down the hill, its exhaust leaving a white trail that swirled to the ground. His breath puffed in the cold air as if in weak imitation. He coughed, and something vile hit his tongue, causing him to fight off an almost overpowering need to throw up.

The Pennycuicks had mocked him. He watched their BMW's brake lights flash as it turned towards Great Western Road without indicating. An image of Geoffrey Pennycuick flickered into his mind. Pinstriped suit, starched white shirt, shining black shoes. Gilchrist looked down at his own feet, at leather that had not seen polish in three days. Grey scuff-marks soiled the uppers. Then Jeanette surfaced beside the image of her husband, her black hair glistening in the light from the window, her white blouse thin enough to reveal the floral pattern of her bra.

Cigars. Periods. Candles.

If it wasn't so serious it would be funny.

Gilchrist faced his Roadster. It looked small and worn compared to Pennycuick's BMW. He turned on the ignition and gripped the steering wheel while the car's engine split the silence of a suburban Glasgow morning. He fought off the crazy urge to floor the pedal, then pulled into Drive and eased away from the pavement.

He replayed the interview, struggling to force his thoughts through the haze of his hangover. It was not until he turned off Hyndland Road and was nearing Glasgow University that he realized his failing. He fumbled in his pocket and removed her business card. He read the company name. *ScotInvest*. The address in Bath Street. Her name and title, Jeanette W. Pennycuick, MBA, Human Resources Director. He scanned the phone numbers. One was her office, another her fax, the last one her mobile.

He flipped open his phone.

She answered on the fifth ring. 'Hello?'

Without introduction, he said, 'I have one more question.'

She let out a tired sigh. 'I didn't give you my business card so you could call to annoy me every five minutes.'

'What did you use to light the candle?'

'Matches, Inspector. What on earth did you think we used?'

Somehow, her answer did not surprise him. His sixth sense was screaming at him, telling him she was not speaking the truth. She could have used a cigarette lighter. Like the one they found in the graveyard. 'How did you meet your husband?' he tried.

'At a party.'

'At university?'

'In the flat in South Street, if you must know. And I'm not sure I like your manner, Inspector. I think I'm going to register a formal complaint. Fife Constabulary, did you say?'

Gilchrist hung up, threw his mobile on to the passenger seat and wondered if Jeanette Pennycuick really was lying to him. She had told him she met her husband at a party in her flat. Which meant Geoffrey Pennycuick had lived in St Andrews at the same time. Or had he been up there on holiday, the same way Gilchrist had met his wife, Gail? Or perhaps he'd been a student at the university. He was a consultant at the Western. St Andrews offered medical degrees. Had Pennycuick graduated from St Andrews? And if so, had his wife tried to fudge her answer to his question?

As a detective, Gilchrist knew that all things were possible. But what was forming in his mind was something ominous. If Jeanette was lying, she had something to hide. Which meant that Geoffrey and Jeanette Pennycuick were now smack dab in the middle of his sights.

CHAPTER 7

It had been two years since Gilchrist last met with Dr Heather Black.

She smiled as he approached, her arm outstretched.

'Good to see you again, Andy,' she said, shaking his hand. 'You haven't changed a bit. Maturing gracefully with age, if anything.'

Not the politically correct introduction, perhaps, but from memory, Heather Black was not a woman who minced her words. Somehow she looked different, her eyes, he thought – larger, sharper, more focused. Brighter, too. Perhaps it was the subtle use of mascara, the hint of kohl on the lids.

'Good to see you, too,' he said. 'You look, eh . . .'

'Stunning?'

He nodded. Yes, stunning would do.

'Laser surgery last year. Best thing I ever did.' She chuckled. 'With three teenage kids and a needy husband, compliments are not something with which I am familiar. If I don't pay them to myself, who else will? Come on,' she said. 'It arrived only half an hour ago.' She strode along the corridor with the enthusiasm of someone half her age.

They entered an open office that reminded Gilchrist of a school laboratory. Desks like drafting tables lined the walls. Tower computers, flat computers, oversized off-white metal boxes that held prehistoric motherboards and hard drives lay stacked under the desks, all seemingly interconnected by what Gilchrist could describe only as cable spaghetti. Six white-coated students sat huddled around a monitor screen on which a face of horizontal and vertical grid lines rotated like a spool of thread on a spindle. Barely a glance as Black led Gilchrist beyond them and into an office at the far end.

A FedEx box lay opened on a grey metal desk, and by a wired window a young Asian woman with black-rimmed spectacles looked up from her computer. Next to her, a familiar skull with its crushed side sat on a raised metal plate like some unfinished sculpture. A camera lay beside it, connected to the computer.

'Yan is one of our more promising students,' Black said, peering at the monitor. 'How's it coming along?'

'Slowly,' Yan replied. 'We could use more memory, faster chips, what can I say? Digital tomography always takes like, for ever.'

'Limited budgets. The bugbear of university research. Here,' she said to him, 'look at this.'

Gilchrist followed her to another monitor.

'How long are you in town?' she asked.

'How long will it take to come up with a visual?'

'Depends,' she replied. 'But if you've something else to do, you should do it.' She eyed the screen, clicked the mouse. 'I'm developing a new technique for fleshing out the skull. It's more time-consuming, but the results are worth it.'

'In what way?'

'Less wooden-looking. More lifelike. I could send a digital image tomorrow. That work for you?'

'That works,' he said.

Another couple of clicks, a password typed and a string of files with numerical identification that meant nothing to Gilchrist flowed down the screen. She clicked again, and the digital waterfall stopped.

'Let me show you,' she said, as the image of a human skull appeared on the screen. She jiggled the mouse and the skull turned left, back to the right, rolled over and around and back to face-on again. 'By holding down the left button and dragging the mouse, you can rotate the image any way you like. Here. Try it.'

Gilchrist obliged, and the skull span on its spot. He clicked again, managed to stop it, but turned it over so that he was looking at it from above. Another couple of clicks and drags and he had the skull stopped, almost back to where it began.

'Three-D imaging,' Black said. 'Helps us develop a more accurate picture. But there's still a lot of guesswork goes into the final image. Skin tone. Hair colour. Eye colour. Shape of the nose. Lips. Ears. We mostly skip the ears. Each of which leaves a different visual impact on the beholder. Here, let me show you.' She spun the skull on its spinal axis, returning it to its original position.

'Certain parts of the face we know have little skin covering.' As she spoke, her fingers worked the mouse. 'Around the eyes, for example.'

The skull took on a ghostly appearance as the bone around the eye sockets seemed to evaporate and fill in with something that spread down both cheeks like fungus. Then the sockets softened and pooled with the same spectral imagery until a pair of eyes took form.

The half skull, half face mask caused the hairs on Gilchrist's neck to stir.

With a click, the eyes changed from dark to light.

'I've got it on greyscale for speed,' she said. 'Colour would show these eyes as blue.' Another click, and the eyes darkened. 'Green,' she said, then another click. 'Or back to brown. Of course, we have no way of telling if the eyes are heavy-lidded, hooded, wide open or narrow. What we can do is give a best-guess estimate of what the face should look like. Sometimes it's best to play the odds.' Another click, and the eyes shut.

Gilchrist watched in silence as Black worked the mouse, filling in the remainder of the skull until he was left looking at a bald head that rotated and rolled before him as if Black was showing off her finished sculpture. Gilchrist puzzled that it looked oddly familiar.

Black turned the skull to profile and placed the cursor on the nose. 'This,' she said, 'in my opinion, is the most difficult feature to portray with any real accuracy. The nose is shaped with cartilage that can deform over the years. Accidents, fights, even the simple act of sticking a finger into the nasal cavity over a period of time can deform the cartilage.' She dragged the mouse over the nose, creating a bulge on the bridge and turned the skull face-on. Another couple of clicks and the nose widened. 'Different. Don't you think?'

She repeated the exercise, this time giving the nose a delicate concave curve.

Straight on again, the bald head had a more refined look to it. Gilchrist studied it. 'Seems familiar,' he said.

Black smiled. 'Would you like me to add glasses?'

Gilchrist almost gasped. He turned to Black, back to the skull, then Black again.

'That's you?' he asked.

78

She nodded. 'Without the telltale markers of hairstyle, colour, glasses, the memory isn't triggered by any recognizable feature. There's nothing locked in memory for the brain to pull up. So it sees the image as a stranger.' She worked the mouse again, until a woman's face with blonde spiked hair rotated on the screen. 'That's what I would look like as a punk rocker.' She added nose and ear piercings, and chuckled. 'Not so stunning. Right?'

'Right,' he agreed.

The blonde spikes melted and shifted to shoulder length. 'How about that?'

'I think I'm used to you not being blonde.'

Another click, and the hair faded to light grey. 'Better?'

'Getting there.'

She clicked the mouse. The skull vanished. 'That,' she said, 'is what I mean by guesswork.'

'Still,' he said, 'it's all we have to go on.'

She nodded. 'We have the sceptics in the profession, of course. The die-hards, the so-called experts who believe that working plasticine over the skull produces a much better result.'

'You don't agree?'

'With some aspects, I do,' she said. 'But no matter which method is used, the skull provides us with certain measurements that dictate certain features. For example, the ratio of the distance between both eyes to that between the eyes and the mouth, gives some indication of the length of the nose. Not precise, by any manner of means. But it's a guide. Where computer-aided facial reconstruction beats the hand-sculpted method hands down is in its ability to produce a number of variations.'

'Would the age of the victim have any impact on the visual

accuracy?' Gilchrist asked. 'I mean, a younger person would be less likely to have been in a nose-reconfiguring accident, or spent years picking their nose. The image could be more lifelike.'

Black let out a short laugh. 'You would have made a wonderful student,' she said. 'The face goes through all its major changes during puberty. Once you're past the teenage years, what you have is basically it for life. Plastic surgery notwithstanding.' She walked towards the door, and Gilchrist had the feeling their meeting was over.

'Once we have an idea of the age,' she continued, and opened the door, 'we can still only reconstruct the face from the skull. Once we have the basic features, we can then age them.' She held out her arm. Gilchrist stepped from her office. 'Bags under the eyes. Wrinkled lips. Chicken necks. That sort of thing.'

'So you will have seen yourself as an older woman?' he tried.

She emitted a high-pitched chuckle like a child's scream. 'I experimented with it once. Found it depressing.'

'And the glasses?'

She surprised him by slipping her arm through his and marching along the corridor.

'That, I believe, was a turning point,' she said. 'My sight was so bad that I had to keep my glasses on to see the image on the screen. I liked what I saw, so I thought I'd give it a shot.'

They reached another door, and she slipped her arm free. 'Can you find your way from here?'

'I'm sure I can.'

'I'll have something with you tomorrow.'

She held out her hand, gave a firm shake, then turned on her heels and marched back to her office.

★ ★ ★

Once Gilchrist was back on the M8, he called Nance.

'That list of names you've got,' he said to her. 'Could you scan and email a copy to Jeanette Pennycuick?' He read off her email address. 'Was Betty Forbes on the list?' he asked.

'Yes. Betty Forbes, née Smith.'

'Address?'

'Somewhere in Glasgow, I think. Give me a minute.'

'Shit.' Gilchrist eyed the motorway signs and pulled across two lanes to the slip road for the city centre.

'Here it is.' She read it out, and Gilchrist assigned it to memory. It made sense, of course. If Jeanette and Betty had remained friends up until only five years ago, he should have guessed they lived in or around the same city. He asked for her telephone number, assigned that to memory too, and dialled it when he hung up with Nance.

'Betty speaking.' She sounded out of breath.

Gilchrist introduced himself, again declining to mention he was with Fife Constabulary. 'Are you available some time this morning for a chat?' he asked.

'Oh.' A pause. 'I'm going to the hairdresser's this afternoon. I have an appointment at two.'

'I could meet you before then.'

He found Betty Forbes' home before 11 a.m., a well-kept, split-level house that sat on a steep hill and seemed ready to fall away from the street. He rang the doorbell, was about to ring again when he was startled by a woman's voice addressing him from the side.

'I'm down in the back,' she said.

She stood at the corner of the building, gloved hands resting on a wooden garden gate. She smiled at him, an open grin that told him she was at ease with herself and the rest of the world.

'Betty Forbes?'

'Last time I checked.' She slipped her right hand from her garden gloves, pushed her fingers through a curl of dirty-blonde hair that dangled over her eyes and held out her hand.

Gilchrist kept his grip gentle.

She slipped her glove back on. 'If you don't mind,' she said, 'I'm trying to finish something in the garden. Can we talk in the back?'

He followed her down a steep grass slope, through another wooden gate and into a level area consisting mostly of stone slabs, some of which had been lifted to expose fill as grey and soft as crushed ash. A fence, dilapidated and overgrown with ivy, defined the end of her property. To the side, the back of the house reared more than two storeys skyward. A few yards away, by a green whirligig, broken slabs lay piled like the beginnings of a concrete bonfire.

'Doing this by yourself?' he asked.

She dragged a gloved hand through her hair. 'Who else is there to help me?'

'No Mr Forbes?'

'Done a runner.'

'I'm sorry to hear that.'

'Don't be. The son of a bitch'd been screwing his secretary behind my back for the best part of three years.' She almost laughed. 'Last I heard, she'd left him for a younger stud.'

Gilchrist heard Jeanette Pennycuick's words remind him, *She tried to have an affair with my husband*, and he wondered if Betty's husband's affair had something to do with that. 'When did this happen?' he asked. 'Mr Forbes doing a runner.'

'Six years ago last Christmas. Can you believe he left on Christmas Day?' She picked up a sledgehammer and raised it above her head with an ease that surprised Gilchrist. 'Watch your eyes,' she said, and slammed the sledgehammer on to the corner of a slab. It cracked with a dull thud.

'You make it look easy.'

'I pretend it's his balls I'm crushing. It's funny,' she said, and laughed as she took another swing. 'I imagine them wrapped up in Christmas paper. It gives me strength.' She hit the broken piece twice more then threw the hammer down. 'There. That ought to sort him out, don't you think?' She bent forward and pulled out chunks of broken concrete, which she threw on to the bonfire.

'Like a hand?'

She screwed up her eyes against a burst of sunlight. Standing like that, in denim jeans and polo shirt, teeth glinting white and strong, Gilchrist thought he had never before seen anyone display such sexual presence without even trying.

'You offering to help?'

'If you'd like.'

'I thought men like you had vanished with the cowboys.' She nodded to the sledgehammer. 'You hit. I'll pick up.'

Gilchrist removed his jacket and threw it over the fence. He spat on his hands and gripped the sledgehammer. Its weight surprised him. 'Same slab?' He caught a quick nod as he pulled the sledge-hammer back, swung it behind him, let its momentum carry it up and over. Then he shifted his weight, stepped forward and aimed for the middle of the slab.

'What would I give to have muscles,' she said, and bent down to pull out the broken pieces.

'They wouldn't suit you.'

She glanced up at him and smiled, then swung her body to the side and threw a chunk of concrete on to the pile.

'You'd get more for these slabs unbroken,' he offered.

'They're too heavy for me to lift. Until you turned up, the only way I could move them was to break them into smaller pieces.'

'Like me to try?'

'I'm only breaking up another four or five,' she said. 'That's all the flowerbeds I'll need. The rest I'll keep as a walkway.'

They worked together for the next half-hour, Gilchrist swinging the hammer, Betty leaning forward, using her arms and her upper body to lug the pieces of concrete to the side. On the last slab, he helped clear the broken pieces, surprised by how at ease he felt being next to her.

Then it was done.

She stood. Sweat glistened on her forehead and at the open neck of her polo shirt.

Gilchrist felt his own shirt stick to his back.

'Thirsty work,' she said. 'Like a drink?'

'Thought you'd never ask.' He stood back as she picked up the sledgehammer, slung it over her shoulder and marched up the side of her house. The physical work had done wonders for his hangover, and he pushed his fingers through his hair, surprised to find how damp with sweat it was.

She dumped the tools at the side of the garage, kicked off her heavy boots and stepped inside. Gilchrist removed his own shoes and followed.

The kitchen was small and airy and smelled of flowers and lemon. The window lay open, and warm air from a sun-trapped corner of the garden wafted in on the breeze. In the bright sunlight it could have been the middle of summer.

'Why don't you have a shower while I rustle up a sandwich? It has to be chicken or tuna, I'm afraid. What'll you have?'

'Whatever you're having.'

'You look as if you could do with putting on some weight, though,' she continued. 'My Bob was turning into a right fat slob. God knows what that bitch saw in him.' She chuckled. 'Come to think of it, God knows what I ever saw in him.' She shook her head as she ducked into a head-high fridge. 'The guest bathroom needs retiling. Use the master bathroom. It's through the back. Towels are hanging over the radiator. Use as many as you like. I do. I just love them all warm and fluffy. Don't you?' She looked at him, and her face split into a white-toothed, blue-eyed grin. 'Are you helpless, or what?'

Gilchrist shook his head. 'I'd like to ask you a few questions, but I'm not sure I'm going to get a word in edgeways.'

She held up a tin of John West tuna. 'I always get it in brine. Never oil. Doesn't taste the same. On you go and have your shower. I'll have one after you. I always like to have a cuppa before I shower. Never understood why, just do. And I promise I'll keep this trap of mine shut while you ask me what you want to know. That suit you?'

Gilchrist nodded.

'What's this about anyways?'

'A thirty-five-year-old skeleton. And Jeanette Pennycuick,' he added, intrigued by the way her face froze and her eyes fired up. 'I won't be long.'

The bathroom was tiled floor to ceiling and had about it an airy freshness he liked. The window was open and looked down on to the neighbour's back garden. He heard voices from below, but saw no movement. In the shower cubicle, he was surprised to find a bar of Aramis soap-on-a-rope hanging from the nozzle. And Brylcreem shampoo. She could have been expecting him.

Ten minutes later, he returned to the kitchen, refreshed and surprised by how hungry he felt from the smell of tea and toast.

'Help yourself,' she said, nodding to the plate. 'I like mine toasted. I've made some with plain bread, too. I'll be back in a mo.'

Gilchrist waited until he heard the bedroom door click shut before he stepped away from the table.

In the utility room off the kitchen, he read handwritten notes pinned to cork boards, mostly names and numbers. A calendar hung on the wall, with printed notes in daily squares. Dentist at ten on Wednesday. May and Rhonda round for a curry on Saturday at seven thirty. Hairdresser today at two.

In the lounge, tucked behind a clock, he came across a number of photographs folded flat. One of a younger Betty, hair sprung in a blonde perm. By her side, an older man with balding head and swelling waist. *My Bob* before he became a *right fat slob*? Another of a once happy couple on a strip of beach, their skin and faces glowing copper red. Caribbean? Spain? He eyed the other photographs, but found none showing any children. A drinks trolley sat in the corner of the dining room, displaying mostly gins. Beefeater. Gordons. Boodles. He picked up the Boodles. It had been a while since he'd tried any—

'Can I help you?'

Gilchrist replaced the Boodles on the trolley. 'I didn't mean to pry,' he said.

'Could have fooled me.' She held his gaze for a long second, then nodded to the kitchen. 'You haven't eaten.'

'Thought I'd wait until you returned.'

'To give you more time to pry?'

'I'm sorry,' he said. 'I shouldn't have, but . . .'

'It runs in your blood. Being a detective. Right?' She smiled, and her face seemed to light up, as if to let him know she couldn't have cared less if she'd found him with his head under the settee. 'Come on,' she said. 'Let's eat.'

They sat opposite each other at a four-seater circular oak table. 'I'll play mum,' she said, lifting the teapot. 'Milk? Sugar?'

'A little milk. No sugar.'

'I like my tea the way I like my men. White and sweet.' She laughed, then patted her stomach. 'I shouldn't take sugar. But there you go.'

'Try sweetener.'

'It's not the same.' She stirred his mug and slid it to him.

Between bites of sandwich and sips of tea, Gilchrist asked about her earlier life, her reasons for attending St Andrews, her family background, and all the while she answered with a willingness he found refreshing. But her answers told him nothing new. She knew of no one who had gone missing from the university. It was not until he tackled her about sharing accommodation with Jeanette Pennycuick that he sensed the first hint of animosity.

'Can you remember the names of any of the other flatmates?' he asked.

She shook her head.

He thought it was important to identify these temporary lodgers, students who may have known about a missing woman, perhaps tell him something that might help shed some light on her disappearance. 'Denise?' he offered. 'Alyson?'

'No idea. None of them stayed long. Cramped our style too much.'

He gave her five seconds or so, hoping a name might emerge, but when she stared at him in anticipation of his next question, he said, 'Your style?'

'Small flat with small bedrooms, and not enough privacy to get up to what any normal teenager in the sixties got up to, if you know what I mean.' She smirked. 'More tea?'

He pushed his mug forward. 'Were you there when Jeanette met Geoffrey?'

'There?'

'The flat in South Street.'

'Jeanette'd been with Geoffrey on and off for years. Even before they went to St Andrews.'

'On and off?'

'Rich little spoiled kids, both of them. Always had to have everything their own way. Used to drive me nuts. One minute they were together, the next with someone else. Sometimes it got to the stage that when I came back to the flat I didn't know who'd be sleeping with Jeanette. She was a looker, I'll give her that. Men fell over themselves trying to date her. Fancied her like mad. Especially when she had a tan. It was her Mediterranean looks: dark hair, dark eyes. Great skin.'

Gilchrist stilled. 'Italian-looking?'

She chuckled. 'By the look on your face I'd say I've surprised you.'

'I spoke with Jeanette this morning,' he said. 'She didn't give the impression of, how should I say it, putting it about.'

'Well, she did. And so did he, let me tell you.'

Gilchrist saddened. Somehow that comment turned his mind back to Gail, and to their first sexual liaison in the Valley of Sin. His wife-to-be's libido had surprised him at the time. But he supposed it should not have. In the sixties and seventies, pre-AIDS, the youth of the day had an almost blasé attitude towards casual sex. Not only were Jeanette and Geoffrey Pennycuick putting it around, but so was almost every other sexually mature youngster in the British Isles and beyond. He forced thoughts of Gail away.

'Can you remember the names of some of the women Geoffrey went around with?'

'Not really,' she said. 'But he would always make a point of trying it on with some of the others who shared our flat. When Jeanette found out, she would toss their stuff out in the street.'

It struck Gilchrist that perhaps Geoffrey Pennycuick kept his affairs close to home just to inflict greater pain on Jeanette. Betty interrupted his thoughts by saying, 'So, tell me. How is the bitch anyway?'

'She said you and she hadn't spoken for five years.'

'She tell you why?'

'Something to do with you trying to start an affair with Geoffrey.'

Her porcelain mug cracked the top of the table with a suddenness that made him jump. Tea splashed on to the oak surface. He watched a flush of sorts work its way from behind her eyes, shift across her face and disappear in a white line at her lips.

'I take it she wasn't telling the truth,' he offered.

She dabbed at the spilled tea with her napkin. 'Twisted, stuck-up bitch,' she hissed.

Silent, Gilchrist waited.

She rolled her napkin into a tight ball. 'Geoffrey can't keep his cock in his pants,' she said. 'Never could. Never will. But that stupid stuck-up bitch refuses to see that.' She grinned, and the anger of moments earlier vanished. 'He had a thing for me at St Andrews. But I shouldn't get worked up about it. Geoffrey had a thing for *everyone* at university. Especially himself.'

'Fancied himself, did he?'

She rolled her eyes. '*Loved* himself. He was a handsome devil back then, I'll give him that. Girls used to have orgasms at the mention of his name.'

'Back then?'

'What's that?'

'You said, *back then*.' Gilchrist sipped his coffee. 'Which I suppose means you don't think he's handsome now.'

'Wouldn't let him touch me with a ten-foot bargepole.'

Gilchrist chuckled. 'Haven't heard that one before.'

'Mae West said that.'

'So, you didn't . . .'

'Here's what happened.' She leaned across the table, and Gilchrist sensed that he was being made privy to some rare secret. 'Jeanette's never trusted her man. And she's every right not to. Geoffrey's a serial shagger. For some reason, Jeanette doesn't want to challenge him. She knew he always had a thing for me.' She shook her head. 'Nothing to do with the way I look, or anything like that. I'm just one of the few who turned him down. Anyway, he still tries, *tried*. We don't see each other any more. But he calls from time to time.'

'Here? At home?'

'Amazing, isn't it? He still thinks he's got a chance.' She seemed to struggle to gather herself, then said, 'Bob had left me about a month, back then. Jeanette calls to invite me to a party. Except it wasn't Jeanette's idea, but Geoffrey's. I didn't know that at the time, or I might not have gone. When I get there, Geoffrey's nice as can be, all attentive, acting like he really cares, making sure I'm all right after Bob and how nothing could have surprised him more. But I'd seen him in action before, and I knew what he was all about.

'Later that night, he tries it on. Shows me the new conservatory he's having built. But I know what's coming. So, I'm ready for him.'

She shook her head, and Gilchrist caught the sparkle of tears. 'When we're out of sight he makes his move. He presses me against the wall, starts telling me how much he's always wanted me. I tell him to piss off. He pushes. I push back. But he just keeps on. He won't take no for an answer. Next thing I know, he takes it out.' She stared at Gilchrist, her eyes and mouth wide open with disbelief. 'His cock. He just took it out.'

After several seconds, Gilchrist realized he was expected to say something. 'Then what?'

'I laughed.' She placed her hand to her mouth. 'I just laughed at him. At it. Well . . .' She shook her head. 'He went wild. Called me all the names under the sun. Fucking trollop. Tight-cunted dog. Next thing, he leaves. So I head to the bathroom to put myself in order. Not that anything was hanging out, mind you, but I was shaking like a leaf. Before I'm finished, in barges Jeanette, accusing me of coming on to Geoffrey, and what the hell did I think I was doing trying to split up a family? Them with two kids and every-thing.' She stared off to some point over Gilchrist's shoulder. 'I gave it to her straight, but the more I tried to sort it out, the more she didn't believe me. In the end, I told her I never wanted to see her or her pencil-dick husband again. That's when she knew.'

Gilchrist frowned. 'Knew what?'

'That Geoffrey had tried it on. She knew I had seen his cock. Long and thin, it was.' She laughed. 'Bob might have been getting to be a right fat slob, but I tell you what, it would take a lot more Christmas paper to wrap his up than Geoffrey's.'

Gilchrist said nothing. He smiled in an attempt to share her amusement, but deep down he burned. Here was a woman who had almost been raped, who had the guts to fight back, only to find her would-be rapist had the barefaced audacity to turn the truth against her, making him the offended, not the offender. As sadness settled over Betty's face, Gilchrist wondered why Jeanette would stand by her husband when—

'And for about five seconds that night,' Betty continued, 'I was scared. *Really* scared.'

'You sounded as if you had it all under control.'

She shook her head. 'For five seconds I had nothing under control. I thought I was going to wet my knickers. For five seconds I saw the real Geoffrey Pennycuick. I had no doubt he would kill to get what he wanted. Kill someone. Me. Anyone. Who knows. I saw it in his face.' Tears swelled, threatening to spill down her cheeks. 'It was his eyes,' she hissed. 'They blazed.' She glared at him. 'Do you know what I mean?'

Silent, Gilchrist nodded, his mind crackling through possibilities until his thoughts clicked into place as firmly as snapping handcuffs on to Geoffrey Pennycuick.

CHAPTER 8

Back in his Roadster, Gilchrist called Stan and asked him to check the university records for Geoffrey Pennycuick. 'And while you're finding out what he eats for breakfast, get someone to comb through police records and see if we've got anything on him. Unpaid parking tickets, drunk and disorderly, spitting in public, flashing his cock at old women, anything and everything, I want to know about it.'

'Gotcha, boss.'

It was not until Gilchrist was crossing the Kincardine Bridge and casting his gaze over the mud-brown waters of the River Forth that Bert Mackie called.

'You OK to talk, Andy?'

'I'm all ears.'

'One of my boys gave that cigarette lighter a good going-over. It's a common-or-garden lighter of the cheapo type, the kind you used to pick up in any shop back in the sixties. Imitation silver-plated, rusted to buggery. One interesting thing though,' he added. 'The scratches look like they're initials after all.'

Gilchrist's thoughts flashed to Geoffrey Pennycuick. Surely it could not be this easy. 'Let me guess,' he said. 'GP?'

'Try JG.'

Disappointment flushed through him, then stilled with a cold shock.

We used candles. Was it possible? Jeanette Pennycuick, née Grant. JG.

'How sure are you of the initials?' he asked.

'Not a hundred per cent,' Mackie said. 'I've ordered an electron-microscope analysis, to try to differentiate between natural scratches and printed scratches. That should clear up any confusion.'

'When do you expect the results?'

'Soon.'

Gilchrist's mind crackled. 'You sure your boy got the initials right? They couldn't be IG, or JC, or something like that, could they?' He had no idea who IG or JC was, but he worried that the initials matching Pennycuick's wife could be wrong.

'I've studied them myself, Andy.' He could almost hear Mackie shaking his head. 'It's JG. I'm almost positive.'

'Almost?'

'Near as damn it. But we'll know soon enough.'

He thanked Mackie for calling and told him to keep in touch.

JG. So, there he had it. Or had he?

The initials could be those of the murdered woman. That was the simple explanation, of course. But the fact that they also matched Jeanette Pennycuick's maiden name forced Gilchrist's logic along a different path.

Perhaps the lighter had belonged to Jeanette but been borrowed by her then boyfriend, Geoffrey. Pennycuick visited St Andrews, and the dates fitted. And if the woman had been a student, like Jeanette, Pennycuick could have met her, perhaps even been intimate with her. *Geoffrey's a serial shagger*, Betty's voice reminded him. Could they have had a liaison that ended in violence, with Geoffrey murdering the woman, battering her to death with a bedside lamp to keep their affair secret from his wealthy wife-to-be? *Sex is always a grand motive*, Mackie's voice confirmed. *Before you know where you are he has a fit and batters her to death.*

Was that what had happened?

And the fact that the cigarette lighter did not point to Pennycuick, but to his wife, did not deflate Gilchrist. Pennycuick was devious, of that Gilchrist was certain, the sort of man who might cover his trail at the expense of others. How simple would it have been to take his girlfriend's lighter and place it in the grave? Or take any lighter and scratch his girlfriend's initials on it? But again, and this was the troubling aspect, why even take the chance? Why risk pointing the finger of accusation so close to home? Why not use someone else's initials?

But Gilchrist thought he knew the answer to that conundrum, too.

Geoffrey Pennycuick believed he was better than everyone else, and if he was ever challenged he would deny it with condescending arrogance. Pennycuick was the kind of man Gilchrist loathed, and he would just love to place him under arrest. And wouldn't Betty be delighted if he added sexual harassment to the charge?

But doubt still tickled his mind. He dialled Nance's mobile.

'Do you have anyone on your list with the initials IG or JC?' he asked her.

He listened to something brush the mouthpiece, a clump as the phone was laid down, then a rustling of sorts, like pages being flicked through.

Her voice returned. 'Nope.'

Gilchrist instructed her to go through the university registers again and make a list of everyone with the initials JG with a three-year spread either side of thirty-five years ago.

'Bloody hell, Andy.'

'My thoughts, too.'

Creating such a list was all good and well, he thought, provided the killer had in fact been a student at St Andrews. They could check other records, of course, but all of a sudden, the task of identifying the victim from an ageing skeleton by filtering a pile of out-of-date information seemed too daunting to be conceivable. Were they even on the right track? Had the killer been a student back then? Or a visitor to St Andrews? Or someone who lived in St Andrews but had not gone to the university? Or who lived nearby? Gilchrist had nothing to confirm the killer was a student, male, female, old, young, local or visitor. Still, the initials on the lighter could be the break they were looking for.

But despite his best efforts to think beyond that daunting task, Gilchrist could not lift his spirits.

Darkness settled over the Fife coastline like a prison blanket. The temperature had dropped close to freezing, and a haar fogged the air like fine mist. Seagulls cried from the invisible distance.

In the Central Bar he ordered a portion of steak pie and chips and a pint of Eighty-Shilling. He remembered Gina Belli saying she would be in the Central around seven, and he thought of taking a seat in a corner at the back so that she might not see him and leave. But in the end he chose a bench seat near the door.

He called Stan for an update, only to be told that Pennycuick appeared to be as clean as his starched white shirts. 'Keep at it,' he said, and grimaced as Stan grunted and hung up.

Nance seemed just as frustrated.

'Why don't you join me in the Central for a beer?' he offered.

She paused long enough to make him think she wanted nothing more to do with him, then surprised him by saying, 'Give me five minutes.' But the tone of her voice warned him that all was not well.

He had finished his steak pie and was on his second Eighty-Shilling when Nance eventually joined him, pushing her way on to the bench seat and sidling up close enough for their thighs to touch. But the look on her face told him she wanted to sit close so that no one could hear what she was about to say.

'Beer?' he tried.

She shook her head. 'Coffee only.'

'Changed days.'

'I'm on duty.'

Well, that said it all right there, he thought. He breathed in her perfume, a fragrance that brought back memories of late nights and secret rendezvous, and he resisted the urge to squeeze her thigh. Instead, he looked around him, at students drinking beer, knocking back spirits as clear as water. And smoking cigarettes, too. He inhaled, searching for the dry hit of secondary smoke. He found some, breathed it in, almost closed his eyes.

'I can't stay long,' Nance said.

'You haven't had your coffee yet,' he replied, and thought he sounded like a man searching for the last straw to clutch.

Her short smile spilled from her face.

'Did you get anywhere with the initials?' he tried, feeling he was only delaying the inevitable.

She shook her head in dismay. 'If I didn't know you better, I'd swear you were trying to bore the pants off me.'

'Seems to be the only way these days,' he joked, and from the tightening of her lips wished he had not even tried.

She turned to face him, and he had a sense that the moment was upon him.

'Look, Andy,' she began, 'I think we—'

'Not interrupting anything, am I?' Gina Belli smiled down at them, her gaze shimmying over Nance's face as she pulled out the seat opposite and sat.

Nance pushed away from the table and stood. 'We'll talk later,' she said to Gilchrist, and shoved past Gina without a backward glance.

Gina watched her go, her mouth forming an ugly grimace that Gilchrist thought did not suit her. She sat, lifting one bare leg over the other, skirt riding high on muscled thigh, and removed a packet of Marlboro Lights from her bag. She flipped it open and pulled out a filter cigarette. 'Not a bit young for you?'

'She's one of my team,' he growled. 'So don't even go there.'

'Purely professional, I'm sure.'

He said nothing as she lit up with a deep draw that sucked in her cheeks, then clicked her lighter shut – not a cheap plastic Woolworth's lighter like the one in the grave, but one that looked as solid and heavy as gold, with initials on the corner, a collection of tiny diamond studs that formed GB. He saw, too, that by not offering him a cigarette she was telling him she knew he had given up smoking. She could probably tell him the exact date, time and place.

'What are you doing here?' he asked.

She turned her head, exhaled a stream of smoke as blue as a car's exhaust. 'I thought we had a date.'

'You thought wrong.'

'I'm here. You're here.' Another pull on her Marlboro.

Gilchrist knew it was pointless arguing.

'You look as though you'd like me to leave,' she said.

'That would be nice.'

'How about I get myself a drink?' She stood and sidled to the bar, her skirt tight, her underwear embossed on its fabric. When she returned, she plonked a gin and tonic on the table. 'Mind if I join you?' she quipped.

He waited until she sat. 'Do I have a choice?'

'You could tell me to fuck off, but you're way too polite to say that to a woman.'

'I've been known to be rude.'

She took another hit of her Marlboro, pulling long and hard, then stubbed the cigarette into an ashtray that Gilchrist had shoved to the end of the table. 'By all accounts you're a nice guy,' she said, 'which made me wonder, what's a nice guy like you doing in a shitty job like this?' She held his gaze, long enough for him to feel a growing need to look away.

He picked up his pint, eyed her over the rim. 'It pays the bills,' he said at length, 'and keeps me busy. Which means I won't be staying here for long.'

'Business, business.' She shook her head. 'That's not good for you, Andy. All work and no play makes *Jack* a dull boy.'

Gilchrist caught her emphasis on the word Jack, and replaced his glass to the table with a crack harder than intended. He glared at eyes that stared back at him, and wondered just what was going on in that sharp mind of hers.

'You wanted to ask me something,' he said.

'I want your agreement to write about you and your cases.' She retrieved her Marlboros, tapped one on the table and lit up with deliberation. Her gold lighter snapped shut, its studded diamonds glinting like a misplaced cluster. She leaned back in her seat, blew smoke across the table. 'I think I'm being reasonable.'

'Why do you need my approval? Why not go ahead and write whatever you like? You're going to do that anyway.'

'Professional pride.'

'Don't give me that.'

'You've got me wrong, Andy. I'm—'

'Oh no I've bloody well not I've got you spot on is what I have. You're a manipulative bitch who'll do anything to get what she wants.' The words were out before he could stop himself. He sat back, stunned by the force of his anger. It was the thought of her digging into his brother's accident that had him fired up. Or perhaps it was her interruption of Nance's imminent dismissal of him.

He pushed his fingers through his hair. 'I'm sorry.' He jerked a smile. 'I shouldn't have said that. I'm just . . .'

'Stressed out?' Her face broke into a grin.

'Most people would have taken offence at what I said.'

'I'm not most people.'

'Maybe it's the American in you.'

'Maybe.' She lifted her gin and tonic and eyed him as she finished it off. Then she replaced the empty glass to the table like a chess player about to declare *check mate*. 'Not going to buy me another?'

He felt regret at his burst of anger, and relief at the opportunity to make small amends. 'Seeing as how it's you,' he said, and slid from his seat. He ordered another pint for himself and a gin and tonic with plenty of ice. As he watched his pint being pulled, he called Maureen on his mobile.

'Thought I'd call,' he said. 'See if you wanted to come up and stay a few days in the cottage. Longer, if you'd like.'

'I can't.'

Again, no explanation. He eyed his reflection in the mirror on the back wall, thought he looked disappointed. What had he expected? 'It's been a while,' he tried. 'You should take some time off. Get away from it all. Give yourself a break.'

A pause, then, 'Thanks, Dad. I'll think about it.'

He knew he could press no further. If he did, Maureen could retreat into that black hole of hers. He wanted to tell her that one day it would be so far in the past that it would mean nothing. But he wondered if it ever would. Defeated, he said, 'Give me a call when you can,' then told her he loved her and hung up.

Back at the table, he noticed Gina on her third Marlboro. Or was it her fourth? The impulse to ask for one had him holding his pint with both hands, not trusting himself.

'So, I have your approval?' she said to him.

Gilchrist tilted his pint, took a long mouthful.

'As you said,' she pressed on, 'I don't really need it. But it could work to your advantage.'

Now she had him puzzled. 'In what way?'

'I would be more considerate about how I address your brother's accident. I'd let you review the draft before it goes to print.'

'You know my views on that.'

'I do.' She exhaled, smoke fogging her face, then narrowed her eyes. 'Jack would have been fifty-four next May. The fifteenth.'

Gilchrist studied his pint in silence.

'He was killed by a hit-and-run driver,' she continued. 'The Traffic Accident Report confirmed that pieces from a broken head-lamp identified the car as an MGB GT, and slivers of paint confirmed the car was blaze. That orange colour was popular back then.

Probably F or G registration.' She sipped her gin and tonic and stared at him.

'And?'

'The accident happened in April '69. Here, in St Andrews. You were twelve. Jack was about to turn eighteen. It was that single failure of the local police to find the hit-and-run driver that led you to become a detective.'

Gilchrist held her gaze.

'Jack's death has haunted you ever since.'

'If you want to write that,' he said, 'go ahead. You have my permission.'

She leaned across the table. 'I want to know how you felt, Andy. I want to know how many nights you cried yourself to sleep, how often you visited the scene of the accident, how often you went to the police. But most of all,' and she leaned closer like a conspirator planning a murder, 'I want to know what you wrote.'

Gilchrist tried to keep the surprise from his face.

She pulled herself back, drew on her Marlboro as if she needed to inhale its fire to live, then exhaled through her nose. 'I know about the diaries you kept after Jack.'

He shook his head. 'There was nothing in them except childish gibberish. Besides,' he said, and gave a wry smile, 'I threw them away.'

'No you didn't.'

He almost laughed. 'Those diaries were destroyed years ago.'

'No, they weren't.'

He frowned. He had kept the diaries for years, even after he married, forgotten them, then discovered them brown-paged and dusty in the attic when he sold the matrimonial home after Gail moved to Glasgow. Then it struck him. Gina must have spoken to

102

Gail. But Gail had been ill for months. 'So when did you speak to my ex-wife?' he asked.

Another draw that pinched her cheeks to the shape of her skull. She crossed her legs, giving Gilchrist a flash of white knickers, then turned her head and exhaled a stream of smoke. 'About six months ago.'

Gilchrist frowned. What else did she know about him?

'Here's what I'm looking for,' she said. 'Your exclusive author-ization to write your story.'

'A biography, you mean.'

'More than just your run-of-the-mill biography. I want a detailed account of how you solved your most famous cases. I want you to tell me about this sixth sense of yours—'

'There's nothing magical about it,' he complained. 'It's just logical deduction.'

'That's not how I hear it.' She drew on her Marlboro, chinned her shoulder and blew it out. 'Besides,' she said, 'I know all about sixth senses. And then some.'

Gilchrist took a sip of beer, not liking the subject.

'And I want sight of all your diaries,' she pressed on. 'In return, we split all royalties fifty-fifty. I'll have my publisher draw up a contract for your solicitor. Once everyone's happy, we sign. Then we talk, and I start to write.' She leaned on the table. 'Sound fair?'

Gilchrist glared back at her, resisting the urge to push his pint away and leave. He could almost make out his reflection in the dark pools of her eyes, just about see his puzzled frown work its way across his forehead. He looked away from her, stared at his pint, picked it up, put it down. Then he held her gaze again.

'Problem?' she asked.

He had never understood how his thought processes worked,

this gut-driven feeling that twisted his insides and forced his logic down one path to reach its conclusion at the expense of all others. Perhaps it was her persistence over his brother's accident, or the way her hands moved or her fingers shifted when she clicked her diamond-studded lighter. But something had triggered his thoughts, worked away at some level deep in the chasms of his mind, almost out of reach of all conscious logic.

He flipped open his mobile, pushed himself to his feet. 'I'll be back in a minute,' he said, half aware of the victory smile on her face, as if she knew what he was thinking.

But how could she? How could anyone?

As he waited for his call to be answered, he walked to the centre of Market Street, breathed in the cold October night, all of a sudden conscious of the heavy pounding in his chest. His convoluted logic had come up with a ridiculous conclusion. He was wrong. He had to be.

But he needed to make sure.

'Mackie speaking.'

'Bert,' snapped Gilchrist. 'The lighter. Do you still have it?'

'What's got you fired—'

'Bert. Please. Have you?'

'Hold on.'

Gilchrist took a deep breath, then let it out in a long release, trying to slow the chatter of his heart. He paced the cobbles in the middle of the road, then faced the Central, the lights from within a warm contrast to the frost in the air, his breath fogging in the cold like steam.

'I've got it,' grumbled Mackie. 'What about it?'

Gilchrist looked to the sky, gave a silent prayer. 'On the bottom,' he said. 'On the edge. Is it nicked?'

'Nicked?'

'Yes. Nicked.' He could think of no other word. He pressed his mobile to his ear, could almost hear Mackie study the lighter with his magnifying glass. He stepped out of the way of a passing car and returned to the bar entrance. He reached out, gripped the door frame. Just in case.

'Yes,' said Mackie. 'It is.'

'How many?'

'Looks like three.'

'All on the same edge?'

'One on one edge, and two on the opposite edge.'

Gilchrist felt his breath leave him. He hung up. How was it possible? He looked around him, as if searching for the answer in the night shadows.

JG. Not Geoffrey Pennycuick. Not Jeanette Grant.

Three nicks. Two on one edge, one on the other. Conclusive. Unarguable.

JG.

The lighter was his brother's.

CHAPTER 9

'*Don't tell Mum and Dad.*'

'*This is our secret, Andy. Just you and me.*'

Gilchrist's fingers trembled as he eased his cigarette into the flame.

'*Now suck in.*'

The heat from the lighter seemed to fire his mouth, and he almost let go.

'*Now take a deep breath,*' *Jack said.* '*Hold it. Then puff it out.*'

Gilchrist inhaled as he was told, felt dizziness surge through him, watched his brother's face shift and shimmer. Then he let it out, but could not hold back a cough.

'*Feel good?*'

'*I think so.*'

'*Don't worry. You'll get the hang of it.*'

Gilchrist sat back, holding the cigarette deep between his index and middle finger, his hand clasped over his mouth. He took another draw and exhaled through his nose, just the way Jack did.

'*Here,*' *said Jack, handing him the lighter.*

The silver lighter gleamed as good as new, except . . .

'*It's scratched,*' *said Gilchrist.*

Jack nodded, blew smoke from his nostrils. 'Two nicks. One for me and one for my girlfriend.' He took a quick draw, pouted it out.

'Do you like your girlfriend?'

'She's special.'

'Will you get married?'

Jack retrieved his lighter and removed a penknife from his back pocket. He snapped the blade open, gouged another nick on the lighter's edge. 'That one's for you, Andy. You're special, too.' He handed the lighter back.

Gilchrist rubbed his finger over the fresh scratch, then said, 'So, will you?'

Jack inhaled, long and deep, held his breath, as if the answer to the question was being formed through the molecules in his lungs. Then he tilted his head, narrowed his eyes as he looked at the bedroom ceiling and exhaled in one long, steady stream.

'One day,' he said.

By the time Gilchrist returned to the bar his mind had already fired a fusillade of questions at him, the most worrying being, how had Jack's lighter found its way into the woman's grave? Was Jack in any way involved in her murder? That thought alone had a cold sweat tickling Gilchrist's neck. But only he knew the nicks could place the lighter with his brother, and he made a pact to keep that to himself. At least for the time being. He could be wrong. There could be some simple explanation. But he found he could give it no further thought, for one other possibility had his mind spinning. Was it possible? Or was he being absurd? After all these years, could he now have a lead to his brother's hit-and-run driver? And did his ridiculous thoughts on his immediate course of action make any sense?

He picked up his pint, downed it in one.

'Thirsty all of a sudden,' Gina said.

'Let's go.'

She caught up with him as he was stabbing the key into the Merc's ignition.

'Whoa there, big boy,' she said, folding herself into the passenger seat, showing more tanned cleavage and muscled thigh than could be considered decent.

Gilchrist snapped into Drive, floored the accelerator.

The Merc twitched as it powered forward.

'Want to tell me what's going on?' She removed the Marlboro from her handbag.

Gilchrist snatched the packet from her, stuffed it back into her bag. 'I'll make you a deal,' he said. 'About the book. I'll agree to it, on one condition. That you tell me the truth.'

'Not even one teeny-weeny white lie?'

He glared at her, annoyed that she would choose that moment to try to joke.

'You're serious?'

Gilchrist gripped the steering wheel, tightened his fingers until his knuckles whitened. 'I can drop you at your hotel if you'd like. Your choice.'

She held up both hands in mock surrender. 'The truth, the whole truth and nothing but the truth, so help me God.'

Gilchrist jerked the wheel and overtook two cars, returning to the safety of the inside lane to the angry blare of a passing horn.

'Of course, the truth doesn't matter a damn if we're both wrapped around a tree,' she said, slapping both hands on the dashboard as Gilchrist pulled in hard behind a Transit van. 'Either you slow down, or I'm going to have a cigarette. And *that's* the truth.'

Gilchrist eased his foot from the pedal, let some distance grow between his Merc and the Transit van. Gina was right, of course. After all these years, what was the point of rushing?

'OK,' she said. 'Let's have it. And I promise to tell you the *truth*.'

He did not like her emphasis, as if she was mocking him. 'Just how good a psychic are you?' he asked, and found himself driving on in a heavy silence that had him thinking the truth was about to catch her out. Hedgerows, trees, walled fields, all passed by in blurred silence. Corners came and went. And still no response.

He kept his speed at a steady fifty, determined to wait her out.

'I believe in what I receive,' she finally said.

'That's not what I asked.'

'How can I answer?' she said, then added, '*Truth*fully.'

'I thought the question was straightforward.'

'That shows how much you don't know.' She faced him. 'I need a cigarette to think straight.'

He depressed a button on the console and her window lowered. He stopped it halfway. 'Start thinking straight,' he said. 'And flick your ash outside.'

She tutted as she dug into her handbag, and a few moments later exhaled out the window. 'I can't explain the unexplainable,' she said. 'I can only tell you what I see, feel, or even hear.' She took another draw. 'After that, it's all up to you. Maybe I should ask, How good are *you* at using the unexplainable? How far do you want to push when no one else believes you? How many resources do you want to use at the ridicule of others? That's what happens. You either believe in what I tell you, or you don't. But you'll find most people don't.' She sucked in hard. In the dark of the car her cigarette glowed red.

Gilchrist gritted his teeth. A few minutes earlier his plan had

109

seemed unequivocal and clear. Now he was not so sure. 'You still haven't answered my question,' he pressed.

She took another draw, this time facing him as she exhaled. 'The best.'

The rust on the cigarette lighter had been descaled in places, the silver plating long corroded. Gilchrist remembered it looking as expensive as solid silver to his twelve-year-old eyes, shiny and gleaming, its perfection marred only by three nicks on its base. He ran his fingers over them, and an image of Jack cupping the lighter in his hands hit him with such clarity that he had to close his eyes.

'Care to share your thoughts?' Mackie said.

Gilchrist shook his head. 'You don't want to know, Bert.' He handed the lighter to Gina Belli, watched her finger it. 'Anything?' he asked.

She rolled her eyes. 'Don't be so goddamned dumb. It's nothing like that.' She turned the lighter over, touched the nicks he had described to her on the drive to Dundee. 'I'd like to have a look at the cold-case files again.'

'You've seen them before?'

'When I thought I was going to need something to persuade you to let me do your biography.'

Mackie said, 'Would someone care to tell me what's going on?'

Gilchrist took Gina by the arm. 'I'm about to find out,' he said, and led her from the room.

Back behind the wheel, Gilchrist said, 'How did you get access to the cold-case files?' But even as that question aired, he saw that with her high-profile police contacts in the States, she could probably gain access to cold-case files anywhere in the world. Even if you thought it was nothing more than witchcraft, what harm

110

would it do to let a psychic with an impressive record sift through your local cold-case files?

As if in tune, she said, 'It's amazing what a simple telephone call can do.'

'Why do you need to see the files again?'

'I now have something that belonged to your brother,' she said. 'It could make all the difference.'

'I can't get hold of them tonight.'

She shook her head. 'How about tomorrow?'

Tomorrow? Tomorrow was too long. He needed to know tonight, right now. He struggled with the rationale. This psychic business made no sense. Everyone knew that. It was nothing more than a hoax, a scam, a way to make money at the expense of others. But he still needed to push as far as he could. He did not have the cold-case files. Not tonight. But having come this far, what did he have to lose by going one step further?

'I can give you a photograph,' he heard himself say.

By the time Gilchrist retrieved three photographs of Jack from his cottage in Crail, it was after 1 a.m. when they pulled up under the portico of the St Andrews Bay Hotel. Like the star attraction she thought she had now become, Gina Belli waited for Gilchrist to open the passenger door and help her out.

'Don't push it,' he said, as she took hold of his hand.

'Charming to the last.' She left him to close the door.

Her room was on the third floor with a view of the sea, its presence noticeable only by a vast and utter darkness that stretched before him like a starless sky. In the distance, the lights of Carnoustie flickered through the night haze, helping him define the limits of the estuary's northern shoreline.

He turned from the window and watched her clear a space on the writing desk. With her tanned skin and designer clothing she seemed ready-made for the surroundings.

'This place is expensive,' he said.

'Uh-huh.' She lit a cigarette.

'Isn't this non-smoking?'

'As you said, it's expensive.' She exhaled from the side of her mouth and switched on a table lamp, adjusting the dimmer until it cast a dull glow over the desk. She took a hard draw of her cigarette, stubbed its lengthy remains into her empty whisky glass and held out her hand. 'Photographs.'

Without looking at them, she laid all three face-down on the writing desk, taking care to line them up in a row. She placed the lighter next to one, taking her time selecting its exact position. Then she placed an envelope on the table – where had that come from? – and removed a dozen or so handwritten pages, which she placed on one corner of the desk with careful deliberation.

'Lights?'

Gilchrist obliged by turning them off.

The room fell into darkness, except for a dim penumbra on the writing desk.

Gina turned over the handwritten pages, one by one, moving them from one corner of the desk to the other.

'What are you doing?'

'Sshh.'

Gilchrist tightened his lips like a chastised schoolboy, and could not help but think that all the fiddly palaver, the precise alignment, the photographs, the lighter, the turning of the pages, the silence and the dimmed lighting were all an act of showmanship to impress him.

She seemed to find the page she was looking for, which she removed from the sheaf and laid next to the lighter. Then she placed her hand over one of the photographs before moving to the next, then on to the last one, until her fingers brushed the cigarette lighter. She closed her eyes, inhaled slow and deep, let it out.

It felt like several minutes, but could have been less, when she opened her eyes and brushed her fingers down the single sheet of handwritten notes from top to bottom, then again, this time stopping about one third of the way down. With her other hand, she turned over the first photograph. Jack with shorn hair, collar and school tie, grinned up at her, teeth and gums sparkling. She flipped over the other two – Jack with flared hipsters, shoulder-length hair and a guitar slung over his shoulder, fretboard down-pointing, Johnny Cash style – Jack stripped to the waist, broad shoulders and ripped stomach muscles making Gilchrist wonder how they could ever have come from the same parents. She brushed Jack's features with one hand, while her other tapped the page with a pen. Another surprise. Where had that come from? Then, with a suddenness that startled him, she pushed her chair back and stood.

Silent, Gilchrist faced her. Was he supposed to switch the lights back on? Say something? But she stood immobile, and stared at him in silence. In the shadowed lighting the swell of her breasts, the curve of her hips added a sexual charge to the macabre image. He returned her stare, not sure what he had just witnessed, and even less sure of what he was expected to do next.

She broke the spell by pushing her hands through her hair. 'I've not been altogether honest with you,' she said.

'Well, that's a start.'

She lit another cigarette, inhaled as if her life depended on it, then sat on the edge of the bed. She eyed him through a shadowed cloud of smoke. 'I received a name.'

'Voices whispering in your ear?'

'In my head.' Her cheeks pulled in for another draw. 'It's the same name.'

'The same name as what?'

'As before. Only this time stronger.'

'Louder?'

'No. Clearer.'

'You've not been altogether honest with me?'

She looked away from him then, her gaze settling on some spot on the wall, as if she could see beyond it and was counting the night stars. 'I read the accident report earlier. Worked through the cold files.' She faced him. 'I also visited the scene of the accident.'

'When?'

'Four or five months back.'

About the same time she approached Gail, he thought.

'That's when the name came to me.' She drew in, inhaled hard and swallowed. 'It was only a whisper.' Her breath rushed in a white fog. 'I couldn't understand what I was hearing. I didn't even think it was a name. It sounded like *fake love*.' She grinned up at him. 'How often is that true?' She pushed herself to her feet, found her empty whisky glass, took another draw and stubbed the stem into it. Then she walked to the window. With her back to him, she stood silhouetted against the night beyond.

Gilchrist waited.

'So I started digging.'

'Digging?'

'Research. I write biographies. It's what I'm good at.' She shrugged. 'I thought I was on to something. I could feel it. I just didn't know what it meant. So I tried another route. I contacted DVLA in Swansea, eventually found someone who would search their database for me—'

'Who?'

She turned from the window and faced him. 'That's not important.'

'Go on.'

'I wanted a printout of the names and addresses of all owners of MGs registered in the UK for 1969.'

Gilchrist felt his eyebrows lift. 'That's quite a task.'

'It was,' she agreed. 'It took me five weeks to get it, and four days to go through it.'

'What were you looking for?'

She shrugged again. 'Anything that came to me.' She strode to the bedside table, removed a fresh packet of Marlboro from her handbag. She stripped it open, removed one and lit it with her diamond-studded lighter. Watching her addiction on full display seemed to douse Gilchrist's own urges. Or maybe his dread of the outcome of her psychic show was killing his desire.

She sat on the bed again, closed her eyes and exhaled. 'When I started going through the printout, I realized that the *fake love* I'd been hearing was really a name. I found seven in total.' She glanced at the writing desk. 'I wrote them down.'

Gilchrist thought he saw where she was going. 'And one of these seven names came back to you tonight. Only clearer.'

'Yes.'

He was almost afraid to ask. 'Whose name?' he tried.

She looked up at him, and something in the shape of her mouth, the glint in her eyes, told him she had not wanted to go this far.

'It's the name of the driver.'

Hearing those words had him struggling with the urge to walk to the door and leave her to play her silly psychic games. But he stood rooted. After all, was this not what he had hoped for, that her psychic powers might somehow give him a lead? But he had not thought it through, had not imagined what she could give him. Not the name of the driver.

He had not expected that.

'On the writing desk,' she said, 'next to the lighter, is the list of seven names. I've underlined the name that came to me tonight.'

Gilchrist strode to the desk, snatched up the sheet.

James Matthew Fairclough.

He scanned the other names, mostly close variations.

Only one was underlined.

James Matthew Fairclough.

He scowled down at her, could not keep the sarcasm from his voice. 'You expect me to believe this?' he said. 'When the entire police force failed to come up with any suspects in their investigation?'

She took a long draw. 'We're going back thirty-plus years here. Forensic science was in its infancy. The east coast of Scotland was a long way from Scotland Yard, if you get my drift. Fairclough was drunk when he killed your brother. Way over the limit.'

'Who have you shown this to?'

'Only you.'

He glared at the name again, his logic screaming that it was all a con, a way for the psychic author, Gina Belli, to land another book on the *New York Times* bestseller list. It would not be the first time he had crossed someone intent on conning him for some ulterior motive.

He stared into eyes as black as oil. 'This is unbelievable.'

'I won't argue with you on that.' She inhaled long and deep, then let it out with a rush. 'But I'm seldom wrong.'

'Which also means you're not always right.'

'But I'm right on this one.'

Silent, Gilchrist waited.

'I knew you would be hard to convince,' she went on. 'So I dug deeper still.'

Now they were coming down to it, he knew, her moment of dishonesty.

'There was a passenger in the car.'

Passenger? Even as the word chilled his skin, his logic was firing two steps ahead, his nervous system twitching at the sudden possibility of a witness to the accident. 'You mean, a woman?'

'You never miss a trick.'

'Fairclough's girlfriend?'

'*Ex*-girlfriend.'

'You've spoken to her?'

'I went to see her.'

'You found her address? How?'

'Don't look so incredulous. Once I had Fairclough's name, the rest was easy.'

'You're not answering my question.'

'My father was wealthy,' she said. 'When he died, he left me a fortune. I don't need to write for a living. I write because it's what I want to do.' Her dark eyes smouldered. 'And it's worth it just to experience moments like this.'

'But how?' he pleaded.

'Money makes people search databases,' she said. 'And it makes people talk.'

Was that all it took, money? The man who had killed his brother had spent all these years free because the police could not throw enough money at the case? Was that what had happened?

'And Fairclough's passenger will come forward only through me,' she continued. 'No one else. She has lived with the memory of that accident for thirty-five years. She can live with it for the rest of her life if she has to.'

'Why doesn't she?'

'She's dying. Motor neurone disease.' She blew a cloud of smoke at him. 'Don't worry, she won't die before she talks to you.'

CHAPTER 10

Sleep eluded Gilchrist.

Images came at him as speeding cars, broken bodies, limbs splayed over damp cobblestones, as if his mind was a screen on which all accidents were replayed. If Gina's information was correct, then he had the name of the hit-and-run driver who had killed his brother and since managed to evade every attempt by the police to track him down.

After thirty-five years.

He pulled himself from bed and stumbled along the hallway in the darkness. In the front room, he opened his notebook and read the name one more time, to reassure himself that it was still there, that he was not mistaken.

James Matthew Fairclough.

Printed in pencil. Each letter gone over half a dozen times.

James Matthew Fairclough.

He would have Stan dig up a current address. But in the meantime, it was the passenger, the sole witness to the accident, he needed to speak to.

★ ★ ★

Pittenweem was one of those fishing villages that featured in holiday postcards and the occasional restaurant menu – *Fresh Pittenweem Haddock Caught Daily*. He turned off the A917 and made his way on to Abbey Wall Road, driving downhill to a picturesque row of houses that looked quaint and fresh-painted and which fronted the sheltered harbour.

That morning, a sea haar dampened the scene.

He parked his Merc and shivered off a chilling sea breeze.

The call from Kara surprised him.

'I don't know who else to talk to,' she began. 'I've tried talking to Jack about it. But you know what he's like. Stubborn as they come. Even when he knows he's wrong.'

'And is he wrong?'

A pause, then, 'He's back on drugs.'

The words were spoken so quietly that he almost never caught them. 'How long?'

'A few months. After we started going out.'

Gilchrist felt his breath leave him. He faced the sea. The haar was lifting, giving a bleak glimpse of swelling waves. In the harbour to his side, anchored boats rocked and creaked as if stirring alive. *A few months*. But Gilchrist suspected differently. Jack was a freelance artist, someone who was perceived to thrive on drug-induced creativity and who mixed in a circle of friends and associates with access to drugs, among other things. Had they sold drugs to Jack? Did any of them know his father was a detective? Would that have mattered?

He struggled to mask the desperation in his voice. 'What's he taking?'

'MDMA.'

Ecstasy. 'Anything else?'

'I don't think so.'

'Where does he get it?'

'I shouldn't have told you.'

'You did the right thing telling me.' He tried a different tack and concentrated on keeping his voice gentle. 'Did you know Jack had taken drugs before?'

'Just dabbled. Nothing hard.'

'But not any more?'

'I think he's becoming addicted.'

Gilchrist gritted his teeth, stared off to the horizon. This was his son she was talking about, his little boy, the same child who cried when a crab gripped him by the toe on the East Sands and who almost died from a combination of measles and pneumonia that had him and Gail taking turns during the night to dab the sweat from his swollen face and the gunk from his welded eyes. How could that boy now be—

'Don't tell him we've spoken,' she said. 'I don't want to lose him.'

'I *will* need to talk to him.'

'I know you will. But please . . . ?'

Gilchrist promised to be discreet, thanked her and hung up.

Well, there he had it. His fears realized. Jack *back* on drugs. Despite his repeated denials. He thought of calling right away, then decided not to. He needed to reason with Jack, not crash over him like a stampeding bull. Besides, even noon could be an early rise for Jack.

He slipped his mobile into his pocket and set off into the village.

He found her house in Routine Row without difficulty – no nameplate, just a number pinned to the door frame in bold brass plates. A brass door-knocker invited him to disturb the early-morning quietness.

He looked at his watch. Not yet eight.

He stepped into the middle of the narrow street. The curtains were still drawn on the upstairs dormer windows. Blinds shielded the downstairs from passers-by. The houses either side had drawn curtains, too, so he decided to give her another ten minutes.

He found a mobile cafe near the harbour, ordered a coffee and a bacon sandwich.

The coffee warmed his hands, and the sandwich dripped bacon fat as he walked along the pier. Seagulls performed hovering aerobatics in readiness of an easy meal, but Gilchrist was too hungry to consider sharing. Down to the crust, on impulse he tossed the remains into the water, only to see it snatched mid-air by a heron gull that swooped inches from the stone wall and wheeled away, others hard and loud on its tail. With the gulls no longer interested in him, he finished his coffee in solitude.

By the time he returned it was 8.27.

The blinds were still closed, but the house next door had curtains opened that gave a view through cleaned windows to a tidy garden that boasted shorn bushes.

He gripped the knocker, gave two hard raps and back-stepped on to the street.

He waited until his watch read 8.30 before giving another two raps, hard enough for the next-door neighbour to stick her head out.

'Rabbie's no here,' she shouted out to him.

'I'm looking for Linda Melrose.'

'That's right. Rabbie's no here.'

Gilchrist failed to follow the logic. 'Does Linda Melrose not live here?'

'Aye. But Rabbie's no here.'

'Forgive me, but who's Rabbie?'

'Her brother.'

Gilchrist waited.

'Linda cannae get up by herself. Rabbie helps her. Come hail or shine.'

Gilchrist glanced at his watch. 'When will Rabbie get here?'

'He's usually here afore nine. Sometimes after. So there's nae need to waken up the whole street. Just bide your time and he'll turn up soon enough.'

She was about to return indoors when Gilchrist said, 'Do you know where Rabbie lives? Or where I can find him?'

'You're right impatient, so you are.'

'It's important,' he said.

She glared at him. 'He walks his dog along the harbour. A muckle Alsatian.'

'Thank you.'

'Wait 'til you see him before you cast any thanks.' And with that, the door closed.

Back at the cafe, Gilchrist ordered another coffee. 'I'm looking for Rabbie,' he said. 'He usually walks his Alsatian.'

'Tam.'

'Tam?'

'Rabbie's Alsatian.'

'Oh, right. Yes. Tam. Have you seen Rabbie walking Tam this morning?'

'Not yet.' She glanced at her watch. 'And I wouldnae expect to see him for another hour or so.'

'Why's that?'

'Heard he got gubbed last night. He can be a right nasty drunk when he's had a few, let me tell you.'

'Do you know where he lives?'

'Somewhere in town.'

'Can you do any better than that?'

'Sorry.'

'Well, in that case, I'll have another one of your bacon sarnies,' then added, 'You wouldn't have a phone book by any chance, would you?'

'You're in luck.'

While he waited for the bacon to fry, he thumbed through the pages, but found nothing under Robert Melrose. Perhaps he had no house phone, only a mobile. He returned the phone book to the counter. 'Can't find Rabbie Melrose's number in here.'

'That's because he's Rabbie McKerihar. Melrose is his sister's married name.'

Gilchrist found the number within seconds, entered it into his mobile and assigned Rabbie's home address in Session Lane to memory. But the phone rang out and did not roll over to an answering machine.

The cafe owner's directions took him across the A917 into Charles Street, and had him at Rabbie's door within ten minutes, in time to finish his coffee and crush the cardboard cup into a rubbish bin.

The cottage reminded Gilchrist of his own before he purchased it. Paint flaked from the door frame and facia. Wet rot nibbled the window frames. Whitewash peeled from stone walls. The small garden was a patchwork of weeds and dog shit and urine-bleach marks. He set foot on the front step and was met by a barrage of growls and snarls. Something hard snapped at the door by his feet.

He tried the doorbell.

Tam let loose with a burst that stirred the hairs on Gilchrist's neck.

He rang the bell again, this time held it down. But it did little to drown the barking. Tam sounded demented. The door shivered as something hit it. Then silence, followed by a yelped whimper and a man's curse.

The door pulled open, and a man stepped into the chilled air, wearing a pair of boxer shorts that had seen better days ten years ago. The air filled with the smell of tobacco and stale beer. Red-rimmed eyes glared at him.

'This had better be fucking good.'

Gilchrist showed his warrant card. 'Detective Chief Inspector Andrew Gilchrist.'

'What's this about?'

'Are you Rabbie McKerihar?'

'What if I am?'

'Let me ask the questions, Rabbie. All right?'

Tam's growls turned Rabbie's haggard face into a mask of anger. He turned and gave a growl of his own. 'Back. *Now.*' A bare foot at Tam rewarded Rabbie with a growl. He tracked Tam down the dark hallway, through an open door that he closed hard enough to loosen hinges.

'Fucking nuisance,' he said when he returned to Gilchrist.

'Good guard dog.'

'I can look after myself.'

Gilchrist caught the grazed knuckles, the cut lip. 'Even when you're drunk?'

Rabbie's eyes narrowed. 'What the fuck've I supposed to have done this time? It was a fair fight. He had it coming.'

'Do you want to tell me about it?'

'No really.'

'Good,' said Gilchrist. 'I don't want to hear it.'

Rabbie's sore eyes widened. 'What's this about then?'

'Your sister.'

'Linda?' Rabbie's face worked through a short display of surprise and confusion, then shifted to anger. 'If anything's happened to my Linda, I'll have the bastards by the—'

'Nothing's happened to her.'

Rabbie brushed the back of his hand across his mouth and chin, the stubble as grey as steel filings.

'I need to talk to her,' Gilchrist continued. 'That's all. Ask her a few questions.'

'What about?'

'There you go again, Rabbie, asking questions. Get dressed before I start on about last night's fight.'

Gilchrist could almost hear the wheels turn.

'Give me a minute.'

The door slammed in Gilchrist's face.

CHAPTER 11

Linda's house was as clean as Rabbie's was grubby. Paintwork glistened. Windows shone. Flowers that Gilchrist thought must have been imported at this time of year filled her home with the scent of spring. He counted three vases in the hall and six in the front room where he now waited. Overhead, the creak of floorboards gave him some bearing on Rabbie's progress.

Once the introductions had been made and Gilchrist had given Tam more ear-scratching than any dog deserved, Tam had shown himself to be soft-mouthed and placid. All he had wanted was his morning walk, and he now lay asleep outside on the front step, a warning to anyone who threatened his master's sister.

Nor was Linda what Gilchrist had imagined. Grey-haired and white-toothed, she greeted him from her wheelchair with a firm handshake that defied her frail appearance.

'Rabbie's telling me you're a nuisance,' she said to Gilchrist.

'I thought he was talking about Tam.'

She smiled for an instant. A flash of sunshine. 'Would you like a cuppa?'

Gilchrist was about to say he was all coffeed out until it struck him that this was her way of keeping Rabbie from listening to whatever he had to ask. 'Just the one, then. Tea. Milk, no sugar,' he said.

'And I'll have my usual, Rabbie. But I've no fresh milk.'

Rabbie slid from the room without complaint.

Gilchrist heard the front door open, Rabbie's words of encouragement to Tam, then a gentle click as the door shut. 'He looks after you well,' he said.

'As well as can be expected at this stage. But I don't think he'll be up for what's coming,' she said. 'I'll need to get a nurse in. To do the personal things.'

Gilchrist lowered his gaze. He wondered how he would feel if he knew he was going to die. Oh, we are all going to die. There is no getting around that. But to know *how* you are going to die, and that it is only a matter of time, that must be a hard thing to acknowledge.

'So why are you here?'

Gilchrist looked into eyes that he saw had once sparkled with the promise of life. Now they glistened with the knowledge that the promise was dashed, that life was nothing more than a routine of wakening and sleeping until one day you didn't waken.

'I met Gina Belli,' he said.

At the mention of her name, something seemed to snuff the light in Linda's eyes. 'She told me you might come.'

'Did she tell you why?'

'Only that you had a vested interest. Whatever she meant by that.'

Annoyance gripped Gilchrist's lips. Gina had veiled the truth. Linda Melrose did not know Jack had been his brother. He decided to edge into it, unsure of how much to disclose.

'You were a passenger in a car,' he said. 'What do you remember?'

She faced the window again, and Gilchrist felt his own gaze following, as if the accident was about to be replayed in the reflective sheen of the glass.

'Not much,' she whispered.

Gilchrist waited.

Seconds turned to minutes. Still, she stared out the window.

Then her shoulders heaved, and her body seemed to rise from her chair before settling once more into immobility. 'It was raining,' she whispered.

Gilchrist strained to catch her words.

'We'd been drinking.'

'We?'

'Me and Jim.'

Something akin to electricity ran the length of Gilchrist's spine.

'Legless, I was,' Linda looked up with a defeated smile. 'I've not had a drink for ten years, and here I am. Legless again.'

Gilchrist tried to offer a smile, but did not pull it off.

'Don't know what I saw in him. Jim wasn't my type, really. Drove a fancy sports car. Just sitting in it made me feel special. Jim was no looker. But when you're young and stupid and drunk mostly every weekend, who cares? I was on the pill. We all were. What did it matter?'

'It was raining, you said.'

She looked to the window, as if searching for her memories. 'I was wearing a mini-skirt.' She shook her head. 'How on earth we wore them I'll never know. I looked good, though.' She slapped her legs. 'Nice and shapely they used to be. I've always wondered, if the

129

style had been different, would that night have turned out different, too?'

'I'm not sure I follow.'

'That's what distracted Jim. My legs. He couldn't keep his hands off them. I told him to stop, keep his eyes on the road, he'd get what he wanted later.' She pressed her hand to her mouth as tears filled her eyes. 'Listen to me, I sound like a wee hairy. But I wasn't. Honest to God, I wasn't. I was just drunk.' She dabbed the corners of her eyes, tucked loose hair behind an ear. 'I never saw him.'

Gilchrist's mind sprang alert. 'Saw who?'

'The man Jim hit. I only heard it. A right hard thud, so it was. Jim stopped the car. He just sat there, gripping the wheel, looking in the mirror. He looked scared.'

'You never saw the man he hit?'

She shook her head. 'No.'

'Why not?'

'I was digging in my handbag for a fag.'

'Then what?'

'Jim drove off.'

'Did he not get out of the car?'

'No.'

Gilchrist raked his hair, fought off an image of his brother lying on the side of the street, blood draining along the gutter in red waves. If either of them had taken a look, could they have saved Jack's life? 'What were you thinking of?' he said. 'Your boyfriend had just killed someone and the next thing—'

'It wasn't like that.'

The snap in her voice coincided with the click of the front door. Gilchrist held his breath, like a lover caught in the act. He felt, more than heard, Rabbie walk the length of the hall, and waited until the kitchen door closed. 'What was it like, then?' he asked.

Linda's fingers gripped her wheelchair, worked the rims of the wheels, wriggled it around until she faced Gilchrist head on. 'I didn't know he'd run over someone—'

'I thought you'd—'

'Let me finish.'

Gilchrist waited while her fingers relaxed their grip. He waited while her eyes welled and tears blinked free.

'I've thought about that night for years,' she began. 'The older you get the more aware you become of your own mortality. And here I am, glued to this chair, waiting to die.'

Gilchrist struggled to contain his anger. 'Jack would have been fifty-four next year,' he growled.

Like a wind uncurling a folded rag, her face shifted. 'Jack? You knew him?'

'He was my brother.'

She held his gaze for a long moment, then looked away, defeated. 'I never knew,' she whispered. 'I'm sorry. So sorry.'

'Tell me what you remember.'

'Jim told me he'd hit a dog.'

'What kind of dog?'

'What difference did it make? A dog's a dog. He said it was OK, that it just got up and ran away.'

'And you believed him?'

'Why wouldn't I? I never saw what happened.'

'A right hard thump, you said.'

'I just thought it was a dog. A big dog.'

'He looked scared, you said. After hitting a dog?'

'But only for a wee while. That's what Jim was like.'

'But you found out later.' A statement, not a question.

She gripped the wheel rims and tugged. 'I heard about the accident on the telly the following week. But I never saw Jim again.'

'Didn't you speak to him about it?'

'No.' She stared through the window again. Clouds curled across a sky as grey as a roadside gutter, and he caught another glimpse of his brother's face. 'I knew something was up,' she whispered. 'All night he'd been talking about doing it. That's all he wanted. He couldn't have given a toss if I was legless or unconscious. All he wanted was a shag.' She backed her wheelchair away from him, as if to distance herself from the memory. 'But he said nothing after the accident, just drove me home and dropped me off without so much as a goodnight grope.' She worked the wheels of her chair so that she faced the window full on. 'But he did say one final thing.'

Gilchrist stared at her. If she lied, he would know it.

'He said, if anyone ever asks, tell them it was a dog.'

A dog. Records had shown that Jack had died from loss of blood. The force of the hit had broken his knee and shattered his thigh, causing a bone fragment to slice his femoral artery. He could have been unconscious in a minute, dead in two. And James Matthew Fairclough had compared Jack's life to nothing more than that of a dog.

'Look,' she said, and spun her chair away from the window, so that her back was to him. 'I've told you all I know. Please, Mr Gilchrist, will you leave it at that?'

'Any problems?'

Gilchrist turned at the sound of Rabbie's growl and, from the glaring eyes and tight lips, caught a glimpse of the wild beast that could be a drunken Rabbie.

'Mr Gilchrist is just leaving, Rabbie. Aren't you, Mr Gilchrist?'

'I would like an answer to one final question,' he said.

'Can you no hear the woman?' Rabbie brushed past and stood between Gilchrist and his sister.

Gilchrist waited while Linda shuffled her wheelchair around to face him. Tears stained her cheeks.

'I'm sorry, Mr Gilchrist. I should have done something about it before now. But I didn't. And that is my regret.'

'Can I ask why?'

Rabbie stiffened. 'Is that your final question?'

'It could be.'

Linda dabbed a shaking hand to her eyes. 'Jim frightened me. It was as simple as that, Mr Gilchrist.'

Gilchrist needed to press for one more answer. 'Would you be prepared to go to court and give evidence?'

Rabbie stepped forward. 'You've had your final question.'

'It's all right, Rabbie, it's all right.'

Rabbie retreated to the side of the wheelchair, placed a hand on her shoulder.

Linda almost smiled. 'I don't have long to live,' she said to Gilchrist, 'so what have I got to be afraid of any more?'

Gilchrist let himself out.

He tried to give Tam a farewell chuck behind the ears, but Tam returned the gesture with a growl, leaving Gilchrist with the feeling that he had upset everyone that morning.

CHAPTER 12

It took Stan less than two hours to come back to Gilchrist with a current address for James Matthew Fairclough – Livingston, on the western outskirts of Edinburgh.

On the drive through, Gilchrist called Jack.

'How do you feel this morning?' he asked.

'Andy? Hey, man. How's it going?' He gave out a hard cough that sounded like gravel turning in a cement mixer. 'What time is it, anyway?'

'You sound a bit rough.'

'Just hungover.'

Hungover? 'Jack,' Gilchrist said, and felt his fingers tighten their grip. 'I'm going to ask you a question, and I want you to tell me the truth.'

'I'm not taking drugs, Andy. I've told you that before. Did Kara say that to you?'

The speed with which Jack had jumped to his conclusion surprised Gilchrist. Maybe his son possessed his own sixth sense. 'Why don't I believe you?' he said.

'I smoked some marijuana not so long ago,' Jack confessed, as if realizing the futility of arguing against a detective parent.

'Define *some*.'

'Not a lot.'

'You'll need to do better than that.'

Another cough, less phlegm-laden. 'I was struggling with the flu,' Jack said. 'I'd taken some stuff to keep my temperature down. We went out for a beer. I had a shandy, of all things. Don't laugh. It was Kara's suggestion. But we met up with an old friend, and one thing led to another. We ended up at some party in the west end, and I crashed out.'

'Crashed out?'

'Fainted, then. Is that better?'

'What did you take?'

'Mostly alcohol.'

'And?'

'And some marijuana. Just a couple of spliffs.'

'Nothing hard?'

'No. I swear.'

'How many other times?' The silence grew, along with Gilchrist's doubts. Jack was lying. He could sense it.

'There were no other times—'

'Come off it, Jack. You don't crash out on alcohol and marijuana. You're talking as if my head zips up the back.'

'I'm telling you, Andy. That's it. The only time. With Kara, at least.'

There. He had it. Jack's confession that he had taken drugs *before* Kara.

'What I mean is,' Jack continued, 'the only time like *that*. I was really sick, man. I had to go to the hospital. Kara insisted they pump my stomach, keep me overnight. I told them I had the flu, that's all. But no one would listen. They thought I was on cocaine

135

or something. But the alcohol must have reacted with the prescription medication—'

'Prescription?'

'Yeah. I went to the doctor. I was feeling lousy.'

Gilchrist felt a spurt of hope. Jack would have seen a doctor only as a last resort. As a child he'd hated the doctor's surgery, with its dismal waiting room and morbid silence. But a doctor kept records. 'Which doctor?' he asked.

'Look, Andy. I've just about had it with you on this. I've told you. I don't. Take. Drugs. OK?'

'I hear you.' But the line was already dead.

Gilchrist slapped his mobile shut and threw it on to the passenger seat. He knew his son. Jack had always been weaker than Maureen. Well, *weaker* was not the correct word. Less strong, perhaps. More telling, he thought, was that whenever Jack lied, he would fight it out to the bitter end, argue black was white if he had to. But caught in an argument over the truth, he would clam shut, just walk away. Or hang up. Which told Gilchrist that Jack was not on drugs. He'd taken them in the past. That was an indisputable fact.

But not now.

He found the housing estate just before midday and eased his Mercedes into it.

Detached homes lined both sides of a quiet road that branched left on to an elliptical cul-de-sac. Trimmed hedgerows bordered tidy lawns. Glistening paintwork edged sparkling windows. All picture-perfect, except for one home that stood out like an old caravan at a car auction.

The rusting body of an old MGB GT that sat on the side lawn beside the tarpaulin-covered hulk of another vehicle had Gilchrist's heart pounding. For a moment he thought it could be the same car Gina Belli identified, but the registration plate dated it in the seventies, years after the hit-and-run. Both cars had not been moved for some time. Grass sprouted around tyres and under the chassis like desert scrub. A dilapidated Ford Sierra huddled half on, half off the pavement, in front of a battered Transit van with taped cardboard where the side window should have been. The only vehicle that looked as if it had moved in the last year was a long-bodied Ford van with the telescopic arm of a cherry picker folded along its roof. *Fairclough Engineering* stood out on its grimy side panels.

Gilchrist parked his Merc four houses away.

When he returned, he lifted the corner of the tarpaulin on the car next to the MGB, just enough to identify the badge of an ancient and dilapidated Ford Anglia. No luck there.

Fairclough's home was no better. The door had not felt the welcome bristles of a paintbrush for at least ten years, maybe twenty. Square lawns either side of a cracked path looked as if the grass had been torn, not cut. Curtains hung askew in the front window. The door split from the frame with a sticky crack on Gilchrist's third pressing of the doorbell.

A pot-bellied man in a grimy T-shirt and baggy sweatpants stood barefoot in the hall. Hair like white wire sprouted either side of a bald head. Swollen bags under bloodshot eyes folded into fat cheeks. The stench of sour milk drifted with him as he stepped forward.

'James Fairclough?'

'Whatever you're selling,' he growled, 'I'm not interested.'

'James Matthew Fairclough?' Gilchrist fingered his warrant card.

'So?'

'Can I have a word?'

'What about?'

'Inside?'

Fairclough coughed, a hard bark that brought phlegm to his mouth. He pulled a filthy cloth from his pocket, spat into it, then slipped it back into his sweatpants. Maybe outside was better.

'You used to own an MGB GT,' Gilchrist said.

'Still do.' Fairclough nodded to the rusting hulk. 'Want to buy it? I'll give you a good deal.'

'I'm sure you would,' Gilchrist said. 'But you had one before that?'

'I've owned a ton of cars. So?'

'A late-sixties model. G reg.'

'Could have.'

'Blaze ring a bell?'

'Don't hear a thing.'

Gilchrist waited. Stan had given him the registration number he downloaded from DVLA's records in Swansea, but Gilchrist did not want to give that out to Fairclough. Not just yet. DVLA had no record of Fairclough's MGB after '76, the last owner's address being somewhere in Stirling, which had him thinking the car had been scrapped.

'Alsatian, was it?'

'What?'

'The dog you hit.'

A tic flickered in Fairclough's right eyelid. 'What dog?' he tried.

'St Andrews.'

'Not been there for yonks.' Fairclough stepped closer, almost filling the doorway with his clatty bulk. 'What's this about, anyways? Dog? What fuckin' dog?'

'MSN 318G?' Gilchrist caught the flicker of recognition at the registration number.

'What?'

'The registration number of your blaze-coloured MGB GT.'

'If you know the number, what the fuck're you asking me for?'

'Because you killed someone in St Andrews while driving that car. You were drunk at the time, so I have to assume it was an accident. But you didn't report it. That was your mistake—'

'I'll tell you what I'm going to do,' said Fairclough. 'I'm going to go inside and have myself a nice cup of tea. Then I'm going to call my solicitor and tell him that some skinny prick in a leather jacket has been slandering my name about, and how much do you think I should sue him for?' Fairclough tried to smile, but his mouth failed to work the way it should.

'You do that,' said Gilchrist. 'And when you're at it, tell him my name. Detective Chief Inspector Andy Gilchrist.' He tried to take some pleasure from watching Fairclough's face pale, but inside he struggled against the almost overpowering urge to pull him from his house and handcuff him face-down on the front lawn. He had no doubts now about Gina Belli's psychic abilities. However she had done it, here was the man who had left his brother dying in the rain-soaked streets of St Andrews, who had driven off without offering help, or calling for an ambulance. How could he now prove Fairclough had done it? Which left him puzzling over his decision to confront him. What had he expected Fairclough to do? Confess?

Gilchrist moved closer. Inches separated them. The stench of bad gums had him holding his breath. 'Gilchrist,' he repeated. 'You know the name because you've never forgotten. I can see it in your eyes.'

Fairclough's throat bobbed. 'What the fuck're you on about?'

'Jack Gilchrist was the name of the man you killed. He was

almost eighteen when you ran him over, and drove off to leave him dying in the gutter.'

'Why don't you go play on the railway?' Fairclough stepped back to close the door.

'I've spoken to Linda.'

Fairclough's eyes flared for a moment, then disappeared as the door slammed shut.

Gilchrist stood on the step for a full minute, his breath fogging the cold air. For one absurd moment he toyed with the idea of kicking the door down and dragging Fairclough to the local police station in handcuffs. Instead, he stuffed his hands deep into his pockets and retraced his steps to his Merc. He made a point of not looking back, even though he knew Fairclough would be following his retreat from behind dirt-laden windows. By the time he switched on the ignition, an idea had come to him. He caught Stan on his mobile, and from the background chatter guessed he was having a pint.

'Let me guess,' Gilchrist said. 'The Central?'

'Le Provençal.'

It was on College Street, almost next door to the Central, a basement restaurant that Stan often used to obtain information from less honest locals.

'Anyone I know?' Stan's rushing breath told Gilchrist that he was bustling from the restaurant for some privacy.

'Wee Jimmy,' Stan said at length.

Wee Jimmy Carslaw. Five-foot nothing and fingers as quick as a snake strike. In and out of your pocket with a touch as light as the wind. Many an innocent tourist had lost more than a few bob to Jimmy's fingers. 'What's he been up to?' Gilchrist asked.

'Just helping out, boss. Keeping him honest.'

Gilchrist accelerated on to the M8. The Merc eased into fast-flowing traffic with barely a murmur. 'I need you to chase something down for me, Stan.'

'Shoot, boss.'

'That MGB we talked about earlier,' he said. 'Can you get Nance to pay the last-known owner a visit as soon as she can?'

'What's the rush?' Stan asked.

What could he tell him? That he had an idea, a passing thought? That this is the car that killed my brother, and I was wondering, if it hadn't been scrapped, was any of his DNA still on it? As he played it through his mind, he realized he was not only clawing at straws, he was making them up.

'It's a long shot, Stan. I don't even know if the car's still around.'

'Leave it with me, boss.'

Gilchrist was about to hang up when Stan said, 'Got a facial on the skeleton.'

True to her word, Dr Heather Black had given Gilchrist's request top priority.

'Any matches?' he asked.

'Not yet. It's just come in. We're working on it. But I'll tell you what, boss. Someone must know her.'

'Why's that?'

'She's a beauty. Can't imagine her not having a string of boyfriends.'

Gilchrist pondered Stan's words. Maybe that had been the girl's downfall. Maybe one of her boyfriends suspected she was playing the field, and jealousy took hold. Maybe she had tried to break up their relationship and a violent argument followed. Or maybe she had been sexually assaulted and was murdered trying to defend herself.

He mulled those thoughts in his mind, trying to work a different angle. But no matter how he worked it, he knew the key to identifying the young woman was to put the computer image on the national news. Someone might recognize her.

If so, that could break the case wide open.

'Get it over to Conway at the Beeb,' he ordered, 'and ask her to put it out on all news channels this afternoon.'

CHAPTER 13

Gilchrist felt his breath catch.

Stan had been correct. The murdered woman had indeed been beautiful.

He gripped the back of the chair, held on tight, tried to still the thick pounding in his chest as he stared hard at the screen.

Dr Heather Black had created a remarkable likeness, but the eyes were not quite right. Gilchrist remembered them being larger, and a darker shade of blue than the sky blue Dr Black had coloured them. Her hair, too, was wrong. Where Dr Black had it long and straight and blonde, the popular style in the sixties, Kelly had worn hers short. He also remembered her teeth being perfect, the whitest he had ever seen. American dentistry could do that. And the tiniest of scars on her chin was not there, although in all fairness to Dr Black, she could never have known.

He brushed his fingers across the monitor.

'What d'you think, boss?'

He had carried her skull, lifted it with his bare hands, held it close to his face, trying to develop a feel for the young woman behind it, never knowing that—

'Boss?'

Gilchrist tilted his head to Stan, but he could not peel his gaze from her eyes.

'You all right, boss?'

'Kelly Roberts.'

Stan looked to the screen, then back at Gilchrist. 'You know her?'

Gilchrist let out a rush of breath. 'She used to go out with my brother Jack.'

Stan pulled a hand over his mouth, down on to his chin. 'Shit.'

'They split up not long before Jack was killed.'

Stan frowned. 'I'm sorry, boss. I never knew your brother had . . .'

Gilchrist nodded. 'I never saw her again. Now I know why.'

Stan pulled out his notebook. 'What was she like? As a person, I mean.'

'Friendly. Vivacious. Confident. She was American. A student at St Andrews University.' He eyed the screen again. 'She worked part-time in Lafferty's, The Criterion back then, which was where he went for his underage drinking. He said she fell in love with St Andrews on one of her father's golfing trips.'

'Were her parents alive back then?'

'I've no idea. But Jack never said they weren't.'

'Any reason why he would keep it from you if they were dead?'

Gilchrist shrugged. 'None that I know of.'

'So why didn't they report her missing?'

'Maybe they did. But in the States.'

Stan scribbled in his notebook.

'The relationship was serious,' Gilchrist said. 'Jack once told me she was special.'

At that, Stan faced the screen, raised his eyebrows.

'He used to bring her round to our home on Friday nights,' Gilchrist pressed on, 'before they went out to the cinema. I was twelve, Jack was seventeen, but mature way beyond his years. When he first introduced Kelly to our parents, I remember our old man couldn't keep his eyes off her legs.' Gilchrist shook his head at the memory. 'Back then, the girls used to wear skirts as short as wide belts.' He nodded as another memory came back to him. 'And she never wore jewellery, Stan. I remember that, too. Only a watch.'

'No watch was found, boss.'

'Taken off and thrown away,' Gilchrist said. He studied the screen, thought her image no longer looked as familiar, as if she had morphed to a sister lookalike. The shape of her mouth seemed wrong to him now, tighter where he recalled her lips being fuller. Her cheeks, too, more rounded where they should have been sculpted. But if he narrowed his eyes, let the image fade out of focus, her likeness returned to the beautiful woman his brother Jack had called *special*.

'See if you can dig up her records from uni,' he said to Stan. 'That should give us her home address. If her parents are still alive, I'd like to talk to them.'

Gilchrist had just taken a sip of his Eighty when Gina Belli said, 'A man of habit, I see.'

Defeated, he gestured to the seat opposite. 'Why don't you join me?'

She did, lighting up another Marlboro before nodding to his plate of bridie, chips and beans. 'That's bad for your cholesterol.'

'It tastes good.' He spread his palms. 'Would you like some?'

145

'I don't do lunch.'

He eyed her through a fog. 'They say the smoking ban will soon be passed into law.'

'That'll do wonders for morale.' She tossed her head, blowing smoke from the corner of her mouth. 'I spoke to Linda Melrose,' she said. 'She seemed upset.'

'She should be. She's remained silent for thirty-five years about a murder to which she was the only witness.'

'Will she cooperate?'

'Eventually.'

Gina nodded, took another pull. 'And Fairclough? Did you find him?'

He noticed a tremor in her fingers, the tiniest of shakes, as if the nicotine had not yet worked through her nervous system. Or maybe her psychic reputation was at stake. Or her bestselling status. 'Different animal altogether,' he said.

'Did he deny it?'

'All knowledge.'

'Do you think he's the one?'

'I'm working on it,' he said, then added: 'Before I forget. Do you have Jack's lighter with you?'

'It's in the hotel room.'

'Have you mentioned what I told you about the nicks?'

She took another draw, blew it out with a gush. 'Give me some credit, for crying out loud.'

'I take it that's a no.'

She scowled at him.

'Good,' he said. 'Let's keep it that way.'

She took another draw, which seemed to kill her anger. 'Be careful, Andy.'

He eyed her over a mouthful of beer.

'I mean it,' she said. 'I'm getting bad feelings about this.'

He returned his pint to the table. 'Voices in your head again?'

She stubbed her cigarette into the ashtray, as if trying to grind it through the glass. Then she pushed her chair back, and stood. 'You know, you can be a real bastard at times,' she hissed, then strode from the bar.

No sooner had she left when a voice to his side said, 'I see you haven't lost your charm with women.'

DI 'Tosh' MacIntosh stood at the bar, no more than four feet from the back of Gina's chair. How long had he been there? But, more worrying, had he overheard any of his conversation with Gina?

Gilchrist tilted his pint. 'Up yours,' he said to Tosh, and took a sip.

'Not going to ask me to join you?'

'Just leaving.'

'I'd buy you a pint, Gilchrist, but I might have to piss in it first.'

Gilchrist pushed from the table and, without a word, walked from the bar.

By two that afternoon, Stan had retrieved Kelly's records from the university. 'She seemed to have it all,' he said. 'Beautiful *and* smart.'

Gilchrist scanned her records. Eighty-six per cent in English, her best subject. He remembered Jack telling him that Kelly lived somewhere north of New York City. He pulled her home address from the records, and a search on Google Maps confirmed that Wilton was a small town about eight miles north of Saratoga Springs in upstate New York. Several phone calls later, State records confirmed that Kelly's father had died five years earlier. The US

Postal Service verified that a Mrs Annie Roberts lived at the given address. This troubled Gilchrist. If both of Kelly's parents had been alive at the time of her murder, why had they not reported her missing?

One way to find out.

He clicked on the recorder, introduced himself and Stan, then placed the call to the States.

'Mrs Annie Roberts?'

'Yes?'

'This is Detective Chief Inspector Andy Gilchrist from Fife Constabulary in Scotland. I have you on speaker phone with Detective Sergeant Stan Davidson. We're recording this call. Can you spare a few minutes to talk to us?'

'Who did you say you were?'

Gilchrist repeated his introduction a little slower, more emphatic. 'We'd like to ask you a few questions about your daughter.'

'My daughter?'

'Yes.'

'My daughter Kelly?'

Gilchrist raised a hopeful eyebrow at Stan. 'Yes.'

'Have you found her?'

Gilchrist frowned at Stan, who eyed the phone with an intensity that almost burned. 'Why do you ask that?' Gilchrist tried.

'Kelly's been missing for thirty-five years.'

'Did you report her missing?'

'We did.'

'Who to?'

'The police, of course. But nothing ever came of it. Have you heard from her? Is she . . . is she all right?'

148

'Mrs Roberts, we're looking into Kelly's disappearance, and need to ask you a few questions that might help us with our . . . enquiries.' He had almost said *investigation* and was already regretting calling. He should have flown out, had a face-to-face.

'I don't understand,' she said. 'From Scotland, did you say?'

'Yes.'

'Why Scotland?'

It was Gilchrist's turn to be confused. 'I'm not sure I follow.'

'What was she doing in Scotland?' she asked. 'She disappeared in Mexico.'

Mexico? Gilchrist leaned forward, placed his hands on the table. 'We have records of Kelly living in Scotland.'

'She took a short-term course in English at St Andrews University, but she left there and went to Mexico.'

Stan spoke into the phone. 'When was that?'

'When she finished her studies.'

'Yes, but which year?'

'Sixty-nine.'

'Month?'

'She said her last exams were in January. She flew to Mexico not long after that.'

'When did you last see Kelly, Mrs Roberts?'

'Christmas sixty-eight. Tom and I flew over for a week.'

'To St Andrews?'

'Yes. Tom loved to golf.'

'Where did you stay in St Andrews?'

'I can't remember the name of it now. Some hotel that overlooked the sea.'

The Scores, thought Gilchrist, an address for a number of hotels with sea vistas.

'And after Kelly left St Andrews,' Stan said, 'when did you next see her?'

'We didn't.'

Gilchrist leaned forward, almost pushed Stan away from the phone. 'Then how do you know she went to Mexico?' he asked.

'She flew there. Straight from St Andrews.'

Flying straight from St Andrews to Mexico was not possible, of course. But a flight from Edinburgh or Glasgow could connect to anywhere in the world. The rationale puzzled him. Kelly was killed in St Andrews. So where and how did Mexico fit in? It made no sense.

'When we reported Kelly missing, the Sheriff's Office checked the flight manifesto and confirmed she'd been on it.'

Kelly had been on it? A flight to Mexico? Gilchrist frowned. What was he missing? 'But you never saw her again,' he said. 'How do you know she actually stayed in Mexico?'

'She sent us a postcard from Mexico City.'

Gilchrist leaned closer, lips almost at the phone. 'Let me make sure I understand,' he said. 'Kelly sent a postcard from Mexico saying she had flown there from St Andrews?'

'No. The one from Mexico said she would be home in a month.' On the end of the line, she stalled. 'That was the last Tom and I heard from her,' she breathed.

The one from Mexico? 'Did Kelly send you another postcard from somewhere else?' he asked.

'She sent one from St Andrews saying she was flying to Mexico.'

'Did she always send you postcards?'

'No. She usually wrote on an airmail letter. One of those lightweight blue envelopes that no one uses any more.'

'So how many postcards did she send you?'

'Only two.'

Gilchrist scowled at the phone. Had the postcards been written by the person who murdered her? That would explain the change in writing material. Was it as simple as that? A thought struck him. Perhaps a mother might have held on to the last keepsake from her missing daughter . . .

'Do you still have the postcards?'

'No.'

Gilchrist felt himself deflate. With today's advancement in forensic science, what might he have been able to recover from—

'Saratoga County Sheriff's Office has them.'

'What?'

'And the letters.'

Gilchrist almost punched the air. 'All of them?'

'Not all of them. I didn't give them every one.'

Gilchrist pulled himself upright. He took a deep breath. Something was still not right. Surely a mother would have recognized her own daughter's handwriting. Unless . . .

'How were the postcards written?' he asked.

'They were typed, not written.'

'Did Kelly sign her name?'

'She did, but it wasn't her normal signature.'

'What do you mean?'

'She hurt her hand and couldn't hold a pen. She said so in the postcards. I didn't think anything of it. Should I have? Have you . . . have you . . . *found* her?'

Stan returned Gilchrist's gaze, and Gilchrist shook his head. This was not the kind of news to drop on someone over the phone. He tried to keep his voice level. 'Mrs Roberts,' he began, 'we are trying to identify the remains of a young woman found in a cemetery on the outskirts of St Andrews. If Kelly had flown to Mexico, the remains are unlikely to belong to her.'

'Oh.'

'For completeness of our records,' he rushed on, 'would you have any objection to giving a sample for DNA analysis? I could arrange for someone from your local police to visit you at home and take a sample. Just a mouth swab. Some saliva would do. Just to be sure.'

'I'm . . . I'm . . .'

'It would really help us with our enquiries,' he pressed.

'Well, if it will help, then I don't see why not.'

'Thank you, Mrs Roberts. You've been extremely helpful. And I'm sorry to hear of Kelly's disappearance.'

'Thank you, Mr . . . ?'

'Gilchrist.'

'Gilchrist?' She repeated his name twice more, then said, 'Thank you, Mr Gilchrist.'

From the muffled sounds on the phone, Gilchrist knew she was crying. 'Our lives were never the same after Kelly disappeared,' she said. 'I'm sure if Kelly had been around, Tom would still be alive. He lost something when she disappeared. We both did.'

Stan sat tight-lipped, scratching his pen on his notepad.

Gilchrist felt his own lips tighten. If Mrs Roberts had been in the interview room, he would have put his arms around her, but he could do nothing for her now, other than find the person who had killed her daughter.

'One final question,' he said.

'Yes?'

'Did Kelly ever receive any letters after she left for Mexico?'

Stan stopped doodling.

'She had her monthly statements from the bank. Tom closed her account a year or so after she disappeared. The statements were just a reminder.'

'What did you do with her mail?'

'After a while, we just boxed it all together and put it in the attic.'

'Is it still there?'

'It is. Yes.'

'Can you remember if she ever received any mail from anyone in Scotland?'

'I'm not sure. I was always looking out for another postcard. But none arrived.'

Of course not, thought Gilchrist. He thanked her and, as her voice broke again, pressed the button to end the call.

He raked his hair. Kelly's mother had kept her hopes alive for all these years. Even her voice at the beginning of their call had soared with hope.

Have you found her?

Yes, he should have said. *Yes, we've found her and I regret to inform you . . .*

Stan switched off the recorder and closed his notepad. 'What's with the mail from Scotland?' he asked.

'Just a thought,' Gilchrist said. 'Email a copy of the computer image to Saratoga County Sheriff's Office, and have them visit Mrs Roberts for an ID and a DNA sample. Put some heat under them. Tell them it's urgent, and that we need to move fast.'

'Got it.'

'And find out where Rita Sanderson lives.'

'Who?'

'Jack's flatmate.'

When Stan left the room, Gilchrist played the recording back.

He paused it when he came to the postcards. Postcards? Two of them? Sent by the killer to make Kelly's parents believe their daughter was still alive, doing well, learning more about life by flying to Mexico? Even though she had not been on the flight, the manifesto confirmed otherwise. Which meant that whoever had taken the cudgel to the side of her head was not a crazed killer but someone with a clever mind, smart, devious.

Intelligent enough to be a doctor?

His earlier worries as to how Jack's lighter had found its way into Kelly's grave could now be readily answered. Jack could have given it to her, or Kelly could have taken it from him and forgotten to return it. Now that conundrum was out of the way, Pennycuick's face shimmered once again in his mind's eye. Calm, controlled, with the foresight, mental acuity and brazen nerves to write two postcards to Kelly's parents. But how could he have faked the flight manifesto? Could that have been done back in the sixties?

All of a sudden, Gilchrist's mind filled with an image of Pennycuick's wife taking her seat on a plane. Could she have flown to Mexico under Kelly's name? Was that possible?

Gilchrist clicked on the recorder and listened to some more.

Did Kelly ever receive any letters after she left for Mexico?

Stan had seemed puzzled by that question. But Gilchrist knew Jack had written to Kelly. He had seen him in his bedroom, eyes red-rimmed, hair ruffled, unkempt, a student struggling with the difficulties of imminent exams. But Gilchrist had known, even at the age of twelve, that Jack was pining for his lost love, his special girl, his lost American girlfriend. Were Jack's letters to Kelly now lying in the box in the attic? What would the local police make of them if they found them? Kelly's disappearance had been reported by her parents, and nothing had come of it. If the local police had taken on the case with any determination and had contacted Fife Constabulary with their suspicions, they might now find something in the local files. But so far, they had not.

So, what had happened?

Was the answer to Kelly's murder in her mail?

We just boxed it all together and put it in the attic.

Which really left Gilchrist with only one option.

He would have to fly out and see for himself.

CHAPTER 14

After checking flights to the States and hotel vacancies in Saratoga Springs, Gilchrist decided to tie up some loose ends in the morning, then fly to the States the following day. He tried calling Nance about Fairclough's car, but ended up leaving a message on her mobile telling her to meet him in Lafferty's. By the time she arrived he had finished his burger and was on his second Eighty-Shilling.

'The usual?' he asked her.

She glanced at her watch, shook her head. 'Soda water and lemon.'

'Driving?'

'To Oban for a couple of days.'

Gilchrist had forgotten Nance had applied for two days' leave, which he'd not had the heart to refuse. Seated at a table in the back, away from the main entrance, they went through Nance's notes together. With the skeleton now having a computer-generated image and a name, he redirected her efforts to having a copy placed on the evening news before she left, and further copies distributed around town. But all the while she seemed distant, as if she was only killing time with him.

She lifted her drink, took a sip, glanced at her watch again.

'Got an appointment?' he asked.

'Can we talk?'

'We are talking.'

'You know what I mean.'

Gilchrist tried a smile, but he sensed what was coming. No Gina Belli to interrupt this time.

'You know about me and John,' she began.

'Nice guy. Bit of a wandering eye, I have to tell you.'

'Well, it's wandered my way.'

'I've noticed.' He took a sip of beer. 'Serious, is it?'

'You could say.' She gripped her glass with both hands, as if ready to squeeze the lemon through. 'Look, Andy, I've enjoyed our time together, I really have. You've been nothing but a gentleman. And I wouldn't want to hurt you in any way. But—'

'I'm too old for you?'

'I don't see it that way.'

Her answer surprised him. 'What way do you see it, then?'

She shook her black mane of loose curls, then fixed her gaze on him, her brown eyes pulling up memories of intimate moments. 'I know this sounds crazy,' she said, 'but I've fallen for John.'

'He's handsome, all right. I'll give him that.'

'It's more than looks.'

Gilchrist didn't like the sound of that. Ending their relationship he could understand, but laying it on thick was not how he imagined Nance would have done it.

'He's asked me to marry him.'

Gilchrist waited a polite three seconds to let her think her words were taking time to be processed. But this was John's

157

modus operandi. As best as he could remember, it would be his fourth engagement. 'How long have you known him? Two weeks?'

'It's not like that, Andy. This is different.'

'Sounds like a sprint, not a romance.'

Nance lowered her eyes.

He had not intended to be mean to her, and wanted to apologize. But how could he when she was intending to marry the office lech? He tilted his glass, chinked it against hers. 'Here's to you and John,' he said. ''Til death do you part.'

She returned his smile, but he could tell it was an effort. When she looked over his left shoulder and her eyes lit up, he knew without having to turn his head that the man of the moment had arrived.

A hand clasped his shoulder. 'Andy.'

John's voice was deep, strong and gentle at the same time, with a timbre trained to ease the knickers down a woman's thighs at the first hello. Gilchrist had always thought it affected. He tilted his drink. 'I hear congratulations are in order.'

John smiled at Nance as if Gilchrist had not spoken.

'Going to join us?' Gilchrist asked, but Nance was already pushing herself to her feet with a determination that told him she could not wait to be out of his sight. She hesitated for a moment, as if remembering something, then slipped her hand into her jacket and removed a folded note.

'Here,' she said.

Gilchrist shoved the note into his pocket.

'We're heading off,' John announced. 'Got a couple of days accrued.'

'Hope the rain stays off,' Gilchrist said. Not that it mattered, he supposed. He could not imagine John doing much sightseeing when he had Nance's body to explore, all fresh and new to him. As Nance slid past, Gilchrist took hold of her arm. She looked down at him, but did not pull away. He leaned up to her. 'Take care,' he said, and gave her a peck on the cheek.

He watched them in the mirror, Nance with her head tilted to John's shoulder, John with his arm already around her, protecting her from dirty old men like Gilchrist. As they walked into the rain, he hoped she would not confess their relationship. That could be trouble.

Thinking about trouble, he called Jack, but it rang out.

He tried Maureen, and she surprised him by picking up.

'Hello?'

He could tell from the heaviness in her tone that she had just risen, or was drunk. 'How are you, princess?' he tried.

'Hello? Who's this?'

'Mo. It's me. Is everything all right?'

'Dad? Is that you?'

'Mo. Where are you, honey? Are you at home?'

'In bed.'

'Are you sick?'

'Why're you calling?'

He thought he heard someone speak in the background, a man's voice, but he could not be sure. 'I was thinking of coming—'

'I'll call back later, Dad.'

'Mo—'

The line died.

He dialled her number again, then slapped his mobile shut before it connected.

Maureen worried him. She was still far from well. But drink was

159

not the cure. He downed his pint with an angry rush and was about to pay for his meal when his mobile rang.

'Got Rita Sanderson's address and phone number for you, boss.'

'Be with you in a minute, Stan.'

The American accent still grated, but something in the tone of Gina Belli's voice had Gilchrist pressing the phone hard to his ear. 'So what are you suggesting?'

'Be careful, Andy. That's what I'm saying. I saw flames, fire—'

'Sounds more like a nightmare than a—'

'Don't minimize me.'

Stan entered the room and caught his eye. 'Look, Gina, I appreciate your concerns,' Gilchrist said, 'but I'm caught up in the middle of something.'

'Sure you are,' she quipped. 'But just remember. It's what you do with what I tell you that makes the difference.' And with that, she hung up.

Gilchrist slapped his mobile shut.

'Problems, boss?'

Gilchrist snatched Stan's note from him.

'She's now Mrs Thomas, boss. Living in Chatham, Kent.'

Gilchrist walked along the corridor into the first interview room. He switched on the recorder, introduced himself and Stan and dialled Rita's number.

As a youngster, he had met Rita when Jack first showed him around his new flat. Gilchrist had been struck by her height, an inch or so short of six foot, and by how long and slender her hands and fingers were. She had told him that was why she was an excellent pianist, but Gilchrist had never been sure if she was joking or not. Not long after, his own growth spurt had kicked in, and by the time he turned fourteen he stood at his final height of six-one, all skin and bone and pimple-faced.

'Rita Thomas, formerly Rita Sanderson?' he asked, just to be sure.

'Yes? Who's this?'

Even from those few words, her voice sounded just as he remembered, its Welsh lilt melodic to his ears. He formally introduced himself and Stan, gave the address of the office in North Street and advised her that the call was being recorded.

Once she placed Gilchrist's name to her memories of Jack and St Andrews, she said, 'Well, I never. After all these years. It's lovely to hear from you. And you're now with the police?'

'For better or for worse.'

She chuckled. 'You sound so Scottish.'

'Some things will never change.'

'Thank God for that. So, what brings you crawling?'

Gilchrist smiled. Some things really will never change. Rita used to tease him about the way he hung around when he was with Jack, never one to be in the forefront. 'It's a case I'm working on,' he said. 'I'd like to scratch your memory, ask a few questions. Are you up for it?'

'What's it about?'

'A missing woman.'

'And you think I might be able to help?'

'Do you remember Kelly Roberts?'

'How could I ever forget her? I could never understand why she left in such a hurry for the States. I remember Jack was devastated.'

Having turned twelve a few months earlier, Gilchrist had never fully understood the emotional change in Jack in the weeks before he was killed. Only now, with the realization of Kelly's sudden disappearance, was he beginning to piece it together.

'After she left,' he pressed on, 'did you ever hear from her?'

'Not a squeak.'

'Did she ever mention Mexico?'

'Mexico? Not that I remember,' she said, as her voice rose. 'Hold on, Andy. Is Kelly this missing woman you're looking for?'

An electronic hiss filled the line.

Her voice came back at him in a whisper. 'Oh, my God. She never went back to the States. Did she?' She paused, waiting for his answer, then said, 'I caught something on the national news. About the remains of a young woman being found. I didn't pay much attention. Is she . . . ?'

Gilchrist let her question hang unanswered. 'When was the last time you saw her?'

'I drove down to Wales for my birthday. When I came back, Kelly had left.' Her voice sounded flat, as if the life had been sucked from it. 'Which was what she had planned, of course. To return home. But she surprised us all by leaving early. Well, at least, that's what we thought at the time.'

'Can you remember the last time you saw her?'

'It was just before I left for my birthday. A couple of days, I think, which would put it around the eighteenth or nineteenth of February. We went out for breakfast together, just the two of us. She promised to keep in touch. I just thought . . .'

Promised to keep in touch. 'Did you write to her?'

'Twice. But I never heard a word. Now I know why. Andy, is it really her?'

'We think so,' he said at last.

'Oh, my God,' she gasped.

He held on to the phone, waiting for her to continue.

'I can't believe it. When she talked about leaving, I always thought we would meet up again. Kelly would visit Wales. I would visit the States. But when she never replied, I just thought she wanted nothing more to do with me. I thought it was something to do with Jack. I just never would have thought. What happened to her?'

Again, he ignored her question. 'After breakfast, then what?'

She sniffed, then said, 'I drove to Wales.'

'Long drive.'

'Old car. When I think back on it, I shudder.'

'When you last saw Kelly, did anything strike you as odd?'

'Not a thing. She was excited, looking forward to going home. She gave me a present. Made me promise not to open it until my birthday. I felt really bad about it because I never got the chance to buy her anything.'

'What did she give you?'

'A pen,' she said, and tried to laugh. But it sounded tired. 'I was going to be a romance novelist. Kelly was going to write a book. The dreams of youth . . .'

Indeed. He had dreams of his own to be Chief Superintendent one day. 'When you came back from Wales, did you notice anything odd?'

'Odd?' A pause, then, 'Yes. I did. Her bed was stripped.'

Gilchrist let that comment filter through his mind, but came up with nothing. 'Why was that odd?'

'They were my sheets. I bought them. Pissed me off at the time, let me tell you. Fitted, they were. And only a couple of months old.'

163

'Why would you buy sheets for Kelly's bed?' Gilchrist had to ask.

'Guilt.'

Now he really was lost. He waited, his silence urging her to go on.

'One of my boyfriends. God, I can't even remember his name. How sad is that? Anyway, whoever he was threw up all over Kelly's bed.'

Still, Gilchrist felt lost. 'What was your boyfriend doing in Kelly's bed?'

'He wasn't. He was trying to make it to the bathroom, opened the wrong door and projectile-vomited on to Kelly's bed.'

Gilchrist let that image settle. 'And where was Kelly?'

'Out with Jack, best I recall. Which was just as well.' She seemed to force a giggle. 'I can laugh about it now, but at the time I was furious.'

The thought of someone bursting into Kelly's bedroom and vomiting all over her had Gilchrist gritting his teeth. He forced that thought away, and said, 'And you promptly washed the sheets—'

'– and scrubbed the bed. But money was always tight back then, and buying a new mattress was out of the question. I offered, of course, but Kelly just laughed it off and helped me turn the mattress over.'

Kelly just laughed it off. If he closed his eyes, he could almost hear her. It was one of the things he had liked about her. Her ready smile. Her joie de vivre. Nothing seemed to trouble her. Whenever Jack brought her home, the entire household seemed to liven. With her blue eyes, blonde hair and sparkling smile, she was like a splash of American colour on a grey Scottish canvas. And she always parted by blowing *Jack's wee brother* a kiss.

'God, how we lived back then,' Rita continued. 'I sometimes wonder. And come to think about it, do you know what else I thought was strange? Her room was spotless. Not like she'd just cleared it out, but like she'd scrubbed it clean.'

Gilchrist felt a shiver tingle his spine. Had Rita unknowingly glanced upon a murder scene? Had Kelly been murdered in her room? Had her killer known Rita as well, known she was in Wales for her birthday? And if so, would her killer also have known of Kelly's intention to return to the States? And with that thought, Gilchrist saw that the killer might have known his brother Jack, too.

But he was still missing something.

'How long did you remain in the flat?' he asked.

'Until the end of my course. Then that was that. Back to Wales to find a job and get back together with my old boyfriend.'

'Thomas?'

'God, no. I never met Rhys, God rest his soul, until I was well into my thirties. I'm afraid the impulsiveness of youth and looking at the world through beer goggles sent most of them packing.'

'What about Kelly's mail?' he asked. 'Bank statements, bills, the usual stuff. What did you do with them?'

'Ripped them up, mostly.'

'Did you not forward any to her address in the States?'

'Now that you mention it,' she said, 'I do remember sending something back. Just the once. A cheque, I think.'

'Who from?'

'How would I know? I didn't open it.'

'Was there no return address?'

'If there was, I never noticed. And if I noticed, I can't remember.'

Gilchrist made a note to check the boxes in Mrs Roberts' attic. 'If anything else comes to mind,' he said, 'please give me a call.' He waited while she rummaged for a pen, then he recited his mobile number and hung up.

Back at his desk, he read through his scribbled notes on Rita, trying to find something that might jump-start his mind, then flicked through those on Kelly's mother. One word leaped from the page.

Mexico, circled in black pen.

Why Mexico?

In the late sixties, Mexico was not the tourist haven it is now. Back then, it would have been barely ruined by greed-driven developers; a sun-scorched land from which simple people eked out a meagre living, with crystal-clear seas from which fishermen fed their families. Like Spain's Costa del Sol in the fifties, perhaps.

So, why Mexico?

In the short time Jack had known Kelly, Gilchrist could not once recall him uttering a single word about Mexico. All of Jack's enthusiasm had been directed towards the States.

Once I get a job, Andy, you can come and visit us. I'll fly you over. We'll have picnics on the beach, barbecued steaks as big as your arm and shrimp as big as lobsters. We'll watch the sun go down on a warm sea, smoke cigarettes and drink beer. You'll get a tan, and grow muscles. I'll get you fit. Every morning we'll run along the beach to a rising sun in a clear blue sky.

Which was what Jack and Kelly used to do – run along the West Sands, sans sun. No matter how he tried, Gilchrist could not conjure up an image of Jack and Kelly jogging on the beaches in Mexico.

But Kelly's parents had received a postcard from Mexico.

Which Kelly had not sent. Of that, Gilchrist was certain.

So who had?

If he could answer that question, Gilchrist knew he had found her killer.

CHAPTER 15

Memories came back at him as he stepped into the living room, like family portraits being unveiled one at a time. The fireplace was still there, although the mantelpiece had since been removed. In its place, a wooden shelf with scalloped edges buckled from the weight of books and ornaments that threatened to slip from its surface. A series of black-and-white photographs covered wood-chip walls that he recalled being as bare as the West Sands.

He crossed the floor to a rear window that overlooked the back garden. The boundary walls seemed higher than he remembered. The gabled outline of a building that once stood in the corner marked its stonework like a martyr's memorial. A concrete slab that used to be the floor of an old wash-house lay like a flattened headstone beneath him. Weeds threatened the base of the boundary walls and crept through the early winter grass.

'When did you say you lived here?'

Gilchrist turned from the window to face Donnie, the owner, an aged gentleman with flyaway hair as wild as Einstein's, and a strip of a moustache that perched above his lip.

'I didn't,' Gilchrist said. 'My brother did, in the late sixties.'

Donnie nodded. 'What did you say the name was?'

'Jack Gilchrist. He shared the flat with Rita Sanderson and an American girl called Kelly.'

'Names mean nothing to me now.'

'Do you remember anything about them? Anything at all?'

'That's too far back for me to remember,' Donnie said. 'But I suppose I could check my records.'

'Records?'

'I used to keep the names and home addresses of every student who rented the place. It started out as a bit of fun,' he added. 'But I stopped about ten years ago. I felt like a dirty old man asking all these young students to sign my book.' He gave out a chuckle that shuffled his shoulders. 'But I always insisted on their phone numbers.'

'Can I see it?'

'If I can find it. It should be somewhere at home.'

'Where's that?'

'Glasgow.'

Gilchrist had hoped Donnie lived locally, but Glasgow was seventy miles south-west of St Andrews. He would have to wait for Donnie to mail it to him.

'How long are you here for?' he asked Donnie.

'We're up for a couple of days. My wife, Kathy, drives. Long drives are too much for me now. Besides,' he said, eyes twinkling with a hint of mischief, 'it's nice to have a designated driver on hand. I don't have to worry about reaching my limit.' His shoulders shuffled again, and his grin revealed the even teeth of a dental plate.

'Do you have anything planned for this evening?' Gilchrist asked.

'Drinking. Napping. Not necessarily in that order.'

'Listen, Donnie, it might shed nothing on the investigation, but I'd like to have a look through these records of yours tonight, if possible.'

Donnie frowned. 'Tonight?' he puzzled. 'They're in the attic somewhere. It'll take me a day or two just to find them.'

'If it's not too much to ask,' Gilchrist said, 'I could have someone drive you home, get you started. If you're lucky you could be back in St Andrews in time for me to buy you a couple in the Central. If I'm out and about, leave them at the office in North Street.'

'Well,' said Donnie, as if trying to warm to the idea. 'I'll see what I can do, but I'll have to talk to Kathy, of course.'

'Of course,' said Gilchrist, 'but before you do, can you show me the back bedroom?'

'Follow me.'

Gilchrist traipsed after Donnie, out of the living room, down a step, across a short hallway, up another step and through a low doorway that opened on to a room that had memories rampaging back at him.

Little had changed. The room was small, rectangular in shape, with a large sash window that overlooked the back garden. He had stood by that opened window when Jack had lit that first cigarette for him. Tired curtains hung either side of venetian blinds half-opened in disarray. A single bed lined one wall, but not where Jack used to have it. A white wardrobe stood lopsided on the slanted floor. The wooden flooring, which had been covered by a threadbare oriental rug years earlier, now lay hidden beneath a footworn carpet that stretched from skirting board to skirting board.

Gilchrist felt his hopes soar. 'How long has this carpet been down?'

Donnie frowned. 'Now you're asking. Ten, fifteen years, maybe. We don't spend much on upkeep any more. Used to. But every year's the same. Place wrecked and needing repainted from top to bottom.' He shook his head. 'My father would have skinned me alive if I'd done half of what these youngsters get up to nowadays.'

Gilchrist eased the wardrobe door open to reveal blouses on hangers, folded sweaters, pressed jeans, scuffed boots on shelves. 'Someone's staying here?'

'They're away for the weekend.'

'Perfect,' said Gilchrist. 'I'll arrange for the SOCOs to complete their investigation before they return.'

Doubt flickered behind the old man's eyes.

'That's not a problem, is it?' Gilchrist asked.

'SOCOs?'

'Scenes of Crime Officers. Forensic investigators. We're investigating a suspected murder.'

'Murder? Here? In this room?'

Gilchrist did not want to tell Donnie that if nothing was found in this bedroom the team would extend their search to other rooms, take over the entire house if they had to, until they found evidence of Kelly's murder, or not. 'Now, about that guest book of yours . . .'

'The less Kathy knows about this, the better,' Donnie said. 'I'll talk to her later.'

'Won't she worry about where you'll be?'

'She'll think I'm having a couple of drams,' said Donnie, and wiped an arthritic hand over his mouth. 'After what you've just told me, I could do with a double right now.'

'How about later?' Gilchrist said.

Donnie glanced at his watch, as if to figure out how to pace himself.

'And they're on me,' Gilchrist added. 'All right?'

That seemed to make up Donnie's mind. 'Let's get on with it, then,' he said, and trundled down the stairs as Gilchrist followed.

Fifteen minutes later, Donnie was on his way to Glasgow, courtesy of Stan, and the SOCOs had the bedroom stripped of furniture, the carpet and underfelt rolled up and all of it carted through to the living room.

Even after thirty-five years, the shadow of where the oriental rug used to lay still showed on the floorboards as a fresher stain. The floor had been varnished at some time in its past, not long before the rug had been placed, Gilchrist thought, but the flooring beneath the rug had retained some of its polished sheen.

The SOCOs hung a thick sheet over the window. The room fell into darkness. They sprayed the floor with Luminol, a chemical that reacts with iron found in blood haemoglobin. It would not matter how old the blood was. If any blood was present, Luminol would glow in the dark.

Gilchrist watched them work around the area of the invisible rug, all the while toying with the thought that they were looking in the wrong place. When the black light clicked on, nothing showed up.

'Would it help if someone told you where the bed used to be?' Gilchrist asked.

Colin, the lead SOCO, looked at him. 'You've been in this room?'

'My brother used to rent it.'

Colin seemed to liven. 'Can you tell me where the bed was, exactly?'

'Over there. By that wall.' Which was closer to the door, and an image of Rita's boyfriend bursting into the room and vomiting all over it burst into Gilchrist's mind. Why else would the sheets be stripped? As he stared at where the bed once lay, an image of the murder weapon shimmered into view; Jack's bedside lamp, an ugly metal thing that stood erect like a ship's decanter, its base wide and round and blunt, perfect for crushing skulls—

'And you think that whatever happened took place on the bed?'

'That's my first thought,' he agreed.

Silent, Gilchrist watched the SOCOs continue their search, spraying the floorboards where the bed used to sit, extending their investigation from one end of the room to the other.

Again, the black light. Again, nothing.

The room was spotless . . . like she'd scrubbed it clean.

Back in the late sixties, forensic science was still in its relative infancy. Whoever tried to destroy evidence could never have known of the advances that would be made in the coming years. Or could they? Geoffrey Pennycuick with his knowledge of medicine jumped to the forefront.

'Here's something, sir.'

Gilchrist kneeled on the floor. Colin pointed a gloved finger at a few smudged spots, glowing luminescent green on the wooden flooring.

'It's not a lot, sir.'

'What do you think?' Gilchrist tried.

Colin shook his head. 'Could have come from a cut foot. Maybe a nosebleed. How did you say she was killed?'

'A blow to the side of the head, powerful enough to crush her skull.'

'That would suggest more bleeding than this.'

Gilchrist stood. He felt helpless, disappointed, so let down by his instincts that he wondered why he had even thought of performing such an investigation.

'Could it be the same bed, sir?'

'Excuse me?'

'I'm thinking of the mattress we moved. Could it be the same one?'

Gilchrist felt a surge of annoyance. He had not asked Donnie. Was it possible, after all these years, that this was the same bed Jack and Kelly had slept in? Despite being a single bed, students made do with what they were given.

'I shouldn't think so,' was all he could say.

'We've nothing to lose, so let's try it, shall we?'

Rather than hang another sheet over the large window in the living room, the SOCOs carried the mattress back through to the darkness of the bedroom and rested it against the wall. When they sprayed Luminol over it, the black light picked up a mass of spots and stains. But Gilchrist could tell from their location that most were due to menstruation leaks, or breaking maidenheads. Nothing showed up at either end of the mattress, where he would have expected to find Kelly's blood. Again, doubts seared his mind like shame.

'Right,' said Colin, 'let's try the other side.' With a combined heave, they flipped the mattress over. Again, the middle of the mattress was an overwhelming mass of stains, but with none that would suggest anything more than a menstruation accident.

Gilchrist felt deflated.

As he watched the SOCOs manhandle the mattress and photograph the stains, he felt a lump swell in his throat. Had this old house, this bedroom, been the place where Kelly's life had been taken, ended by a blow that had crushed her skull and spilled her lifeblood? Why had she been killed? What had happened? But more troubling was the question that kept resurfacing in his mind.

Where had Jack been when Kelly was battered to death?

At that question, a shiver as cold as an Arctic wind ran the length of his spine. The thought was almost inconceivable. But Gilchrist knew anything was possible. The cigarette lighter, Kelly's disappearance, Jack's emotional crash, his out-of-character mood swings and vocal ragings in the weeks before his hit-and-run accident – were all of these connected, somehow? Gilchrist had always believed that Jack had been pining for his lost American girlfriend. Now more crippling thoughts wormed to the fore. Had Jack killed Kelly? If he had, could he have lived with the burden of what he had done? Had Jack committed suicide by stepping in front of a speeding—

'Sir?'

'Yes?'

'I was asking if you remembered which way the bed faced.'

Gilchrist pointed to the wall opposite the door. If anyone rushed through that door and projectile-vomited, the bed would be the unlucky recipient. 'This way,' he said.

'So the pillows would be at this end? About here?'

Gilchrist nodded. 'Give or take. Does it matter?'

'Just a thought, sir. But if the mattress was turned this way, and her head was on the pillows, then the bloodiest stain would be closest to the wall.' He kneeled on the floor and fingered the wallpaper where it overlapped the skirting board. 'See here, sir?'

Gilchrist kneeled beside him.

'Several layers of wallpaper. See? No one does a proper wall-papering job any more. My old man used to strip the walls back to the plaster before papering. Then he'd rub them down and fill the cracks before sizing the walls. Nowadays, they just plaster new paper over old, which got me thinking, just how many layers could have been put up in thirty-five years?'

He gripped the edge of the paper between thumb and forefinger, eased it from the skirting board, pulled it back to reveal a white layer underneath. He continued to scrape until he loosened another layer. Then he grunted. 'Looks like there's three layers. Could be one more. Maybe multiple coats of emulsion in between, depending on the damage left by the students. What do you think?'

Gilchrist nodded. 'It's worth a try.' He stepped back as the other two SOCOs brought the bed frame back into the room, laid the mattress on top and adjusted it as if readying to make the bed.

Colin removed a pencil from his pocket and drew a rectangle on the wall, from just beyond the head of the bed to about three feet along its length, and four feet above the level of the mattress. Then he manhandled the bed away from the wall, pushing it into the middle of the room.

'Right, Joe,' he ordered. 'Set it up.'

One of the SOCOs spent the next two minutes setting up the camera on a tripod, and once done, pressed the shutter. The room flashed.

'OK, here we go.' Colin sprayed Luminol within the rectangle on the wall.

Gilchrist counted a full minute before Colin clicked on the black light.

Nothing.

'Keep going,' Colin said.

The other SOCO stepped up to the wall with a pail of warm water, and painted over the rectangle with a pasting brush. Another minute passed before he looked at Colin for his nod of approval, ran the sharp edge of the scraper along the pencilled lines and eased the wallpaper back.

'One layer at a time,' Colin said.

Gilchrist watched the top layer peel back to reveal white wood-chip. Strips of the first layer remained, half-peeled slivers as drab as pith.

'Joe?'

The camera flashed once, twice.

Colin pointed his arm to the wall and sprayed the woodchip with Luminol.

After another minute, the black light revealed nothing.

Silent, Gilchrist watched them peel back two more layers, until a series of luminescent spots glowed.

'Well, well, well,' Colin said, peering closer. 'What have we here?'

The room flashed as the camera clicked, then Joe unscrewed it from the tripod and moved closer, capturing the spatter pattern on the wall. In his mind's eye, Gilchrist watched Kelly lying in bed facing the wall, defenceless, as the killer struck down at her, crushing the right side of her skull, spattering blood and brain matter on to the wall. And no matter how he tried, in his mind's eye flickered an image of Jack in a rage.

'Let's try for some DNA,' Colin said.

'We should cut the lot out,' Joe said, 'and take it back to the lab.'

'Let's do that. But first shoot off some more, Joe. Make sure we've got it covered from all angles.'

Gilchrist slipped from the room.

In College Street, the air felt cold and damp, the wind fresh and lively. He breathed it in, felt its chill bring life back into his lungs. He walked towards Market Street and turned right. He had no destination in mind, no idea where he was walking to, knowing only that he was walking away from something, some terrible event in the past.

Perhaps the scene of his brother's murderous crime.

CHAPTER 16

Gilchrist was nearing the arches of the West Port when his fingers found Nance's note.

He unfolded it. At the top, in her neat printing, was *MGB*, and beneath, *John Betson*, followed by an address in Edinburgh, a phone number and a note that John Betson was the last recorded owner of the MGB GT that Fairclough had once owned.

The call to Betson put Gilchrist through on the first ring. Without introducing himself, he said, 'I understand you own an MGB GT.' Betson paused long enough to make Gilchrist think he had lost the call. 'Do you still have it?' he tried.

'You *are* joking, right?'

Gilchrist frowned. 'What's so funny?'

'Some other punter called me first thing this morning and asked if I still had the GT. I mean, I've had it for over twenty years, and in the same day I get two calls about it. Is that crazy, or what?'

Excitement surged through Gilchrist. Had his surprise visit to Fairclough flushed him out? Was he now too late? 'Have you sold it?' he asked.

'No. And that's another funny thing,' Betson said. 'We talked money, but he sounded disinterested. Like he didn't want to buy.'

'Did you get his name?'

'He hung up before I could ask.'

It had to have been Fairclough, and for a moment he thought of telling Betson that he was with Fife Constabulary. But Betson seemed so loose and ready with his words that he worried that doing so might clamp him up. Instead, he said, 'Has anyone come round to have a look at it?'

'I wouldn't know. I've just got back.'

A thought hit him. 'Is it still there? The car, I mean. It's not been stolen—'

'Not a chance,' Betson said. 'It's under six feet of rubbish in the garage. Tell you what, though, I could do with selling it at the moment. It's up on blocks, and the engine's filled with oil, so it should be spotless. Are you interested?'

It occurred to Gilchrist that Fairclough might already be on his way over with a tow truck and a pile of cash that Betson could not resist. That could be Fairclough's style. Which also meant that, after all these years, time might now be running out. 'I might be,' Gilchrist said. 'Can I see it?'

'Sure. But it's buried in my garage.'

Which should keep it safe and secure for a while longer. 'Did the man who called earlier say anything that seemed odd? Did he say how he knew you had the car?'

'No.'

'Did he just ask if you had it, then hang up?'

'He asked if it was roadworthy, and I told him it was in my garage.'

'Then he hung up?'

Betson paused, then said, 'You know, come to think of it, he did ask one question I thought was odd.'

Gilchrist pressed the phone hard against his ear.

'He asked if I'd stripped the front end or changed the headlights.'

The headlights? 'Both of them?'

'I assume that's what he meant, yes.'

Gilchrist stared off to the distance, to a bank of clouds as dark as his mood. An image of a body being thrown over a car like a stringless marionette hit his mind, the same image he had dreamed ever since entered brother's death – always the same – Jack's body tumbling and hitting the ground, to be left bleeding and dying.

And the only damage to the car, a broken headlight. Or was it?

'And had you?' he asked.

'No. There's nothing wrong with the headlights. I've done nothing to the car since I bought it, except keep it clean and in storage. And when I told him that, he swore, which I thought was odd.'

'At you?'

'No. Just a *fuck*, then click.'

Why had Fairclough asked if the headlights had been changed or the front end stripped? He would have repaired the broken headlights himself before selling the car on. But had the front end been damaged in the accident as well?

All of a sudden, he saw other possibilities.

'What year is the car?'

'Sixty-eight,' said Betson. 'And in great nick,' he added, and launched into his sales spiel.

Silent, Gilchrist listened to Betson quote brake horsepower, engine size in cubic inches and cubic centimetres, length of wheelbase, turning circle and a litany of other things that Gilchrist could not care less about. He could hardly wait to call Stan, get him to check something out for him.

And all the while the Mercedes was eating the miles to Betson's home.

Stan called Gilchrist back before he reached Edinburgh.

'You were right, boss. McKinley, who bought the car from Fairclough, said it had a dent in the front end, which he patched up himself.'

'Patched up?'

'Hammered out, buffed down, repainted. His own words.'

Gilchrist gripped the steering wheel, eyed the road ahead.

Was it possible? After all these years?

By the time Gilchrist reached his destination, night had fallen.

Betson's garage was remote from the house, one of a row of identical lock-ups that lined a cobbled lane at the back of the tene-ment building. Light from the kitchen windows cast a dim glow over parts of the lane. Each lock-up seemed too narrow to park a car in, the turning circle too tight. A number on a metal plate screwed into the frame above double wooden doors matched Betson's home address.

'Here we are.' Betson inserted a key into a rusted padlock. 'Haven't had a look at it for some time, but back here's as safe as houses. We've lived here for over thirty years and never had a spot of bother. Not even any graffiti. Amazing, when you think about it.'

Gilchrist eyed the narrow lane. The lock-ups extended in a row to a high stone wall that bordered the back gardens of houses one street over. On the opposite side of the lane, a wall as high as the other bounded Betson's building. The lane faded to a dark mouth as it kinked on a forty-five-degree bend out of sight to the main road. Betson's garage sat at the farthest end, where the lane dead-ended against the back of a brick building. No matter how skilful the driver, manoeuvring in and out of any of these garages had to be a feat in itself.

Most of the lock-ups were secured with rusting padlocks and wooden doors that seemed to have taken root among the weeds. Paint and slivers of wood had flaked off at the foot of Betson's garage door, but the cobbles fronting it had the worn pattern of wood scraping stone.

Someone could die back here, and remain undiscovered for days.

'When did you say you were last down here?' Gilchrist asked.

'Months ago. Just after Easter, I think.'

'Looks like these doors have been opened recently.'

'That would be the wife. She's forever stacking stuff down here.'

Betson hooked the opened padlock on to the clasp, the key dangling from it like an earring, and eased one of the doors open. The strangely pleasant smell of petrol and oil mixed with ageing leather hit Gilchrist.

'There's a light switch in here,' Betson's voice came back at him.

The inside of the garage opened up to Gilchrist like Aladdin's cave.

Folded tables, chairs, cardboard cartons stacked with comics, books, children's toys, lined both sides of a grey tarpaulin stretched across the ghostly outline of some low-slung vehicle. Framed pictures and posters wrapped in tissue paper perched on the tarpaulin, as if placed there as an afterthought.

Betson pushed his way through the muddle like a man wading

183

through water, to squeeze past a rusted barbecue stand, a bag of golf clubs, then step over what looked like a chaise longue, its yellow fabric spotted with oil or mould. A gunmetal toolbox sat in the mildewed folds of a garden umbrella that lay like a quilt over boxes of comics.

Gilchrist followed.

'The wife refuses to throw stuff away,' Betson said to him. 'If you're going to keep that car, she says, then I'm going to keep everything else.' He chuckled. 'One of these days I'm going to have to clear the lot out. A friend of mine says he could sell it on eBay and make a fortune.' He grunted as he bent beneath a pedal bike suspended from hooks on the ceiling. 'Maybe I'll take him up on that offer. Split the proceeds fifty-fifty. That would be better than having all this stuff just lying here doing nothing.'

From where Gilchrist stood, the tarpaulin that covered the bonnet and front grille was clear of all jumble, whereas the roof seemed to double as additional storage space. From outside, he thought he heard the grumbling of a running motor echo off the lane's stone walls.

'Christ knows how we'd manage to live if she couldn't dump her mess here,' Betson said. He kicked something out of the way, then bent down. 'Grab an end, will you?'

Gilchrist obliged, conscious of a car door shutting in the lane outside. 'Neighbours?'

'Who?'

'Someone's in the lane.'

'It gets quite busy from time to time.' Betson steadied himself. 'When I say three, pull it up and over. OK? One, two, three and up . . .'

Gilchrist pulled the tarpaulin back and folded it over the front windscreen of a gleaming sports car. The smell of polish engulfed him.

'Beautiful, isn't she?' Betson beamed down at his car, fingers caressing the shining metal. 'God, I should take her out next summer.'

'Thought you wanted to sell it.'

'I do and I don't,' Betson said. 'I'm prepared to let her go for the right price. But other than that, I'm not interested.'

'And the right price is?'

'That's for you to decide. I have a number in mind, but I wouldn't want to spoil it for you.'

Gilchrist leaned down to inspect the front headlights. Condensation dotted the inside of the glass like beads of perspiration. 'The paintwork looks new,' he said.

'Got her resprayed not long after I bought her.'

Something slumped in Gilchrist's stomach. He had expected that, had known it was more than likely. Repainting would have destroyed any evidence of his brother's hit-and-run. Still, it was amazing that the car was around after all this time. And in such condition. He ran a finger around the rim of the headlights, touched the orange indicator light. The chrome bumper shone like a metal mirror. The car looked showroom-new.

'The person who called earlier,' Gilchrist said. 'Would you have any objection if I pulled your phone records to find his number?'

Betson frowned at Gilchrist. 'What do you mean?'

Gilchrist explained that he was with Fife Constabulary investigating a cold case, but did not give further details. 'And I'd like to impound your car,' he added.

'You've got to be joking.'

'We'll take care of it. Do what we have to do with it, and return it to you. You won't even have noticed it missing.'

'I'm not sure I like that idea,' Betson said.

Gilchrist thought he caught a faint whiff of petrol. 'I'd like to—'

The first bottle missed Betson's face by inches, smashed against the back wall with a hot roar. Gilchrist had time only to shield his face with his arm as flames billowed around him. He heard Betson scream to the floor as flames as fluid as liquid swallowed him, then caught the dull thud of another bottle as it landed unbroken on the roof of the car. Entangled in the picture frames, its lighted rag set off the packing tissue and threatened to flare down the neck of the bottle. Through the orange glare and roiling smoke, Gilchrist caught the silhouette of someone closing the door.

He backed from the heat of the flames, picked up the bottle on the roof, prayed it would not explode in his hands and threw it out. Too late, it bounced off the closing door and landed on the concrete floor with an eye-blinding flash.

The door slammed shut.

Gilchrist turned to Betson, but already the smoke had created a black fog through which he could see nothing. His eyes stung, his throat burned, and as he fell to his knees he heard the unmistakable click of a padlock being snapped shut.

The speed with which the contents of the garage ignited almost stopped his heart.

Flames licked the roofing. Along one wall they jumped from box to box. Toys and gifts stored for years in the dry warmth of the garage were more efficient than fuel-soaked kindling. Comics roared to life, pages curling in the heat. Cardboard boxes squirmed and blackened. Plastic toys flared and melted.

No time to think. Only to act.

Back on his feet, he tried to make a run for the door, but the heat from the second bottle was too great. He backed off, felt his face burn. He kneeled and grabbed the tarpaulin.

Shouting with all his strength, he peeled the tarpaulin back, running it up and over the roof of the car, tilting picture frames and burning paper. The tarp fell from the car like billowing sacking and folded over the flames of the second Molotov cocktail.

Something popped – the single lightbulb – and the garage went dull for a moment, to be replaced with a hellish landscape of flickering black and orange. Gilchrist kicked the door. It bounced back at him. He tried again. Same result. He slammed his shoulder into it and gasped with pain. The wooden doors may not have looked solid, but they were more than he could burst his way through.

He slumped to his knees, eyes closed.

Christ, not like this, he thought. Not trapped and burned alive.

If he could somehow smother the flames at the other end of the garage, he might have a chance. But where was Betson? He tried to open his eyes, but the heat and the smoke were too much. He crawled on the concrete floor along the side of the car, one hand over his face and mouth, the other outstretched like a blind man's cane.

Barbecue stand. He knocked over the golf clubs. Chaise longue, and his fingers groped and curved around the metal toolbox. He picked it up and threw the lot at the door.

The toolbox burst open and bounced on to the smouldering tarpaulin.

He fell after it, sprawled among the tools, cut his fingers on the edge of a saw blade. His coughing body contorted. His eyes burned. Fingers of flames tickled overhead and stung him with their dripping touch. He gripped a cold metal handle, felt the head of a claw hammer. His heart soared as he realized this was his way out.

He swung the hammer at the door, once, twice, but the wood was solid. He staggered to his feet, felt the framework, found the spot where one door met the other and thudded the claw end into the wood.

He missed. Tried again.

Missed again. Christ, he was going to die.

What about Jack? What about Maureen?

He could no longer find air to breathe, only the acrid fumes of hot, choking smoke that heaved in and out of his lungs with every cough. He thudded the claw hammer into the door one last time, but it bounced off.

Dear God. This was where it was all going to end.

He slid to his knees, hammer clasped tight in one hand, its claw head scraping down the wooden—

It caught.

He tugged, felt it catch. He tugged again, heard the wood crack, the nails and screws rip free. He pressed the head in deeper, eased the handle back and pulled hard. The door was giving. Dear God, it was giving. He was going to—

He grunted in pain as the hammer slipped free and his knuckles hit wood. He heard the hammer land with a metallic thud somewhere in the smoke-filled corner. In desperation, he tried tearing the damaged frame with his hands, felt his nails break, his skin tear.

But he could not pull the wood free, could not break it loose.

This was it. He was going to die.

No. Not like this.

He slumped to the floor, his body wracking with spasms, felt his back hit the car, his feet the garage doors. If he straightened his legs, pushed with his back against the car, he might find enough purchase to force one of the doors open.

He closed his eyes, pushed and pressed as hard as he could.

Nothing.

He could tell from the burning pain in his chest that he was running out of time. The body could keep this up for only so long before succumbing. He tried again, forced his legs straight with his last breath, held it and, with a surge that jolted the length of his spine, his right foot broke through a length of wood close to the ground.

He kicked again, heard the dry crack of rotted wood, then heard it break and snap. He pulled forward, forced his head through the jagged opening and breathed in air that hit his lungs like ice and had him wracking up phlegm as black as soot. Using the car as leverage, he forced his shoulders through the tight gap, ignoring the slivers of cracked wood that gripped his clothing and tore at his skin.

He wriggled from the hole, rolled on to the lane, clothes smoking and smouldering.

Smoke billowed from the hole at his feet like a misplaced chimney.

Where was Betson?

He staggered to his feet, grabbed the padlock. The clasp was good and tight. When he pulled one door and pushed against the other, he saw a gap in the frame where none had existed before. He thudded his shoulder to the garage doors, forced them against the hinges.

They creaked, but bounced back.

But if he concentrated on one door only?

189

He crossed the lane, pressed his back against the wall, took a deep breath and pushed off as hard as he could.

He hit the door like a battering ram.

The frame splintered. Hinges tore from the wood, screws hanging loose like stubborn roots. A wall of smoke hit him. The heat almost had him backing off, but he kicked the door loose, broke it from its frame, pulled his jacket around his face and bruised his way back inside the garage.

The rush of air gave new life to the fire. Flames licked in rising tongues across the garage roof. Beneath, the car seemed to shimmer in the heat. He fell to the floor, hugged the concrete, finding that if he kept his face to the garage floor the smoke did not choke him.

He wormed along the side of the car, worried that any one of the burning pile of cartons could tip over and trap him. But he made it to the passenger door where he found Betson by feel, lying headlong on the concrete floor. He grabbed his collar, pulled him along the floor like a sack of meat. As he neared the garage door, he knew he could not drag him over the tarpaulin, so he got to his knees, grabbed Betson by his belt with one hand, his collar with the other and hauled him up and over and out into the lane.

He dropped Betson on to the cobbles and collapsed beside him on his hands and knees, heaving with coughs that seemed to come from the pit of his lungs. A strong hand gripped his shoulder. He grabbed it, ready to tear Fairclough's throat from his neck, but toppled over.

Stone cobbles rose up to meet his head with a dull crack.

He lay there, stunned.

At that angle, the lane looked as busy as Market Street. Shoes and legs came at him from all sides. A wriggling snake turned itself into a hose that sprayed water from tiny leaks. Something hissed like a rush of air, and the metallic clang of a fire extinguisher told him they were trying to put out the fire.

A pair of hands helped right his world.

'Is there anyone else inside?' a man's voice asked.

He tried to say, 'No,' but coughed instead. He shook his head. 'Only two of us,' he managed to whisper.

'He's badly burned,' a voice from behind said. 'He needs to go to the hospital.'

Gilchrist dragged his hand across his lips, freed phlegm that hung from his chin like slime. 'A car,' he tried to say, but it came out as a cough. He cleared his throat, spat a mouthful of soot to the ground. He tugged at the trousers by his side. Warm hands pulled him to his feet.

'You're bleeding,' the man said. 'Are you all right?'

Gilchrist choked back a cough. 'A car,' he said. 'Did you see a car?'

'What kind of car?'

Gilchrist pushed away, removed his mobile, dialled the office.

'Put me through to Stan,' he rasped, and when Stan came on the line, said, 'Talk to someone in the correct jurisdiction and have them pick up James Fairclough for questioning. You have his home address.'

'On what grounds, boss?'

'On suspicion of arson.' He eyed Betson. His head and neck looked like charred plastic, and the side of his face shone tight from blistering skin. But it was the stillness of his body that worried Gilchrist. He coughed again, turned to the stone wall and spat black phlegm over the weeds. 'It could be upped to murder,' he added.

'Boss?'

'Give me a call when it's done,' he said, and hung up.

He checked Betson's pulse. Alive, but not doing well. He looked up as a woman rushed towards him, almost tripping in her efforts to reach the scene.

'John,' she cried. 'John, are you all right?' Then she was on her knees, cradling Betson's head in her hands, sobbing and hugging and begging him to waken.

Gilchrist faced the garage.

The fire was almost out, but thick smog continued to roll along the ceiling and swell in black billows from cardboard boxes. A young man powered water from a hose into the smoking depths. Pockets of embers popped and exploded in angry bursts before dying under the onslaught. Even from where he stood, Gilchrist could tell that the car had suffered no significant damage. Paint blistered along the sides and roof, and a box had toppled from one of the piles and spread books over the bonnet like lumps of wood. The very material that had fed the fire had acted like a protective blanket in places.

He hoped the front end was unscathed.

He approached the man with the hose, showed him his warrant card and ordered him to make sure no one took anything from the garage. Then he returned to his Merc and removed a pair of rubber gloves from the boot.

Forty minutes later, he had recovered what he could of the Molotov cocktails, and with the help of a local policeman placed the pieces of glass into two separate boxes. He thought it unlikely that Lothian and Borders Police would be able to lift any prints from the glass, but identifying the bottles themselves might give them a lead.

His throat and lungs still felt clogged with soot, and he hawked up a gob of blackened phlegm, walked to the end of the lane and spat into a clump of weeds. He ran his hand across his mouth and eyed the scene.

Betson had been removed to the hospital, his wife by his side, and the fire brigade had converted the lane into a temporary storage unit. Three firemen were still clearing the garage of debris and junk, while another two clambered on top of the lock-ups, tracking down telltale flumes. With quick action from Betson's neighbours, the fire had been contained to Betson's garage only, and as the concrete floor continued to be cleared, the MGB GT stood alone, its blaze paintwork bubbled and blackened in the firemen's spotlight.

Gilchrist entered the garage and ran his hand over the front panel. The front bumper jutted out from the chassis, and he thought it might be possible for it to be damaged in a hit-and-run while the headlights were not touched. Linda Melrose mentioned nothing about the lights being different. If one headlight had been broken, she would have noticed on the drive home, would she not? Or had she been too drunk? He moved to the front nearside, the part most likely to clip a pedestrian, and tried to imagine what his brother might have heard, might have done, as the car powered its way into him.

Had he tried to jump out of the way? Had the car swerved and hit him?

Or had he been overpowered by murderous guilt and stepped into its path?

Gilchrist's mind whispered Linda Melrose's words.

I told him to keep his eyes on the road.

Distracted by a pair of legs, and a life lost for ever.

He ran his hand over the bonnet. Although some paintwork had blistered, by the headlights it was fine. Why had Fairclough asked about stripping the front end? The vital evidence that would put his brother's death to rest was something to do with the front panel, of that Gilchrist was certain.

CHAPTER 17

Gilchrist won the jurisdictional fight over the MGB on the basis
that it might have been involved in a fatal hit-and-run accident
within the town of St Andrews. However, the idea that this car
might now be the cause of two deaths worried him. Betson's third-
degree burns to his face, neck and shoulders had landed him in
intensive care, and Gilchrist had seen enough burns victims to
know he might not pull through.

He stood back as the tow-truck driver hauled the MGB from the
garage and secured it with chains to the truck's flatbed. Six spot-
lights mounted on a bar running across the cabin roof exposed the
MGB in all its glistening, yet blistered, glory. Despite the fire, the
damage appeared superficial. Paint bubbled along the nearside
front panel, door and rear panel like coloured blisters streaked with
soot. The bonnet, roof and hatchback boot lid were blackened but
not blistered. The wire wheels were scorched, and one of the tyres
looked like skin ready to slough. The nearside headlight and brightwork looked intact.

He signed the paperwork and checked that the car was to be
delivered to SK Motors, a ramshackle garage in the town of

Strathkinness on the outskirts of St Andrews. Shuggie may not run the most profitable business, but when it came to things mechanical, his layman's terms were like gold in a court of law.

With the MGB secured and Betson removed to the hospital, Gilchrist slid into his Merc, leaving the firemen and neighbours to restock the garage and secure it for the night. He was fifteen minutes from St Andrews when he called Stan.

'What's the latest on Fairclough?'

'Bad news, I'm afraid, boss. He's not at home or work. No one's heard from him since yesterday. And his mobile's been disconnected.'

'You mean the battery's flat?'

'No. Disconnected. He called the phone company and cancelled his contract.'

Gilchrist had once tracked a scam artist through the calls he made on his mobile to his girlfriend, and who was now serving two years at Her Majesty's pleasure. But Fairclough was a different animal. Having already killed once and lived with that knowledge for over thirty years, was he now prepared to kill again to keep his freedom?

And yet, something did not fit. Why would Fairclough think anyone would connect him to the fire in Betson's garage? He would have fled while the fire took hold, and must have thought Gilchrist had been trapped and killed, the car destroyed. So why cancel his phone contract? If he did not want anyone to track him to Betson's, why not just leave the phone at home? It took a few seconds for Gilchrist's logic to work out that Fairclough must have cancelled his phone contract before the arson attack, and that he had a different SIM card, one of a number that were more than likely untraceable.

'Call the press, Stan,' he said. 'Tell them we want to question Fairclough about a hit-and-run accident in the sixties. And get them to run it beside a story about a garage fire.'

'What garage fire, boss?'

Gilchrist explained. 'And tell them to lay it on thick,' he added.

'Will do, boss. One other thing. I've now got hold of old Donnie's records. I've had a look at them, but nothing jumps out at me. I had to hand the originals over to Greaves, but I made you a copy.'

'Why does Greaves want the originals?'

'I'm not sure. But something's going on, boss. They've got Tosh working with some high-flying chief inspector they pulled in from Tayside.'

Gilchrist felt something skip in his chest. Pulling in a senior CI from another Force signalled the start of an internal investigation. Why had Chief Superintendent Greaves done that? And why had Greaves wanted old Donnie's original records, which were all to do with Gilchrist's case? Was he about to initiate an investigation into Gilchrist, or some other member of his team? Were these questions related, or were they simply coincidental? But just as troubling was the inclusion of Tosh.

As if in tune with his thoughts, Stan said, 'Have you ever wondered how Tosh has managed to keep his job? His record is next to useless.'

'What are you not telling me?'

'It's only just been revealed that his wife's uncle and McVicar are stepbrothers.'

Gilchrist took a moment to digest Stan's words. Assistant Chief Constable Archie McVicar. Tough but fair, a man who went by the rules. He would not bend any rules for nepotism, of that Gilchrist

197

was certain. But if an internal investigation was about to start, Tosh was the last person Gilchrist wanted to be pitted against.

'Where are you, Stan?'

'At home.'

'Do you have Donnie's records with you?'

'Where else, boss?'

'I'll pick them up in ten minutes.'

Back at his cottage in Crail, Gilchrist took off his clothing in the bathroom. His leather jacket stank as if it had been smoked, and was torn and scratched beyond repair. Stripped naked, he was astonished to find that even his underpants smelled of smoke and soot. He threw the lot into the wash to soak overnight.

He showered, and examined his new cuts and bruises.

He had almost lost one fingernail on his right hand, and the palms of both hands were sliced and scarred with skelfs that he removed as best he could. A nasty cut on the back of his shoulder had him wincing with pain when he wiped the wound clean. He applied some antibiotic cream, but no bandage, deciding to let the air do its stuff, then a dollop or two on the fingernail, which he covered with a plaster. His right cheek blushed as if slapped, and felt tender. He rubbed some cream over it, figuring it might scab in a day or two. A limp that seemed to originate from somewhere deep in his left hip forced him to take his time.

Was he too old for this any more?

By the time he was seated at the dining table, stripped to the waist, with old Donnie's records laid out in front of him, it was almost midnight. The list was hand-printed on the letterhead of an architectural firm that bore the same name as Donnie's. He flicked through a total of eleven pages, all neatly printed and in chronological order, starting in June 1965 and ending in September 1985. He was not sure what he expected to find, but found himself searching for any name that jumped out at him, like Pennycuick or Grant. And it struck him how readily his mind was prepared to settle on these two.

He came across neither, but found Kelly's name and home address in the States after Jack's, his own old home address. Kelly's phone number, too, was the same as he'd already dialled. Next on the list was Rita Sanderson and an address in Wales, a convolution of consonants and vowels he could not pronounce. He recognized with a flicker of surprise the third person who had shared the flat with them that year. Lorena Cordoba.

He had met her only a few times, once when Jack had brought all his flatmates home for New Year, several months before the fatal hit-and-run. He recalled her being a slight woman, anorexic in appearance, with the black silken hair of the South Americas. And he remembered being surprised that she could not speak much English, and that she would choose to live in a foreign country so alien to her homeland.

He felt a cold frisson as he eyed her home address, and country. Mexico.

He scanned the records again.

Mexico? He had always thought Lorena was South American. He read the phone number and wondered if it was possible. After all this time, could she still live at the same address, still have the same telephone number?

Two minutes later, he had the international code for Mexico. He dialled the number.

'¿Aló?' A woman's voice.

He tried, 'Lorena Cordoba?'

199

'¿Córdoba?'

'Yes. Lorena Cordoba. You speak English?'

'¿Aló? ¿Quién llama?'

'Can I speak to Lorena, please?'

'¿Lorena? ¿Quién llama? ¿Aló?'

'Lorena? I want to speak to Lorena?'

'Creo que tiene el número equivocado.'

The call was cut.

If he had asked for a dead-end he could not have found a better one.

Or was it?

Kelly's mother had received a postcard from Mexico. Could Lorena have mailed it? Was she somehow involved in Kelly's murder? Gilchrist stood, walked around the table, letting that thought fire his mind. Lorena had been small, verging on fragile, surely too small to manhandle Kelly's dead body.

But what if she had a boyfriend?

That thought stopped him. Lorena had been attractive; nice features, smooth skin and a permanent tan. But in the few times he had seen her, he could not remember her being with a boyfriend.

He glanced at his watch. Twelve twenty-nine. How inconsiderate could he be? If he was any man at all, he would wait until the morning.

He found her number stored in his mobile.

'Hello?' her Welsh sing-song voice said.

He thought she sounded awake. 'I'm sorry to disturb you at this late hour.'

'Andy? Is that you?'

'It is. I'm sorry.'

'It's OK, I couldn't sleep. I can't get Kelly out of my mind.'

'Do you mind if I scratch your memory again?'

'Scratch away.'

'Do you remember the fourth flatmate in St Andrews?'

'Barely. It wasn't Lorna, but it was something like that.'

'Lorena?'

'That's it. But don't ask me her last name.'

'What was she like? I mean, did you ever see her with anyone?'

'She was odd, I remember that much. She didn't speak very good English, which didn't help. But I remember seeing her with one boy she used to go out with.'

'Boy?'

'Man. But young-looking. Not much facial hair. No sideburns, that sort of thing.'

'You have a name?'

'I'm hopeless with names.'

She had to know more, he thought. He just hadn't asked the right question. 'Describe him,' he said. 'Was he Scottish?'

'Yes.'

Well, at least that was a start. 'Dark hair? Blonde hair? *Any* hair?'

She laughed out loud, a sharp surprise. 'Dirty blonde,' she said. 'Almost light brown. Whenever I saw him he always looked unclean, like his hair needed washing or combing.'

'Were they going out?'

'You could say. But they never seemed close, if you get my meaning. I never saw them holding hands. Even when they were together, they hardly spoke to each other. I remember thinking it was a really odd relationship.'

'Were they having sex?'

'Now how would I know about that?'

'I meant, did he sleep over?'

'Not that I recall. She kept herself to herself, and often she would slip out without letting anyone know. Kind of creepy when I think about it. But back then we had plenty to keep ourselves occupied.'

'Was he a local?'

'I couldn't say.'

'A student?'

'Don't know.'

'What height was he?'

'I'm no good with heights.'

'Small, medium, large?'

'Medium.'

'Less than six foot?'

'Definitely.'

Gilchrist paused. 'So he was more small than tall,' he confirmed. 'Fat?'

'No. Skinny. Like her.'

Gilchrist ran through his notes. He was looking for a skinny, medium-built Scotsman, scruffy, with light brown hair. He might as well look for a sheep in a white flock—

'There is one more thing I remember,' she said. 'He had bad teeth.'

'In what way?'

'It was really noticeable, especially when they were together. Lorena had such white teeth, and his were so yellow.'

'Any missing?'

'No. Just yellow.'

'Crooked? Buck-toothed?'

'No. Just normal.'

They talked for a few minutes more, but he sensed Rita had

given him as much as she could. He thanked her and asked her to call if she remembered anything else, to which she elicited a promise from him to keep in touch.

He revisited his notes. The more he puzzled over them, the more distant the answer seemed. Sleep crept up on him, urging him to lay his head on his hands. His muscles ached from their recent abuse, and his right hand felt as if it was on fire. He flexed his fingers, expecting to see the seeping telltale signs of infection, but all his cuts looked clean.

He fingered his cheek. It felt tender, nothing more than a graze from flesh on wood. His back hurt, and his spine seemed to have locked. He had to stretch upright, arms in the air, twisting at the waist, before he felt any comfort. He resisted the urge to have a Scotch nightcap, and limped off to his bedroom.

As he drifted off, his last waking image was of a thin Mexican woman smiling up at him. And in that smile he thought he saw the reflection of her lover with the yellow teeth.

CHAPTER 18

Gilchrist opened his eyes.

Overhead, his Velux window glistened with rain. He tried to pull himself to his feet, but his body seemed not to work.

He twisted his head, squinted one eye at his radio alarm. Seven forty-two.

He ran his hand around the back of his neck, felt the dampness of sweat and worried that he was running a fever. Feet on the floor, up and over to the bathroom, his body racking with coughs that brought up phlegm as black as coal. He popped a couple of Ibuprofen and downed them with a handful of cold water.

Showered and shaved, he dialled Edinburgh's Royal Infirmary and managed to get through to Betson's ward. Betson had survived the night but was still in critical condition. Gilchrist thanked the nurse and was about to call Stan when his mobile rang.

He recognized the North Street number.

'You're wanted at the office.'

It took Gilchrist a full second to place the voice as Tosh's, and one more for him to decide against hanging up. If Greaves was in any way involved, he had better be careful.

'Wanted by whom?' he asked.

'Oh, listen to that. Wanted by *whom*?' A pause, then, 'You're wanted by me. DI Walter MacIntosh. That's *whom*. And let's make sure there's no misunderstanding about what's what. I couldn't give a flying fuck how far up the ladder you think you are. You'd better get that smarmy arse of yours to the office pronto, or I swear I'll issue a warrant for your arrest.'

'In your dreams, Tosh.'

'Try nightmares, Gilchrist. I'm gonnie nail you this time.'

The connection went dead.

Nightmares? Gilchrist almost smiled.

If he had only known.

'This is Chief Inspector Jeffrey Randall,' Tosh began.

Gilchrist took Randall's hand. The grip felt dry and firm.

'Jeff's from the Complaints and Discipline Department, and assisting me with our enquiries.'

'Into what, exactly?'

Tosh smiled. 'We're coming to that. But first I'd like to show you these.'

Silent, Gilchrist watched Tosh remove a number of X-ray images from a large yellow envelope and slap them on to the table in front of him.

Gilchrist stared at the images for a moment, before picking them up.

Someone's dental records. He read the name printed in felt-tip pen along the bottom.

Not just any someone. His brother Jack's.

He slid them back to Tosh. 'Where did you get these?'

'Wrong question. Try *why*?'

Gilchrist let his gaze shift to Randall, then back to Tosh, trying to play his best poker face. He would be damned if he was going to be forced to play Tosh's game.

Tosh pulled the X-rays to him. 'Didn't know your brother had a crown.'

'He had two, actually.'

Tosh nodded. 'But I'm more interested in this,' he said, stabbing a finger at the X-rays. 'A missing tooth. Upper right.' He squinted at the X-ray image. 'And the date's intriguing. Extracted on 19 February 1969.'

'Is that supposed to mean something to me?'

'It's five days before Hamish McLeod's funeral.'

Gilchrist tried to ignore the significance of that, pretend it was harmless.

Tosh placed a plastic bag on the desk and slid it over to Gilchrist. 'We found this on the woman's clothing. It's a tooth. Your dead brother Jack's, to be exact. The one extracted on the nineteenth.'

As feared, the date made sense. He felt his brow furrow. Without a DNA analysis, how could Tosh be so confident? But even as he asked himself that question, he realized Tosh must have accessed his brother's cold files and carried out a comparative DNA analysis on his clothing, all of which had been soaked through with Jack's blood.

'We had a DNA analysis done on the tooth. Mitochondrial. Quicker, cheaper, but every bit as damning.'

'Define *damning*,' Gilchrist said.

Tosh pressed close enough for Gilchrist to catch a whiff of underarm sweat. 'You removed critical evidence from an ongoing murder investigation. You withheld further evidence vital to the enquiry. You could be charged with attempting to pervert the course of justice.' Tosh sat back. 'However, seeing as how we're all part of the same team, we'd like to hear your side of the story first.'

Gilchrist did not miss the unspoken threat in the word *first*. He felt a bead of sweat trickle down his back. How had Tosh managed to move so quickly? Had Mackie told them about the nicks on the lighter? But even if he had, what would that have proven? Gilchrist had told no one of the connection to his brother. Except Gina Belli. Her rush of anger came back to him. Had she lied?

As these questions flickered through his mind, he realized his error in not informing Mackie of his concerns. But more damaging had been his failure to return the lighter. He had been so consumed by Gina Belli's psychic results – the driver, the passenger – that he had forgotten the lighter and left it lying on the table in the St Andrews Bay Hotel. With its connection to his brother now leaked, any competent Fiscal could turn that against Gilchrist and nail his head to the legislative wall for removing critical evidence. They might even argue that he was culpable in some way. Had his brother confessed to him all those years ago? Was that why he had removed a vital piece of evidence? What other secrets did he know about his brother, or Kelly's murder? Gilchrist needed to limit the damage, somehow recover control.

'Where did you find the tooth?' he asked.

'Let me ask the questions—'

'Unless and until someone directs me otherwise, I am the senior investigating officer on this murder enquiry. And if you refuse to cooperate by not telling me where the tooth was found, I'll have *you* charged with attempting to pervert the course of justice.'

Tosh sat back with a forced grin. 'Listen to him, Jeff. Back's against the wall and he thinks he can still call the shots.'

Randall leaned forward. It struck Gilchrist then that Randall was not assisting Tosh, but the other way around. If Randall had been drafted in from Complaints and Discipline in Tayside, it was odds on that his next step was to chop Gilchrist from the case. 'It was found wrapped in silver foil in the remains of the pocket of her nylon jacket, by . . .' Randall referred to his notes, '. . . a Ms Geraldine McNab, an assistant with Dr Bert Mackie, the forensic pathologist.'

'Thank you,' Gilchrist said. 'Why wasn't I notified?'

'You were, but your mobile was switched off.'

Gilchrist retrieved his mobile from his pocket, flicked it open, checked the log and, sure enough, there they were, two calls from the office.

He slapped it shut.

'Do you have any idea how the tooth got there?' Randall asked, his voice purring with an ingratiating English accent.

'No.' At least that was the truth.

Randall smiled, but Gilchrist sensed the worst was yet to come. 'So, Andy. You don't mind if I call you Andy?'

'That's my name.'

'So, Andy, although we can all take a stab at why the tooth was in the jacket pocket in the first place, and why the lighter was on the body, too, what I don't follow, you see, is why you would remove critical evidence from an ongoing murder investigation. Do you see my problem with that?'

Gilchrist clasped his hands. Gina's words came back to him. *How far do you want to push using something that no one else believes in . . . at the ridicule of others?* His explanation for removing Jack's lighter would sound ridiculous. What could he tell them? Who would believe him? On the bare face of it, it looked like he had removed it for no other reason than to protect his brother's name.

'Well?' Tosh grinned at him.

'I put it in my pocket by mistake,' Gilchrist said at length.

'Don't give us that shit, Gilchrist. You put fuck all in your pocket by mistake. You were—'

'Walter,' purred Randall. 'Let's stick with the facts, shall we?'

Tosh shifted in his seat, eyes blazing. If ever there was a portal to the soul, Tosh's eyes were it. He pressed forward. 'Here's how we see it,' Tosh growled. 'The lighter's your brother's. Fact one. The tooth's your brother's. Fact two. Both were found on the belongings of a dead woman. Kelly Roberts, to be exact. Fact three. A woman your brother was screwing when she died. Fact four. And the night Kelly was killed, your brother was involved in a fight outside the Keys. Fact five.'

Gilchrist almost jolted. 'Who told you that?'

'Did you not know that, Andy?' Randall again.

'No.' Not strictly correct.

Tosh pulled his chair closer to the table. 'So that puts—'

'I asked, who told you that?'

Tosh screeched his chair away from the table and stood. He raked his hair, then tried a smile. 'No one told us. It's in the files. Your brother had a record. And don't try to tell us you didn't know *that.*'

Record might be the correct word, but being charged for under-age drinking was hardly a serious offence. The fact that Jack had been attacked by two older youths as he was leaving the Keys, and in the act of defending himself knocked one of them unconscious and put the other in hospital, was something Gilchrist had always admired as a youngster. But Jack had been charged with assault and jailed for the night. In court the following day, the charges were dropped, thanks to three eyewitnesses.

Gilchrist returned Tosh's riveting glare, seeing in his pig eyes an anger verging on the manic. 'Which means what, exactly?' he asked.

'That your brother's fingerprints are all over this case.'

'Have you found any fingerprints?'

Randall raised his hand to stop Tosh from launching himself. 'Let's stay focused, shall we?' He pulled himself closer to the table. 'Andy, I have to ask you. Are you able to tell us why you withheld evidence regarding the cigarette lighter?'

'What evidence?'

'That it belonged to your brother.'

'You don't know that.'

Randall sat back, seemingly surprised by Gilchrist's answer. But the truth of the matter, whether they liked it or not, was that the only person who could confirm the lighter belonged to his brother was himself. Which had him cursing under his breath that he had told Gina Belli.

'It has three nicks,' Tosh said. 'You mentioned that to Mackie.'

'And your point is?'

Randall stared at him, dead-eyed, and Gilchrist made a mental note to keep an eye on the man. Too smart by far. Cool and calculating.

'Run through it for me,' Randall said. 'Your reasons for removing evidence on one count, and for withholding evidence on the second count.'

'And if I don't?'

Randall's ice-blue eyes never flickered. Here, thought Gilchrist, is a man who could look the Devil in the eye and not flinch. He thought of calling the interview to an end and asking for his solicitor. But what would that prove? Requesting a solicitor could send the wrong message.

Randall placed both hands palms-down on the table, as if to show how harmless he was. 'I'm with you on this, Andy. We both are. We're on the same side. We don't want to make accusations that could tarnish the Force's reputation. We have enough problems with our image as it is. But you must see how it looks, Andy. The body of a young woman is found thirty-five years after she disappeared, and the brother of one of our own boys in blue, the SIO in charge, no less, was going out with her at the time she was murdered.'

Randall paused, lifted both hands from the table in a gesture of helplessness. 'And to make matters worse, this SIO removes an important piece of evidence, and withholds further evidence, both of which are critical to the case. Which puts us in a bit of a dilemma, Andy.' Randall tried a smile of sympathy, but he was fooling no one. 'What we're hoping for is that you can help us explain away this . . . this damning evidence, if you'll pardon the expression.'

Gilchrist sat motionless. He had heard some pretty persuasive arguments before, but never with such self-serving guile. If Randall was a fox in a henhouse, he would have convinced the chickens he was laying their eggs for them.

'So, Andy. Can you help us? Can you tell us why you removed your brother's lighter?'

'Who said the lighter was my brother's?'

'Isn't it?'

'How would I know?'

'If it wasn't, why did you remove it?'

'I took it by mistake.'

'That doesn't cut it,' Randall said, shaking his head.

'You have the tooth,' Gilchrist said. 'That's enough to try to nail my brother to the cross, if that's your aim.'

'But we found the tooth only after you removed your brother's lighter, Andy. Do you see our problem with that? If we hadn't found the tooth, what evidence would we have had?'

'The only problem I see is that you continue to assert, without one shred of proof, that the lighter is Jack's.'

Randall gave a tired smile and sat back.

Gilchrist returned a smile of his own, but his mouth refused to work the way it should. If he was in Randall's position, the only course of action he could recommend would be to remove the SIO from the case. The facts were almost unarguable. The SIO had a personal stake in this case and could not be trusted, evidenced by the fact that he had removed his brother's lighter. They would argue that if Gilchrist had been around when they found the tooth, he would have removed that, too.

'I see,' said Randall. 'I would remind you, Andy, that we are trying to help you here. Give a bit, take a bit, that sort of thing. Back and forth. But if you're holding anything from us, it really isn't helping anyone. Do you understand, Andy?'

Loud and clear, Gilchrist thought. He struggled with the sudden impulse to get up and leave. He was the SIO, and the case was still his until instructed otherwise. He made a conscious effort to breathe slow and deep.

Randall shifted in his seat. 'What can you tell us about the jacket?'

'What jacket?'

'The one in which the tooth was found.' Randall scanned his notes. 'We've established that it was a man's jacket.'

Where the hell was he when all this investigation was going on? Chasing a lead to his brother's hit-and-run accident, came the answer. No wonder he was so far out of touch.

'Maybe she liked to wear men's clothes,' he said.

'Not just any man's clothes,' Randall said. 'But your brother's.'

Gilchrist said nothing. He knew they had found something on the jacket to tell them it belonged to Jack. In his mind's eye, he watched his mother sew a name-tag into the seam of the collar. She had done that on all their clothing, from the first day he had gone to school, for as long as he could remember.

'Do you see where this is going, Andy? We need you to be more open. We need you to help us out. Can you do that for us, Andy? Can you?'

'What colour?' Gilchrist said.

Randall frowned. 'Colour?'

'The jacket. What colour?'

Randall referred to his notes, flustered for a moment. 'Dark blue, we think.'

'Material?'

'Nylon-based.' Randall smiled, pleased to be back in control. 'Just an ordinary waterproof jacket.'

'You sure?'

'Positive.'

'I never knew Jack to wear any kind of waterproof jacket.' Gilchrist pushed his chair back and stood.

Tosh sprang to his feet. 'What are you doing?'

'Ending this charade,' Gilchrist snapped. He looked down at Randall. 'This is still my investigation. And I will bring formal charges against anyone who keeps anything from me or interferes with it. Got that?'

213

Randall pushed his chair back. He stood a tad taller than Gilchrist, six-two, perhaps, to Gilchrist's six-one. 'I'm prepared to put matters on hold for the time being,' he purred. 'But I have to advise you that I am not altogether *au fait* with your answers.'

Au fait? In which country was this investigation being carried out, exactly?

'But I would be grateful if you could find a way to return the lighter,' Randall said.

Gilchrist nodded.

'You still have it, I presume?'

For one disconcerting moment Gilchrist suspected it was a trick question, but he said, 'I do,' and prayed that Gina Belli had not checked out of the St Andrews Bay.

Outside, he breathed in clean cold air. The wind had picked up, carrying with it the taste of the open sea. Overhead, gulls wheeled and dived in the swirling winds. He needed to clear his mind, try to think straight.

At the end of North Street, he crossed into Gregory Place, a narrow access road that paralleled the cathedral wall towards the harbour. He changed course at the ruins of Culdee Church, doubled back along the pathway that led to the castle ruins. He stopped at the path's peak, gripped the black wrought-iron fence and stared out to sea.

Sixty feet beneath him, waves thrashed the rocks.

A tooth. Had it come to that? And a jacket. Why had he not told them the truth?

He remembered the jacket clearly now. Dark blue, a present from Kelly to Jack, a Christmas gift that she seemed to wear more often than Jack. She wore it to the New Year party – dark blue jacket and dark blue jeans. With her blonde hair and even tan,

Gilchrist thought he had never before seen anyone as beautiful. Jack had told him that she loved to slip it over whatever she was wearing, to keep out that cold Scottish weather, that dreich and dreary dampness. He smiled at the memory of her American accent tripping over the Scottish words.

'Dreich,' Jack had said to her, 'with an eegh not an eek.'

'Dreek,' she had replied.

Gilchrist watched a pair of gulls tumble in the wind, then he fixed his gaze on the grey horizon. Was this what it was all coming down to? Thirty years of a police career sucked down the drain because of a cigarette lighter and a tooth?

CHAPTER 19

He called Gina Belli on the number registered in his mobile's log, but it rang out. He then tried the St Andrews Bay, managed to confirm that she was still resident and asked the receptionist to pass a message to her to hold the lighter until he collected it.

Then he went to find Stan.

The jacket was barely recognizable as a piece of clothing. What appeared to be rotting strips of material had been the collar and sleeve and part of the front, the rest having disintegrated to more or less nothing. The name tag had been removed for forensic analysis. But what had looked like a clump of dirt in a pocket, had been a tooth wrapped in the silver foil from a chewing-gum packet.

Gilchrist remembered it now, the rugby game the weekend before, in the days before gumshields were the norm. Jack had dived at a loose ball and been booted unconscious by a poorly aimed clearance kick. The tooth had cracked above the root, and had to be extracted.

'So where does that put us, boss?'

'Nothing changes, Stan. We still have a murder to solve.' And even as he said the words, he knew he did not have long to go.

'It's not looking good for Jack.' Stan scratched his head. 'Is it, boss? With the fight outside the Keys, and the assault charge and everything.'

'Jack could take care of himself,' Gilchrist said, 'but he would never harm a woman. That you can bet your life on.'

Stan nodded and turned away, as if unconvinced.

Who could blame him? 'I think Kelly was sexually assaulted,' Gilchrist said.

Stan turned around. 'Boss?'

'Think about it, Stan. She was wearing a jacket. When they found her, she was not wearing knickers. Jacket with no knickers? Doesn't sound right, does it?'

'Maybe she was changing and got interrupted.'

Gilchrist shook his head. 'The jacket, Stan.'

'Maybe the killer put it on after she was killed.'

'Why?'

Stan scratched his head, for once out of ideas.

'And now they have Jack's tooth, Tosh will try to force-fit the evidence to get the result he wants. And have me fired or demoted at the same time.' Gilchrist pursed his lips, raked his hair. Or even charged, he thought. *Tosh.* He wished he had never met the man, never confronted him. But looking back, he would have done it all over again.

'What are you doing?'

Tosh had turned, chest heaving with the anger of the moment. At his feet, a woman sat huddled in a puddle, arms protecting her head, strands of hair striping her face like wet string. Gilchrist had not known if she was shivering from the cold, or from the kicking.

'What are you doing?' he asked again.

Tosh adjusted his jacket, his muscles bulging. 'Making an arrest,' he panted.

Gilchrist stepped around him, aware of the animal strength of the man. He reached down, took hold of the woman's hand, pulled her to her feet. Her clothes clung to her, cheap and sodden. Mascara streaked her cheeks like oil. She could have been sixteen, maybe younger. She ran the back of her hand under her bloodied nose.

Gilchrist removed his leather jacket and hung it over her shoulders. 'Would you like to register a complaint?'

'She's a fucking hoor, is what she is.'

She lowered her eyes, shook her head.

Gilchrist drove her to the hospital and filed a complaint on her behalf. But she signed herself out the following morning and fled back home to Falkirk. With no formal statement, Gilchrist was stymied. Two weeks later, he had taken a beating of his own from two thugs who were never found—

'Andy?'

Gilchrist was aware of a silencing in the room, a subtle change in the mood, as if someone had eased the doors shut on an outside noise. Chief Superintendent Greaves stood half in, half out of the office.

'You got a moment?' Greaves said.

Not a request, but an instruction, evident by Greaves closing the door on his way back to his office. By the time Gilchrist stepped into the hallway, Greaves was already marching up the staircase without so much as a backward glance. Gilchrist reached the upper landing in time to catch Greaves slipping into his office.

Gilchrist opened the door.

Greaves lifted his suit flap and sat on the edge of his desk, facing Gilchrist. 'Come in, Andy. Just had a word with Randall and

MacIntosh.' He clenched his jaw, shook his head. 'Randall's not buying it, I'm afraid.'

'And Tosh?'

'The same.'

'How about you?'

Greaves paused, as if giving consideration to his question. But Gilchrist knew that his decision had already been reached. This face-to-face was only a matter of courtesy, the way Greaves always liked to handle things. Silent, Gilchrist waited for the words that could end his career.

He did not wait long.

'Under the circumstances, Andy, I don't believe I have any option but to remove you from the case.'

'I really don't—'

'Andy.' Greaves raised his hand. 'Let me finish, please.'

Gilchrist struggled with the urge to turn around and walk from the office. But he had known Greaves for many years, found him to be fair and reasonable. Better to sit tight, he thought.

'I don't believe you have any ulterior motive for removing evidence,' Greaves said. 'I want to make that perfectly clear. Your record speaks for itself, and I would stand by you to the death in support of that. But . . .' Greaves raised his eyebrows as if seeking some revelatory explanation, '. . . as Jeff pointed out, we really are in a bit of a dilemma.'

Greaves slid his backside off his desk and shuffled around to the other side. 'The dilemma being,' he continued, 'that we can't be seen to have the slightest influence in the outcome of any ongoing investigation.' He studied Gilchrist. 'Do you get my meaning, Andy?'

'You can't have your SIO being suspected of cooking the books, is what I believe you are trying to tell me.'

'I wouldn't want to use the term *cooking the books*.'

'What term would you want to use?'

Greaves frowned. Two lines creased his forehead. Gilchrist thought he had never before seen a man so torn. 'Regrettably, there appear to be some question marks hovering over this one,' Greaves went on. 'And regrettably, Andy, they're hovering over you. I will say that Jeff's a good policeman, a strong man to have on your side, but he seems disinclined to believe you. I've challenged him on your integrity, of course, but until we clear up what I'm hoping will be nothing more than a simple explanation, I have to carpet you, Andy. I'm sorry.'

Well, there he had it. Suspended once again.

'You'll be on full pay, of course.'

'Of course.'

'Yes. Well. Any questions?'

'No, sir.'

Greaves leaned forward, resting both hands on his desk. 'I don't like this, Andy, not one bit. It upsets me when I see a ready willingness to find blame among our own. That would never have happened in the old days. We were all part of a team back then, and proud as punch to be cops. Don't let anyone know I told you this, but if you need to lay your hands on anything to do with this investigation, let me know and I'll do what I can to get it to you. God forbid if the press ever got hold of that. So, I'm relying on you to keep that between us.' His eyes burned. 'All right?'

'Thank you, sir.'

Gilchrist strode towards the door, gripped the handle when Greaves said, 'One other thing, Andy.'

Gilchrist stood in the open doorway. 'Sir?'

'Why *did* you remove the cigarette lighter?'

'Do you believe in ghosts?'

Greaves frowned, tilted his head, as if looking down his nose. 'Can't say that I do.'

Gilchrist backed from the room. 'I never used to either, sir.'

He closed the door.

'Same again, Andy?' asked Fast Eddy.

'You talked me into it. You don't happen to have a phone book in here, do you?'

'Sweetheart,' Fast Eddy shouted to a woman Gilchrist had not seen before. 'Phone book for the gentleman at the bar.' As he eased a fresh pint from the tap, Fast Eddy said, 'You look a bit out of sorts, Andy. Everything all right?'

'Same old same old.'

'Tell me about it. Sometimes I wonder what I'm doing in here, pulling pint after pint. Nothing but a shopkeeper is what I am. And the shite I have to take from some customers? One of these days I'm going to nail one of the pricks to the wall. Thanks, sweetheart,' he said, handing over the phone book. 'I don't believe you've met Andy,' he said. 'Andy, this is Elspeth. She's just joined our happy little outfit.'

Elspeth wiped her hand on a bar towel and held it out to Gilchrist.

'Pleased to meet you, Andy.'

Andy took her hand. 'And you, too. Haven't we met before?' he asked her.

'Can't think where.'

'Watch Andy's patter, love. He's a charmer, that's for sure.'

'I'm only here for the beer.' Gilchrist opened the phone book and within thirty seconds had the number of the travel agency.

Five minutes later, he was booked on a Continental flight from Glasgow to Newark the following day, connecting with Continental Express to Albany, New York. 'Going on holiday?' Fast Eddy asked.

'Not quite.'

'Haven't seen much of that Gina Belli woman for the last day or so. One week she's in here every minute of every day, it seems like, and the next, poof, she's gone from sight. Bit of a looker, I'd say.'

'Not my type,' Gilchrist offered.

'But you'd give her one. Right?'

Gilchrist lost his answer in a mouthful of beer. He was in no mood for Eddy's sexual banter. Since his divorce, he could count on four fingers the number of women he had been to bed with. Not promiscuous by any stretch of the imagination, but he wondered if it had been his love for Gail, or his love of his work, that had kept him faithful. He tried to recall the last time he and Gail had laughed together, but the image failed. Gail was gone, and he was suspended once again, only one step away from losing it all.

He gripped his pint, took a sip. If he was off the official case, then that would give him the rest of the day to take care of the other one. He pulled out his mobile.

'Anything new on Fairclough?' he asked.

'We're still looking, boss.'

'If Betson dies on us,' he said, 'we're looking at murder.'

'We think he might be in Rothesay.'

Rothesay? 'What's there?'

'That's where his secretary comes from.'

'Keep going.'

'Fairclough owes one of his subcontractors close to a hundred grand, and this guy's been calling every day for the last six months, threatening to take legal action if he doesn't cough up. He also knows Fairclough's been boinking his secretary for years, and when neither of them turned up yesterday morning, he flipped.'

'They could have gone anywhere,' Gilchrist tried.

'Not a chance, boss. Apparently it's where they go. They've done it before.'

Still a long shot, but Stan's positive manner had him struggling to maintain his composure. He managed to make Stan promise to call the moment he heard anything.

He closed his mobile, Fairclough once again in his sights.

The drive to SK Motors took fifteen minutes.

The garage was a converted barn that pulsed to the beat of music. Gilchrist located the culprit, a black box of a radio from the sixties that seemed to defy the laws of electronics with the power of its speakers. Shuggie gave a snarl for a smile, rubbed his hands clean with a filthy rag and shook Gilchrist's outstretched hand. Gilchrist tried to say it was good to see him again, but he could not hear his own voice.

The MGB was already up on a ramp raised to shoulder height.

'What's it looking like?' Gilchrist shouted.

'It might look as if it's in good nick,' Shuggie replied. 'But it's a cheap rebuild. All fur coat and nae knickers.'

'How can you tell?' It was like trying to talk in a disco.

Shuggie lifted a hammer out of his toolbox, stuck his head under the ramp and hit the underside of the car with a blow that should have shattered the chassis. Bits of dirt fell to the floor. Shuggie picked some up and showed it to Gilchrist. 'Rust,' he said. 'Big no-no when it comes to classics.' He slapped the side of the car. 'Heap of shite's nothing but a rust bucket.'

Gilchrist eyed the paintwork, gleaming showroom-new in parts, black and blistered in others. Up on the ramp, the car looked more fire-damaged, the classic style more dated.

Shuggie removed a crumpled sheet of oil-stained paper from his pocket – Gilchrist's handwritten instructions. 'So what kind of stuff are we looking for?' Shuggie asked him. 'Something about the front panel and the nearside headlight?'

'I believe this car was involved in a fatal hit-and-run accident in the late sixties,' he began. 'I need you to find something that might give credence to that theory.'

Shuggie snorted. 'Like what? A body part stuck to the front grille?'

'The victim was someone I knew.'

Shuggie looked at Gilchrist as if waiting for the punchline.

'My brother,' Gilchrist said.

Shuggie glared at the car. 'Nearside headlight, you say?'

'The headlights might have been replaced, and I suspect some damage to the front panel's been repaired. But since the accident, it's only had the one paint job.'

Shuggie ran a hand as big as a bear's paw over the metal, scratched one of the bubbles with a fingernail as black and thick as a claw. 'Cheap job, too,' he said, then looked back at Gilchrist. 'You got the accident report?'

Gilchrist shook his head. 'Not on me. My brother was struck down crossing the road. His body was found straddling the pavement.'

'How did he die?'

'Bled to death. The femoral artery, that's the one in his leg,' he added, 'was sliced open.'

'Is that above or below the knee?'

'Above.'

224

Shuggie palmed the front of the car. 'Any broken bones? Crushed knees? That sort of stuff?'

Gilchrist recalled the details. Multiple breaks in the lower and upper right leg. Meniscus cartilage shattered. Bones poking through skin. Jack had not died immediately, but lain on the side of the road, probably unable to move. Assuming he had been conscious, the pain from his shattered bones would have had him clutching his leg. By the time he realized his artery was cut, the loss of blood would have had him in shock. With the drop in blood pressure he would most likely have passed out in less than a minute, been dead in two.

'His right leg was a mess,' Gilchrist said.

'So he was walking on to the road, no off it.'

'It looks that way.'

'Back then,' Shuggie continued, 'these chrome bumpers and nifty-looking sidelights and stuff was as good as being hit with an axe. You don't see them any more. Against the law. I remember seeing a Jaguar mascot once, you know, the one with the leaping cat on the bonnet? Well, this was covered in blood and stuff. The guy it hit went flying over the bonnet, but no before the mascot ripped a hole in his stomach. Guts and stuff everywhere.'

Gilchrist eyed the radio. It was difficult to think with all the noise. But he did know one thing. There had been no *guts and stuff* in Jack's accident. A bone splinter that sliced the femoral artery had been his fatal injury.

'I like this one,' Shuggie said, and turned the radio up an impossible notch.

'What is it?' Gilchrist shouted.

'Green Day.'

'I meant, the radio.'

Shuggie gave a friendly grimace. 'Brother's into electronics and stuff. Jake put in new speakers. Small as shite and stuff. You should hear it at full blast.'

Gilchrist shouted, 'It can go louder?'

Shuggie gave a proud grin that revealed broken teeth. 'It's idling, man. Just ticking over.'

Gilchrist choked back a cough. 'How long do you think it'll take?'

'If I concentrate on the front panels, a couple of days, maybe less, maybe more. Depends on what kind of stuff I find.' He scratched his beard with a grimy finger. 'Want me to strip it down all the way?' He seemed pleased with his question.

Gilchrist felt a clammy sweat grip the nape of his neck, whether from his fever or the thought of presenting Greaves with the bill, he could not say. Or maybe from the thought of uncovering proof of the hit-and-run. 'Concentrate on the front end,' he said. 'If you find something, let me know, and I'll tell you if I want you to dig deeper.'

Shuggie nodded, disappointed.

As Gilchrist walked from the garage, he hawked up a lump of black phlegm and spat it into thick grass at the base of a stone wall. In the car, he wiped his face of sweat and tried to ignore a shiver that flushed down his arms.

Back in town, he popped into Boots on Market Street for a box of Ibuprofen. He took two, had to work up spittle to swallow them dry. He clicked his remote fob and was about to step into his Merc when he saw old Donnie. He caught up with him as he was turning into College Street.

'I got your records,' Gilchrist said.

'Were they any help?'

'Too soon to say, but thanks for your trouble. I owe you a half or two.'

Donnie frowned. 'It's too early for me,' he said. 'I'd fall asleep in my soup if I had a half now.'

Gilchrist nodded. It was almost too early for him. 'Do you remember any details of any of your female renters?' he asked Donnie. 'Back in the sixties, I mean?'

'The sixties?' Donnie frowned, as if stunned that all these years had passed. 'What sort of details?'

'Anything that might stick out in your mind. Such as an American accent . . .'

'We had more than a few Americans renting the place over the years. Can't you just look at the addresses on my records? That should tell you who's American or not.'

'I was hoping you might recall something that seemed odd at the time.'

Donnie shook his head. 'They were just wee lassies giving me their names and addresses. That's the only dealings I ever had with them. Sometimes I never even got to talk to them. Sometimes I got the information from the property manager, and just updated my records.'

Gilchrist nodded, not quite finished yet. 'How about Mexican accents?' he tried.

'Mexican?' Donnie shook his head. 'Not that I remember. Which doesn't mean much nowadays. But I'm sure I would have remembered a Mexican. Particularly if she was giving me the eye.' His shoulders shuffled at his joke.

Gilchrist had known it was a long shot.

'One thing I do remember about the sixties, though,' Donnie added, 'was the sexual promiscuity.' He licked his lips, as if at the thought. 'Used to make me wish I was young enough to join in. Musical fannies was what it was.' His shoulders shrugged at the missed opportunities.

On his walk back to his Merc, Gilchrist well remembered the days before AIDS put the fear of God into unprotected sex, and the pill was a life-saver popped like sweeties. Gail had been on the pill when they first met. He had thought nothing of it at the time, instead had been swept off his feet and her on to her back by her air of sexual liberation. Had her carefree attitude been a precursor to her marital infidelity? Should he have noticed the warning signs, even way back then? But the thought that he sometimes sensed those same signs in his daughter's recovery worried him.

He turned the ignition, backed out on to Market Street and was manoeuvring around a parked delivery van when his mobile rang. He recognized the office number and cursed under his breath when he heard Tosh's voice.

'You're off the case, Gilchrist. I want that lighter.'

'I told you I would turn it in.'

'You did. But I don't believe you. Where are you? I want it *now*.'

Gilchrist hung up, and floored the pedal.

CHAPTER 20

The Merc's tyres squealed as they bit into asphalt and powered Gilchrist up and over Kinkell Braes. He tried calling Gina Belli again, but her mobile rang out until the call ended. No luck at the St Andrews Bay, either. He gripped the wheel and forced his thoughts into overdrive.

He had experienced Tosh's obsessive mania once before, when Tosh had carried out a personal vendetta against the family of a petty criminal who had conjured up witnesses to help him duck a charge of assault. After the case was dropped, one by one the family members found themselves in front of the sheriff for cooked-up charges that were driven home by questionable evidence. Fines and custodial sentences were the order of the day, until Tosh had been called into the sheriff's office and ordered to lay off.

Gilchrist had no doubt that Tosh would do everything in his power to press charges against him for wilful removal of evidence in a murder investigation. And with Tosh's track record of fabricating evidence and lying in court, the fight to clear Gilchrist's name was not a foregone conclusion. He was also troubled by the likelihood of being hindered in his search for Kelly's killer and his efforts to clear Jack's name. He needed to talk to Kelly's mother, face to face, before Tosh shackled him. No matter what, he needed to be on that flight to the States in the morning.

He glanced at his watch. He had no time. For all he knew, Tosh might already have finagled a search warrant for his cottage in Crail, God forbid. That thought had him gritting his teeth and his eyes glued to the road as the Merc zipped through sweeping bends like a greyhound after a hare. Out and past a minibus, and again for three cars that swept past him as if going the other way. He eyed the dash, caught his speed pushing ninety and eased back.

He reached Crail without mishap, and crawled through the town at the speed limit. Back at his cottage, he powered up his laptop and connected to the Internet. He accessed MapQuest, typed in the address, requested directions from Saratoga Springs and printed out the result. He threw trousers, underpants, socks, shirts, sweaters and a waterproof jacket into a suitcase and his laptop, passport, Donnie's records and copies of the case files into his computer case.

In his bedroom, he opened his wardrobe and kneeled on the floor.

He pulled out a shoe rack to reveal a wall safe. He entered the four-digit code – the months of Jack and Maureen's birthdays – and pulled out a roll of one-hundred-pound notes. He unravelled twenty and returned the remainder to his stash. From his bedside drawer he removed another mobile phone.

Five minutes later, he locked the cottage behind him.

Hasty departures were good reasons not to have pets.

He took the coastal road south, and called Maureen on his regular mobile.

'Hi,' he said.

'Dad?'

'The one and only.'

'Long time,' she said.

He did not have it in his heart to remind her that she had hung up on his last call. 'Listen, Mo,' he said, 'I'll be out of town for a few days, heading down to the south coast. If anyone's looking for me, that's where I'll be.'

'OK.'

He asked how she was holding up after Mum, what she was doing, if she was back at work, but received only grunts in response. After a few more efforts, he said, 'Got to go, princess. Catch you later. Love you.'

When he hung up, he swore under his breath. Her psychiatric reports confirmed she was making steady progress. Sometimes he found it difficult to convince himself of that. But she *was* alive, and she *was* recovering, no matter how slowly. He had to take that from it at least.

He called Jack next.

'Heh, Andy, how's it going, man?'

'Good,' was all he offered. 'How about you?'

'Never been better.'

'Why don't I believe you?'

'Because you've been a policeman too long and you don't trust anything you hear any more.'

It pleased him to see that simple things like speaking to his children could still pick him up. 'If you say so,' he replied. 'Listen, Jack, I'm driving down to the south coast for a few days.'

'Anywhere nice?'

'Cornwall.'

'Cool.'

'Yes, it will be.'

Jack laughed. 'Heh, Andy, have a great time. And don't forget to call.'

'The phone works both ways, young man.'

'I can never remember your number.'

'Haven't you got it saved yet?'

'That's too complicated, man. I prefer the simpler things in life. Beer and sex. But not in that order.'

'Stick to the beer.'

They exchanged promises and farewells, then hung up.

He felt bad at having lied to both of them, but if Tosh called for information on their missing father, at least their stories would match.

He drove straight to Glasgow International Airport and parked in the long stay car park. In the terminal building, he converted fifteen hundred pounds into US dollars, then slipped the lot into his computer case. An airport bus dropped him off at a hotel in Paisley, and he checked in under Harry Jamieson, a combination of his ex-wife's husband's name and her unmarried name, and paid for the room with cash. The whole place stank of cigarette smoke, which almost had him tapping his pockets for a packet.

He resisted the urge to take a walk into town for a pint. The fewer people who saw him, the better. Instead, he had a shower. He eased back the plaster from his finger, pleased to see he was not going to lose his fingernail, and took care not to open his shoulder wound, which was healing nicely. Even his cough seemed to have cleared. But he took another couple of Ibuprofen to stave off any fever.

Once showered and towelled, he called Edinburgh Royal Infirmary using the room phone, and was assured that Betson was expected to make a recovery. He fought off the urge to call Stan from his new mobile, or the room phone. Either number would appear on the office phone system. Instead, he slipped under the covers and clicked the TV remote.

He picked up nothing of concern on the evening news, no mention of missing DCIs, or upgrades in Fife's murder enquiries. He clicked the TV on to mute, picked up the room phone and dialled her number.

'This is becoming a bit of a habit,' Rita said.

'It's that accent of yours that I find irresistible.'

Even her chuckle sounded Welsh. 'Any luck with your investigation?'

'Still sniffing around,' he said. 'Do you mind if I ask you some more questions?'

'Sniff away.'

It had been his comment to Stan that made him revisit his deductive reasoning. Jacket and no knickers. Had Kelly been sexually assaulted? But just as troubling was his inability to recall exact dates. When exactly had Jack's emotions changed? After Kelly disappeared mid-February? Or had it been closer to New Year? Had Kelly taken on a new lover? If so, that raised the possibility, no matter how slender, that Jack had been unable to handle the break-up and killed her in a fit of jealous rage. Was that possible? Could his brother really have been a murderer? And again the thought that Jack had deliberately stepped in front of Fairclough's MGB slipped into his mind. All of a sudden he was not quite sure how to broach the subject.

'Did Kelly ever confide in you?' he blurted.

'We were quite close, if that's what you mean.'

He thought her evasive response gave him his answer, but he

needed to be sure. 'Did she ever talk to you about seeing anyone else?'

The pause on the line told him that Rita was having trouble breaking a long-held confidence. 'What do you mean?'

'Do you know if she slept around?'

'While she was with Jack?'

'Yes.'

'I'm not sure, Andy.'

'But you have your suspicions.'

She paused long enough to worry him, then said, 'Andy, I really don't like this.'

At last. He had hit on something, or rather, some*one*. He tried a different tack. 'I'm sorry,' he said. 'I don't mean to pry into your personal relationships, but it sounds to me like it might have been someone common to you both.' He pressed the phone to his ear.

Silence.

'If I gave you a name, could you just say if I'm wrong or right?'

She sniffed. Was she crying? 'Depends.'

'Geoffrey Pennycuick,' he said.

'Never heard of him.'

Gilchrist frowned. Not quite the answer he had expected. He decided to go straight for the heart. 'We can do this unofficially,' he went on, 'or I can have you brought to the office for a formal interview.' He let his words sink in. 'I really don't want to go down that road.' He hated lying to her, but she would never know he was suspended. 'But I'm in charge of a murder investigation. Any information you provide could prove critical.' Another pause. 'If it's personal, it won't go any further.'

'I can't tell you, Andy.'

'I *will* have you pulled in,' he pressed.

234

'It won't do any good,' she said. 'I don't know their names.'

Gilchrist felt himself slump. *Their* names. 'Rita?'

'She had men back all the time, Andy. I'm sorry.'

Men back all the time. Well, there he had it. He wanted to ask where Jack had been while Kelly took others at her leisure. But he knew Jack had played rugby, practised with the team during the week, spent most weekends on the field, at home or away. He took a deep breath. In terms of finding Kelly's murderer, this was about the worst thing that could have happened. Instead of narrowing the suspects, Rita had opened up the field, thrown in an entire rugby team. Maybe two teams, for all he knew. They could have made a right good game of it. But more troubling were his thoughts on how Jack would have reacted if he had ever found out.

'Are you still there, Andy?'

'I am.'

'I'm sorry.'

'Don't be,' he said, wondering if *all the time* meant not as often as he first thought. He decided that was what he would choose to believe. Kelly had not been a sex-craving slut, but a young woman living away from home, attractive, vivacious, looking for comfort where she had found none in her relationship with her boyfriend.

'Rita,' he said, 'I have to ask you this. It might help. Can you remember any of their names?'

'She didn't exactly introduce them to me.'

'So how do you know Geoffrey Pennycuick was not one of them?'

'I didn't say that. I said I'd never heard of him.'

There he was again, missing the obvious, hearing only what he wanted to hear and jumping to conclusions. Which at least meant that Geoffrey Pennycuick was still not ruled out. Not just yet. He was undecided if that pleased or disappointed him: pleased that he might bring down the King of Condescension himself; disappointed that Pennycuick might have shared intimate moments with his brother's girlfriend.

He tried to settle his thoughts by thinking ahead.

Maybe he would find something in Kelly's mother's attic that would throw light on what had happened. He wanted to believe that. Without that, the case was toppling against him. And with those thoughts, he could almost feel the wheels of justice crushing his memories of Jack.

CHAPTER 21

Morning arrived dark and wet.

Before boarding the airport bus, Gilchrist dismantled his mobile phone, dropped the SIM card through the grating of a road drain and threw the phone case into a waste skip. Seated in the departure lounge, he half expected Tosh to come bounding along the corridor, brandishing a pair of handcuffs. But the flight was called sans Tosh, and he boarded without incident.

Clearing customs at Newark was a different matter. The grilling he received over such a short visit had him wishing he had ticked the business box for the purpose of his trip. But he had worried that he might have needed a business visa to do so, and had not checked the requirements before leaving.

Compared to Newark, Albany was a breeze. His luggage cleared the carousel in no time at all, and he was driving his rental car within thirty minutes of landing, paying for two days in cash.

He drove north on the Thruway, surprised by how cold the landscape looked. Trees bared of leaves rolled over hills as grey as a jailer's crew cut. Heavy clouds threatened snow. Summer could have been a forgotten season.

He took exit 13N for Saratoga Springs, which brought him into the north end of town, close to Route 9 north to Wilton. He tried calling Kelly's mother on his new mobile, but was connected to her voicemail and hung up. Checking into the Holiday Inn off Broadway, he booked the cheapest room they had.

He unpacked, showered and confirmed that all his wounds were doing fine. Then he phoned Kelly's mother again but was connected once more to her voicemail. He worried that she might have left town or arranged to meet someone, and cursed himself for not calling ahead. He checked his watch. Seven forty-three.

Although night had fallen, he decided to try to locate her home.

Route 9 north was a two-way highway that ran dead straight for a number of miles through the foothills of the Adirondacks. Commercial yards spilled off the road to his left and right, their lighted signs announcing landscaping supplies, RV trailers, swimming pools, kitchen cabinets made to order. As he travelled farther north, traffic thinned and the highway darkened to a long tunnel lit by his high-beams. The Wishing Well restaurant opened up on his left, its parking lot overflowing, its dull wooden structure brightened by windows that beckoned him inside for a drink and a meal.

Then back to darkness and silent highway driving.

He checked his MapQuest printout to confirm the house number. Driveway reflectors alerted him to nearing mailboxes glowing with luminescent numbers. House by house, he drove closer, slowing to a crawl as he neared. He caught a glimpse of Kelly's home through a narrow stand of trees bordering a deep front yard. His high-beams brushed bushes on the opposite border as he made the turn, then fell along the driveway.

The house sat well back from the road, at least a hundred yards. Windows glowed with light from within. He checked the time on the dashboard. Nearly nine. It had been only two days since he had first spoken to Kelly's mother and it seemed surreal that, after all these years, here he was, pulling into the driveway to the home in which Kelly had been raised.

He parked in front of a double garage that sat back from the house. Light flickered at the edge of the closest window. Kelly's mother said she lived alone, and he worried that a strange car driving into her yard at that time of night might cause her concern. He flipped open his mobile and dialled her number. He got the busy signal, and wondered if she was on the phone after seeing his car.

Three attempts later, she picked up.

'Hello?'

'Mrs Roberts?'

'Yes?'

'This is Detective Chief Inspector Andy Gilchrist of Fife Constabulary,' he said, conscious of the strength of his Scottish accent. 'We spoke a couple of days ago. About Kelly.'

'Yes?'

'I'm parked in your driveway. I'm sorry it's a bit late, but could we talk?'

'Oh. It's you. I was wondering who that was. I'm just getting ready for bed.'

'That's not a problem,' he said. 'I'll come back to—'

He jumped as a double-barrelled shotgun tapped the side window once, twice, then jerked in a *get out of the car* motion.

'Take it nice and easy, mister,' a voice said as the car door was opened for him.

'I'm here about Kelly,' Gilchrist said, and realized the error in his statement.

'Is that a fact?'

'I mean, I—'

'Both hands where I can see them.'

Gilchrist gripped the steering wheel, mobile phone in one hand, and kept his eyes on the shotgun. The man behind it was six foot plus, twenty stone at least, with a gut that threatened to pop the buttons off his shirt.

Gilchrist nodded to the shotgun. 'I hope that's not loaded.'

'She's loaded all right.'

'I'm a detective,' Gilchrist said, 'with Fife Constabulary in Scotland.'

'Helluva long way to come for a ride.'

Gilchrist eased his hands from the steering wheel. 'I'm investigating a missing person,' he went on, trying to ignore the shotgun as he pulled himself from the car.

Face to face, at six-one, he was still a good six inches short.

The man's gaze shifted over Gilchrist's shoulder, and Gilchrist turned to see Kelly's mother standing at the front door.

'It's all right, JD. It's Mr Gilchrist. From Scotland.'

'You got ID?' JD asked. 'And move those hands real slow.'

Gilchrist ended his call, then eased his hand into his jacket. He removed his wallet, pulled out his driving licence and handed it over.

JD raised the muzzle of his shotgun, breached the barrel, then slung it over his left arm. 'Can never be too careful,' he said, and held out his right hand. 'Name's Jonathan. Everyone calls me JD. Live next door and keep an eye out for Annie here.'

Gilchrist shook a shovel-sized hand as rough as bark. 'Everyone calls me Andy.'

As they walked towards the front door, Gilchrist said, 'Did the Sheriff's Office visit Mrs Roberts in the last day or so?'

240

'Not that I'm aware.'

Gilchrist felt his heart sink. No one had followed up as he had asked. He'd come all this way from Scotland unprepared to break the news. 'In that case,' he said to JD, 'I'm not sure how much Mrs Roberts knows about our suspicions. I think she believes Kelly may still be alive.'

'Until she sees Kelly's body one way or the other,' JD growled, 'she ain't gonna give up hope. That's all she's got.'

All she's got. He had flown thousands of miles to take even that away from her.

JD stepped on to the porch and leaned down to give Mrs Roberts a hug. 'How're you keeping, Annie?'

'Just fine, JD.' She beamed at Gilchrist. 'Are you related to Jack Gilchrist?' she asked. 'Kelly said he had a younger brother.'

Gilchrist jerked a smile, surprised not only by her question, but struck by the shape and colour of her eyes – Kelly looking at him from an older face. 'That's me,' he said. 'I'm Andy. Andy Gilchrist,' and showed his driving licence.

She barely glanced at it.

'I never realized until I put two and two together,' she said. 'I'm not as bright as I used to be, you know, but I'm not altogether dumb.'

'Still sharper than a double-edged deer knife,' JD retorted.

'Please come in, Andy. You don't mind if I call you Andy, do you?'

'Not at all, Mrs Roberts.'

'Annie,' she said. 'Call me Annie. That's what Kelly called me, and I've been known as Annie ever since.'

JD remained at the door and tipped an imaginary Stetson. ''Night, Annie. If you need anything, just give me a holler.' With that, he walked along the front of the house and melted into the darkness.

Gilchrist followed Annie along a narrow hallway that opened on to a spacious living room with a stone fireplace that filled most of one wall. Shelves lined the walls, laden with ornaments, books, framed photographs, houseplants that dangled or climbed.

'Why don't you sit here?' Annie asked, leading him to a long four-seater that fronted a slate-topped coffee table. 'Can I get you anything to drink? You must be tired after such a long flight.'

'I'm fine, thank you.'

'Coffee, then?'

'If you're having one.'

'I have a nice Colombian Roast. I won't be long.'

Gilchrist remained seated until he heard the clatter of kitchen utensils.

On one of the shelves by the fireplace, Kelly smiled back at him. She looked younger than he remembered, her face more full, her hair longer, folded over her shoulders. Another one showed her squinting against the sunlight, her jeans showing off the curve of her hips, her blouse the swell of her chest. In a china cabinet by the entrance to the dining room, family photographs jostled for space between crystal glasses and ceramic ornaments. He opened the glass door and removed a photograph of Kelly with her arms around her parents. Her likeness to her father struck him.

'That's one of my favourites,' Annie said, placing a silver tray on the coffee table. 'And Tom is so handsome in it, too.'

Gilchrist felt the warm flush of embarrassment at being caught holding a personal memento. 'Kelly's beautiful,' he said, and returned the photograph to the cabinet. He took his seat back on the sofa.

'Help yourself, Andy. Please. I don't know how you take your coffee, so there's milk here, and sugar there. And some cookies, too.'

He tipped milk into his cup from a white porcelain jug.

Her gaze drifted to the cabinet. 'I miss Tom,' she said. 'I miss them both.'

Gilchrist took a sip of coffee, dreading the way the conversation was going. Annie seemed pleased to see him, the bearer of good news. 'At the door,' he began, 'you said you had put two and two together.'

'Kelly was seeing someone during her stay in Scotland. I hadn't realized who you were until I thought about your call.' She smiled at him. 'And how is Jack?' she asked.

Gilchrist pressed his lips together, found himself wringing his hands. He had not expected this, to be the bearer of nothing but bad news. He had not given it any thought, that she would have known about Jack, known nothing of his accident.

'Jack died, I'm afraid.'

Annie placed her hand to her mouth. 'Oh. Oh, dear. I'm so sorry. I had no idea. When . . . ?'

'It was many years ago,' he said, and hoped she would leave it at that. He sipped his coffee, tried to gather his thoughts, find some way to change the subject. 'You mentioned on the phone, a couple of days ago, that Kelly wrote to you,' he began. 'And that you gave some, not all, of her letters to the Sheriff's Office.'

'Yes. Some were far too personal for the Sheriff's Office to keep.'

Gilchrist returned his cup to its saucer. 'Would you mind if I had a look through them?'

'Of course not. I brought them down from the attic after you called the other day.' She smiled, and he caught the glimmer of tears. 'I had a wonderful time reading them again. It was lovely to have Kelly back in my life, even if it was only through her writing.'

Gilchrist thought he saw an opening. 'Mrs Roberts—'

'Annie.'

He clasped his hands. 'Annie,' he began, 'has anyone from the Sheriff's Office visited you recently?'

'Yesterday morning.'

Thank goodness. 'What did they say?'

'They asked for a blood sample and a mouth swab for a sample of my DNA.'

'Did they say why?'

'No.'

He realized he was wringing his hands again, and he separated them, placed them on his knees. He tried to hold her gaze, but found he could not look at Kelly's eyes and talk about her murder.

'Are you all right, Andy?'

He shook his head, defeated. 'No. I'm not.'

She frowned, as if not understanding.

'It's about Kelly,' he said. 'That's why I'm here. I'm sorry.'

He watched tears swell in her eyes, her lips press together and the tiniest of tremors take over her chin. He reached for her then, and she surprised him by taking hold of his hand.

'Kelly never flew to Mexico,' he said.

'She didn't?'

He shook his head. 'She never left St Andrews. We believe we've found her remains.' He felt her grip tighten. 'I'm sorry, Annie,' he whispered. 'I'm so sorry.'

She stood then, and came around the table to sit down beside him. And it surprised him that she was the stronger, not what he expected at all.

'I've prepared myself for many years for this moment,' she said to him.

Which helped him understand his own pain.

Kelly's death was still a shock to him.

CHAPTER 22

Seeing Jack in Kelly's photographs did little to lift his misery.

He recognized the West Sands and Jack and Kelly in running shorts; Jack's minuscule and tight, his white thighs rippling with the powerful running muscles of an inside-centre. Beside him, Kelly's tanned legs looked lean and lithe, her hair ruffled by a strong sea breeze, her hand raised as she pushed it back from her brow.

He slid his hand into the box again, like a lucky dip, and removed another. This one showed Kelly, Rita and Lorena Cordoba seated in some bar, the table crammed with pint mugs, cigarette packets, filled ashtrays. There seemed to be more beer on the table than in the glasses. He pulled out another photograph and stared at it. Kelly faced the camera, her eyes smiling, her hand to her mouth, time locked in the moment of her blowing a kiss. He felt Annie's interest in his stillness, and he buried the photograph in among the others.

Back into the box. This one a black-and-white image of the castle ruins, taken with a low-lying sun, the direction of the shadow telling him that Kelly had shot it in the morning. She had introduced him to the art of photography, given him a camera for his twelfth birthday and explained how to adjust the lens aperture for depth of field, or frame a study for effect.

'Here,' Annie said, and handed him another.

Gilchrist stilled. Jack stared back at him, another black-and-white on fast film, the natural light from the window by his side creating a hard contrast that sculpted his face. How young he appeared. It struck Gilchrist then that Jack and Kelly had been killed in their prime, their ambitions, aspirations, all snuffed out at the hands of some callous killers. They had never been given the chance to live, to marry, to have a family, and here he was, browsing through images they should have been looking back on with fondness.

He cleared his throat. 'This is quite a collection,' he said.

'All of her time in St Andrews,' Annie said. 'She had more albums of her days at Skidmore. Would you like me to get them?'

'Maybe later,' he said. 'At the moment, I'm more interested in anything you can show me of her stay in St Andrews. Perhaps her letters?'

'Let me get them for you.'

Annie left the room, and Gilchrist dug his hands into the photographs, letting them fall from his fingers like playing cards. What had become of Kelly's camera? Had that been stolen when her flat had been cleared out? Could that have contained a photograph of her last day, perhaps of her last moments, her killer captured on film?

Annie returned with a shoebox tied with string. 'Here it is.' She untied the knot and removed the lid. 'Tom opened every one in the hope of finding something that could tell us where Kelly had gone, even though he felt as if he was violating her privacy. In the end, after he closed her bank accounts, they just stopped coming.'

Gilchrist glanced at his watch, surprised to find it was almost eleven o'clock. 'I've kept you up way past your bedtime,' he said.

'Don't worry,' she said. 'I won't be able to sleep tonight. In a way I'm pleased you came. It's difficult to explain. But it's the not knowing that's the worst. At least I now know where Kelly is.'

Gilchrist realized that the subject had not come up. 'I can arrange for Kelly's remains to be transported to the States,' he ventured.

Annie shook her head. 'Kelly had nothing but nice things to say about Scotland, and especially St Andrews. Tom's grandparents came from Scotland. I'm sure Tom would not object to returning Kelly to the home of her forefathers,' she said. 'And I would like to make one last trip to Scotland before I die. To say my farewells to Kelly there.'

Gilchrist nodded, not trusting his voice.

'Can I ask you to arrange that for me, Andy?'

'Of course,' he said, and cleared his throat. 'When they took your DNA sample yesterday, did they ask you to identify a computer-generated image?'

'An image? What of?'

The fact that the police had failed to ask her to identify the computer image formally only injected doubt into his mind of their willingness to assist in solving this crime. Their apparent disinterest in her case troubled him. He had the computer image in his case in the car. But what good would it do showing it to Annie now? It could only upset her, an image of her missing daughter manufactured from death. Not like this box of photographs that provided images of her while alive.

'Just a thought.' He pushed himself to his feet, picked up the photographs and letters. 'Do you mind if I borrow these?'

She stared at him for a long moment.

'I'll return them tomorrow,' he pressed on. 'Give you a call before I drive over.'

'Please,' she said, as if realizing the futility of it all, 'help yourself to any you would like. They're just going to lie in the box until I die.'

Back in Saratoga, he drove along Broadway and found a spot in a parking lot between Lillian's and Professor Moriarty's. He chose the Professor and ordered a Sam Adams, which came in an ice-chilled glass with beer frothing over the rim. He took a long sip, removed the lid from the shoebox and began to sort through Kelly's letters.

Most were statements from Provident Bank. He counted twenty-seven in total, and wondered if he would have done the same if Maureen had gone missing. Would he not have notified her bank for over two years? If hope was all you had, why destroy that? He made a note of the account number and sort code, then continued sifting.

Two letters from the IRS, which Kelly's father would have checked to make sure his daughter did not fall foul of tax demands. Next, four statements from Visa, which surprised him. He would have expected more. He checked the dates and confirmed that the oldest one was dated one year after Kelly had gone missing, and had a balance of $761.00. The remaining statements had a zero balance, and he realized her father must have settled her account and closed it about the same time he closed her bank account. Gilchrist would have liked to have seen her Visa account at the time of her disappearance, to check if any of her purchases threw light on her final days. He scribbled down her account number and laid the four statements on the bar.

He pulled other letters from the box: one from Skidmore

College about an upcoming reunion; four statements from Macy's for the same closing months as her Visa account; one from a photographic studio in Albany thanking her for her response to their ad and asking her to contact them on her return from Scotland. Nearing the bottom of the box, he recognized the striped edging of the old-fashioned airmail letter, two in total, addressed to Kelly, but no letter from Kelly to her parents. Had Annie withheld that from him?

He removed the airmail letters. The St Andrews franks would have had Kelly's parents' hearts racing. One of them did not have the return address filled out, while the return address on the other was to Rita Sanderson at the flat in College Street.

He unfolded Rita's letter. The first thing he noticed was the date, 22 April 1969, two months after Kelly disappeared.

Hi Kelly,

I must say that I am disappointed. I expected to have heard from you by now. Your departure left me in a bit of tizzy to say the least, and it would have been nice if you had left me some note of explanation. What did you do with the sheets? Why did you take them? And can I please have my scarf and gloves back, and my books, especially my Jane Austen? I wouldn't have expected that of you. Anyway, now I've got that off my chest, and I have to say that my chest is getting bigger, much to Brian's liking I hasten to add, I am pleased to tell you that my final exams are over, and I am quietly confident that I have passed them all. I will be returning to Wales at the end of next week, that is if my old banger of a car can survive the trip. Brian says he is going to visit me, but I'm not holding my breath. I like him a lot, but that's about it. I've enjoyed our time together, but I really want to start something new, not lug the old about. I will be back in

St Andrews for graduation in the summer, and if there is any way you might be able to make it, please drop me a line. Lorena sends her regards, as if she cared, the little tramp. Oops, I must watch that tongue of mine. And I was able to find someone to take over your share of the rent, some Scotch bimbo with bigger boobs than mine. Margaret's her name, although she wants everyone to call her Megs. Ughh!!!! Nothing but a beer-guzzler. Anyway, I hope all is well, and I would love to hear from you again. Please please please write.

> *Love,*
> *Rita*

Other than confirmation that Lorena shared the flat, nothing else jumped out at him. Confirmation that Megs also shared the flat, perhaps. He presumed the missing scarf, gloves and books had all been taken by Kelly's killer while clearing out her room. He read through her letter again, strangely disappointed that she made no mention of Jack to Kelly. Yet again, why should she? He eyed the date again, and realized Rita's letter had been written one week before Jack's death. Had Rita written to Kelly later and told her about Jack? Or had she returned to Wales never knowing about his fatal accident?

He lifted the other letter and opened it. It was dated 28 February 1969, not long after Kelly's murder. He searched for the signature at the end and felt a shiver course through him when he saw it had been written by Jack.

Dear Kelly:

How are you? Well, I hope. I was sorry to miss you on your last night in town, and had hoped that we could have parted on a happier note. I'm sorry for accusing you of things I know you never did, and I'm sorry for shouting and leaving the flat the way I did. I hope you can find some way to forgive me. I am thinking of flying out to the States in the summer, and would like it if we could meet up. If you think you can stand a sorry Scotsman visiting you, please write and let me know. If I don't hear from you, I'll understand that you don't want to see me again. I'm sorry, Kelly, for arguing the way I did. I just wish I could have those last two days back so that I could make everything right again, the way it used to be. I miss you. I miss our runs along the beach. I miss the sound of your voice. I miss the smile in your face. I miss you.

Yours,

Jack xxx

There it lay, in simple black and white, his brother's appeal to a lost girlfriend in words that left no doubt how he felt for her. Gilchrist read the letter again, wondering what had caused them to argue over *those last two days*. And what had Jack accused her of? – *things I know you never did*. Had Jack uncovered Kelly's infidelity? Had he accused her of sleeping around? He had been *sorry for shouting and leaving the flat the way he did*. What had he done?

But the more Gilchrist read Jack's letter, the more he realized how explosive it could be in the hands of someone like Tosh. Here was clear evidence of a major falling-out between two lovers, an argument that had Jack storming off from the flat in a fit of rage. In the hands of a competent lawyer, Jack would be painted as a man of violence, a jealous lover, a fit-as-a-fiddle rugby player who had no idea of his own strength as he battered a defenceless woman to death. This letter did not prove Jack's innocence. Far from it. It might even be argued that it showed how devious he was, having killed Kelly, then written to her in a ploy to prove he cared, the behaviour of someone so callous, cruel and cunning that they should be locked away for life. A competent solicitor might make that stick.

Gilchrist folded Jack's letter and slipped it into his pocket. For the time being, it was better to remove it than have others read it. He rubbed his hands over his eyes. Despite the rush from the discovery of Jack's letter, he felt a wave of sleep wash over him. His watch told him it was almost midnight, which put it at five in the morning in Scotland.

A long day, to say the least.

He returned the letters to the box, left ten dollars under his half-finished Sam Adams and nodded to the barman on the way out.

The night was cold, the sky clear and stars seemed to shimmer in a black void. He stood for a while, breathing in the crisp cold air, eyeing the length of Broadway, noting the side streets that fell off to the right, streets that Kelly would have walked, bars and restaurants she would have visited. A high-pitched laugh reached him, and he watched a young couple stroll along the opposite side of the road, arm in arm. Something in the way the girl clung to her partner, both arms holding his, as if for warmth, struck Gilchrist. That could have been Jack and Kelly. If she and Jack had lived, would they have walked this street arm in arm? Would they have married?

And what of Gilchrist's own marriage? He had never thought of himself as being impulsive, but his marriage to Gail had been achieved in record time: sixty-five days from first sight to register office, he had once worked out. Had Gail come along at the right moment and filled a void in his life? Or had he filled one in hers, up from Glasgow to the east coast on her summer holidays without a care in the world, except to snag herself a husband?

The walk along Broadway seemed to revitalize him. Back in his hotel room he raided the minibar, removing an assortment of liquors. He cracked the top off a miniature Jack Daniel's and tipped the photographs on to the bedroom floor, where he split them into two piles, one of landscapes and places, the other of Kelly and friends. Sipping the Jack straight from the bottle, he set to work.

Twenty minutes later, and on his second bottle – Captain Morgan's Dark Rum – familiar scenes of St Andrews lay before him. Images of the harbour, the East Sands, the cathedral ruins, St Rules, the West Sands and the university itself, all spread out around him. But it was the less familiar images that grabbed his attention – Kelly with her friends, in groups of three, four, as many as eight, mostly much the worse for drink and few he recognized.

He picked one at random.

A party in someone's house. In the background, couples dance-hugged in a dimly lighted room. No Jack. No Rita. Just Kelly in the foreground, her arms around someone he did not recognize, their bodies pressed close. Another of Kelly with her arms draped over the shoulders of two male students either side, grinning faces tilted towards the all-American girl. The university archway fixed the locale.

Where had Jack been when all this was going on?

He further split the Kelly-and-friends pile into Kelly with women, Kelly with men, Kelly with both and those without Kelly. He had no idea where this would lead him, but he thought it might prove something. Perhaps the extent of her infidelity. Rita's words echoed in his mind – *men back all the time*. Could Kelly not be true to her boyfriend? As he stacked the photographs in their respective piles, the answer became clear to him.

No, she could not. Not one bit.

He studied another photograph – Kelly seated on a sofa, being kissed with passion, returning it with passion of her own. Another of her seated at some bar, the Central perhaps, a friend's hand dangling over her shoulder, his fingers daringly close to the tip of her left breast, the nipple proud through her summer blouse. If Gilchrist had not known better, he would have thought these were photographs of a free-spirited girl with no steady love interest, intent on enjoying life to the full.

He finished the dark rum, stripped open a bottle of wine.

Never mix the grape and the grain. Why the hell not? He almost finished the wine in one go, and spread the photographs across the floor. He picked up the closest one.

Rita stood shoulder to shoulder with Kelly on the beach, scarves and gloves and flushed faces beating off the chill. Behind them, waves frothed. Anywhere else in the world it would have been a winter scene. In Scotland, it could have been the middle of summer. He searched for others of Rita, found one of her with Brian. He remembered Brian playing rugby with Jack, but nowhere near as gifted, or committed. Beside Brian stood Kelly, and next to Kelly stood Jack, slim and fit. But where other photographs showed Jack smiling, this one showed him dark and brooding. He had always thought Jack and Kelly made an attractive couple, always happy in each other's company. But that photograph told him otherwise. He flipped it over, looking for a date, but the back was clear.

Had this been the start of Jack's dark period, his emotional change? How intense he looked, how unhappy. Had he found out about Kelly's infidelity? Had he confronted her with his suspicions?

As Gilchrist studied the photograph, he came to see in Jack's eyes the desperation of a lover knowing he was being cast aside and not knowing how to stop it.

He thought of Jack's letter to Kelly, his cry for her to come back to him.

I hope you can find some way to forgive me.

Having now seen these photographs, did Jack not have that the wrong way around?

I just wish I could have those last two days back.

Would two days have made any difference? By the looks of things, he would have needed two years.

Gilchrist finished off the wine, pressed his thumb and forefinger into the corners of his eyes. The desire to sleep swept over him in waves. He glanced at his watch: 1.42. Back in Scotland, he would be on his way to the office by now. He gathered the photographs from the floor. Those he had already looked at, he stacked in their respective piles and placed on top of the television stand. The others he swept together and threw into the box.

In doing so, one caught his eye.

Kelly and Rita in a bar. Where else? But standing in a group of three men behind them lounged a young Geoffrey Pennycuick, his face at an angle, his eyes captured in a lustful look at an American blonde. Gilchrist studied his face. No doubt about it – Kelly was his focal point, or rather, her backside was.

The other men in the group were out of focus, their faces turned to the bar. Only Pennycuick seemed aware of the sexual possibility before him. Others in the periphery tugged at Gilchrist's attention. Was that the profile of a young Jeanette Pennycuick? He pulled the image closer, thought of having it digitally enhanced.

But what would that prove? That Pennycuick went out with his wife before they married?

He scooped up another photograph, a close-up of Kelly by herself, smiling her white American smile, wrapped up against the winter chill, her scarf covering her chin. She did not look like someone who would be dead before spring. He was about to return the photograph to the box when he paused. Something about Kelly's scarf caught his eye – black, with an unusual red edging, of material as fine as silk but without the sheen. Merino wool, he thought, or maybe cashmere. He had seen that scarf before.

He flicked through the photographs as fast as a card trickster and found what he was looking for. Rita and Kelly on a windblown West Sands, black scarf around Rita's neck, matching gloves on her hands. And there was the red edging. He compared the photographs. The same scarf. He thought he knew enough about women to know that buying identical outfits was tantamount to sacrilege. But students, especially close friends, would not have been averse to sharing.

Can I please have my scarf and gloves back, and my books, especially my Jane Austen? I wouldn't have expected that of you.

Bills, food, drink, make-up, scarves, gloves. Boyfriends, too?

That thought struck him. Would Rita and Kelly have shared the same boyfriend? Could Brian have been persuaded to participate in a threesome? Maybe the answer to Kelly's murder lay not in her own list of one-night stands, but in Rita's infrequent lovers. Had Brian been pulled in by Kelly's blonde charm? Had they consummated a forbidden relationship in Rita's absence? The opportunity was there. Hormones, too. But a session on the side with your girlfriend's flatmate was no reason to commit murder.

He pushed the photographs aside. He could not go on. Sleep pulled him bedside.

He staggered to his feet, dumped himself on to it.

By the time he wriggled up to the headboard, he had drifted off.

CHAPTER 23

Morning brought a quiet stirring of different sounds – a door closing, a heat pump switching on, a melange of noise that rustled in
the background.

Shaving and showering did little to bring Gilchrist awake. His
back felt stiff and his neck hurt, and by the time he pulled on his
leather jacket it was almost nine thirty. One part of his brain told
him it was morning, while another computed five hours ahead
and reminded him it was 2.30 p.m. in Scotland. Another day had
almost passed, and he wondered if Tosh had made any progress
with his vendetta against him, or if he'd had the audacity to
phone his kids.

He called Mo's number first, but it rang out. Jack's did, too, not
even kicking into voicemail. He peeled back the curtains with a
grunt, and faced a grey sky. Pockets of snow spotted the sidewalks
and property lines. Beneath him, his rental car sat in a distant
corner of the parking lot where he had abandoned it.

Downstairs, reception gave him a phone number for Saratoga
County Sheriff's Office and an address in Ballston Spa, some eight
miles south on Route 50. He called the number and set up an

appointment with a Detective Latham of the Records Department for ten thirty, which gave him plenty of time.

But once off Route 50, and on Fairground Avenue, Gilchrist drove past the turn-off for County Farm Road and had to double back. By the time he found the Sheriff's Office, a relatively modern building that sat alone in what seemed like acres of open ground, he had six minutes to spare.

He asked for Detective Latham and was instructed to take a seat.

At ten thirty on the button, Detective Latham walked through the double swing doors, blonde hair pinned back and a uniform two sizes too small for her chest.

They shook hands and introduced themselves.

'You're interested in the Kelly Roberts case, right?'

'Right.'

Latham strode off, and it took Gilchrist a full second to realize he was supposed to follow. They pushed through swing doors, then up a flight of metal stairs that echoed with their footsteps, into a room filled with racks of shelves loaded with boxes.

'Cold cases are in here,' Latham said.

Gilchrist watched her work her way between two rows of shelves, eyeing the printed boxes and mumbling from the alphabet.

'Here we are.' She stooped to remove a cardboard box from a lower shelf, and he could tell by the ease with which she did so that it did not contain much. She carried it to a metal table and slit it open. 'Sixty-nine,' she said, peeling the top back. 'It's been a while. There's not a lot in here. What's the deal?'

'She was murdered in Scotland.'

'Right. This is the one that's causing some dust to fly.'

'Excuse me?'

'We got a call yesterday from someone with an accent just like yours. Wanted us to send him two postcards. He was told we would need to see something on his letterhead. We gave him our fax number and haven't heard from him since.'

'Did he give his name?'

'Nope. He hung up. We called the number back and got a restaurant.'

'Which one?'

'Pad something. A Thai restaurant. These must be what he was asking for,' she said, and handed him the postcards. 'I'll leave you to it. But let me know when you're done.'

Gilchrist thanked her, then dug through the box. More letters, a hairbrush, nail file, toothbrush, all to retain samples of Kelly for DNA. In the late sixties, a way to analyse DNA had not yet been refined, but most police forces around the world knew it was coming.

He turned his attention to the postcards.

After all this time, and having passed through countless hands on their way to this box, the likelihood of lifting fingerprints from either of them would be non-existent. But the underside of the stamps might provide a DNA sample.

One postcard was of a busy Mexican metropolis. The printing on the back told him it was Mexico City. The other he recognized as St Andrews Cathedral, twin entrance spires in the foreground, St Rules Tower in the background.

He turned the St Andrews postcard over.

The date stamp was still legible, but only just.

12 Feb 1969

He read the date again. It could not be correct. The killer should have sent this *after* Kelly was dead and buried, not before. This date was too soon. But if the date was correct, it could mean only one thing.

Kelly's murder had not been spur-of-the-moment, but planned.

His mind pulled up Rita's words, when she last saw Kelly.

Not long after my birthday. Around the 18th or 19th of February.

Rita had driven to Wales after breakfast with Kelly that day. The killer must have known that, must have been waiting for his chance to move in. He would have known of Kelly's imminent return to the States and grabbed that narrow window of opportunity, which had Gilchrist thinking of Rita's boyfriend, Brian.

Where was he now?

Just as Kelly's mother had said, the postcard was typed. He scanned the letters for inconsistencies, a missing dot, a slanted letter, a crooked serif, but found none. The address was correct, to Kelly's parents – Mr and Mrs Roberts – which the killer must have known through his friendship with Kelly. Again, Brian popped to the fore.

Just how well had Brian known his girlfriend's flatmate? And if Brian was the killer, what had he done with all Kelly's stuff? Burned it? Buried it? Discarded it in rubbish bins around town? Gilchrist pulled the card closer. No full-stop after either title, not the way an American would have typed it. *Mr. and Mrs.* Which confirmed his thinking that the killer was Scottish, or at least not American. Mexican? Was that a possibility?

He read on.

Typing this because I hurt my hand. Tripped up on the beach. Going to Mexico for a short break. Won't be back in the States until March. Will be in touch. See you soon.

Love you both. Kelly. xx

Gilchrist read it again.

Typing this because I hurt my hand.

Good enough reason for using a typewriter, yet vague enough to explain why medical records would show no visit to the doctor or hospital.

Won't be back in the States until March.

The killer must have known Kelly was planning to return home after her final exams, and would have needed to make sure her parents received the postcard in advance. If not, Kelly's parents would have been on the phone to the Scottish authorities for news of their missing daughter.

This further proved to Gilchrist that he was dealing with someone who had not acted on impulse, who had not killed Kelly in a spontaneous fit of rage and disposed of her body in a rush. In other words, Kelly's murder was premeditated.

No one would have missed her. She was leaving Scotland, returning home. And who better to know the perfect moment to commit the deed? None other than Rita's boyfriend, Brian.

Gilchrist pulled up what he could remember of Brian.

Not tall, but physically strong from playing rugby. Much shorter than Rita, five-six or -seven or thereabouts. Bad skin and straggly hair. Gilchrist remembered thinking Rita and Brian looked an odd couple, Rita tall with smooth skin and shining hair, and Brian short and scruffy with hair like a tramp. Perhaps the thought of having sex with a blonde American girl with a reputation for putting it about could have been too much for Brian to resist.

Gilchrist picked up the postcard from Mexico. Again, addressed to Kelly's parents. Again, typed. And date-stamped the American style, with the month first – 03/14/69. He compared the postcards. The letter 't' on the Mexican postcard had a slight tilt to it, and the serif on the letter 'y' had a break. He searched the St Andrews postcard and confirmed his thoughts. Two different typewriters. Had this been typed in Scotland, then mailed from Mexico? Or had the killer flown to Mexico and typed it there? At that thought, an image of Lorena Cordoba tried to form in his mind, beside it, the grey shadow of someone else. But his mind refused to pull them up, and they both faded from view.

He focused once more on the postcard.

Having a great time. Staying on in Mexico a bit longer. Expect to be back at the end of April. Will give you a call. Love, Kelly xx

What had Kelly's parents thought when they received this postcard? It gave no details of where she was staying, no town, no hotel, no names of friends, no phone number. How long had they waited before they realized their daughter was never coming home? The killer had built a wall of time and created a belief that Kelly had left Scotland for Mexico.

The plan was simple, ingenious.

But was it foolproof?

How had the postcard been mailed from Mexico? Had the killer given it to Lorena and asked her to post it when she visited her parents over New Year? Had the killer sent it in an envelope to a friend in Mexico with instructions to post it to the States? Or had the killer visited Mexico with Lorena and mailed it himself?

Himself? Had Kelly's mother not told him that the Sheriff's

Office had checked the flight manifesto and confirmed that Kelly had been on the plane to Mexico? Which meant someone had purchased a ticket to Mexico and travelled as Kelly Roberts. Did the next logical step not indicate that the killer was therefore a woman?

Again, Lorena's face popped into Gilchrist's mind.

And again, too many questions, too few answers.

The rest of the files revealed nothing more, and Gilchrist slipped the postcards into his jacket pocket, closed the lid and returned the box to its shelf. Downstairs, he told the clerk that he had to leave to take a personal call, and could he thank Detective Latham for him.

Back in his car on Route 50, he was thinking he was no further forward than he was two days ago when his mobile rang. He felt a cold chill as he recognized the international code followed by the number of his office in North Street. Spreading the white lie that he was on the south coast of England was one thing. Being tracked down in the States with a new phone and SIM card was another. He chose not to answer; instead, he slipped it into his pocket and did not retrieve his message until he returned to his hotel.

'You're up to your neck in shite this time, Gilchrist. South coast, my arse. I'm preparing a warrant for your arrest, and if I don't hear back from you by five o'clock tonight, and that's Scottish time, so don't even think about trying to fuck around with me, you're mine. You know the number, so give me a call.'

Gilchrist listened to the message again.

South coast, my arse.

So, Tosh must have spoken to Jack or Maureen. The fact that he would even consider doing that, dragging Gilchrist's family into an internal investigation, had Gilchrist gritting his teeth and making a silent promise that when all of this was over, when all was done and dusted, he would find a way of having Tosh removed from the Force.

For one illogical moment, he thought of returning the call. But what would that prove? That Tosh had indeed located him in the States?

Right then, denial sounded good.

He let his anger settle, then he dialled Rita's number again.

She laughed when she recognized his voice. 'Haven't heard from you in umpteen years, and now you're making a nuisance of yourself.'

Gilchrist felt as if his days were shortening, so he chose the direct approach. 'How long did you go out with Brian?'

'Brian Fletcher?'

That was it. *Fletcher*. 'The one and only.'

'About ten months. Why?'

'Ever hear from him?'

'No.'

'Know where he lives?'

'No.'

'What he does for a living?'

'He was studying medicine when I knew him. But he didn't want to be a doctor. He was more into pathology, that sort of stuff.'

'Is pathology what he ended up doing?'

'I think so, but I really don't know. And don't know if I want to know.'

'Was he ever unfaithful?'

'Unfaithful? That's a bit much. We only went out together.'

'Well, then,' said Gilchrist, 'did he ever screw around when you were seeing him?'

'Probably.'

Gilchrist soldiered on. 'Did you?'

'Screw around when I was seeing Brian?'

'Yes.'

'Not much.'

Well, there he had it. Rita shared a flat with Kelly. Why not share her lifestyle as well? 'So it's likely that Brian reciprocated,' he offered.

'Probably.'

'Do you think he and Kelly were ever . . . an item?' he tried.

'If they were, I never knew.'

'And you're sure you don't know Geoffrey Pennycuick?'

His change of tack almost threw Rita. 'Positive,' she said.

'How about Jeanette?'

'Who?'

'Geoffrey's wife. You would have known her as Jeanette Grant.'

'The name doesn't ring a bell. But nowadays, not much of anything rings bells.' She gave a short laugh, and Gilchrist wondered if she had been drinking.

'When you went to Wales that Christmas, do you know what Lorena had planned?'

'No. I didn't spend much time with her, even less after Megs took over Kelly's room.'

Megs. Rita mentioned Megs in her letter to Kelly. 'I thought you didn't like Megs,' he said.

'Who told you that?'

'I, eh . . .' His thoughts jumped to Rita's letter. 'I must have heard it somewhere.'

'It was Lorena who didn't like Megs,' Rita said, as if not hearing him. 'Megs was too big and pushy for her. Whenever Megs was around, Lorena wasn't.'

'Made herself scarce?'

'You could say.'

'Stay over at her boyfriend's?'

'No. Once Megs came on to the scene, they split up.'

'Lorena and her boyfriend?'

'Yes.'

'And you still can't remember her boyfriend's name?'

'No. But I think Megs went out with him for a while.'

'For a while?'

'For what it's worth, my memory of Megs is that she was always either splitting up or making up. I think they split up after about two weeks or something, then it would be back on, then off again. Bit of a bitch, if you ask me. Stealing someone's boyfriend. But she was always on the lookout.'

'So, going back to Lorena, you thought their relationship odd?'

'It seemed that way. He'd come by to see Lorena and the two of them would watch TV without saying a word, and sometimes not even on the same chair. Like strangers. But it takes all kinds, I suppose.'

Gilchrist thanked her for her help, then hung up.

Back in his hotel room, he pulled Donnie's records from his computer case, flicked through the pages and found it.

Margaret Caulder. *Megs* to all her friends. Married Dougie Ewart in the early eighties. But not for long. Less than two years, as best as he could recall. And he thought that if he could find out where Megs now lived, and talk to her, she might be able to tell him the name of Lorena's boyfriend. Her address in Donnie's records was noted as Cupar, beside it her phone number.

A long shot, he knew, but he punched in the international code and the number.

'Hello?' A young woman's voice.

'I'm not sure if I've got the right number,' Gilchrist said, 'but I'm looking for Margaret Caulder.'

'She's not here.'

'Is this her number?'

'I don't know anyone called Margaret Caulder. She's not here.'

Gilchrist was about to hang up when he said, 'Do you know anyone called Megs Caulder?'

'Megs?'

'Yes. It's an odd name, I know—'

'That's my mum's name.'

'Can I speak to her?' he asked.

'She's just gone down to the shops for some fags.'

'I'll call her back, then.'

The line went dead. So much for telephone etiquette.

He closed his mobile, powered up his laptop and plugged in the Internet connection. A few minutes later, he googled *Brian Fletcher* and got 1,859,574 hits. He narrowed his search by typing *Scotland*, then again by typing *forensics*, and after several further variations managed to narrow it to four hits. He opened the first article, which turned out to be an excerpt of some court hearing and did not help. The next one confirmed that Dr Brian Fletcher was employed at Queen Margaret's Hospital in London. Did Queen Margaret's have a pathology department? He continued his search, but after fifteen minutes decided he needed help.

He checked the time, then called Stan.

Stan answered with a curt, 'Yep?'

'Can you speak, Stan?'

'Boss? Where are you? Tosh has got the ear of the ACC on this one. Wants to put out a call to you on the evening news.'

'What for?'

'To get you to turn yourself in, of course. What do you mean, what for?'

'Tosh knows where I am, Stan. He's not interested in me turning myself in. He's only interested in furthering his career. He knows I'm in the States—'

'The States?' A pause, then, 'You're at Kelly Roberts' place, aren't you?'

'Not quite, but close. Listen, Stan, I think I've found something, but I need your help.'

'Hold on, boss. You can get me into trouble.'

'Not at all, Stan. You've used your head, been talking to a number of people listed on old Donnie's records and come up with a few names. Could get you noticed by the likes of McVicar,' he added.

Stan paused, as if weighing the scales. 'I hate that bastard Tosh, so let's have it.'

'I need you to track Brian Fletcher down for me.'

'Who's he?'

Gilchrist told him.

'And you think he might have killed Kelly?'

Too early to say, he thought. But all things were possible. 'He needs to be questioned about his relationship with Kelly,' he said, then thought of his imminent call to Megs. 'I might need you to do one more search for me. But let me get back to you on that, Stan.'

'One other thing,' Stan said. 'That Gina Belli bird stuck her head in here yesterday, wanting to know about the fire in Edinburgh.'

'What did you tell her?'

'Told her to read the newspapers.'

'Did she mention the cigarette lighter?'

'Not to me, boss.'

If Gina Belli got his message at the St Andrews Bay, she would hold the lighter until he collected it in person. He had no idea of her travel plans, when she was scheduled to return to the States, or if she was planning to stay on in St Andrews. He thought of asking Stan to track her down and retrieve the lighter. But the thought of Tosh triumphing over the return of Jack's lighter in his absence made him decide against that.

After hanging up, he returned to the photographs and shuffled his way through them with a fresh pair of eyes, setting aside those of Kelly's friends. But it was a photograph of Lorena that grabbed his attention.

There she stood, with a small, straggly-haired individual by her side, whom Gilchrist realized was her mystery boyfriend. He pulled the image closer.

Was this the photograph of a murderer? Was he looking at Kelly's killer? Who better to visit Mexico with Lorena and mail a postcard to the States, than her boyfriend? Gilchrist saw for the first time the muscular strength of the man. Shirtsleeves pulled above his elbows revealed forearms striped with muscles like cable. What Gilchrist had taken as a thin face he now saw were the sculpted features of a man carrying a deep-rooted hatred of those around him. Black eyes glared back at the camera, as if demanding what right the photographer had to take his picture. Even his grip around his beer mug looked as if it threatened to crush the glass. Gilchrist placed the photograph to the top of the pile.

All he needed was a name.

He picked up his mobile and flipped it open.

CHAPTER 24

'This is Megs. Who's calling?'

As soon as he heard her voice, a short backlog of memories swept into his mind. She had accompanied Dougie to a number of police nights out when they were husband and wife: Megs, following a pint with a double Scotch in short order, guffawing at Dougie struggling to keep up; Megs, big and loud and red-faced from the weather or the drink, a real-life farmer's daughter if ever there was one.

'Andy Gilchrist,' he replied.

She gave a short intake of breath. 'Of Fife Constabulary?'

'The very same.'

A pause, then, 'Why are you calling?'

He thought her voice sounded nervous. 'Just want to ask a few questions.'

'What about?'

Her answer seemed too quick, almost defensive. 'Do you remember Kelly Roberts?' he tried.

'Who?'

'When you went to university, you shared a flat with Rita Sanderson and Lorena Cordoba.'

'Yes . . .'

'So you remember?'

'That's going back a bit.'

Gilchrist thought silence his best response.

'So, who was Kelly?' she asked.

'You took over her room when she left.'

'Never heard of her.'

Not quite the answer he expected. He was almost certain Megs would have noticed Kelly around town. Few Americans attended St Andrews University back in the sixties, and with Kelly's blonde looks and American accent, she would have stood out. Maybe Megs had known Kelly by sight, not by name. But that thought, too, seemed flawed. The local news had been full of the skeleton discovery, with Kelly's computer image being shown on national TV. It seemed unbelievable that Megs would be so clueless.

'Do you remember Lorena Cordoba?' he tried.

'That little dago bitch?'

Her change in mood almost threw him. 'And her boyfriend?'

'Why would I know her boyfriend? Come on . . .'

'Didn't you go out with him?'

'Oh. Now I remember. Are you talking about Wee Johnnie?'

Her response seemed too fast, too glib, but he scribbled down the name. 'Could be,' he said. 'What's his surname?'

'Walker.'

For someone who had denied knowing Lorena's boyfriend two breaths ago, Megs displayed remarkable recall. 'Aren't you getting his name confused with a whisky?'

'That's why I remember it. His name was Wee Johnnie Walker. And *wee* fitted the bill, if you get my meaning.'

'What did Lorena do when you started going out with Johnnie?'

'Do?'

'You'd moved into her flat, stolen her boyfriend—'

'Is that what she told you? Well you can tell that little tramp that Johnnie wanted a woman, not a Mexican bimbo.'

Megs had never been a mincer of words. He remembered that, too.

'Did your relationship with Johnnie last long?'

'Long enough.'

'For what?'

'Use your imagination.'

Gilchrist did, but it was not a pleasant image. 'It sounds to me like it was an acrimonious ending.'

'Not for me. I was glad to see the back of him.'

Gilchrist wondered if it wasn't the other way around. 'How long did you stay in the flat?' he asked.

'End of the year. Then I left.'

'Graduated?'

'That'd be the day.'

'You jacked it in?'

'Couldn't stand it any more.'

'Where did you go?'

Megs seemed to give his question some consideration. 'What's my leaving uni got to do with Kelly?' she finally asked.

He thought the first-name familiarity odd. But Megs had already shown how good her memory could be. 'Just wondering if you ever saw Wee Johnnie again?'

'Not a chance. Wasn't interested.'

'I think you've been helpful in answering my questions,' he said. 'If I think of anything else, I'll give you a call.'

He was about to hang up when Megs said, 'Are you looking for Wee Johnnie?'

'Do you know where he is?'

'Haven't a clue. But would a photograph help?'

Gilchrist pressed the phone to his ear, intrigued by her sudden enthusiasm. 'Do you have one?'

'I'll have a look-see,' she said, and gave him her address. 'If you want to come by and pick it up.' Before he could tell her to deliver it to the office, she said, 'See you soon, Andy.'

Gilchrist hung up to what sounded like laughter. He picked up the photograph of Lorena with her boyfriend. Was that Wee Johnnie Walker? Maybe Megs' photograph would confirm that.

Somehow, the thought of visiting Megs for an ID did not appeal to him, but if doing so could clear Jack's name, then what choice did he have? A face-to-face with her might reveal some more of the past, but having Stan do more legwork for him could give him a heads-up for the visit. He flipped open his mobile.

'Long time,' joked Stan.

'As well as Brian Fletcher,' Gilchrist began, 'I need you to track down Johnnie Walker.'

'Any clues?'

Gilchrist gave Stan what little he had, and surprised himself by not mentioning Megs. But a thought had struck him during his call to Stan, that if Megs could identify the person standing next to Lorena, could she identify those Gilchrist did not know in the other photographs? A visit to Megs was fast becoming a must.

He placed Lorena and Wee Johnnie to the side, and spent the next three hours going through every photograph, numbering them lightly in pencil on the back, making notes against each, cataloguing them in order of names he knew and those he did not. By the time he finished, it was almost five o'clock. The thought of a beer and a bite almost had him wrapping the lot up and heading to Professor Moriarty's. Instead, he called Kelly's mother, told her he was flying back to Scotland the following afternoon and asked if she would be interested in accompanying him to the Wishing Well.

'That would be wonderful,' she said. 'I haven't been back since Tom died. Why don't I make a reservation? It sometimes gets busy.'

'Perfect,' he said. 'I'd like to return your photographs. But if you don't mind, I'd like to borrow a few.'

'Of course, dear.'

'And you mentioned letters you and Tom received from Kelly. I think you may have forgotten to let me see the last one you received.'

'Did I? I'll look it out and bring it along.'

The bar at the Wishing Well was unavoidable. Patrons had to walk past it to enter the restaurant beyond. Gilchrist escorted Annie by the arm, and she surprised him by saying, 'Do you mind if we have a cocktail at the bar?'

'Not at all.' Gilchrist pulled out a stool and helped Annie to sit.

'Thank you,' she said, as he pulled his stool beside hers. 'Tom and I always had a cocktail before we ate. Sometimes we never even made it to the restaurant. We would just start talking and before we knew it we were on our third cocktail and ready to go home.' She shook her head with a sad smile. 'I miss Tom.'

Gilchrist surprised himself by squeezing her hand.

'I miss Kelly, too,' she said.

Gilchrist felt his lips tighten. The thought that he had held Kelly's skull in his own hands only two days earlier, had watched

Dr Black build virtual skin and tissue around it, while this woman seated beside him had longed for some sight of her daughter for over thirty years, had him not trusting his own voice.

Annie forced a smile at the bartender. 'I'd like a vodka martini, Gray Goose, and go light on the martini. With extra olives.'

'Certainly, ma'am. And you, sir?'

'Sam Adams.'

The bartender placed two coasters on the bar and removed a frosted glass from the fridge. As Annie leaned closer, Gilchrist thought she looked troubled.

'I was so sorry to hear about Jack,' she said to him. 'Tom and I met him once, that Christmas we visited. Such a nice young man. So handsome, too.' She looked at him then, her eyes a cold blue. 'Can you tell me what happened, Andy?'

So Gilchrist did, eking out details in a level monotone, as if the person he was talking about was someone he did not know. He did not mention that Jack was fast becoming the prime suspect in Kelly's murder, or that his hit-and-run driver was now being sought for a recent arson attack, and more. When he finished, Annie gripped both his hands in hers.

'Such a tragic story,' she said. 'Two young lives lost. With so much to live for.'

Gilchrist nodded, not trusting his voice.

'You still miss him,' she said.

'I do.' It was all he could manage to say.

Annie pulled back and smiled. 'I think Kelly and Jack would have kept in contact after she left Scotland. And I think Jack would have visited her in the States. Who knows?' she added with a wink. 'He might even have emigrated.'

'Why do you think that?'

She delved into her handbag and removed an envelope. 'Here,' she said. 'Kelly's last letter. This might help you understand how she felt.'

Gilchrist took it, resisting the urge to read it there and then.

'When you're done with your investigation, I would like you to send it back to me. It's all I have left of her.'

'Of course,' he said, and slipped the envelope into his jacket pocket.

Their drinks arrived, and Annie lifted her glass and forced a smile. She chinked her martini against Gilchrist's frosted beer and said, 'To the memory of Kelly and Jack,' and took a sip that made her face crinkle with pleasure. She replaced her glass on the bar and licked her lips. 'That tastes wonderful. I can't tell you the last time I had a vodka martini. Tom usually had Scotch. They used to keep a bottle of Glenfiddich in the gantry, just for him. That was before the previous owner passed away.'

Gilchrist waited for some more history, but Annie seemed content to stir her olives. He felt hesitant to press on with the morbid subject, but after a few beats said, 'What are *your* memories of Kelly?'

Annie looked into his eyes for a long second, then her gaze shifted and settled over his shoulder, focusing somewhere in the distance. 'The blondest hair,' she said, 'and baby's tears. I can still see her in her little swimsuit, running across our backyard, her arms sticking through those life-ring things you used to see. Tom bought one of those plastic swimming pools and set it up in the backyard, just for Kelly. We have albums of photographs of her. Hair so blonde it was almost white. She got that from Tom, not me. I'm fair, but nowhere near as fair as Tom was.'

She chuckled then. 'The first time Kelly went into the pool with all her life-rings on and flippers, too, it was so funny. She was scared she would drown. But the water was too shallow. Tom made sure of that. Once she got more confident, he put more water in it. But that first time, she splashed in the pool all day long like she never wanted to come out. And that's when the tears came, when I brought her in. She cried for hours. She could be quite stubborn when she put her mind to it, Kelly could.' She took another sip of martini, almost finished it. 'Would you mind if we just ate here? At the bar?'

'Not at all,' Gilchrist said, and asked for the menu.

'That's what Tom liked to do. Sit at the bar. Don't get me wrong, Tom wasn't much of a drinker. He preferred the informality of sitting at the bar. I liked that about him. So down to earth. But he could wear a business suit as well as any man.'

Gilchrist noticed Annie's drink was almost done, and his Sam Adams had helped lift his spirits, so he ordered another round.

When the menu came, Annie selected a fish sandwich, fries on the side and hold the bun. Gilchrist chose a chicken sandwich with fries, and what the hell, 'Hold the bun,' he ordered.

They chinked glasses again, and Gilchrist found himself warming to Annie, catching glimpses of Kelly in the way she laughed – plenty of teeth, pleasing eyes, an almost beguiling innocence in her manner that could have men misinterpreting her meaning.

'Are you married, Andy?'

'Divorced.'

'Any children?'

'Two.'

Annie seemed to give that some thought. 'Kelly was an only child. I wanted more. We both did. But that was God's will. Only the one. Which I suppose made it all the more painful when we lost her.'

Gilchrist tried to hide his feelings in his beer. It felt surreal sitting in a bar in the States, talking to Kelly's mother about the past, about Kelly and Jack, about their families, after all these years, as if two individual yet separate parts of his memory had been released to hit him with their joint demands.

Kelly. Jack.

Could he ever put them to rest?

And he realized the only way to fight those demons was to find their killers.

CHAPTER 25

Back at his hotel, he pulled Kelly's letter from his jacket, not an airmail envelope but a business envelope with two blue *par avion* stickers straddling either side of the address. He eyed her handwriting with its curling tails to upper-case letters and tidy, almost individual letters throughout. He removed a single A4 sheet with floral borders, a daughter's letter to her parents, and read the date:

January 30th 1969

About three weeks before she would be murdered.

He read on.

Dear Mom and Dad:

Happy New Years (sorry it's a bit late). It was so lovely to see you both at Xmas. I promise I'll be back in the States for Xmas next year. How is life in good old US of A? Life in sunny Scotland is so much fun I am sad that my stay is nearly at an end, and I will be sad to leave. I have loved every minute of my time here, even the weather. Everybody complains about the weather, especially the rain, but it is the rain that makes the countryside so beautiful. And I am going to miss St Andrews with its cathedral ruins and cobbled streets and all these old stone buildings. I am going to miss university life and all things Scottish, like fish and chips, and pints of beer, and driving on the wrong side of the road, not that I've driven much. But most of all I am going to miss Jack. He has been so kind to me. He brought me flowers yesterday to tell me he loved me, and to tell me he didn't want me to go. He is sooooooooo sweet. But if the truth be told it is me who should be saying sorry. I can be such a b**** at times. I was so pleased you got to see him at Xmas. He doesn't know it yet, but I'm going to invite him over for the summer (if I can wait that long). I have enclosed some more photographs. In case you've forgotten, Jack is the tall handsome man standing beside the good-looking blonde (ha ha). He is so sad that I'm leaving. One part of me is sad that I'm leaving, too, while another part is looking forward to coming home. I can't hardly wait. Do you know if I received any response to my job application? If not, I'll give them a call on my return. See you soon. Tell Scamp I'll be back soon. I'm going to bring her some Scottish treats and some tartan catnip.

Love you both,

Kelly xxxxxxx

Gilchrist read the letter again, letting his eyes linger over every word. Any thoughts he may have held about Kelly going to Mexico were dispelled then and there. This was a homecoming letter from a daughter to her parents, her excitement about returning, her sadness about leaving, written down in black and white.

He scanned the page again, his eyes settling on his brother's name.

. . . most of all I am going to miss Jack.

How could he have been so wrong? Jack and Kelly could not have split up before she disappeared. This letter told him they were two young people in love, both saddened by the prospect of her imminent return home.

He brought me flowers yesterday to tell me he loved me . . .

Gilchrist thought he now understood Jack's despair in the weeks before his accident. With Kelly's sudden disappearance, he would have thought she had ditched him in a hurry, perhaps taken up with one of her other lovers. With no explanation, Kelly's non-response to his own letter would have convinced Jack she wanted nothing more to do with him. Gilchrist knew that Jack would have been too proud to try to win her back. Instead, he had withdrawn into his own shell of bitterness, hurt and isolation.

He read the letter one more time, but found nothing that would indicate anything other than Kelly's love for Jack. No indication she was planning to do anything other than return to the States, and that she was sad about leaving Scotland. She even planned to invite Jack to the States for the summer, to continue their romance. And the reference to the job suggested she had every intention of settling down for the long haul. If Jack's emotional collapse had been caused by thoughts of Kelly no longer loving him, then he'd had it so wrong.

Gilchrist folded the letter and returned it to its envelope.

He now had a clearer understanding of Kelly's emotional state in the weeks before her disappearance. But he was no further forward in his search for her killer. What he did know was that Jack had not killed Kelly. Of that he had no doubts. But without physical proof, how could Gilchrist convince Tosh and others?

He tried to recall the last time he saw Jack, what they had said.

Had Jack spoken the last word, or had he? But each image he pulled up vanished at the moment of its appearance. One instant Jack would be grinning, the next his face would fold into sadness, then vanish. In his mind's eye, he saw himself reach out to Jack. But the closer he came, the more Jack faded from sight. It was like trying to start a conversation with a ghost.

Or maybe it was the lack of sleep catching up with him.

His watch told him it was 9.37. His body told him otherwise.

Sleep came at him in waves, their heavy undercurrent pulling him down.

He struggled to stay awake, but Jack's ghost whispered in his mind, telling him he loved Kelly. And in his mind's eye he watched Jack lie down beside her, wrap his arms around her, heard her husky voice say, *You're so sweet. So sweet.*

I love you, too, Jack whispered.

Sleep took him in its warm breath.

Gilchrist wakened to the blackness before dawn, his heart pounding.

Silence filled the room.

His fumbling fingers found the bedside lamp, then the switch. He clicked it on.

Light stunned him. He lay still, letting his heartbeat slow. Something had jerked him awake. But what? The bedside clock told him it was 5.42, as his memory fought to recover slivers of his dream – fire, smoke, blistered skin, and in the background, Gina Belli's voice whispering its psychic warning.

He pulled himself to his feet, flipped open his mobile phone.

His call was answered on the third ring.

'SK Motors.'

Music thudded in the background. 'Shuggie, it's Andy Gilchrist.'

'Ah, Mr Gilchrist. What can I do for you this morning?'

'Any luck with the car?' he asked.

'Depends.'

Gilchrist fired wide awake. 'On what?'

'On what evidence you still got available.'

'Such as?'

'Clothes.'

Clothes? Gilchrist paced the room. 'What've you found, Shuggie?'

'Fibre.'

'After all this time?'

'Told you it was a shitey paint job.'

Gilchrist opened the curtains to a black morning. The sky was starless, covered by clouds he could not see. His own thoughts seemed just as blind. 'Start from the beginning, Shuggie, and tell me what you've got.'

'You wanted me to keep the costs down, so I concentrated on the front end, where any damage would have occurred. If I found nothing there, I was gonnie start stripping her back bit by bit.'

Silent, Gilchrist stared into the darkness.

'Took lots of photographs so there'd be nae problems down the road. Got one of them digital cameras, with seven megapixels. Jake told me that'll let you blow them up without loss of detail. But I took them close, just to be sure. Hang on . . .'

Gilchrist thought the background music dropped a notch, but he could not be sure.

'Once I started stripping the brightwork, I seen the paint job had been done by an absolute beginner. Nae attention to detail. Just cheap and nasty and throw the stuff back together again. One coat of paint to hide the shite. What you're supposed to do is—'

'Shuggie. What did you find?'

'Haud your horses. I'm getting there. What?' His voice faded, directed to someone else, then returned. 'Hang on . . .'

Gilchrist closed his eyes, took a deep breath, forced himself to stay calm. After all these years had Shuggie found something that could link the MGB to the hit-and-run?

Shuggie's voice came back at him. 'You're supposed to buff it back to bare metal, especially around the bits that could rust, like around the headlight and indicator housings, where they're screwed in. Then build the paint back up in layers. But in a cheap job like this, there was none of that.'

'Shuggie?'

'The paint job covered dirt and rust and something else that might interest you.'

Gilchrist opened his eyes, felt his throat constrict.

'Now, I'm no a hundred per cent sure, but it looks like a piece of torn fibre. Just a tiny bit, mind you. So I got out my magnifying glass and my tweezers—'

'Don't tell me you pulled it off without someone being present.'

'Mr Gilchrist,' Shuggie grumbled. 'You should know me better than that. I got Phil to take photos as I was peeling it back, paint and all, and placed it into a *clean* jam jar.'

Gilchrist caught the emphasis on the word *clean*. Years ago, when Shuggie had been involved in his first forensic examination, he had deposited lumps of windscreen glass into a cardboard box that had once contained God only knew what. The procurator fiscal declared the entire sample contaminated. It had been a hard lesson for all involved.

'But better than that,' Shuggie went on, 'my magnifying glass also detected what looked like hair—'

'What kind of hair?'

'I'm no an expert—'

'Long hair short hair blond hair what?'

'Short hair. Dark.'

Gilchrist reached down, steadied himself on the window sill. 'Jesus.'

'That's what I was telling you, Mr Gilchrist. The paint job was shite. Just spray the fucker and cover it up. I was able to peel a chunk of it off. I've got two hairs stuck to the back of the paint. It's perfect, Mr Gilchrist.'

'Yes,' Gilchrist whispered, 'it is.'

He hung his head. Beneath him, the parking lot glowed a faint orange from the overhead lights. A car shifted in the morning chill, headlights brushing the asphalt.

It's perfect, his mind repeated.

Or was it?

Not long after he joined the Force, he had asked to see the records of his brother's hit-and-run and, to his disgust, had learned that much of it had been lost during repainting of the premises. They still had his blood-soaked socks and shoes, but no trousers or shirt. Without any samples of his brother's trousers, which would have taken the brunt of the hit, the fibre might not be conclusive. The procurator fiscal would argue that it came from a trouser leg, unequivocal proof that the car had been involved in an accident in which someone had been hit. But the defence would argue that it was nothing more than a piece of rag torn off while its careful owner had been meticulously cleaning his car. Why, just look at these photographs. The car is immaculate.

But it could be perfect. Shuggie had found two hairs. If those hairs matched Jack's DNA, which Tosh had already forensically

288

analysed, then no defence solicitor in the land would be able to explain it away.

'Are you still there, Mr Gilchrist?'

Gilchrist turned. 'Listen, Shuggie,' he said, 'I need you to hold those hair samples for me. I need you to keep them in a safe place until I have someone pick them up.'

'Where are you?'

'Will you do that for me?'

Shuggie agreed, and Gilchrist hung up.

He dialled Stan's number and approached the window again. Narrow slivers of white, orange, yellow streaked the skyline. He had a domestic flight to catch that afternoon, then an international connection in Newark. He would be in Glasgow the following morning, by which time Stan would already have started the chain of custody that could bring his brother's killer to justice.

Maybe Megs would have found a photograph of Wee Johnnie by then, too. Or maybe Stan had managed to find out where Wee Johnnie worked, even spoken to him, perhaps had already set up an interview. But if they could lift DNA from the back of the post-cards' stamps . . .

That could solve the case right there.

CHAPTER 26

At Glasgow International Airport the following morning, Gilchrist passed through customs with barely a pause. He collected his suitcase from the baggage carousel, strode into the arrivals lounge and was powering up his mobile when a hand slapped his shoulder.

'That's as far as you're going, Gilchrist.'

He spun around.

Tosh had a wide grin on his face. Nance stood beside him, expressionless.

'Aren't you out of your jurisdiction?' Gilchrist tried, but from the way Nance went for her handcuffs, he knew what was coming.

'Sorry to have to tell you, old son,' Tosh went on, 'but you're being detained under Section 14 of the Criminal Procedure Scotland Act for attempting to pervert the course of justice in the investigation into the murder of a Ms Kelly Roberts. You are not obliged to say anything . . .'

As he listened to Tosh continue to read him his rights, he slid his computer case from his shoulder and placed it on the tiled floor.

He turned his back to Nance while she cuffed him, quite gently, he thought, and forced his mind to work through the logic.

He was being detained, not charged. So a warrant for his arrest had not been issued. Which meant they had insufficient evidence against him. Or, more correctly, he imagined, they had not concocted a strong enough case. Not yet, that is. With Greaves in Gilchrist's corner, he felt sure Randall would want Tosh to play by the rules. They would interview him in North Street, and surely charge him then.

Handcuffs on, he faced Nance. But she could not hold his gaze.

'Car's over in the car park, Gilchrist. Not yours. Ours. We'll have someone drive that fancy little Merc of yours all the way back to the office for you. How fair is that?'

He shrugged off Tosh's grip and nodded to his computer case. 'I'll take that,' he said, and leaned forward as Nance slipped the strap over his head. 'The suitcase is yours,' he nodded to Tosh, and headed for the exit with Nance by his side.

The doors slid open and a cold Glasgow draught stopped him. A drizzle as fine as a St Andrews haar dampened his hair. 'Collar,' he said to Nance, and tried to engage her eyes as she tugged his jacket collar up around his neck and adjusted the computer-case strap. But her vacant look told him he was on his own, and she took hold of his arm and escorted him from the terminal building. Not quite like old times, he thought, but something in the way they fell into each other's stride warmed him.

Tosh caught up with them as they entered the multi-storey car park, and the rest of the walk was carried out under his monosyllabic commands. Left. This way. Stop. Gilchrist tried, 'Everything all right, Nance?' But she only gave him a blank look that told him she was having none of it.

The car was parked on level four, and the ride in the lift was done in silence. Tosh beeped his remote and the boot clicked open. He threw in Gilchrist's suitcase, while Nance folded the driver's seat forward to let Gilchrist take his seat in the back.

He turned his back to her. 'Do you mind taking these off?' he said.

Silent, she obliged, then stood back as he leaned forward and squeezed into the car. Tosh jumped into the passenger seat, while Nance sat behind the wheel. Alone in the back, Gilchrist laid his computer case on his knees and placed both arms over it.

'What's in there? The Crown jewels?' Tosh quipped, clicking in his seatbelt.

'You're a laugh a minute these days,' Gilchrist said. 'Practising for stand-up?'

'Not like you, eh?' Tosh caught Nance's snapped glance, but it did little to stop him. 'So how was Kelly's old dear?'

'If you're trying to impress me with your skills of detection, Tosh, forget it.'

'Not at all. I was thinking maybe you'd given her one. Nice tits on her, like Kelly, had she?'

'Give it up, Tosh.' Nance that time.

From the look on Nance's face, Gilchrist was not alone in his misery. Or maybe she was not getting much sleep around John. But having now gone through Annie's collection of Kelly's photographs, Gilchrist saw that Dr Black's computer image had done little justice to Kelly, more like a wax dummy than a vibrant young woman with the eyes and voice and an inner energy that thrummed with the promise of life yet to be lived. For Tosh to talk of Kelly in those terms he must have found photographs of her, and Gilchrist made another mental note to be more wary of the man.

'What made your brother snap, Gilchrist? Eh? I bet you've been thinking about it, haven't you? High-flying detective all these years and here you are, nothing but a murderer's brother. Makes you think, doesn't it?'

Nance stabbed the ignition key into the switch and gave a hard twist. The engine revved and the car jerked forward.

'No comment?' Tosh said. 'Is that you getting in some practice for the cameras?'

'Give it up, Tosh, will you?' Nance again. 'You're giving me a headache.'

Tosh shifted his gaze from Nance to Gilchrist then, as if seeing in Nance's comments the first glimmer of some other possibility, gave the tiniest nod of understanding. And in that instant, Gilchrist promised, for Nance rather than for himself, that if Tosh even so much as hinted at their past sexual relationship, he would have him.

He stared out the side window as a surge of anger threatened to fire up his muscles. He tightened his grip on his computer case as Nance powered the car down the spiral exit ramp. Kelly's photographs and letters and old Donnie's records were in his case, on his lap. He could hand everything over to Greaves, explain his theory, ask him to carry out a DNA analysis on the stamps. But without Johnnie Walker or Lorena Cordoba, what would that prove? That someone other than Kelly licked the stamps? Weak as water did not even come close. He was clutching at straws, maybe even inventing them. He needed more time to fight his corner. He needed to come up with more evidence, something, anything. Without that, Jack would be proven a killer and Gilchrist would be found guilty of withholding evidence to protect his brother's name, then convicted.

Of that he was certain.

A cold sweat tickled the back of his neck. No matter how he looked at it, he was in serious trouble. He could not let himself be taken to the office in North Street. But seated in the back of a car, with no means of exit other than the front passenger or driver door, what could he do? Even if he did manage to escape, resisting arrest would not profit his case. But what choice did he have? Fight from behind bars? Leave it to his solicitor to—

'Did Jack tell you what it was like to shag an American?' Tosh had turned in his seat and was looking at Gilchrist with grim interest. 'Was that little blonde pussy of hers tattooed with stars and stripes?'

Gilchrist returned Tosh's stare, thought he caught Nance give a supportive glare.

'She was murdered,' Gilchrist snarled. 'Is this how you talk about all murder victims?'

'Oh, she was murdered all right.' Tosh gripped the back of his seat, pulled himself closer to Gilchrist. 'By *your* brother. And you removed vital evidence to protect his name, and in doing so, tried to protect your own. The brother of a murderer? When that little lot comes out, I wouldn't bet tuppence on your career.'

Gilchrist levelled his gaze at Tosh. 'Johnnie Walker,' he said.

Tosh frowned, struggling to find the joke.

'Wee Johnnie Walker,' Gilchrist repeated. 'That's who killed Kelly.'

Tosh shook his head. 'You're as slippery as they come, Gilchrist. I told them you would try to pass it on to someone else.'

'Have you located him? Do you even know where he lives?'

'The only Johnnie Walker I'm interested in is the stuff that comes in a bottle.'

'He went out with Lorena Cordoba,' Gilchrist went on. 'Lorena's from Mexico. Same place the postcard came from.'

'You're making it up as you go along,' Tosh snarled.

'Personal vendettas are not good for business.'

'Maybe so, Gilchrist. But at the end of the day, you're the one going to prison. Not me.'

'All you can prove,' he argued, 'is that Jack once went out with Kelly. Unless you have more than a tooth, you're on a loser.'

'How about a jacket and a cigarette lighter?'

Gilchrist tightened his lips.

'And Jack and Kelly argued a lot,' Tosh said.

A lot? How did Tosh know that? Had he spoken to someone who had known Jack and Kelly all those years ago, someone who would say in court whatever was necessary to support Tosh's charge? All of a sudden Gilchrist was aware of Jack's letter to Kelly in his computer case. If he was taken to North Street and charged, they would go through his personal belongings and find it, clear evidence that Jack and Kelly argued – *a lot*. That's how the procurator fiscal would present the letter in court. The damage would be done, the seed of doubt planted in the minds of the—

'He must have really bopped her one to crush the side of her head like that,' Tosh continued. 'Did he boot her when she was down? I bet he did, the murdering fucker.'

Gilchrist shifted in his seat. 'Jack never hit a woman in his life.'

'Maybe not after Kelly, he didn't.'

Gilchrist forced a laugh. It sounded faked. 'The tooth, the jacket, the lighter. All of it's circumstantial. Nothing direct. Kelly happened to be wearing Jack's jacket, with his tooth and lighter in it. Of course she did. It's what lovers do. Please tell me you have something else with which to go to court, before you waste all that taxpayers' money.'

Tosh shifted in his seat and glared out the window, and Gilchrist caught the corners of Nance's mouth shift in a smile. But his mind was made up now. If circumstantial evidence was all they had, then the last thing he wanted was for them to read Jack's letter to Kelly, the single piece in the jigsaw that could arguably meld the individual parts of the case into a cohesive whole.

Gilchrist realized that he could not be taken to North Street. The more he thought about it, the more conceivable it became that he could be locked up for days, maybe weeks, even longer. He could not let that happen. He would need to find some way to escape, or ditch his computer case. Or the letter? Could he do that? Throw the letter away? He heard the echo of his promise to Annie to return everything when his investigation was over. Well, that was that, then.

Again, thoughts of making a run for it flooded his mind.

At the office in North Street, Nance would drive through the arch and park the car in the back. From there, he had one chance before he was taken into custody: the boundary wall. It was six feet high. If he was quick enough, if he took them by surprise, he could pull himself up and over and into someone's back garden. Risky, for sure. They could follow his progress on CCTV until he got out of St Andrews. As his mind struggled to calculate the risks, he came to see that fleeing was the beginning of the end of his career. And so, too, would being found guilty of attempting to pervert the course of justice.

In the centre of Cupar, the traffic thickened. Nance eased forward in stops and starts.

'It's always the fucking same, this place,' Tosh grumbled.

'Jam-packed solid. I've never understood why.' He tapped his jacket's side pockets, then twisted in his seat as his hands worked into his trousers. He tutted, then said, 'Stop at the first newsagent's. I'm out of cigarettes.'

'Can't you wait?'

'What's your bloody problem? You'd think the car was yours.'

Nance shook her head, gripped the wheel.

Fifty yards on, Tosh pointed. 'There,' he said. 'Pull in over there.'

'In the middle of the road?'

'Just double-park the fucker. I'll only be a minute.'

Gilchrist felt his senses come alive. He had not expected any stops en route. Could this be a chance, perhaps his only one? He tightened his grip on his computer case.

Tosh had his seatbelt off and the door open before Nance drew to a halt, and jumped out and slammed the door with a grunt.

Gilchrist watched him cross the street and step into the newsagent's, heart thudding at the possibility presented to him. If he made a run for it now, there could be no turning back. Resisting arrest was a jailable offence. He would need to find proof of his innocence before he could turn himself in. All of a sudden, the magnitude of what he was about to do reared over him like some physical presence that kept him rooted to his seat.

In front of him, Nance eyed the traffic as if conscious of being double-parked.

Gilchrist looked at the newsagent's. How long had Tosh been gone?

Or more to the point, how long until he returned?

Then it would be too late.

He had to do it. And do it now.

He depressed the lever on the passenger seat, pushed forward and opened the door in one fluid movement. 'Give me five minutes,' he said, and was out of the car before Nance could react. 'Andy. Don't—'

He ran, clutching his computer case to his side. He glanced back to see if Nance would chase him. But he had known from her eyes that her heart had not been in it, and the car remained stationary with its hazard lights blinking, Nance at the opened door, staring after him, her mobile already to her ear. And as he ran, he tried to work out how much distance he would have to put between him and Tosh to be safe.

He remembered Tosh being a sprinter, his shorter legs and thicker muscles powering him faster than Gilchrist could ever run. Long legs and slender build made distance running more Gilchrist's style.

He glimpsed over his shoulder, caught Tosh crossing the street, stripping a cigarette packet, then the hesitation and a hand thumped on the car's roof, followed by a quick look left, then right, until their eyes locked.

Tosh vaulted over the bonnet of a parked car with an agility that had Gilchrist cursing under his breath. He forced himself to concentrate on just running. Tosh might be a sprinter, but like all sprinters he could not keep it up for long before his muscles burned out. How long would it take? Already Gilchrist's lungs were burning, and the computer case seemed to be gaining weight with every step.

He turned into a side street, relieved to recognize familiar territory. Two years ago he had been called to a domestic dispute in a house at the end of the row, and had chased the husband across the back gardens, along a little-used communal path.

He raced into the path. But his memory had tricked him.

Ten yards in, the path dead-ended at a brick wall.

He doubled back, veered down another length, cursing at having lost valuable seconds in his race with Tosh, and almost crashed into a higher-than-remembered hedge. With no way to go except forward, he lugged his computer case up and over.

He forced himself through the hedge, caught a glimpse of Tosh skidding into the pathway. Their eyes locked for an instant, then Tosh tucked his head forward and powered towards him in a determined sprint that would have him on Gilchrist in seconds, it seemed.

Gilchrist pulled himself free and hurtled along the communal path. But he knew it was no use. He could not outrun Tosh, and his lungs were not working the way they should. He coughed up phlegm blackened from Betson's fire. His breath rushed in hard rasps that burned his throat. Tosh would catch him and he would have to give himself up. What else could he do? Assault an officer of the law while resisting arrest?

The communal path rounded a gable end then split into two, one branch leading back to the main road, the other deeper into the back gardens, the hedgerows taller, the bushes thicker. From behind, he heard Tosh fight his way through the overgrown hedge.

Gilchrist saw his chance.

He turned into the longer of the two paths, ducked out of sight, pushed his computer case through the bottom of the hedgerow into a grassed area and shuffled in after it. He only just managed to pull his legs in when Tosh came bursting past, crashing into the hedge where the path split.

'Fuck,' he gasped.

Tosh's legs were no more than two feet from Gilchrist's face. He watched them turn in one direction, then the other, and from the rushed breathing knew that Tosh was hard-pressed to keep going. His own breath was coming at him hard and fast, and a spasm gripped his body as his lungs convulsed to cough up more phlegm. He clenched his jaw, closed his eyes, forced his body to ignore the overpowering need to cough, then felt all hope leave him as he heard the beeping of numbers being tapped into a mobile phone.

Who was Tosh calling?

Gilchrist could not power down his mobile. Not now. The slightest movement would attract Tosh's peripheral vision. If Tosh was calling his number, then it really was all over.

At that moment, Tosh chose the deeper path and ran off.

Gilchrist tugged out his mobile, powered it down and coughed up phlegm. He waited until the spasm ceased and he could no longer hear footsteps before pulling himself and his computer case from the bottom of the hedgerow.

He ran back the way he had come.

He had just cleared the hedge, stepped back into the street, when he came face to face with Nance. She stood no more than ten feet away, barely breathing, arms by her side. He might be able to outrun Tosh, but he could never tire Nance.

'Johnnie Walker,' he said. 'He went out with Lorena Cordoba, murdered Kelly and sent the postcard from Mexico. You need to find him.'

'Too late.' She shook her head. 'Stan's just found out he committed suicide sixteen years ago.'

Nance's words fired through Gilchrist's mind with the power of a lightning strike. Without Wee Johnnie, could he prove his case? With all the evidence, circumstantial or not, the procurator fiscal would have no trouble laying Kelly's murder at Jack's feet with a damning case. Any competent lawyer could. And as for his own dilemma? He could now see no other way out of it except through a custodial sentence.

He stood there, helpless, waiting for Nance to pull out her handcuffs.

'I need more time,' he tried.

'To do what, Andy? Think about what you're asking me to do.'

'Jack's innocent.' He held her dark eyes, prayed she knew him well enough to know he had to be telling the truth, that his brother was no murderer.

She glanced along the communal path. 'Oh, fuck it,' she said. 'Just go.'

Gilchrist turned and ran.

His knowledge of the backstreets of Cupar was nowhere near as good as he thought it was and he had to backtrack twice. Once, when he had to cross the main street, he saw Tosh about a hundred yards away, giving instructions to two motorcycle policemen, arm stabbing and waving in the air. Even from that distance, Gilchrist could sense the man's anger.

He slipped down a narrow lane and continued jogging.

By the time he worked his way to his destination, a tidy bungalow in a quiet neighbourhood, police sirens called from the distance like waning birdsong.

He rang the doorbell and prayed she was in.

CHAPTER 27

The door opened to reveal a slimmer version of the Megs he had last seen twenty years earlier. Her eyes widened with surprise. 'Well,' she said, stepping back to invite him in, 'it's been a while.'

Gilchrist pushed past her into a narrow hallway.

'Kitchen's straight ahead.'

Gilchrist opened a pine door and entered a room brightened by a conservatory that overlooked a rock garden, the soil turned over for the winter. The sweet smell of pineapple had him searching for fruit going off, and he found a glass bowl on the work surface by the sink filled with chopped pineapple, grapefruit, oranges. A half-skinned mango lay on a chopping board, ready to be added.

'Tea?' Megs asked. 'Or something stronger? You look buggered. What've you been up to?' She pulled out a chair. 'Here. You'd better sit before you fall down.'

Gilchrist slid his computer case to the floor. 'Tea's fine.'

'You sure you're all right?'

'Just flew in from the States.'

'Well that explains it. Jet lag's pure murder, so it is. I swear it's a disease. Milk and sugar?'

'Milk. No sugar.'

'Would you like a biscuit?' She removed a tin from a glass-fronted cupboard, tipped an assortment of biscuits on to a plate. 'Tell you what,' Megs went on, 'you look like you could be doing with a bit of filling up. If you were a woman, I'd hate you. All skin and bone. Not like me. Look at this.' She lifted her skirt, farther than he thought decent. 'Farmer's legs are what I have. Fat thighs.' She slapped her right one. It barely wobbled. 'Some men like them. Not me. I hate them.' She lowered her skirt and eyed Gilchrist, as if waiting for comment.

'You look as if you've lost some weight,' he offered.

She laughed, and Gilchrist regretted having spoken. 'You still haven't lost that charm of yours, Andy. And the grey sideburns suit you.' She plonked a mug on the table, pulled out a chair and sat next to him. Her closeness caused him to pick up his computer case and set it down on his lap. He opened it and removed a photograph.

'I'd like to show you something,' he said.

Megs pulled closer, leaned forward to examine the photograph.

Gilchrist was conscious of cleavage swelling by his side, her skirt slipping high on white thighs. 'Do you recognize him?'

Megs nodded. 'That's Wee Johnnie,' she said, 'with his dago bimbo.'

'You said you had another photograph. Were you able to find it?' He bit into a biscuit, followed it with a sip of tea.

Megs seemed to shift closer still. Her hand landed on his thigh.

'I'm in the middle of a murder investigation,' he said, taking her hand and placing it on the table. 'I really need to see that photograph.'

She pulled her head back and laughed, but it sounded forced. 'You always were the quiet one,' she said. 'Do you know what women used to say about you?'

'Megs? Please? The photograph?'

She pushed herself to her feet, the sound of chair legs on tiles announcing her change in attitude. 'You know what I remember most about you, Andy? You had all these women just gagging for it, and you never seemed to notice.'

Gilchrist raised an eyebrow. 'The photograph, Megs?'

'Right,' she said, with some finality in her voice. 'Follow me.'

In the lounge, Megs kneeled on the floor, opened a cupboard door and removed a pile of photo albums. 'This could take a while,' she said, and dug deeper. By the time she stood, Gilchrist counted twenty-four albums around her feet, some small and tight as a wallet, some large and padded as a cushion.

'Can I help?' he offered.

'You could help by bringing me my tea.'

Gilchrist obliged, carrying both mugs and the plate of biscuits. By the time he brought them through to the lounge, the coffee table was covered with albums.

'Give me my cup,' Megs ordered, 'and put the biscuits over there.'

Gilchrist did as he was told, and placed the plate on top of a cabinet next to a bookshelf that seemed stuffed with paperbacks two deep. 'You read a lot,' he said.

'Like crazy. It keeps me sane. Got another bookshelf in the dining room and two in the bedroom, all filled with books. I never lend them out or throw any away. I've kept every book I've ever bought, been given, or stolen. And do you know what's funny?' she said. 'I never go the library. I only read books I buy, or are given to me. Which of course makes Maggie's Christmas and birthday shopping easier.'

'Maggie?'

'My daughter. Well, Dougie's and mine. Before I threw him out.'

Gilchrist realized it must have been Maggie who answered his call from the States.

'Where's Maggie now?' he asked, and from Megs' smile regretted asking.

'Staying over at a friend's. So we have the place to ourselves.'

He looked at the scattered piles of albums, realized it would take Megs hours to go through them all and said, 'Maybe you should look at some other photographs first.'

'Who's in them?'

'Kelly.'

'Oh, that.'

Yes, that. Gilchrist retrieved his computer case from the kitchen and spilled Kelly's photographs on to the carpet. He watched for any reaction as he passed them to her one at a time. But she showed remarkable disinterest. Only when she lifted one in which she was caught in the background did she pull it closer.

'I don't remember that being taken.'

One of Geoffrey Pennycuick intrigued her, too.

'He was such a randy sod. Screwed his way to a degree, so the story goes. I wasn't his type. Must have been the only one.'

But the photograph of Kelly and Rita stopped her.

'What is it?' he asked.

'The scarf,' she said. 'I used to have one just like it.'

305

Gilchrist retrieved the photograph, then eased out his question. 'Can you remember where you bought it?'

'I didn't. It was a gift. A birthday present.'

'Who from?'

'Who knows? Probably Dougie.'

Silent, Gilchrist stared at her. From Rita to Kelly to Johnnie to Dougie to Megs? Or had Dougie bought it brand new? 'Where did Dougie buy it?' he tried.

'I didn't say he did.'

'No,' said Gilchrist. 'Wee Johnnie, then?'

'I wouldn't know.'

'Thrift shop?'

'Could've done.'

Gilchrist stared at the scarf. As a student with not much money, thrift shops could be a cheap way to keep in fashion. Or had Johnnie passed it to Dougie after murdering Kelly? Why keep it at all? Why not simply dump it? As Gilchrist stared at the scarf around Kelly's neck, he felt as if he was standing at the brink of some chasm over which he had to cross to find the answers. The same scarf? Could there be more than just a scarf? Or was he searching for the improbable?

He pushed to his feet, walked to the bookshelf, fingered a couple of books. 'Who's your favourite author?' he asked.

'Don't really have one.'

The books seemed to be sorted in alphabetical order, which in itself was some kind of feat. This bookshelf started at the letter H, and the thought persisted. 'Do you mind if I look through some of your other books?' he asked.

'Help yourself.'

'Where did you say the other bookshelves were?'

'There's one in the dining room.'

Gilchrist found it, a tall oak shelf stacked from top to bottom. He scanned the books a row at a time, and came to see that although they were intended to be sorted alphabetically, several broke the system. He found Jackie Collins beside a long row of paperbacks by John Grisham, and two by Debbie Macomber next to Faye Kellerman. He removed several from the front row to check those in the back, then restacked them the way he found them.

The dining room had another door that led to the kitchen. Gilchrist opened it, crossed the kitchen and entered the hallway. He listened for movement in the lounge, heard none, and tried the first door on his left.

It looked like a spare bedroom, the bed made up and curtains open, with a dusty smell that told him no one had slept in it for months. He closed the door, tried the next one.

Posters of boy bands littered walls painted deep pink and light purple. More posters clouded a dark-blue ceiling, and wardrobe doors sported full-size images of young men he had never seen before. Rows of dolls crowded a lower shelf like some memorial to a lost childhood. CDs lay scattered over every surface.

He eased the bedroom door shut.

Only one door left. He opened it and stepped inside.

The room lay in twilight from half-drawn window blinds. A queen-sized bed faced a TV cabinet. Two shoulder-high darkwood bookshelves backed against the wall either side of the window. Gilchrist crossed the deep-pile carpet, regretting that he had not taken his shoes off.

In the dim light he could just make out the book titles and

author names on the spines. He found what he was looking for, surprised to come across two of the same book. He pulled one out by the spine, eased open the cover flap to a blank page, then returned it. He did the same with the other, taking care to hold it by the edges, and grunted with surprise when he saw the tribute. He was too deep in thought to hear the door open.

'Find one you like?'

Megs filled the doorway. From where he stood, and in the room's half-light, he could not tell if her smile was one of annoyance, or something more troubling.

'Sorry,' he said. 'I was looking through them.'

'And here was me thinking you didn't want to see my bedroom.' She closed the door behind her, pressed her back to it, one hand by the neck of her blouse, the other running over her thigh. 'Your move, Andy.'

Gilchrist walked towards her. 'Megs,' he said, 'I need to ask you—'

'Yes?'

He reached the end of the bed, held the book by its spine, almost balancing it on his hand. 'I need to ask you where you got this.'

She frowned, disappointment etched on her lips. 'What are you talking about?' She held out her hand. 'Let me see.'

Gilchrist turned it so she could read the title. '*Pride and Prejudice*, by Jane Austen.'

'I've had it for years.'

'You have indeed,' he said. 'But that's not what I asked.'

'Why?'

'Just answer the question, please, Megs. Where did you get this book?'

'How would I know?'

'Try another answer.'

'What answer would you like me to give you?'

'The truth.'

Megs laughed, a sharp cackle that sounded eerie in the darkened room.

Gilchrist pulled the book to him. 'You have two copies of
Pride and Prejudice, but only one of others by Jane Austen. Why
is that?'

Megs shrugged. 'Sometimes I buy books I've forgotten I've
read.'

Maybe Gilchrist was mistaken. 'One copy looks new,' he said.
'The other is second-hand. This one.'

Megs glared at him. 'What's this about, Andy?'

'You said all your books were bought, gifted, or stolen.' He
glanced at the cover. 'Which was this?'

'If it's second-hand, it would have been given to me. If it isn't
new, I didn't buy it.'

He nodded. 'So it was given to you,' he said. 'From who?'

'I can't remember.' She reached out. 'Let me see.'

Gilchrist pulled it back. He would be interested in seeing whose
fingerprints they could lift. On the other hand, the absence of
fingerprints might confirm who had not touched it. He opened the
front cover and read out the penned tribute.

'Happy Birthday. Lots of love, Brian.'

She looked at him. 'Who's Brian?'

'I thought you might tell me.'

'How would I know? It was given to me second-hand.'

'But who by?'

'What d'you think I've got? A photographic memory? I can

barely remember what day of the week it is, and you're asking who gave me a book I haven't read in years?'

'How many years?' He did not want to prompt her by putting words in her mouth. He needed to hear the name from her own lips without hint or coercion. 'I'm asking you to think,' he tried. 'What was going on in your life when you read this?'

Megs frowned, as if giving his question some thought. 'I can't remember.'

'Try when you were at university.' Not a direct hint, but as close as he wanted to go.

Something seemed to spark behind her eyes. 'It's Wee Johnnie, isn't it? That's why you want me to show you a photograph.'

Gilchrist would have preferred direct recall rather than deductive reasoning, and felt saddened that it had come down to this. 'Think,' was all he said.

'It might have been Johnnie,' she said. 'He sometimes gave me stuff. Mostly drink, so he could get me drunk and screw me. That's all he really ever wanted to do, drink and screw. And he was no good at either.'

Not quite the recollection Gilchrist had hoped for, but it opened up other possibilities in his thinking. Was it possible Megs had taken the book herself? Could she be involved in Kelly's murder more directly? Kelly had been fit and strong, but she would have been no match for Megs in terms of muscled bulk.

'Maybe you picked it up at a party some night and didn't return it.'

'What d'you mean? That I stole it at a party? Whose party?'

Megs was either telling the truth, or was a decent liar. 'Rita's?' he offered.

Something seemed to settle into Megs' mind at the mention of

Rita's name. She stared at the tribute, at the cover, back to the tribute, then glared at him. 'That cheapskate bastard.'

'Who?' Gilchrist asked.

For an instant, she seemed lost. 'Wee Johnnie,' she blurted.

But in that moment's delay, Gilchrist thought he caught her lie.

CHAPTER 28

Megs found the photograph she was looking for.

Wee Johnnie Walker, not quite so *wee* in this image, with an arm as tight as steel around Megs, one hand firm on her biceps, the other holding a bottle of San Miguel. Ripped muscles striped his stomach, pecs cut square like a boxer's. Megs looked bloated and white beside him. They could have been any Scottish student couple, happy in each other's drunken company, except that the location did not fit. Palm trees lined the street. Off to the side, the lazy waters of some sea lay as smooth as glass.

'Loret de Mar,' she said. 'Costa del Beer. Thought I was going out for a week's romancing in the sun. All Johnnie wanted to do was drink.' She glared at the photograph. 'That was us after breakfast. When I look at this now, I don't know what he saw in me. Laurel and Hardy were a better-looking couple.' She let out a laugh like a cough. 'I think he was just racking up his score.'

Why take you to the Mediterranean? Gilchrist wanted to ask. Wee Johnnie looked as if he was nursing a hangover. Beer for breakfast. Hair of the dog? His body was tight, trim. Sinewed muscles seemed to invade his face, making him look hard and unforgiving. Wisps of a chin-only beard added to the Mexican bandito look. Was that what had attracted Lorena? Megs, on the other hand, looked more like baby-fat grown old. Laurel and Hardy might be considered a compliment.

'Just you and Johnnie?' he asked.

'Dougie and Brian came, too.'

Brian? Of Brian and Rita? He thought it odd that Megs had not remembered Brian moments earlier. But she seemed not to have noticed. 'Was Rita there?' he asked.

'No, just Dougie and Brian. The three of them went everywhere together. Worse than musketeers.'

'So you were the only woman?'

'Not for long. A pair of pick-up artists, they were, Johnnie and Brian.'

'But not Dougie?'

She gave a hard cough again. 'Johnnie and Brian were as cocky as they come, but Dougie just hung around.'

'So Johnnie and Brian picked up some Spanish women and—'

'English,' Megs grumbled. 'From London or somewhere.'

'So Johnnie just . . . ?'

'Pissed off and left me.'

'Left you with Dougie?'

She smiled, and something touching warmed her eyes. 'That's when Dougie and I first started going out. Romantic, don't you think?'

Well, that might explain Johnnie's invitation to Megs to go to Spain. Three friends studying the same course at university, one of them hopeless with women, too awkward or shy to ask her out directly, and all by himself. But on holiday, with plenty of drink, it

313

would be easier to establish a relationship, even take over when one ended. Particularly if that had been the plan all along. It might be considered a convoluted way to start a romance, but he had heard of stranger beginnings.

'You and Dougie didn't marry for years.'

'Off again, on again. I liked to go on foreign holidays, see a bit of the world. Dougie didn't. I could have lived in South America. Definitely my favourite. But Dougie was so undecided about everything. In the end, I had to take the bull by the horns, or in Dougie's case the boy by the balls, and make up his mind for him.'

'And the divorce?'

'I made up his mind on that, too.' She shook her head. 'How he got to where he is defies logic. But I wish him no harm.'

Gilchrist held up the photograph. 'Do you mind if I keep this?'

'You can have it, for all I care. Don't know why I can't throw stuff out. Worse than a magpie, so I am.'

'Do you have a plastic bag?' he asked.

She gave him a Ziploc bag from the kitchen, into which he slipped the book. Her Mediterranean photograph of Johnnie he placed with Kelly's.

'Did the three musketeers ever go on holiday anywhere else?' he asked her.

'Once or twice, I suppose. But they all ended up going their separate ways. Why?'

'Did they ever go to Mexico?'

Megs frowned. 'I think so, but don't quote me.' Then her eyes lit up as some long-forgotten memory returned. 'They did,' she said. 'I remember it now. They had just come back. It was not long after

I moved into the flat with Rita and that Mexican brat. We all went over to the boys' place one night.'

'All of you?'

'Me, Rita and Miss Mexico.'

Gilchrist gave that some thought. Brian and Rita. Johnnie and Lorena? Which left Dougie and Megs. 'Was this before or after the trip to Loret?'

'Before,' she said, a bit too quickly. 'I had just moved in.'

Lorena would still have been seeing Johnnie. 'What was so memorable?' he asked.

'We got drunk on tequila. That's what happened. The real McCoy. Duty-free in Mexico City Airport, I think. I remember it because Johnnie ate the slug. I never knew tequila had slugs. Why do they do that, anyway? I thought it was some sort of joke.'

That would be Wee Johnnie's style, Gilchrist thought. Macho man. But was he a killer? 'And what about Dougie? He was free. You were free. Did you, eh, get together?'

'Nope. Just got drunk.'

The thought of Megs being in the presence of a man and turning down the opportunity for sex seemed out of character. Perhaps Dougie had been too shy for someone as bold as Megs. 'So, when did you and Johnnie start going out?'

'I wouldn't call it *going out.*'

'What would you call it, then?'

'Sex on tap.'

'And Lorena? Did she just sit back and let Johnnie walk away?'

'She was looking to leave him. She fancied Dougie.'

'Your Dougie?'

'Not any more.'

'And did she go out with Dougie?'

315

'Dougie fell head over heels for the tramp.'

Now Gilchrist thought he understood. Hell hath no fury like a woman scorned, or a woman whose man was having sex with the local Mexican. After all these years, Megs still held a grudge. The atmosphere in the flat must have been like touchpaper looking for a light.

'So the Mediterranean beer outing was the end of Lorena's relationship with Dougie and the start of yours?'

Megs grimaced. 'A beer outing it was, that's for sure. But yes, Dougie and I, how should I say it, consummated our relationship during that short week.'

Gilchrist thought he saw Lorena's dilemma. First, her Johnnie was lost to Megs, then her Dougie. So how did that explain Megs' hatred? Should it not have been the other way around? 'You and Dougie didn't last long, did you?'

'Not that time.'

'Lorena persuaded Dougie to stay with her?'

Megs frowned, and a hint of anger flitted behind her eyes. 'What is it about men?' she grumbled. 'Spread your legs and they're like putty in your hands. Drooling all over you until they get what they want. If it wasn't so pathetic it'd be funny.'

'So, it's safe to say that you and Dougie split up not long after Costa del Beer?'

'Very safe.'

'For how long?'

She shrugged. 'Can't really remember. Months, I suppose.'

'When did he give you the scarf?'

'My birthday,' she said, without missing a beat.

'Which was . . . ?'

'Beginning of March.'

'Before you moved into the flat on College Street?'

'Just after.'

He thought it amazing how memories could improve. 'And *Pride and Prejudice?*'

'The same, I think.'

Gilchrist tried to work through the logic. Johnnie, Brian and now Dougie. Each one of them might have had some personal reason to kill Kelly, but what that reason was he could not say for certain. Jealousy? Rejection? Rape? But if he pushed his thoughts beyond the actual murder itself, and fast-forwarded to the disposal of the body, he found he could think of only one name.

He needed help. But with Tosh on the rampage, he would have to call in for it.

He powered up his mobile and noticed he had three messages, the first over an hour ago. He listened to Tosh's breathless voice tell him, 'I'm going to have you for this, Gilchrist. You're in deep fucking shite now.'

Gilchrist worked out the time, figured that must have been Tosh on the run, the call made as he was chasing him along the communal path. The second was from Tosh again, this time in control of his breathing.

'I know you're going to listen to these messages some time, Gilchrist, and when you do, I want you to know that I now have a warrant for your arrest. So my advice to you, old son, is to do the right thing and turn yourself in.'

The third was Tosh again. Did he have nothing better to do than leave voicemail?

'Got some good news I thought I should share with you. You're going to be on the telly tonight, Gilchrist. The evening news.' Then a voice close to the speaker. 'You really are fucked this time.'

Gilchrist deleted Tosh's messages and powered down his phone.

'Got some problem with my mobile,' he lied. 'Do you mind if I use your phone?'

'If you want some privacy, use the one in the bedroom. And I'll not come in.' She waved him off with a flap of her hand. 'Go on with you. I'm only joking.'

In the bedroom, Gilchrist closed the door. He dialled 141 to shield Megs' number from caller ID, then got through on the first ring.

'Stan. It's me. Don't hang up.'

'Boss?' A pause, then a breathy rush. 'For crying out loud, boss, what's got into you? This is serious. Even McVicar's calling for your blood. And as for that prick, Tosh, he's prancing about like he's been awarded a knighthood.'

'Nance told me Johnnie Walker committed suicide. How did he die?'

'Drugs overdose.'

Somehow, from the images he had seen of Walker, that did not surprise him. 'I need you to do something else for me, Stan.'

'No chance. I can't do it, boss. This is all the way to the top. I can't afford to lose my job over this—'

'I need you to find Lorena Cordoba for me, Stan. She flew to Mexico that Christmas. I need you to find out who was on the flight with her.'

'I'm sorry, boss.' The line went dead.

Shit. This was worse than serious. Stan was his fallback, someone he could rely on when everything was against him. He dialled

Nance on her mobile. Busy. He tried again. Still busy. On the third attempt, she picked up.

'Stan told me you'd call,' she said. 'You've really done it this time, Andy. I don't know what else to tell you. All the big guns are out. Rumour has it McVicar is going to make a personal appeal to you on the evening news.'

Assistant Chief Constable Archie McVicar. For McVicar to take this unprecedented step, Tosh must have been able to pull some mighty big strings. 'What's Tosh telling everyone?'

'That you hit him.'

'I didn't lay a finger on—'

'He's got cuts on his face to prove it.'

From fighting his way through hedges, he thought. But Tosh would gut him to the hilt, do as much damage to Gilchrist's reputation as he could. Assaulting an officer of the law was a serious offence. And with the charges piling up, Gilchrist had no doubt which of the two of them, Tosh or himself, the jurors would believe. Jesus, he really was in—

'Besides,' Nance went on, 'he's threatening to pull me into it.'

'How can he do that?'

'Someone saw us.'

Gilchrist raked his hands through his hair. 'I'm sorry, Nance.'

'Don't be, Andy. Just turn yourself in.'

The call ended.

Gilchrist felt the strength in his legs leave him. He sat on the bed, the phone still pressed to his ear. Christ, without Stan or Nance kicking the ball for him, he really was on his own. He thought of phoning Greaves, but knew Greaves would not risk his career for such a maverick detective, and he came to see that he really had only the one choice.

The phone was picked up on the third ring. 'McVicar speaking.'

'This is DCI Andrew Gilchrist, sir. I need to—'

'Good Lord, Andy. Where on earth are you?'

He could not tell McVicar that he knew about his imminent appeal on the news. That would point the finger to others. Instead, he said, 'I intend to turn myself in, sir.'

'That's a wise move, Andy. Tell me where you are, and I'll have someone pick you up. I'll do what I can for you, but I'm going to have to play this by the book. You understand?'

'I do, sir.'

'I have to ask you, Andy.'

'Sir?'

'Is there any truth to these allegations?'

'None whatsoever, sir.' Not strictly correct. He still had the lighter.

McVicar seemed to give thought to Gilchrist's words. 'I have to tell you that you've got yourself into one hell of a mess in this one, Andy. You do understand that, I'm sure. So I'm going to insist on Dugard representing you. He's one of the best—'

'Sir, I'm not turning myself in right away.'

'You're not? Good Lord,' McVicar's voice boomed. 'The media have already got hold of this. God knows how they get on to things so quickly.'

'Tosh, sir?'

'Pardon?'

'Tosh told them.'

'Can you prove it?'

'Probably not.'

Silence, while McVicar digested his words. 'That's too bad.

320

There's something about that man that worries me. But regrettably we can't go bending the rules where our own staff are concerned. We can't be seen to be above the law. Do you understand what I'm saying, Andy?'

'I do indeed, sir, but I do intend to turn myself in this evening.'

'When and where?'

'The *where* is the office in North Street. The *when* I'm not so sure about.'

'You'll need to do better than that, I'm afraid.'

'I can't, sir. All I can tell you is that I *will* turn myself in.'

'I can give you until six o'clock, Andy. After that, you're on your own.'

Six o'clock meant that McVicar was intent on putting out an appeal on the evening news if Gilchrist was a no-show. Six was too early. 'I'm going to have to ask you to trust me, sir.'

'What do you think I'm doing, Andy? A warrant has been issued for your arrest. After six, I'm afraid I can't help. Think about it, Andy. Will you do that?'

With that, McVicar hung up.

Gilchrist replaced the phone. McVicar's tone warned him that this case had climbed to the topmost branches, probably to the Superintendent. Could he blame them? Tosh would have presented a compelling case – Jack's tooth, his DNA, a secret witness to confirm he and Kelly argued *a lot*, Jack's fight outside the Keys with Branscombe. Even Jack's letter to Kelly could be used against him. How would it look to the public if one of Fife's finest was found guilty of removing evidence that could convict his brother for murdering his girlfriend over thirty years ago? It would be seen as a cover-up. How could the public ever trust the Force again? Heads would roll. McVicar's, Greaves', maybe even Superintendent Blanefield's. Nothing would ever be the same. And all the while, praise and glory would be piling on to Tosh's head.

But Gilchrist also knew that as all the stops were out on this one, his calls to Stan and Nance's mobile phones would be in the process of being tracked. He figured he had about ten minutes, probably less, before Megs' house would be overrun with police officers, cars, dogs and anything else Tosh could throw his way.

He found Megs in the kitchen.

'What's got you in such a tizzy?' she asked.

'Do you have a car?'

'If you can call it that.'

He grabbed her by the arm. 'I need you to do me a favour.'

'Steady on, Andy,' she said, tugging her arm free. She looked at him as if seeing him for the first time.

'Get the car keys,' he said. 'I'll explain on the way.'

Gilchrist stuffed everything into his computer case and lugged it over his shoulder. He followed Megs out the back door, along a slabbed path to a single garage that sat back from the house and could not be seen from the road. Megs seemed to take for ever to unlock it. By the time he swung the door up and over to reveal an old Vauxhall surrounded by a household's worth of bric-a-brac, he caught the sounds of police sirens in the distance.

He threw his computer case into the back seat. 'You drive,' he ordered.

'If it starts.'

'When did you last have it out?'

'Couple of months ago.'

Gilchrist wondered if he should just skip over the neighbour's hedge and make a run for it. 'Megs?' he urged.

She glared at him as she opened the door. Then her look softened as she focused on something in the distance. 'Those sirens,' she said. 'They're after you, aren't they?'

'It's a long story, Megs. Please?'

'Right.' She bundled herself on to the driver's seat. 'Fingers crossed.'

Gilchrist groaned as the engine clicked. Nothing. The battery was as flat as—

Another click, followed by the empty rattling of an engine running on no fuel.

Not flat battery. Faulty starter motor.

Another click, but this time the starter motor engaged and the engine burst into life. It held for a moment, threatened to stall, then gave a healthy snarl. A blast of grey exhaust erupted from the car, causing Gilchrist to cover his mouth.

Megs backed out of the garage and swung the car around, tyres crunching the gravel.

The sound of approaching police sirens told him they were almost upon them.

He slammed the garage door shut and jumped in beside Megs.

The Vauxhall seemed to hobble down the driveway.

'Doesn't it go any faster?'

'It takes some time to get going.'

Shit. Time was not something he had.

The Vauxhall bounced on to the road with a lunge that convinced Gilchrist its suspension was shot. Ahead, a police car careened into the housing estate, lights flashing, sirens howling. Gilchrist flipped a lever at the side of his seat and pushed back. The seat folded flat with a jerk that made him grunt in surprise. But at least he was out of sight.

He almost felt the rush of air as the police car tore past them.

He pulled himself up and watched out of the rear window, worried that the trail of exhaust would lead them to Megs' house. But the police car passed it and slid to a broadside stop as the driver made a mess of a U-turn. Smoke poured from its wheels as it backed up, then again as it leaped forward and screeched to a stop in front of Megs' driveway.

Tosh was first from the car. Three constables spilled out after him, bodies thickened with body armour, carrying tasers and what looked like baton guns. What the hell had Tosh told them? At the entrance to the driveway, Tosh gave directions with one hand, mobile pressed to his ear with the other.

The scene vanished from sight as they rounded a corner that brought them to a junction.

'Which way, Superman?'

'Right.'

Megs obliged, powering the Vauxhall forward into a sweeping turn.

Two motorcycle policemen passed them before Gilchrist had time to duck. But with the siege action up ahead, they did not so much as glance at Megs' Vauxhall.

Gilchrist pulled his seat upright, felt himself breathe a little easier as the seconds ticked by. How long would it take Tosh to realize no one was home and he could kick down the door? One second? Two? Something seemed to have snapped in him. He had heard it in the phone messages, seen it in the angry flush of his face as he led the assault on Megs' house. An image of a cowering prostitute on a rain-soaked street flashed into his mind, and he felt a surge of regret at not having followed up to the hilt all those years ago.

They reached another junction, and Gilchrist gave directions. He glanced at Megs, saw she had paled. 'Are you all right?' he asked.

'It's about Kelly, isn't it?' she said, and looked at him.

'Eyes on the road, please.'

'I never thought that of you, Andy, that you would harm a woman.'

Gilchrist understood her dilemma. In her eyes she was helping a murderer escape the law. What else was she supposed to think?

'When they question you,' he said, 'just tell them that I asked you to give me a lift, and that you had no idea I was on the run.'

'You killed her, didn't you?'

'No, Megs. I didn't kill her. But they've found evidence that links Jack to her.'

'So why are you on the run?'

Gilchrist smiled at the logic of that question. 'It's personal,' he said. 'Someone doesn't like me and is out to get me.'

'Why?'

She's a fucking hoor, is what she is.

Gilchrist shrugged. 'Who knows,' he said.

They drove on in relative silence, Gilchrist giving directions, Megs obeying without a word. They turned into Cupar's main thoroughfare, and Gilchrist directed her through the backstreets. Five minutes later, they pulled into a small office complex and parked at Gilchrist's instruction.

'Thanks for the lift,' he said to her.

325

'I'm not stupid, you know.'

'I didn't say you were.'

'There's only one reason you're here,' she said, and nodded to the square building.

'I'm only going to ask some questions,' Gilchrist said.

He slipped from her car and walked towards the surgery.

CHAPTER 29

The waiting room murmured with the subdued stirrings of a seated group.

Someone coughed. Behind Gilchrist, a door clicked shut. He was instructed to take a seat and told he would have to wait at least forty minutes. Dr Ewart had appointments through to midday. Gilchrist did as ordered, but kept his eyes on a board that displayed four names, each with a small light beside them. All glowed red.

He did not have long to wait until the light next to Dr Ewart's name turned to green. He marched down a short hall to Ewart's office, gave a hard rap and entered.

Ewart looked up from his desk, down at his files, then gave a twisted smile. 'You don't look like Mrs Forrester.'

A small voice from behind Gilchrist said, 'I'm sorry, Doctor. I couldn't stop him.'

'That's all right, Annette. Inspector Gilchrist won't be staying long. Will you?'

'I shouldn't think so,' Gilchrist agreed. He waited until the door closed behind him, then pressed his back against it. They would not be disturbed so readily next time. 'I have a bit of a problem,'

Gilchrist began. 'It seems that the case I'm working on has turned a bit too personal.'

'I don't understand.'

'I'd like to ask you a few questions.'

'Sit down, sit down. Take a seat.'

'I'd rather stand.'

'Well in that case, I'll join you.' Ewart pushed his chair back and walked around his desk. He was a good three inches shorter than Gilchrist, but seemed to prefer that to being seated. Gilchrist thought the polished, dark-brown brogues and tartan trousers with inch-high turn-ups were a bit over the top, even for a Highland doctor. But Ewart had never been renowned for his sartorial wisdom.

'How long did you go out with Lorena?' Gilchrist asked him.

Ewart frowned. 'Who?'

'Lorena Cordoba. And don't even think about denying you know her, Dougie. I've got photographs.'

'Photographs?' Ewart paused as if some thought had just struck him. 'Lorena,' he said with some emphasis. 'Cordoba? From way back when? That Lorena?'

'Were there any other Lorenas?'

'I didn't go out with her at all, as best I can recall.'

'Not even for a few days?'

Ewart pressed his lips together, shook his head.

'Not go on holiday with her?'

'No.'

That was the first lie, Gilchrist thought. 'Ever been to Spain?' he asked.

'Once,' he said, too quickly, as if Gilchrist was asking questions to which Ewart was primed for the answers. 'And no, Lorena wasn't with us.'

328

'Us?'

'Me, Brian and Johnnie.'

'Brian Fletcher and Johnnie Walker?'

Ewart nodded. 'What's this all about?' he asked. 'Has she been murdered?'

Right question. Wrong woman. 'Why would you think that?'

'Isn't that what you do? Investigate murders?'

'And missing people.'

'Ah,' Ewart said.

'And what about Mexico?'

'What about it?'

'That's where Lorena's from.'

'I don't follow.'

'Ever been there?'

'Never.'

Gilchrist let the second lie of the day pass. He would come back to that one, catch him out later. 'Not even with Lorena?' he asked.

'Look,' said Ewart, 'I'm not sure I like—'

'I take it that's a no.'

'No. I mean, yes, it's a no.'

Ewart was becoming flustered, losing some of his guile. Gilchrist pressed on. 'Do you know where Lorena lived?'

'What?'

'Can you remember the address?' Gilchrist watched Ewart's face crease into an amazed smile. 'The name of the town, then?'

'Look, can you tell me what this is all about, please?'

'As you said, I'm investigating a murder.' Gilchrist moved away from the door, swung his computer case from his shoulder, laid it flat on the desk. He caught his image in a mirror on the wall, thought he looked tired and bruised.

'I'd like to show you some photographs,' he said. 'For identification purposes.'

'If you must.'

'We could do it at the office later, if you like. Have you come into St Andrews, this evening, if that would—'

'No, no, this is fine,' Ewart grumbled, and stood by Gilchrist's side.

Gilchrist repositioned himself. From where he stood, Ewart's face filled the mirror. He unzipped the back of his case and removed the envelope containing the photographs. 'I don't need you to see them all,' he said. 'Just a few.' He watched Ewart nod as he slid his hand into the envelope and removed the postcards.

Ewart seemed to still, as if time had stopped for an instant. Gilchrist fumbled inside the envelope and removed a batch of photographs. He spread them over the table.

In the mirror, Ewart paled.

Gilchrist picked up one of the photographs – Kelly alone, her eyes and teeth smiling in the bright sunshine. In the background, a bed of daffodils fixed the date as spring. He held her image up. 'Can you identify her?' he asked.

'That's the American,' Ewart whispered.

'Yes,' said Gilchrist. 'That's Kelly.' He looked at Ewart as a thought squeezed into his mind. 'Did you ever go out with her?'

'Wasn't your brother seeing her?'

'Let me ask the questions, Dougie.'

Ewart shook his head. 'No. Never.'

'Ever go to her flat in College Street?'

Ewart raised an eyebrow. 'Well, I'm sure I must have,' he said.

'Must have?'

'Didn't she share with Megs for a while?' Ewart shrugged his shoulders. 'Megs and I were an item for years.'

'Before she moved in with Kelly?'

'Before she even went to uni.'

Well, that was news. 'On again, off again?' Gilchrist suggested.

Ewart gave a grim smile. 'Megs can be difficult to live with.'

'And in between, you'd have relationships with others?'

'Hardly.'

'And what about Megs?'

'She'd mope around, make life difficult and then we'd get back together and everything would be fine for a while.'

'And what about Lorena? Did you go to Mexico with her?' he asked again.

'I've never been to Mexico.'

'I don't believe you.'

Ewart's eyes flickered left and right, as if his mind was working out which way to jump.

Gilchrist picked up another photograph. A winter shot of Kelly with Rita. In the mirror, Ewart's tongue ran across his top lip. 'Remember Rita?' Gilchrist asked.

'Vaguely.'

'She shared the same flat.'

'Look,' said Ewart. 'I don't see what I have to do with any of this—'

'Almost done.' Gilchrist delved into his case, removed the computer-generated image, placed it flat on the table like a trump card. Kelly stared up at them, half ghost, half alive. 'We found her.' he said.

Ewart's lips tightened, as if to make sure he did not say something he would later regret.

Gilchrist turned over one of the postcards. 'From Kelly to her parents. *Going to Mexico for a short break. Won't be back in the States until March. Will be in touch. See you soon. Love you both. Kelly. Kiss kiss.*'

Ewart frowned. 'I didn't go with her, if that's what this is about.'

'She never flew to Mexico. She was murdered in Scotland and her body buried in someone else's grave.' Gilchrist picked up the Mexican postcard. *'Staying on in Mexico a bit longer. Expect to be back at the end of April. Love, Kelly.'*

Ewart scratched his head. 'You have me confused,' he said. 'If she never flew to Mexico, how could she have sent the postcard?'

'She didn't.'

Ewart paused. 'I'm not sure what you're trying to tell me, Andy.'

Gilchrist noticed the use of his first name, a ploy to soften him up, perhaps, keep it friendly. But sometimes you had to go in with the boot. 'Someone sent the postcard from Mexico on her behalf.' He stepped forward, closed the gap. 'That someone was you.'

Ewart frowned, his forehead a mass of intersecting furrows that seemed to move in waves as his eyebrows lifted and fell. 'I've never been to Mexico.'

'Why don't I believe you?'

'How would I have got there?'

Gilchrist almost stumbled. 'Flown. How else?'

'I don't fly. I've never flown. Not once. Ever.'

Something fluttered in Gilchrist's chest, then kick-started with a rush of blood that threatened to scald his face. 'You went to Spain,' he tried, but he already knew the answer.

'We took Johnnie's car.' Ewart's voice seemed to ring with renewed confidence. 'Aviatophobia,' he pronounced. 'I have a fear of flying.'

'People take pills for that.'

'I'm allergic to most of them.'

Even then, Gilchrist tried not to lose face. 'I'll check passport records, look into—'

'No need to,' Ewart said. 'I've kept my original passport. The only one I've ever had. The only stamps on it are the exit and entry to Spain that year. First and last time I've ever left the country.'

Gilchrist stepped to the end of the desk and stared out the window, trying to find the flaw in the logic. Ewart could have had a false passport, used it to fly to Mexico, then destroyed it. Or maybe lost his passport and had another issued. But if his fear of flying and his allergies were for real, then he really was accusing the wrong man—

He jerked at the sound of squealing tyres.

From the tilt of Ewart's head, he knew he had heard it, too.

He squinted through the blinds. By the corner of the building, a team of policemen spilled from the opened doors of a white Transit van, followed by Tosh, all wild arms and red face, shouting out orders.

Gilchrist swept the photographs and postcards off the desk and into his laptop case. 'Give me five minutes, Dougie, all right?'

Ewart seemed puzzled to the point of grinning.

Gilchrist leaped over the desk and pulled open a drawer.

'Hey, hang on—'

Gilchrist slammed the drawer shut, opened another and pulled out a set of car keys with a BMW keyring. 'Tell them I left five minutes ago. If it comes down to it, I'll swear under oath that I threatened you.' He zipped up his case, swung it over his shoulders, pulled the blinds to the side and opened the window. A final check confirmed that Tosh was out of sight, probably running his way through the main door. Others would surely follow.

He swung his feet up and over and dropped to the ground.

It never failed to amaze him how the mind worked. Even as he ran, his brain fired up in some part of his subconscious, sprang alive somewhere deep within its neural network and, with the logic of a computer, dissected and analysed and spat out the answer.

By the time he powered up Dougie's BMW, he thought he had it worked out.

CHAPTER 30

He found her in the back garden, pegging washing to a whirligig.

The look on her face shifted from shock to surprise, then settled into a strained grin that warned him – here was a woman who could slide a knife deep into the heart of your gut and tell you she loved you. Cracking a bedside lamp against Kelly's head would have raised about as much emotion as tapping a nail into wood.

'You've decided to come back,' she said.

Gilchrist followed her into the kitchen where she shoved the clothes basket into the utility cupboard. Before she could turn, he clamped both her arms to her side and pushed her through to the lounge, away from the kitchen with all its cleavers and knives.

They reached the safe haven of a bookshelf in an alcove to the side of the fireplace. He let his computer case slide from his shoulder to the floor.

She turned to him, her face an odd mix of surprise and determination, her hands hoisting the hem of her skirt. 'When did you last have a woman, Andy?'

Five weeks ago, his mind whispered. But Nance's heart had not been in it.

He pushed away from her. 'Give it up, Megs,' he said. 'It won't work.'

'What? Percy won't rise to the occasion?' She guffawed. 'I think we'll have Percy popping out of his pants and just gagging for—'

'Megs.'

He had not intended to shout, but the strength of his voice made her freeze. She stood for a long second, stilled like an image trapped on film. Then he caught the movement in her eyes, the quickest of glances to the kitchen door, and realized she was not just one step ahead of him, but probably four.

'Let me get a drink to loosen you up,' she said, and moved towards the kitchen door with the speed of someone half her weight.

He managed to slam the door shut as she opened it.

She faced him, her back pressed against the wood. With one hand holding the door shut, they stood closer than he liked. Her breath rushed hot and hard by his face. He sensed her panic, her fear, her inability to work out how to stop it.

'Let's talk, Megs. Shall we?'

'Verbal foreplay? I'm all for that.' Her smile came off all wrong, a baring of teeth that gave him a glimpse of her dark side.

Hand still flat to the door, he nodded to the sofa. 'Take a seat.'

With pained reluctance, Megs shuffled to the sofa and slumped down on it.

'It took me some time to work it out,' he said, 'but once I did, I wonder why I never thought about it sooner.'

She patted the sofa, an invitation for him to sit beside her.

He returned to the bookshelf, stood with his back against it. From there, he felt in control. Megs stared at him as if preparing to listen. But behind her façade, he knew an active mind was trying to work out some way to trick him.

'You phoned the office,' he said, 'and told them I was at Dougie's.'

She pouted. 'Why would you think that?'

'How else would they have known?' he replied. 'They had nothing to go on, nothing to point them there. Until you told them.'

One hand played with the hem of her skirt. 'You look shot, Andy. Come and lie down. Let me help you relax.'

'Did jealousy make you do it?'

Her tongue slid over her lip. She shifted her skirt higher.

'I think that's what happened,' he said. 'Kelly was a young woman from another country, with a free spirit, living away from home, not afraid to sample life to the full. She was blonde, beautiful, slim. Everything you're not.'

Her skirt flapped to her knees with a speed that startled him. Anger blazed behind dark eyes that settled into a dead gaze and seemed to focus on something miles behind him.

'She could have had any man she wanted,' he pressed on. 'Even Dougie. The love of your life.'

Her gaze returned, as black and sullen as a betrayed señorita. And it struck him then, that Megs might have been the woman who had comforted Mrs McLeod at her husband's graveside all those years ago.

'Bitch,' she spat.

Now they were coming down to it.

'You travelled a lot,' he went on. 'South America was your favourite. You could have lived there. You said so yourself. Was it even better than Mexico?' He kept his eyes on her as he bent down, opened his case and removed the postcards. 'But you never went anywhere by yourself. You went to Mexico for a mid-term break with Wee Johnnie. It took me a while to work out how the flight

337

manifesto checked out, because Kelly never flew to Mexico – *you* did, under her name.'

He waited for her reaction, but he could have been talking to a wax dummy. 'Then later, you went to Spain,' he went on. 'That was when Dougie tagged along, but also where I slipped up. You see, I thought Dougie and you got together *after* Spain. But I never knew until Dougie told me that you had been out with him before.'

Not even a glimmer.

He held up the Mexican postcard. 'Remember this?'

Her lips tightened.

'Want me to read it?'

'Go on,' she said. 'Bore me.'

'This one first.' He flipped over the St Andrews postcard. Her eyes never wavered. *'Going to Mexico for a short break. Will be in touch. Kelly.'* He stared at her, felt hatred stir and simmer deep within him. 'This is clear evidence of premeditation,' he said.

Megs eyed him with a dead stare.

'And this one. Written after Kelly was murdered,' he said. *'Staying on in Mexico a bit longer. Expect to be back at the end of April.'* He lowered the postcard, gave a dead stare of his own. 'Still deny it?'

'Deny what? Murdering her? What for?'

Her answer confused him for a moment. Was she questioning her reason to deny it, or her reason for committing murder? 'For Dougie,' he tried.

'Dougie was a man. She was a woman. Men and women screw on the side. We were all doing it back then. What's the big deal?'

He noticed the past tense, wondered if it meant anything. 'The big deal was that Dougie wasn't just any man. He was *your* man.'

'You're off your head, Andy. Look at you. You're knackered. You need a break. Forget all this stuff about murder. You're barking up the wrong tree. I didn't do it.' She patted the sofa again. 'Come here. Sit down.'

'Of course, back in the late sixties, forensic science was not what it is today,' he pressed on. 'Fingerprint technology—'

'You can't get fingerprints off that postcard,' she objected. 'I'm not stupid enough to believe that. It's been through the mill, that has.'

'So you're saying you've touched it?'

Her face closed down as if he had slapped her.

'I wasn't thinking about fingerprints,' he went on. 'I was thinking more along the lines of DNA.'

Her eyes came alive then, shifted from side to side as if trying to recall where she had slipped up, what she had missed.

'The stamps,' he offered.

Her eyes stilled, her lips pressed together.

He turned the postcard over, pointed to the stamp. 'Our forensics boys will lift it off, peel it back and take a sample—'

'Of what?'

He cocked his head, looked out the window, thought he heard a car door closing. Had Tosh returned? Outside, the street lay deserted. He strained to hear the faintest sound. Had he imagined it?

Megs stood, the move so sudden that Gilchrist almost jumped. 'Waste of bloody time trying it on with you. You always were a cold bastard, Andy. Just like Jack. That's why that American bimbo screwed around. She wasn't getting any at home.'

Her words stunned him, but he just managed to beat her to the door again.

'Are you going to open this fucking door,' she said, 'or am I going to have to fight my way through it? One thing's for sure, Andy. I am going into my own kitchen.'

He caught a glimmer of madness in her eyes, had a sense of her brute strength. In full attack mode, Kelly would have been no match for her. He readied to open the door, put his hand on her shoulder—

She struck at it with the speed of a snake.

'Keep your filthy fucking hands off me.'

The venom in her voice surprised him. He wondered if he should just arrest her there and then. But the instant he stepped into the office, even with Megs, he would be locked up before he could make a case. Tosh would see to that. Maybe McVicar, too. He realized he needed to play along a bit, try to trip Megs up, trick some confession from her. So far she had denied everything. Even his threat of DNA sampling had failed to evoke a response. If he was going to turn himself in, he needed more than his own convoluted logic and two postcards.

'I'm waiting.'

He cocked his head, strained to catch the metallic rattle of something.

But again, nothing. He was too tense, by far. He had Tosh on the brain.

He stepped back and Megs barged into the kitchen. She clattered a kettle under the tap, smacked it on to the tiled surface, spilling water. Even through her moments of anger, he came to understand that she would not attack him, for doing so gave him some form of confession, without which he had nothing.

Except the stamps.

Who could he give them to? Who could he trust?

He laid the postcards on the nearest shelf, on top of a pile of hand-printed recipes that acted as a makeshift bookend for a row of paperback cookbooks. One toppled over as he lifted the wall phone from its cradle. He noticed the message light was blinking.

'Why don't you use the phone?' A drawer opened, spoons rattled. 'Then get the hell out.' The drawer slammed.

He turned his back to Megs, but kept sight of her reflection in the window, just in case, and pressed the button.

He puzzled at the sound of the voice . . .

Megs? Andy Gilchrist's been here . . .

Took a fraction of a second to recognize it . . .

I think he's on his way . . .

And an instant too long to sense the rush of movement behind him . . .

Don't say anything to—

A blow like a hammer-hit struck the back of his neck and the floor swept up to meet him with a thud that pulled a grunt from his throat.

His day sank into darkness.

But not before his dying sight caught tartan turn-ups and brown brogues.

CHAPTER 31

When Gilchrist came to, he was trussed and gagged and naked.

And lying on a sheet of plastic that crinkled with every move.

A dull pain burned the nape of his neck. The taste of oil and dirt lay thick on his tongue. A piece of sacking was jammed into his mouth, held in place by a rough rope that cut into his face and crushed his ears. His hands were twisted behind his back. When he tried to move, something tugged at his ankles, telling him he was hog-tied.

For a second, panic swept through him in an acid attack that threatened to heave bile from his stomach and choke him to death. He tried to still his heart, take long breaths through his nose, force his mind away from even the thought of throwing up.

Just keep breathing. Deep and slow. Deep and slow.

He could not tell how long he had been out, only that it was dark. Despite the cold, sweat tickled the corner of one eye. He felt light-headed from lack of air, and fought off the overpowering need to have the gag removed. He tried to force his thoughts awake, work out what had happened, or more to the point, what was about to happen.

His legs felt cramped, and a deep ache worked its way through his thighs and buttocks and into his back and shoulders. He tried to ease the pain, rolled on to his side and cursed when the cartilage of his ear hit something hard and metallic. He held still for several seconds while the pain faded.

Where was he? What time was it? It felt cold enough to be night.

He lifted his head to the metal thing that had cut his ear, and tried to feel it with his nose. He could not tell what it was, only that it seemed to form part of the lid of whatever box he was in, and that it had a hard, straight edge. He twisted his body, pressed his cheek against the metal bar, felt the rope that held his gag catch, then slip off.

He tried again, pressed harder, ignored the pain in his cheek as he eased back, hoping he was not tearing skin from his face. The rope slipped from the edge of the bar, but it felt different, not so tight, and cut across his cheeks at a different angle.

Four attempts later, he was able to shake the rope free and spit the sacking and oiled dirt from his mouth. He breathed in long cool gulps of fresh air that brought life back to his body. It took him a few seconds longer to work out that he was locked in the boot of some car. The smell of petrol and oil, musty and unclean, reminded him of Megs' old Vauxhall.

Was he in Megs' garage?

He worked his way around the confined space, contorting his body to probe the tiniest of corners with his fingers, touch some wires, lift the edge of some boot covering, search for anything sharp enough to cut the rope.

As he struggled, his powers of reasoning came back to him.

Dougie and Megs were in it together. Of that he was certain.

Between them they had concocted a string of events that had delayed the discovery of Kelly's disappearance and even had the wrong police force searching for her. But which of them had killed her, Gilchrist could not say.

Perhaps Dougie. With his fear of flying, he would have needed someone he could trust, someone he knew would keep his secret, someone who would fly to Mexico for him and send the postcard to Kelly's parents, that single piece of evidence that would clear the crime from the shores of Scotland. Who better than his soulmate, Megs?

Or maybe Megs had caught Dougie and Kelly in flagrante delicto and, in a fit of rage, the stirrings of which Gilchrist had witnessed earlier, had decided to put a permanent stop to their sexual liaison. Or perhaps Megs and Dougie had done it together, taken advantage of Kelly's inquisitive sexual nature, maybe convinced her to engage in a threesome and, at the moment of truth, or penetration, or whatever, one of them changed their mind and—

He stilled.

His fingers gripped a plastic cover on the side of the boot, with a knob that released it and gave access to what felt like a plastic toolbox. He battled against the pain of the rope as he groped in the darkness, worked at the toolbox latch, opened it and felt inside.

His hand landed upon a socket with a bent handle, for loosening wheel bolts. He searched for a blade-headed screwdriver, one he might use to cut through the rope, but from the way he was trussed, he worried he could not twist his wrists sufficiently to cut himself free.

The sound of a padlock being unclasped and a garage door opening stopped him. He listened to the screech of the door-spring and the rattle of the wheels as the garage door rolled overhead, then puzzled as the noise seemed to reverse and it closed again.

He thought he caught the soft shuffle of shoes on concrete, then the unseen presence of someone close by, the click of the boot lid—

The burst of light blinded him.

Ewart stood over him like some colossus, the closed garage door in the background.

'Ah,' he said, 'I see you've been busy.' He reached inside the boot for the oiled rag and discarded rope. 'And this, too.' He removed the toolbox. 'I'm going to have to tie it tighter.' He leaned forward, grabbed the rope that secured Gilchrist's wrists to his ankles and gave a hard tug.

'There's no need for this, Dougie,' Gilchrist gasped. 'Think of what you're doing—'

'What I'm doing is making sure we don't go to prison.'

'You could strike a deal, work something out with—'

'Premeditated murder is what you told Megs. We won't be working anything out. But I'm surprised you found the postcards,' he said. 'What did you do with them?'

'What postcards?' Gilchrist tried.

Ewart shook his head. 'We'll find them. And if we don't? Well, after tonight, it won't matter a damn.' He leaned forward, placed one gloved hand behind Gilchrist's head, pushed the oily rag into his mouth with the other. He tried to work the rope around Gilchrist's head, but Gilchrist spat out the rag.

Ewart stood back and smiled down at him. 'Your choice,' he said, dangling the rope with one hand, removing a syringe filled with clear fluid from his pocket with the other.

Gilchrist stared at the needle, fighting back the rising panic. If

Ewart injected him with whatever concoction the syringe contained, he would be unconscious in seconds, never to be revived, of that he was certain. Why had Ewart not already done that? His hesitation gave Gilchrist the answer.

'A post-mortem would reveal drugs in my blood,' he said, 'which could point to someone in the medical profession.'

'A detective to your dying breath, Andy. I'm impressed.'

'And you don't want to take that chance. Do you?'

'As I said, it's your choice.'

Gilchrist eyed Ewart, stunned that he had never before seen the killer in him. Dead eyes belied a beguiling smile. A career as a doctor had made him immune to the feelings of the dying. But it seemed surreal to be having a conversation with his executioner-to-be. Like choosing from which side he would like his throat slit. Oh, from the right, please.

'I'm waiting.'

Gilchrist really had no decision to make. An injection ended it there and then. An oily rag in the mouth kept him alive, at least for the time being.

'I won't shout,' he tried.

'I know you won't,' Ewart agreed.

Gilchrist opened his mouth to accept the rag, and Ewart leaned down and pressed it in with gloved hands. The rag was pushed in deeper than before and that, along with the stench of petrol and oil, nearly brought up the contents of his stomach. He worked his tongue and pushed the gag behind his teeth as Ewart, true to his word, tied the rope tighter around his face with a roughness intended to confirm he was not fooling around.

'You won't get out of that so easily,' Ewart said, and left Gilchrist to stare out of the opened boot.

The sound of chains rattling and something being dragged across the concrete floor caused the hairs on the back of Gilchrist's neck to rise. He needed no explanation as a length of chain was lugged with some effort into the boot, the car settling on to its suspension springs from the added weight of an anchor.

'You're going for an eight-hundred-metre swim,' Ewart said. 'Straight down.'

The boot lid slammed shut.

Gilchrist lay still in the darkness, listening to the sound of the garage door opening, the crunch of Ewart's shoes across gravel. The rope tight around his face brought tears to his eyes. Or was he really crying, knowing he was trapped, knowing he would never see his children again, and knowing that whatever Dougie and Megs had in store for him, this time no one would ever find the body?

Eight hundred metres. Straight down.

Was that any way to leave this world?

He recalled the murder cases he had been involved in over his lifetime. How many other poor souls had left it the same way? How many innocent victims had lived their last minutes petrified with fear, helpless with despair and crying at the futility of it all?

He felt his eyes burn, blinked away his own tears.

Christ, he could not die. Not now. Not like this.

He had to find a way out.

By not giving him an injection, was that Ewart's mistake? By keeping him trussed and alive, was Ewart giving him false hope of escape? Or had Ewart kept him alive because he needed Gilchrist to help him in the final act, by walking towards whatever death awaited him—

The crunching sound of gravel again, the lopsided beat of the different steps of two people, and he sensed someone walk past the boot to the front of the car. The door opened, and the suspension settled as the driver took his seat.

The engine started with the recognizable rattle of Megs' old Vauxhall, and his head hit the boot lid as the car pulled from the garage and jerked to a halt.

The suspension settled again, a bit more to the left side, he thought. So, Ewart was driving, with Megs as his passenger. The Vauxhall accelerated down the drive and lunged on to the road with a hard bump that cracked his head on the boot floor.

Where were they going? Somewhere far from St Andrews, of that he was certain. If one of Fife Constabulary's detective chief inspectors went missing, teams of experts would scour the countryside, starting at his last known position, spreading wider until his body was found, or his case eventually closed and filed, unsolved. The irony of it all did not escape him. He would end up just like Kelly.

No, he thought, he would be dumped in some little-known spot at sea. Eight hundred metres deep. He wondered why Ewart had been so precise. As best he could recall, Dougie had never been a sailor, so bathymetrical details would be of no interest to him. Gilchrist had no idea if Megs was sea-wise, and he struggled to pull up a memory of anything in her house or garage that would suggest so. Other than the anchor, his mind remained blank.

Were they taking him out on the North Sea? Or to some loch? Many of Scotland's lochs were hundreds of metres deep. But eight hundred? Or maybe they would throw his body into some long-abandoned quarry pit.

The car's motion threw him around the boot, jarring limbs that were already burning from being hog-tied. His thighs cramped, his back ached, his shoulder muscles screamed for release. He twisted and turned, contorting himself in the tight confines, trying to work into a position that would lock his body in place, stop the reckless rolling about. He forced his head back, and found that doing so slackened the rope that tied his wrists to his ankles and relieved the pain, if only for just a moment—

The car pulled to an abrupt halt that forced a curse from Dougie, and threw Gilchrist hard against the side.

Hope soared in his heart.

For one fleeting moment he had felt it.

He forced his head back some more, put pressure on his neck, twisting more and more until his fingers just managed to touch the one thing that could set him free.

The rope around his ankles.

CHAPTER 32

By the time the car stopped, they had been travelling for two hours, the last ten minutes of which had thrown Gilchrist around the boot as they weaved and splashed along what felt like a potholed dirt track.

He estimated they were a couple of miles deep off the beaten track.

When the boot opened, he blinked against the glare of a torch that wavered over his nude body, then settled on his groin.

'I see I wasn't missing much,' Megs quipped.

Gilchrist groaned from behind his gag.

Ewart bustled in beside Megs. 'Give me a hand,' he said, and leaned into the boot space. 'Come on. We don't have much time.'

'You mean *you* don't have much time. You've got to get back to that stuck-up wife of yours. I've got all night.'

'You take his ankles. I'll take his arms.'

Gilchrist waited until Ewart's gloved hands touched him.

Then he rolled over, gripped the anchor with both hands and swung it up and into Ewart's shocked face. His stiff joints and aching muscles caused him to miss with full force, but Ewart still

350

slumped to the ground with a hard grunt. Gilchrist snatched the rope from his mouth, spat out the gag and scrambled out of the boot to confront Megs, who stood transfixed as he heaved the anchor to shoulder height.

They stood no more than three feet apart.

'Don't make me hit you with this,' he said to her. 'Chain him to the bumper.'

Ewart groaned.

Gilchrist's effort to free himself, twist his body to reach the rope, then hold that position while his fingers worked the knot behind his back had almost exhausted him. It had taken him the best part of an hour to free his ankles, and the pain when he at last straightened his legs brought tears to his eyes. He then worked the rope around his wrists, slackening it enough to let him bump and shuffle his tied hands under his backside. Slipping his legs free had almost cost him a broken wrist, but he persevered, and when he slid the rope from his head and pulled the gag from his mouth, he had cried with relief.

The anchor felt like it was doubling in weight, and his legs begged him to sit. If they put up a fight now, he knew he could not take on both of them. Perhaps not even one.

Ewart pressed his hands to the ground.

'Stay put,' Gilchrist ordered.

Ewart spat out blood, pushed himself to his knees.

Gilchrist brought the anchor down on his shoulder with a force that broke bone.

Ewart slumped to the ground, moaning as he gripped his shoulder.

'I'll break the other one if you make a move.' He flashed a look at Megs. 'Now tie him up.'

Silent, Megs reached for the chain and pulled it rattling over the rim of the boot where it slinked to the ground like a living thing.

'How do you expect me to tie him up with this?' she complained.

Here we go again, Gilchrist thought. He needed to be careful around Megs. 'Just wrap it round him and loop it to the bumper.'

She gathered in the chain. 'I had nothing to do with it,' she pleaded. 'I only mailed the postcard from—'

'Shut up.' Ewart glared up at her.

'It's all your fault—'

'For God's sake, woman—'

'If you'd kept your cock in your pants, none of it would have happened—'

'Don't say anything—'

'You didn't have to get rid of her. You didn't have—'

'Shut up—'

' —to kill her.'

Gilchrist thudded the anchor into the ground.

Ewart and Megs flinched into silence.

'Tie him up. Just get on with it.' If Gilchrist had not been so exhausted, he could have listened to them argue all night, each accusation bringing him one step closer to the truth of what happened all those years ago. And standing naked in the cold night air did not help. A tremor gripped his legs, and a shiver rattled his upper body.

Megs laid the chain on the ground, doubled it over. 'What's going to happen to us?'

'That's for others to decide,' he said.

She pulled a doubled-up length of chain to her, moved in front of Ewart, her back to Gilchrist. 'I don't want to go to prison,' she said. 'I couldn't stand it.'

'You'll get a fair trial.'

She stood still for a moment, as if working out the logic of his words, then twisted her hand around and through a length of doubled-up chain and, like a hammer-thrower at the moment of release, spun around and swung it at Gilchrist in a slicing arc.

Gilchrist had time only to lift his arm as the chain whistled towards his head like a scythe. He cried out in pain as a heavy blow caught him on the wrist, and back-stepped in panic as a second caught his other arm. It was all he could do to hold on to the anchor. He backed up, stumbled, fell to the ground on his back, managed to roll to the side as the chain thudded by his head with a force that brought up dirt and grass.

Up and over and on to his feet, one hand dangling useless by his side, the other gripping the anchor for all he was worth.

He pulled back in time to miss another scything blow. And another.

The next one caught him on his knee, sending a flash of pain the length of his body.

Any thoughts of making a run for it were killed there and then.

She came at him like a crazed demon, hissing and spitting and scything.

'I warned Dougie about you . . .'

Gilchrist backed away, stumbling over rock and grass in his bare feet, just managing to stay out of reach of the whistling chain. If he tripped, it was over.

'But would he listen . . . ?'

The chain scythed left then right.

'Would he fuck . . .'

He stepped to the right. Megs cut him off.

Then to the left. She did likewise.

But he saw some logic in her missing swings. She was backing him up, guiding him to some point where he would be trapped, left to face the onslaught head on, his back to the wall, so to speak. It did not matter that her blows were not connecting. It mattered only that he kept back-stepping into the night.

A quick glance behind him left him none the wiser and had the chain whistling past his throat, a warning to keep his eyes to the front, on Megs. Another swing scythed past his thighs, close enough to feel the draught of its passing.

And with each sweep of the chain, Megs vented her anger.

'Who killed her?' he shouted back.

'Not me . . .' Another sweep.

'Why did Dougie do it?'

'She told him she was pregnant . . .'

Pregnant? The chain clipped his elbow, sending a jolt like an electric shock to his shoulder, reminding him to keep backing up.

'I see that got your attention.' She swung the chain at his face, and almost connected. 'You bastard . . .'

But he could tell she was tiring, the scything taking its toll, her words punctuated by gasps. He noticed, too, that she was now swinging the chain with one hand, gathering it in with the other, like a climber easing her way up a length of rope to the summit of Gilchrist's anchor. It would not be long until she reined him in.

He clung on to the anchor. Its weight fired the muscles in his arm and shoulder.

If he could swing it back and forward, somehow use it to—

His heel caught.

He landed on his back with a force that emptied his lungs and cracked his head on a rock. He struggled to stay conscious. For one confusing moment his body failed to work. Megs seemed to sense this as she widened her stance, readied to swing the chain up and over and down in a crushing death blow.

The anchor. It was his only hope.

He lifted it, tried to throw it, but on his back, with his weakened arm, its weight was too much. He gasped in disbelief as it slipped from his grip.

Megs' eyes widened at the logic of something that was beyond Gilchrist's thinking.

The sound of metal ringing by his ear had him turning his head.

The chain rattled and scurried over the rocky surface like a burned snake.

Megs was trying to unwrap the other end from her wrist, her mouth gaping in panic, her arm flapping. The chain seemed to shoot up from the ground, take hold of her arm and jerk her towards him. She belly-flopped by his side, threw an arm over him in the passing. But in the nude, he had nothing to offer.

He had time only to turn to his side, respond in like fashion. He managed to grab the hem of her skirt, felt the strain in his arm as her body fell over the edge, the shock of pain in his wrist as her deadweight transferred with a sharp snap through the broken bone.

He could not hold on.

He pushed himself to his knees in time to see her tumbling off the rock face, her body spinning like a toy, deep into the dark void. Moments later, the sound of her death-splash echoed up at him. He lay still for several seconds, then pushed back from the edge.

A violent tremor took hold of his body then, chattering his teeth, shaking his limbs. He could not tell if it was from the rush of

355

fear, or from the cold night wind that seemed to rise up the rock face from the quarry pit below.

Or perhaps it was from the passing of Megs' cold soul as it rose from the depths to embark on its final journey.

CHAPTER 33

Tosh was all spittled mouth and flushed face.

'You fucking set it all up, Gilchrist. I know you.'

'Give it up, Tosh.'

'Ewart's telling us you attacked him and his wife—'

'Ex-wife—'

' —Trussed them up and drove them to the quarry.'

'Of course he would.'

'Then you tied a chain around his wife's wrists and kicked her over the edge.'

'You're not listening.'

'Oh, I'm listening, all right. I'm listening to Ewart tell me what really happened.'

'If he was telling the truth, why would I not have shoved him over the edge, too?'

'Then you'd have no reason to come back to the office,' he said, without missing a beat. He closed in on Gilchrist, his face growing impossibly redder. 'And act all hurt and innocent.'

'The postcards,' Gilchrist said to him.

Tosh stumbled. 'What postcards?' he tried.

Gilchrist knew Tosh was bluffing, waiting to see how he would play it. Tosh could not know that Gilchrist knew of his call to the Sheriff's Office from the Thai restaurant. 'The postcards Kelly was supposed to have sent from St Andrews and Mexico,' he said. 'You need to talk to Bert.'

'Bert? What the fuck's Bert got to do with any of this?'

'He's having DNA lifted from the back of the stamps.'

'Who told him to do that?'

'Now you really are making me think you're dumber than I—'

'You don't get it, do you? You've fucked up, Gilchrist. I have a warrant for your arrest.'

'Well, here I am.' He pulled himself forward, his face close enough that he could smell the man's hatred. If he was not so exhausted, he might have tried some anger of his own. 'If you had listened to me,' he said, 'instead of playing Rambo and running up a ton of man hours trying to settle some personal vendetta, Megs would not be anchored to the bottom of some water-filled quarry pit.'

'Don't try and slime your way out of this one so—'

'If you hadn't been so pig-headed,' Gilchrist pressed on, 'Megs would still be alive. Have you thought about that, Tosh? Have you thought about how your brainless stupidity caused a woman's death?'

Tosh's eyes flared with a flicker of madness. He pushed back, slapped his hands on the table with a smack that should have cracked the frame, then stomped from the interview room, leaving Gilchrist with CI Randall.

Gilchrist slumped back into his chair. His body demanded rest. His left wrist was swollen and bruised, and burning from the fire of broken bones. His right arm throbbed from shoulder to fingertips. His hair was matted with blood where he had split his skull from his lucky stumble by the quarry edge. Several more backward steps and it would have been his body the police divers were searching for, if they would ever have known where to look.

He tugged the blanket around his neck.

Randall pulled up his chair and faced him. 'Can I get you anything, Andy? Tea? Coffee?' He eyed Gilchrist's wrist, raised his eyebrows. 'A doctor?'

'I'm all doctored out.'

Randall gave a soft chuckle in response, but it was short-lived. He leaned forward. 'I'd like to ask a few questions of my own, Andy,' he said, glancing at the recorder to make sure it was still on. 'Tell me once again what happened.'

Gilchrist did, taking fifteen minutes to explain events leading to Megs being dragged over the quarry edge.

'And then you phoned Bert?'

'I did.'

'You were naked. Where was your phone?'

'I used Dougie's. It was in his jacket.'

'I see.' Randall looked down at his notes. 'And what did you tell Bert?'

'That he should go to Megs' house and retrieve two postcards. Megs kept a spare key under a flowerpot at the back door. It's how Dougie used to get in.' Gilchrist smiled at Randall's puzzlement. 'Although Dougie and Megs are divorced, they've been having an affair for over twenty years.'

'And Dr Ewart gave this information willingly? About the key?'

'He spoke to Bert of his own free will.' Which was Gilchrist's first lie. It had taken a foot pressed to Ewart's broken shoulder to force him to agree to speak to Bert. Ewart's squeals still rung in his ears. Well, the man had intended to kill him, after all.

'That's not what Dr Ewart is saying.'

'Of course not.'

'You didn't coerce his cooperation by force.'

'Is that a question?'

'It is.'

'When I told him what had happened to Megs, he collapsed. It was over for him, and he knew it.' Which was his second lie. Ewart had cursed Megs to hell and back for having spoken out in Gilchrist's presence. Then he had smiled up at Gilchrist, swore blind he would deny everything, until Gilchrist mentioned the postcards. The look that flashed across Ewart's face told Gilchrist all he needed to know.

The postcards were still intact, lying on the shelf, hidden by a cookbook.

'I'm sure you realize, Andy, that without a warrant, any evidence obtained by Bert in an unofficial search of Megs' house would be inadmissible in court.'

'That's true.'

Randall seemed to rise up in his chair. 'Then why did you order Bert to do it?'

'I didn't. Bert's next-door neighbour is Sheriff Tyler.'

'So Bert had a warrant?'

'Of course.'

Randall's ice-blue eyes narrowed. For the first time that morning, resentment seemed to shimmer in them. But Gilchrist had sound reason for being unhelpful. Randall was senior to Tosh, and should have reined Tosh in. Not doing so broke whatever trust Gilchrist might have been prepared to extend to the man.

'When did you next speak to Bert?' Randall went on.

'About an hour or so after I first spoke to him.' Which was not exactly correct. By the time Gilchrist had limped naked into the nearest police station, to the shocked smiles of a young WPC, Bert had already called back and confirmed he had a warrant.

'What did he tell you?'

'That he located both postcards in Megs' kitchen, next to the phone.'

'Anyone with him?'

'Sheriff Tyler.'

Randall frowned. 'At that time of night?'

'According to Bert, Sheriff Tyler was on his way out for a midnight fishing trip when he called. He told Bert he'd like to come along for the ride.'

Randall studied his notes, then said, 'You drove yourself back.'

Gilchrist had stuffed Ewart into the boot of Megs' car, unbound and ungagged, and set off across the countryside, following the tyre marks of Ewart's earlier passing. When he reached the paved road he turned right, remembering being flung across the boot space as Ewart had slammed on the brakes and veered sharp left.

'Yes,' he said.

'How did you know where you were?'

'I didn't. I asked.'

'With no clothes on?'

'How else?'

It had felt odd being naked behind the wheel. The Vauxhall's heater was shot, giving out little warmth even though the temperature gauge wavered on the hot side of normal.

'And then you made your way here, with Dr Ewart locked in the boot, what, for how long? Two, two and a half hours?'

361

'Yes.'

Randall closed his notebook and held Gilchrist's gaze in a long hard look. 'I have to tell you that this maverick approach of yours has been noted by senior staff members. You should have called into the office—'

'And done what? Turn myself in?'

'You were causing this Division to utilize unnecessary manpower. You should have at least kept us informed—'

'And what would that have achieved?'

'We would have listened to—'

'You saw how Tosh listened. He wasn't interested.'

Randall tried a smile, but he was fooling no one. 'Tosh can be a bit wild at times.'

'Tosh is on his way out of St Andrews.'

Randall stilled, as if Gilchrist's words had struck a nerve. 'Tosh is well connected,' he said at length.

'I know,' said Gilchrist, and stood.

Randall pushed back and stood, too. Worry etched his brow. 'We wouldn't want you to leave the office,' he said.

'We?'

Randall's calm demeanour seemed cracked at the edges. 'Until we complete our search of Mrs Caulder's home.'

'And you want me to do what, exactly? Let myself be locked up until you decide I'm free to go? You have the postcards. You have Dougie. Why not let Tosh take him out the back and beat the truth out of him?'

'I don't think there's any need to take that attitude.'

'There's every need.'

'We don't have any physical evidence linking Dr Ewart to the—'

'Bert will lift DNA from the postcards' stamps.'

'I hope so,' Randall purred, his voice back in control.

Without replying, Gilchrist pushed past.

In the hallway, he ordered a taxi, then took a seat in one of the interview rooms.

Bert would find Megs' DNA on the back of the stamps. Christ, he would have to.

CHAPTER 34

They found Megs at the bottom of the quarry pit, her body chained to the anchor like a balloon in air. Not quite eight hundred metres deep, but deep enough to have kept Gilchrist's body hidden for a long time, perhaps for ever.

Ewart was grilled for six straight hours, and for six straight hours, despite having identified Kelly earlier from Gilchrist's photographs, denied all knowledge of her, swore blind he never had sex with her, that Megs was his one true love. He troubled his inquisitors by insisting that Gilchrist had broken into Megs' home and interrupted an embarrassing moment, then trussed them together like pigs and driven them for two hours in the back of Megs' car to the quarry.

'The back seat, not the boot?' Ewart had been asked.

'Back seat. Have your boys take samples from there. Then we'll see who's telling the truth.'

When challenged by Greaves, Gilchrist suggested Ewart and Megs used the back seat for reliving their student years, which had him worried that he had underestimated Ewart.

But he still had a few questions of his own to ask.

'Megs said you didn't have to kill Kelly,' he had said to Ewart.

'Your word against mine.'

'So why did you do it?'

'I didn't.'

'Kelly was pregnant,' Gilchrist said.

Ewart glared at him, as if seeing him for the first time.

'Did she tell you the child was yours? Were you frightened your parents would disown you, or that you'd be thrown out of university? That your dreams of becoming a doctor would be lost? With a wife and child to support, how would you—'

'Shut up.'

Gilchrist leaned closer, tried to engage Ewart's guilt-laden eyes. He wanted to tell him that Kelly could never have been pregnant. She had been on the pill. Jack had let that slip one night. With her promiscuous lifestyle, she had taken no chances. Telling Ewart that she was pregnant had been her way of ending whatever relationship Ewart thought they had. He saw that now. Kelly must have known Ewart would run a mile. But had he been scared enough to kill her? Gilchrist thought not.

'And Hell hath no fury like a woman scorned,' he pressed on. 'Once Megs found out, she threatened to do what, exactly?'

Ewart lifted his eyes, as if pleased to be discussing something he knew about. 'Megs is not right in the head,' he said. 'But other than my wife, she's the only woman I've ever loved.'

'So you went along with her plan to kill Kelly. The postcard was sent. By the time it arrived in the States, Kelly was already dead and buried.' Gilchrist leaned closer. 'Did you not try to talk her out of it?'

Ewart closed his eyes, shook his head.

Gilchrist decided to try another tack. 'I see you're right-handed.'

Ewart's eyes sprang open, as if in surprise at the comment.

'Kelly's fatal injury was on the right side of her head. Just about here.' Gilchrist tapped his temple. An image of Kelly in bed, rolling away from Ewart to face the wall where they found the blood spatter, forced its way to the front of his mind. 'You waited until she turned her back to you.'

Ewart's eyes seemed to glaze over, as if recalling the memory of that fatal blow.

'You never even had the courage to look her in the eyes.' Gilchrist leaned closer, hoped Ewart could feel his hatred. But the man appeared to have switched off. 'I checked the weather records. It rained heavily that week. You dressed Kelly up in a jacket so you could lug her, like a drunk, out of the flat and into your car.'

Nothing.

'When Hamish McLeod died, the opportunity presented itself. You had to act when the grave was fresh. You killed her that night. Or maybe the following night.' He counted thirty seconds before saying, 'Which one of you buried her body?'

'Don't know what you're talking about.'

'I must say, I never would have thought you were Kelly's type.'

Ewart tried one more defiant look. 'And your brother was?'

'Thought you didn't know her.'

'I didn't.'

'But you knew Jack was going out with her.'

Ewart seemed confused by Gilchrist's simple statement. Saying he agreed would only confirm his lie. He dug himself deeper with, 'That's what I heard.'

'Who from?'

'One of the idiots who questioned me.'

366

'We'll replay the recording, check it out, see who said what.'

Ewart stared at some point on the wall.

'You scratched Jack's initials on the cigarette lighter.'

Ewart blinked once, twice, at the memory.

'Then dropped it in beside Kelly. If her body was ever found, then there was the evidence pointing to Jack, his own personalized lighter that must have slipped from his pocket as he was burying the body.'

Ewart lowered his head, tightened his lips.

'Talk to me, Dougie. Tell me what happened.'

But Ewart seemed to have decided it was safer to say nothing.

As Gilchrist was preparing to leave the office, Stan caught up with him.

'Would you like an update on Fairclough, boss?'

Trying to convince Greaves of his own innocence in Kelly's murder investigation had caused Gilchrist's mind to switch off all thoughts of Fairclough. His career had effectively been put on hold, pending DNA results from the postcards' stamps. As he struggled to interpret Stan's expression, he felt a need to swallow a lump in his throat.

'We've got him.'

Gilchrist frowned, his thoughts entangled.

'He's got a record,' Stan went on. 'And the fingerprints we lifted from the broken bottles are a match.'

'The Molotov cocktail?'

Stan nodded. 'If the DNA tests from the MGB are positive, we have a connection and enough evidence to throw the book at him.'

Gilchrist reached out for Stan, felt strong arms clamp his own.

'You all right, boss?'

Gilchrist shook his head. 'I'm fine, I'm fine.' Something clamped his chest, like a steel band that squeezed and tightened until the light went out of his world and he felt the hard wooden seat of a chair hit the back of his thighs.

'Boss?'

Gilchrist waited until Stan's face reappeared in a shimmering haze. 'Fingerprints?'

Stan nodded. 'Plain old-fashioned fingerprints.'

Gilchrist dabbed his eyes, sniffed his running nose. 'We did it,' he whispered. 'We got him, Stan. We got him.'

'Yes,' Stan said. 'You did—'

'What did I tell you?'

The American accent had Stan and Gilchrist turning their heads like a choreographed act. Gilchrist thought Gina Belli looked softer somehow, as if the passing of a few days had helped her shed an outer layer of skin. As she neared, he thought *less severe* might be more appropriate. She surprised him by leaning forward and pecking him once, twice on the cheeks, leaving behind a fragrance that teased his senses.

'Believe me now?' she asked.

Upright again, she removed a Marlboro and lit it up, her penetrating stare never wavering from his, as if she were trying to speak to him through her psychic thoughts. She took a couple of deep breaths, exhaled from the side of her mouth.

'Here,' she said to him, 'you look as if you could use this.'

He inhaled, hard, the heat and acrid taste hitting his throat with a force that had him coughing. But he stuck it out, fought off the dizziness that threatened to overpower him and took another draw, pulling in for all he was worth.

She grinned at him as she lit another. 'I know you better than you know yourself,' she said, and removed a small blackened metal case from her bag and handed it to him.

Jack's cigarette lighter. Gilchrist nodded, half-closing his eyes against the nip of smoke, an overwhelming sense of relaxation flowing through his being. If he closed his eyes, he could be floating through air. He took another draw, long and deep and hot.

'Maybe,' he said to her. 'Maybe you do.'

Stan and Gilchrist took the CalMac ferry to Rothesay, and found the flat in Bishop Street without any difficulty. They reached the top floor of the refurbished tenement building and confirmed the number on the door.

Gilchrist shivered off the cold air and gave a hard rap.

It took a full minute before the door opened. A stocky woman eyed them with suspicion from beneath a mass of blonde tousled hair. She tightened her bathrobe.

'Mrs Clarke?'

'Yes?'

'We understand a Mr James Fairclough is living here.'

'Says who?'

Gilchrist flashed his warrant card, but she showed no interest in it. 'We need to talk to him. Is he here?'

'Naw, he's no.'

The smell of bacon drifted along the hallway, followed by the clatter of a metal pan sliding on a stove.

'Are you alone?'

'What if I am?'

That was enough for Gilchrist. He pushed her aside, marched

down the hallway and burst into the kitchen. Fairclough jerked his head in surprise, and Gilchrist managed to pin him to the wall before he could swing the frying pan at him. Fat and bacon strips splashed the tiles and dripped on to the cheap linoleum floor.

'A dog,' Gilchrist growled into Fairclough's ear. 'That's what you compared my brother to.' He spun Fairclough around, pressed his face against the wall with more force than was necessary and twisted his arm up his back, hard. 'A *dog*.'

Fairclough gasped from the pain.

'The good news for you is that Betson's out of intensive care.'

'Who?'

'You know who,' Gilchrist said, and cuffed Fairclough's wrists with a hard click. 'Betson's going to live,' he growled.

'My arm—'

'So you're only going to be charged with the one—'

'*Boss*.'

Gilchrist gave Fairclough's arms a parting jerk up his back, heard the hard crunch of gristle tearing and stood aside as Fairclough slid down the wall with a groan and slumped to the floor. For a moment, Gilchrist puzzled as to why Stan's face was so tight. From the hallway, Fairclough's secretary stared at the scene with white eyes. 'Read this fat piece of shite his rights,' he said to Stan, and bruised his way from the kitchen.

Outside, wet streets sparkled like glass. The sky shone blue-white.

Gilchrist raked his hair. His chest heaved as if he had sprinted a hundred yards. He removed a packet of Marlboro, took one and had to steady one hand against the other as he raised his lighter to it.

He inhaled, long and hard, held it in his lungs as he felt its heat flood through him, its poison settle his jumping nerves. A dog. That's what had set him off. The memory of that single word. He took another pull, then studied the burning tip as if surprised to see what he was holding. He exhaled, dropped the cigarette on the pavement, ground it out by stirring it into the asphalt. A dog. He pulled the cigarette packet from his pocket, crushed it in his hands and dropped it into a rubbish bin, followed by his lighter.

By the end of the week, Gilchrist had his answer.

Forensics confirmed Ewart's DNA on the St Andrews postcard, and Megs' on the Mexican one. Confronted with the evidence, Ewart claimed he remembered Megs asking him to mail some postcards for her. He'd had no idea what she'd written on them, of course, or where they were going to, and had simply done as he was told. In those days, no one argued with Megs, he joked.

Two hours later he was formally charged with the murder of Kelly Roberts.

And Fairclough, too. Jack's DNA was confirmed from the hairs trapped in the paint, and a perfect thumbprint lifted from pieces of the broken bottles recovered from Betson's garage matched Fairclough's. An investigation of Fairclough's offices revealed a crate of Irn-Bru bottles in a storage cupboard, providing the critical connection to the arson attack. The final nail was hammered deep by way of Linda Melrose's statement confirming the hit-and-run, leaving Fairclough with no way out.

The procurator fiscal confirmed she had enough evidence to charge Fairclough with death by dangerous driving, and attempted murder for the arson attack. Additional charges of failing to report the collision and attempting to pervert the course of justice would guarantee that Fairclough would be an old man by the time he got out of prison. If he ever lived that long.

CHAPTER 35

Two weeks later

The funeral was small, more memorial service than burial, as they interred the bones in a coffin in the tiny plot. A simple black headstone gave tribute in neatly etched words to the memory of a young life lost.

KELLY ANNABELLE ROBERTS
MARCH 17, 1949 – FEBRUARY 23, 1969
FOREVER IN OUR HEARTS

Gilchrist thought the final date at least gave some closure to the open-ended question Ewart continued to refuse to answer. It could be a day out, no more than two. But as best he could figure, the twenty-third was when Ewart took Kelly's life.

Somehow, staring at the dates seemed to strike home to Gilchrist just how young Kelly and Jack had been at the time of their deaths. Kelly had been a teenager, about to turn twenty in March of that fateful year, and yet she had been two years older than Jack.

Kelly's mother surprised him by taking hold of his hand. 'Are you all right, Andy?'

He nodded, not trusting his voice. He turned with her, away from the grave, and said nothing as their feet crushed the gravel pathway to his car.

'It's such a beautiful place,' Annie said. 'Kelly would be pleased. And Tom.' She turned her face to the wind as if testing the air. 'And such a beautiful day, too. Kelly used to write Tom and me about days like this, with the trees and the grass glistening fresh and smelling damp from the rain. It's what she loved most about Scotland.'

She squeezed Gilchrist's hand. He squeezed back.

At her insistence, he dropped her off at Leuchars Station.

'I'd be more than happy to drive you to Edinburgh Airport,' he offered again.

'I'd rather take the train,' she said, 'if you don't mind.'

'Of course not, it's just . . .'

'It's just that Kelly wrote about the train journey to Edinburgh. I'd like to travel that same route now, see the same things Kelly might have seen. For Tom, too,' she said, almost as an afterthought. 'I don't think I told you, but Tom and I visited St Andrews three years after Kelly disappeared. We went back to that same hotel, but checked out after only two days. We couldn't stand it, knowing this was where Kelly used to live. Tom never came back to Scotland again.'

Gilchrist felt his lips tighten.

'It's a bit silly, I know,' Annie went on, 'but now I know where Kelly is, I feel as if I'm seeing the beauty of the Scottish country-side for the first time. I don't suppose I'll ever return here, not at my age, so I'd like to take back what memories I can.'

Gilchrist carried her suitcase to the platform and, when the train arrived, helped her on board. She turned and faced him, eyes glistening, and placed her arms over his shoulders as if to give him a lover's hug.

'Take care, Andy,' she whispered. 'And take care of Kelly for me.'

'I will,' was all he could say.

He returned her hug, then stood alone on the platform as the train pulled into the distance. His last glimpse of Kelly's mother was of her face at the window, her hand to her lips, blowing him a kiss, a simple action that made him raise his hand in a belated farewell to his own memories of Kelly.

When the train rattled out of sight, Gilchrist shoved his hands deep into his pockets.

Take care of Kelly for me.

The wind rose then, a cold burst that shivered the station windows and carried with it the faintest whisper of the departed train. He looked to the skies, thought the rain might stay off. He had one more grave to visit, one more string of memories to fold away. He would repay his final respects to Jack, tell him his killer had been found, then drive to Glasgow and visit his children.

Take care of Kelly for me.

The echo of Annie's voice pulled up an image of blonde hair whipping in the wind and a young couple running along the West Sands, unaware of what the future held for them.

And blue eyes that laughed and could bring a smile to his lips.

Even now.

He leaned into the wind and walked to his car.